15 30 45 60 75 90 105 120 135 150 165 180

Moscow
Berlin
Rome
Istanbul
Jerusalem
Cairo
+4.5
+3.5
Dubai
New Delhi
+5.75
Mumbai
+5.5
+6.5
Bangkok
Beijing
Seoul
Shanghai
Tokyo
Pacific Ocean
Singapore
Jakarta
Indian Ocean
+9.5
Sydney

+1 +2 +3 +4 +5 +6 +7 +8 +9 +10 +11 +12

WORLD TIME ZONE

15
30
45
60
75
90
105
120
135
150
165
180
Moscow
Berlin
ris
Rome
Istanbul
Jerusalem
Cairo
+4.5
+3.5
Dubai
New Delhi
+5.75
Mumbai
+5.5
+6.5
Bangkok
Beijing
Seoul
Shanghai
Tokyo
Pacific Ocean
agos
Singapore
Jakarta
Indian Ocean
+9.5
Sydney
+1
+2
+3
+4
+5
+6
+7
+8
+9
+10
+11
+12

WORLD TIME ZONE

180
165
150
135
120
105
90
75
60
45
30
15
Arctic Ocean
Vancouver
Seattle
Chicago
-3.5
New York
San Francisco
Los Angeles
Atlantic Ocean
Miami
Mexico city
-4.5
Lima
São Paulo
Rio de Janeiro
International Date Line
-12
-11
-10
-9
-8
-7
-6
-5
-4
-3
-2
-1

開口就會
商貿英語

Business English

實踐大學應用外語系專任講師
黃　靜　悅
Danny O. Neal ◎著

五南圖書出版公司 印行

推薦序

麥克魯漢（Marshall McLuhan）於上世紀六〇年代首度提出了「地球村」的概念，當時他原本用這個新名詞來說明電子媒介對於人類未來之衝擊，實不亞於古騰堡（Johann Gutenberg）印刷術對西方文明的影響；曾幾何時，「地球村」在今天有了新的涵義：天涯若比鄰！

現代科技進步昌明，往昔「五月花」號上的新教徒花了六十幾天，歷經千辛萬苦才橫渡大西洋，今日搭乘超音速飛機只要四個多小時就可完成；網際網路的普及，世界上任何角落發生的事情對千里以外的地方都會有不可思議的影響，亦即所謂「蝴蝶效應」；語言文字的互通理解；東方的「博愛」和西方的「charity」使得普天下心懷「人溺己溺」之心的信徒，都能為營造開創一個由愛出發、以和為貴的世界而一起努力！這一切都說明了一個事實：人與人之間不再因距離、時空、障礙和誤解而「老死不相往來」！

當然，在這一片光鮮亮麗的外表下，隱憂依然存在。「全球化」（Globalization）對第三世界的人而言，竟成為新帝國主義和資本主義的同義字！造成這種誤解，甚至於扭曲的主要原因是對不同於自己的文化、風俗、傳統及習慣的一知半解；是不是用法文就顯得比較文明？使用義大利文就會比較熱情？德文，富哲理？英文，有深度？而美語，就「財大氣粗」？是不是有一套介紹書籍，雖不一定包含了所有相關的資訊，但至少是對那些想要知道或了解異國風物的好奇者，能有所幫助的參考工具書？

放眼今日的自學書刊，林林總總，參差不齊。上者，艱澀聱牙或孤芳自賞；下者，錯誤百出或言不及意！想要找兼具深度和廣度的語言學習工具書，實屬不易。現有本校應用外語學系黃靜悅和唐凱仁兩位老師，前者留學旅居國外多年，以國人的角度看外國文化；後者則以外國人的立場，以其數十年寄居臺灣的經驗，兩人合作撰寫系列叢書，舉凡旅遊、日常生活、社交、校園及商務應用，提供眞實情境對話，佐以「實用語句」、「字句補給站」讓學習者隨查隨用，並穿插「小叮嚀」和「小祕訣」，提供作者在美生活的點滴、體驗與心得等的第一手資訊。同時，「文化祕笈」及「旅遊資訊站」更爲同類書刊中之創舉！

學無止境！但唯有輔以正確的學習書籍，才能收「事半功倍」之效。本人對兩位老師的投入與努力，除表示敬意，特此作序說明，並冀望黃唐兩位老師在教學研究之餘，再接再厲，爲所有有志向學、自我提昇的學習者，提供更精練、更充實的自學叢書。

前實踐大學　校長

張光正

自序

學習外語的動機不外乎外在（instrumental）及內在（intrinsic）兩類：外在動機旨在以語言作爲工具，完成工作任務；內在動機則是希望透過外語學習達成自我探索及自我實現的目標。若人們在語言學習上能有所成，則此成就也必然是雙方面的；一方面完成工作任務而得到實質上的利益報償，另一方面則因達成溝通、了解對方文化及想法而得到豐富的感受。

現今每個人都是地球公民中的一員，而語言則是自我與世界的連結工具。今日網路科技的發展在彈指間就可以連結到我們想要的網站，人類的學習心與天性因刺激而產生對未知的好奇心及行動力，使我們對於異國語言文化自然產生嚮往；增進對這個世界的了解已不是所謂的個人特色或美德，而是身處現代地球村的每個人都該具備的一種責任與義務！

用自己的腳走出去、用自己的眼睛去看、用自己的心靈去感受世界其他國家人們的生活方式、用自己學得的語言當工具，與不同國家的人們交談；或許我們的母語、種族、膚色、性別不同，或許我們的衣著、宗教信仰、喜好以及對事情的看法、做法不同，但人與人之間善意的眼神、微笑、肢體動作、互相尊重、善待他人的同理心，加上適切的語言，對世界和平、國際友邦間相互扶持的共同渴望，使我們深深體會到精彩動人的外語學習旅程其實是自我發現的旅程！只有自己親自走過的旅程、完成過的任務、通過的關卡、遇到的人們、累積的智慧經驗、開拓的視野、體驗過的人生，才是無可替代的眞實感受。世界有多大、個人想爲自己及世人貢獻的事有多少，學習外語完成自我實現內在動機的收穫就有多豐富！

今日有機會將自己所學與用腳走世界、用心親感受的經驗交付五南出版社出版叢書，誠摯感謝前實踐大學張光正校長慨爲本叢書作序、前鄧景元主編催生本系列書，眾五南夥伴使本書順利完成，及親愛的家人朋友學生們的加油打氣。若讀者大眾能因本系列叢書增進英語文實力，並爲自己開啓一道與世界溝通的大門，便是對作者最大的回饋與鼓勵！

願與所有立志於此的讀者共勉之。

作者　黃靜悅　謹誌

目錄

Unit 1 尋找客戶 Finding Customers

Unit 2 國際參展準備 Preparation for International Trade Fairs

Unit 3 參加國際商展 Participating In International Fairs

Unit 4 接待客戶 Receiving Clients

Unit 5 作商業簡報 Giving Business Presentations

Unit 6 討論產品製作 Discussing and Manufacturing Products

Unit 7 報價與議價 Offering and Negotiating the Price

Unit 8 協商交易條件 Negotiation on Terms and Conditions of Transaction

Unit 10 處理產品問題 Handling Problems with Goods

Unit 11 危機處理 Handling Crises

Unit 12 商業書信 Business Letters

附錄 Appendices

Unit 1 Finding Customers

尋找客戶

雖然每個公司行業屬性及預算有所不同，但無不想盡辦法開拓商機（business expansion），網路時代除了以電子郵件開發潛在客戶外，企業透過建置自己的網頁、社群（networking）或登錄貿易網路平臺（business platforms）及參與各類工商協會的管道增加被搜尋到的曝光率（如參展、觀展、刊登廣告、工商目錄等）。有幸經由人脈（connection）介紹的客戶，更應輔以電話聯絡，製造多一點的互動，增加商機。

1.1 電話聯繫潛在客戶—陌生接洽未獲轉接
Calling a Potential Client: The First Contact - Not Getting Connected on the Phone

（電話鈴聲 Ring）

A: 我是傑生，是家用工具的製造商，從臺灣打電話來，我看到您的網站在賣家用工具，您可以將我轉接給負責家用工具的人員嗎？

A: My name is Jason. I'm a home tool manufacturer calling from Taiwan. I saw on your website that you're selling home tools. Could you please transfer this call to the person responsible for home tools?

B: 好，等一下（幾秒鐘）。抱歉，他現在不在辦公室。

B: OK. Just a moment. (a few seconds) Sorry, he's not in the office right now.

A: 我可以問他的分機號碼、大名跟職稱嗎？

A: May I ask his extension number and his name and title?

B: 很抱歉，我們公司不允許洩漏資料。

B: I'm sorry. Our company does not allow me to release that information.

A: 我了解，您可以給我一個有效的電子郵件地址讓我寄一些資訊過去嗎？

A: I see. Would you give me a valid email address that I can send some information to?

B: 你可以寄到我們網站上的電子郵件地址。

B: You can write to the email address on our website.

transfer [træns'fɝ] v. 轉接
responsible [rɪ'spɑnsəbl̩] adj. 負責的
extension number 分機號碼
title ['taɪtl̩] n. 職稱
release [rɪ'lis] v. 釋放，洩漏
valid ['vælɪd] adj. 有效的

1. 我是傑生，是家用工具的製造商，從臺灣打電話來。
   This is Jason. I'm a home tool manufacturer calling from Taiwan.
2. 我可以跟負責家用工具的人員談話嗎？
   May I speak to the person who handles home tools?
3. 您可以將我轉接給負責家用工具的人員嗎？
   Could you please transfer this call to the person responsible for home tools?
4. 我可以問他的分機號碼、大名跟職稱嗎？
   May I ask his extension number and his name and title?
5. 您可以給我一個有效的電子郵件地址讓我寄一些資訊過去嗎？
   Would you give me a valid email address that I can send some information to?

不入虎穴，焉得虎子，電話行銷（telephone marketing）最重要的是不怕被拒絕，不害羞有自信才能讓對方想聽下去，在通過總機或助理的電話過濾（screen phone calls）後才有可能被轉接給重要人物（指明找「負責」某部門的人員，被轉接的機會較大）。如果無法找到人，必須設法問到資訊（名字、分機、職稱、致電時間、有效郵件地址等），以免無功而返白忙一場。

1.2 陌生接洽—被轉接給助理
The First Contact - Getting Connected to the Assistant

（電話鈴聲 Ring）

A: 我是傑生，是家用工具的製造商，從臺灣打電話來，我看到您的網站在賣家用工具，您可以將我轉接給負責家用工具的人員嗎？

A: My name is Jason. I'm a home tool manufacturer calling from Taiwan. I saw on your website that you're selling home tools. Could you please transfer this call to the person responsible for home tools?

B: 好，請等一下（幾秒鐘），我將為您轉接到他的助理。

B: OK. Just a moment. (a few seconds) I'll connect you to his assistant.

A: 謝謝！

A: Thank you !

（電話轉接 call transferring）

B: 哈囉，（這裡是）羅伯特的助理，瑪麗，我如何幫你？

B: Hello. Robert's assistant, Mary speaking. How may I help you?

A: 嗨，我叫傑生，是家用工具的製造商，從臺灣打電話來，我看到您的網站在賣家用工具，我可以跟負責家用工具的人員談話嗎？

A: Hi, my name is Jason. I'm a home tool manufacturer calling from Taiwan. I saw on your website that you're selling home tools. May I speak to the person who handles home tools?

B: 那是我的主管，羅伯特彼德森，但他現在不在。

B: It's my supervisor, Robert Peterson, but he is not in right now.

A: 何時打電話給他最好？

A: When is the best time to call him?

B: 你明天早上可以試試。

B: You can try tomorrow morning.

A: 好，謝謝！

A: OK. Thank you.

connect [kə'nɛkt] v. 連接
assistant [ə'sɪstənt] n. 助理
supervisor ['supɚˌvaɪzɚ] 或 [ˌsupɚ'vaɪzɚ] n. 主管

1. 我看他是否可以接電話。
   I'll see if he is available.
2. 我應該說是誰打來的？
   Who shall I say is calling, please?
3. 彼德森先生現在很忙，他想要知道你想跟他談什麼？
   Mr. Peterson is rather busy right now and would like to know what you wish to speak to him about.
4. 何時打電話給他最好？
   When is the best time to call him?

1.3 陌生接洽—被轉接給負責人 The First Contact - Getting Connected to the Person in Charge

B: 哈囉，（這裡是）羅伯特的助理，瑪麗，我如何幫你？

B: Hello. Robert's assistant, Mary speaking. How may I help you?

A: 嗨，我叫傑生，是家用工具的製造商，從臺灣打電話來，我看到您的網站在賣家用工具，我可以跟負責家用工具的人員談話嗎？

A: Hi, my name is Jason. I'm a home tool manufacturer calling from Taiwan. I saw on your website that you're selling home tools. May I speak to the person who handles home tools?

B: 那是我的主管，羅伯特彼德森。我會問他是否現在可以跟你說。

B: It's my supervisor, Robert Peterson. I'll ask if he can talk to you right now.

（幾秒鐘後，轉接中 a few seconds, call transferring）

C: 哈囉，（我是）羅伯特彼德森。

C: Hello, Robert Peterson.

A: 彼德森先生，我是傑生，是家用工具的製造商，從臺灣打電話來，我看到您的網站在賣家用工具，我們想要提供您品質良好且價格極具競爭力的產品，我相信您一定會有興趣。

A: Mr. Peterson. This is Jason. I'm a home tool manufacturer calling from Taiwan. I saw on your website that you're selling home tools. We'd like to provide you good quality products with very competitive prices. I'm sure you'd be interested.

B: 我了解了，再說一次你的名字是？

B: I see. What's your name again?

Word Bank 字庫

quality products 優質產品
competitive [kəm'pɛtətɪv] adj. 有競爭力的

Useful Phrases 實用語句

1. 我幫你轉接給彼德森先生。
   I'll put you through to Mr. Peterson.
2. 我們想要提供你品質良好且價格具競爭力的產品。
   We'd like to provide you good quality products with competitive prices.
3. 我可以有您的 Skype 帳號嗎？
   May I have your Skype account?
4. 我相信您一定會有興趣。
   I'm sure you'd be interested.

被轉接後，雖然仍可能被客戶掛電話，但客戶有許多種，總會有想聽你說下去的客戶，也有些客戶在拒絕幾次後會給你機會，因此在練好自我介紹及打電話目的說詞後，務必以客戶的立場來打動對方。此外，首次接洽被成功轉接後務必要問到負責採購者的有效郵件地址及直接聯絡電話以打開溝通管道。

使用網路即時通訊軟體（online instant messaging，如Skype）有其利弊須衡量，好處是使用者可以看到誰在線上及其顯示狀況即時打字或（使用視訊）電話溝通，但壞處是忙碌的時候，如果客戶一直敲你要回覆，甚至好幾個人同時敲你的話，可能讓人疲於應付。此外，即時通訊講求即時反應，反而較容易出錯，加上語言文化及時差因素，以及過往紀錄不好找、不易保留，影響其法律效力（legal effect）等諸多缺點，加總起來可能超越即時性的優點。電子郵件相較之下優缺點正好與其互補，因此可以將即時通訊軟體作爲即時通知工具，而以電子郵件作爲主要訊息傳遞的工具。

1.4 電話聯繫潛在客戶—朋友介紹
Calling a Potential Client - A Friend's Reference

（電話鈴聲 Ring）

A: 哈囉，這裡是泰瑞莎陳，從臺灣打電話來，我想要跟銷售經理史蒂夫瓊斯先生談話， 他在嗎？

A: Hello, this is Teresa Chen calling from Taiwan. I'd like to speak to the sales manager, Mr. Steve Jones. Is he in?

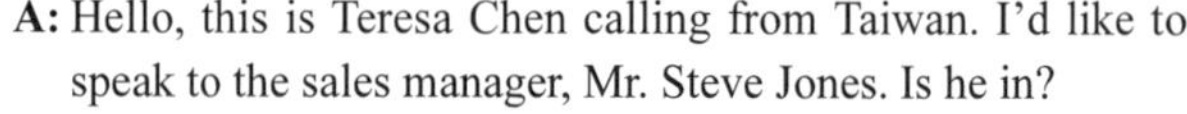

B: 陳女士，我可以有您的公司大名嗎？

B: Ms. Chen, may I have your company's name?

A: 是的，LH 集團，我們有一個共同的朋友，艾倫史奈德先生。

A: Yes, LH Group, but we have a mutual friend, Mr. Allen Schneider.

B: 請等一下（兩秒鐘後），陳女士，您被轉接到瓊斯先生了，請說。

B: Please hold. (two seconds later) Ms. Chen, you are connected to Mr. Jones. Please speak.

A: 哈囉，瓊斯先生，早安！我是泰瑞莎陳。

A: Hello, Mr. Jones, good morning. This is Teresa Chen.

C: 哈囉，陳女士，早安！凱文有提過你會打電話來。

C: Hello, Ms. Chen. Good morning. Kevin mentioned that you'd call me.

A: 是的，瓊斯先生，您可以叫我泰瑞莎，我知道你對品質好的家用工具有興趣，我們是臺灣超過 20 年的供應商。

A: Yes, Mr. Jones, you can call me Teresa. I know that you are interested in good quality home tools. We have been a supplier in Taiwan for over twenty years.

C: 好，你何不先寄給我你的網址，然後我們再來談談。

C: OK, why don't you send me your website address first, and we can talk later.

A: 好，瓊斯先生，我應當寄到您的哪個電子郵件帳戶？

A: Sure, Mr. Jones. Which email account should I send it to?

C: 寄到stevejones@gamil.com。

C: Send it to stevejones@gamil.com.

A: 史蒂芬與瓊斯中間有標點符號嗎？

A: Is there any punctuation between "steve" and "jones"?

C: 沒有，沒空格也沒標點符號。

C: No, there's no space and no punctuation in between.

A: 好，瓊斯先生，我會馬上去做，並且介紹一些您可能有興趣的產品。

A: OK, Mr. Jones. I'll do it right away and recommend some products that you may be interested in.

C: 謝謝，我們晚點聊。

C: Thank you. Talk to you later.

mutual ['mjutʃuəl] adj. 共同的
mention ['mɛnʃən] v. 提及
punctuation [ˌpʌŋktʃu'eʃən] n. 標點符號

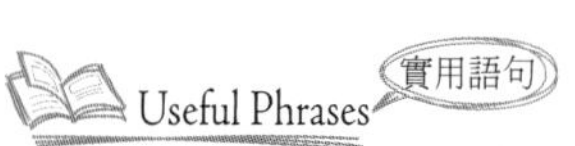

1. 我想要跟銷售經理史蒂夫瓊斯先生談話。
   I'd like to speak to the sales manager, Mr. Steve Jones.
2. 我們從美國商會〔全球資源/阿里巴巴/eBay〕得知您的資訊。
   We learned about you from the American Commerce Chamber [the Global Source/Alibaba/eBay].

3. 我們經由艾倫史奈德先生介紹。

   We were introduced by Mr. Allen Schneider.

4. 我們有一個共同的朋友，艾倫史奈德先生。

   We have a mutual friend, Mr. Allen Schneider.

5. 張先生介紹你給我。

   I was referred to you by Mr. Chang.

6. 我應當寄到您的哪個電子郵件帳戶？

   Which email account should I write to?

7. 史蒂芬與瓊斯中間有標點符號嗎？

   Is there any punctuation between "steve" and "jones"?

8. 我會介紹一些您可能有興趣的產品。

   I'll recommend some products that you may be interested in.

陌生接洽總是充滿挑戰，但透過朋友口碑（through word of mouth）的介紹或推薦就像獲得一張入場券，被介紹的客戶（referrals）通常有更高的機率成爲固定客戶，並且可能成爲你的下一個介紹人，爲你帶來更多的人脈及商機。要注意的是，不要給新客戶緊迫盯人的感覺（Don't be pushy.），而應注重提供良好的資訊及服務，因雙方之聯繫產生商機，在彼此合適的條件下自然有機會達成交易。

在電話上拼字爲辨別起見，可用簡短淺顯單字輔助。

例如：

b as in "boy"

d as in "dog"

@英文爲 at

(.)爲 dot

(-)連字號爲 hyphen

(_)下標線爲 underscore

寫下後應該與對方確認無誤。

1.5 電話聯繫國際商展之潛在客戶 Calling a Potential Customer after an International Fair

（電話鈴聲 Ring）

A: 哈囉，這裡是泰瑞莎陳，從臺灣打電話來，我想要跟銷售經理約翰羅傑先生談話，他在嗎？

A: Hello, this is Teresa Chen calling from Taiwan. I'd like to speak to the sales manager, Mr. John Roger. Is he in?

B: 陳女士，我可以有您的公司大名嗎？

B: Ms. Chen, may I have your company's name?

A: 是的，LH集團，我與羅傑先生兩星期前在拉斯維加斯會展談過話。

A: Yes, my company is LH Group. I've talked to Mr. Roger at the Las Vegas Fair two weeks ago.

B: 請等一下（兩秒鐘後）。陳女士，您被轉接到羅傑先生了，請說。

B: Please hold. (two seconds later) Ms. Chen, you are connected to Mr. Roger. Please speak.

A: 哈囉，羅傑先生，早安！我是泰瑞莎陳。

A: Hello, Mr. Roger, good morning. This is Teresa Chen.

C: 哈囉，陳女士，早安！

C: Hello, Ms. Chen. Good morning.

A: 是的，羅傑先生，您可以叫我泰瑞莎，我們兩星期前在拉斯維加斯說過話。我知道你對品質好的家用工具有興趣，我們是臺灣超過 20 年的供應商。

A: Yes, Mr. Roger, you can call me Teresa. We talked at the fair in Las Vegas two weeks ago. I know that you are interested in good quality home tools. We have been a supplier in Taiwan for over twenty years.

C: 好，泰瑞莎，我記得跟你談過話！ 你何不先寄給我你的網址，然後我們再來談談。

C: OK, Teresa, I remember talking to you! Why don't you send me your website address first, and we can talk later.

A: 好，羅傑先生，我應當寄到您的哪個電子郵件帳戶？

A: Sure, Mr. Roger. Which email account should I send it to?

C: 寄到johnroger@gamil.com。

C: Send it to johnroger@gamil.com.

A: 約翰與羅傑中間有標點符號嗎？

A: Is there any punctuation between "john" and "roger"?

C: 沒有。

C: No.

A: 好，羅傑先生，我會馬上去做，並且介紹一些您可能有興趣的產品。

A: OK, Mr. Roger. I'll do it right away and recommend some products that you may be interested in.

B: 謝謝，晚點談。

B: Thank you. Talk to you later.

打鐵趁熱，參加國際商展時當場問客戶何時與他聯絡最好，掌握黃金聯絡時間（best timing），以免客戶先下訂單給別人，而自己卻因蹉跎而喪失先機。

1.6 初步交涉—以電話回覆報價
Preliminary Contact - Replying to an Inquiry by Phone

A: 哈囉，我可以跟麥迪遜先生說話嗎？

A: Hello, may I speak to Mr. Madison?

B: 我可以問你的名字及你打電話給麥迪遜先生的理由嗎？

B: Could I have your name and the reason of your call to Mr. Madison?

A: 是的，我的名字是泰瑞莎陳，從臺灣LH集團打來，是關於他在我們網站的詢價。

A: Yes, my name is Teresa Chen calling from LH Group in Taiwan to talk about his inquiry on our website.

B: 好，請稍待（兩秒鐘）。

B: OK, one moment please. (two seconds)

Dialog 2 對話2

（稍後 Later）

A: 嗨，麥迪遜先生，這裡是泰瑞莎陳。

A: Hi, Mr. Madison. This is Teresa Chen.

B: 嗨，陳女士，我收到妳的郵件了。

B: Hi, Ms. Chen. I got your mail.

A: 好，你認為目前如何呢？

A: Good. What do you think so far?

B: 看起來不錯，但是我需要更多資訊。

B: It looks fine, but I need more information.

A: 好，我可以幫你什麼呢？

A: Sure, what can I help you with?

B: 呃，我需要知道你的生產線，你是供應商或是貿易商？還有，基地設在哪裡？

B: Well, I need to know more about your production line. Also, are you a supplier or an agent? And where are you based?

A: 我們是在臺灣的製造商，麥迪遜先生，我們的產品外銷到全世界超過 20 年了。麥迪遜先生，您是批發商或是零售商？您通常進口家用工具嗎？或是還有其他產品？

A: We are a manufacturer based in Taiwan, Mr. Madison. Our products have been exported around the world for over twenty years. Mr. Madison, are you a wholesaler or retailer and do you usually import home tools or other goods, too?

B: 多數是家用工具，我們是批發商，你的產品價格及出貨條件是什麼？

B: Mostly home tools. We are a wholesaler. What is the price of the product and your payment terms?

A: 價錢要看你的量而定，我們要求 30% 預付款，剩下的用電匯付款，你們的付款條件為何？

A: The price depends on the quantity of your order. We ask for 30% deposit in advance, and the rest paid by T/T. What about your payment terms?

B: 我們用記帳。

B: We use O/A.

A: 麥迪遜先生，你們每年購買家用工具的頻率及購買量有多少？

A: How often and how many home tools do you buy each year, Mr. Madison?

B: 每年 4-5 次，超過 200,000 件。我下訂單後你們多久可以完成生產？

B: 4 to 5 times a year, and over 200,000 of them each year. How long does it take for you to finish production after I place an order?

A: 大約 3-5 週。

A: About 3 to 5 weeks.

B: 你的產品有任何一種認證嗎？

B: Do your products have any certification?

A: 有的，我們通過世界主要市場的要求標準。

A: Yes, we do. We have passed the standards required by the world's major markets.

B: 很好，你的最低訂貨量是多少？

B: That's good. What is your MOQ?

A: 500 件。麥迪遜先生，你有特定的需求或是需要其他產品資訊嗎？

A: 500. Mr. Madison, do you have specific requirements or do you need other product information?

B: 我要再看看你寄給我的照片後想一想。

B: I have to look at the product pictures you sent me again and think.

A: 好的，麥迪遜先生，請看我們的網站有任何你感興趣的產品，當你有疑問時，隨時讓我知道。

A: OK, Mr. Madison. Please have a look at our website for any products of interest and let me know any time when you have a question.

B: 好，謝謝！

B: Alright. Thank you.

A: 很樂意幫忙，再見。

A: My pleasure to help. Goodbye.

B: 再見。

B: Goodbye.

Word Bank 字庫

reply [rɪ'plaɪ] v., n. 回覆
inquiry [ɪn'kwaɪrɪ, 'ɪnkwərɪ] n. 詢問
T/T (telegraphic transfer) 電匯
O/A (open account) 記帳
certification [ˌsɝtəfə'keʃən] n. 認證，證明
require [rɪ'kwaɪr] v. 要求
MOQ (minimum order quantity) 最低訂貨量
specific [spɪ'sɪfɪk] adj. 特定的，明確的
requirement [rɪ'kwaɪrmənt] n. 需求

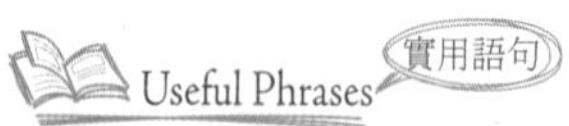

Useful Phrases 實用語句

1. 您是批發商或是零售商？
   Are you a wholesaler or retailer?
2. 您通常進口家用工具或是還有其他產品？
   Do you usually import home tools or other goods, too?
3. 你有任何特定的需求嗎？
   Do you have any specific requirements?
4. 你的產品價格及出貨條件是什麼？
   What is the price of the product and your payment terms?
5. 你們的付款條件為何？
   What about your payment terms?
6. 你們每年購買家用工具的頻率及購買量有多少？
   How often and how many home tools do you buy each year?
7. 你們的主要市場在哪裡？
   Where is your major market?
8. 你的產品有任何一種認證嗎？
   Do your products have any certification?
9. 我們通過世界主要市場的要求標準。
   We have passed the standards required by the world's major markets.

10. 你有特定的需求嗎？

Do you have specific requirements?

11. 價錢要看你的量而定。

The price depends on the quantity of your order.

12. 我晚點會寄給你報價（單）。

I'll send you a quote later.

13. 你在美國有任何經銷商嗎？

Do you have distributors in any part of the US?

14. 你在美國有多少客戶？

How many clients do you have in the US?

15. 你可以給我美國經銷商的地址嗎？

Can you give me the addresses of the distributors in the US?

16. 我們在加州有幾個經銷商。

We have several distributors in California.

17. 讓我先寫下你倉庫的地址。

Let me have your warehouse address first.

18. 我下週前會詳細地回電子郵件給你。

I will email you in detail by next week.

19. 我需要跟同事確認後，再給你回覆。

I need to double check with my colleague and get back to you later.

價格可說是一開始接洽最根本卻也最關鍵的問題。正因如此，陌生接洽總是充滿彼此攻防的諜對諜情節，因爲對方提供的資訊虛實更有待經驗及時間證明，切記不要在對方詢價時馬上提供報價單或目錄，以免對方獲得資訊就不再聯絡。

此外，一開口就要樣品的對象可能志在收集樣品而非交易。對方詢價時，正確的做法爲反問對方問題，看他的回答反應判斷對方實力，如公司性質、進貨量、產品、材質、款式、付款方式、市場等。讓對方知道你問這些問題是爲了提供最適合的產品及報價。

當然對方也會打探（prying）他們所要的足夠資訊，所以打電話前需要準備充分以爲應對。如果對方有所要求，或是對方的問題你無法當場回答，在掛斷電話前要重述確認，並在電話後做筆記，著手進行後續。即使對方暫無所求，也要記下他們的反應或意見，以利後續商機。電話聯繫後，還是要以電子郵件簡短敘述雙方談話重點留下書面紀錄。（報價議價請詳見第七章）

1.7 透過電子郵件及網路主動開發客戶 Starting First Contact with a Potential Client by Emailing and Networking

樣本 Sample

Subject: To Mr. Carl Reed
主旨：致卡爾瑞德先生

Dear Mr. Carl Reed,
親愛的卡爾瑞德先生，

How are you doing today? We got information from your website, indicating that you are interested in home tools.
今天過得好嗎？我們從您的網站得知您的資訊，顯示您對家用工具有興趣。

As a highly professional factory in Taiwan, we have been satisfying our customers with high quality products(please see the attached photo)since our establishment in 1975. We are also experienced in making products for famous brands.
作為臺灣高度專業的工廠，我們從 1975 年設立至今即以優良產品滿足客戶（請參見附件照片），並擁有為許多知名廠牌製作產品的經驗。

If you need professional, quality products, please feel free to contact us. We look forward to cooperating with you in your market and hope to hear from you soon.
如果您有需要專業品質的產品，請不吝聯繫我們。我們期待能在您的市場與您合作，並期待您近日的回音。

Thank you very much！
非常感謝您！

Sincerely yours,
誠摯地，

Teresa Chen
Sales Executive
LH Group
Contact information
泰瑞莎陳
銷售執行
LH 集團
聯絡資訊

1. 我們很高興收到來自美國商會的資料，了解您對家用工具有興趣。

   We are glad to have received your information from the American Commerce Chamber and learn that you are interested in home tools.

2. 我們是臺灣的一個可靠的供應商，有最新的技術及研發團隊。

   We are a reliable supplier in Taiwan with the latest technology and a R&D team.

3. 我們相信您會滿意我們的物美價廉。

   We believe you will be satisfied with our high quality products with very competitive prices.

4. 我們期待與您建立一個雙贏的商業關係。

   We look forward to establishing a mutually beneficial business relationship with you.

5. 有關我們公司資訊請看附件。

   Please see the attached file for more information about our company.

6. 請上網看我們的工廠照片及全部的產品。

   Please visit our website for our factory photos and a full range of our products.

7. 我們感激您給我們任何意見。

   We'd be grateful if you could kindly give us any feedback.

8. 您的儘早回覆會讓我們非常感激。

   Your early reply will be greatly appreciated.

9. 我們期待儘快收到您的回覆。

   We look forward to hearing from you soon.

為避免寄出的開發信被對方視為垃圾郵件刪除，主旨打上收件者（銷售經理）全名以保證該信被閱讀。如不知收件者姓名，但知道相關人員姓名，可致歉請求代轉。完全不知對方姓名時可用「致：銷售/採購經理」（To: Sales manager/purchase manager）或「關於____產品詢價/訂單」（Re: price inquiry/purchase inquiry/your possible order for____products），但效果就差多了。

開發信宜簡明扼要，並點出自己的優勢及強調能為對方創造何種利益（例如：獲得的服務更好，產品價錢更低，客戶付出的各種成本更低，並因此能創造出「一系列」產品銷售利基）。記住署名時職稱不要寫「銷售助理」顯得人微言輕，換成「銷售執行」或其他夠份量的頭銜，對方才有可能回信。

以公司信箱寄出之開發信如果被擋，可能是短時間大量發信之故，有時需要修改主旨去除廣告字眼後（如 price, sale, cheap）重寄，有些信箱設有驗證或過濾名單，如果始終無法寄達，就用電話代替。（商業書信請見第十二章）

1.8 網路平臺回覆
Responding to a Reply on the Internet

電子郵件 Email

Subject: price inquiry from Mr. Robert Hughes
主旨：羅伯特休斯先生之詢價

Dear Mr. Robert Hughes,
親愛的羅伯特休斯先生，

Thank you for visiting our website. We are pleased to receive your inquiry on floor bike stands. Since we offer many kinds of materials, sizes, and products, we need your annual quantity of purchase and shipping terms in order to provide you a competitive quote.
感謝您拜訪我們的網站，我們很高興收到您關於地板型腳踏車架的詢價，因為我們提供許多材質、尺寸及產品，我們需要您每年的購買量及運輸條件，才能提供您最具競爭力的報價。

Thank you.
感謝您。

With warm regards,
獻上誠摯關懷，

Teresa Chen
Sales Executive
LH Group
Contact information
泰瑞莎陳
銷售執行
LH 集團
聯絡資訊

在網路什麼都有什麼都不奇怪的今日，商業間諜（business espionage）同樣無孔不入，所有想在網路平臺做生意的人第一步都必須先從防止公司及個人資訊遭駭（hacking prevention）開始。

網路詢價比電話詢價更隱密，你甚至無法從對方何種口音（accent）去做任何判斷，因此必須篩選信函，根據對方是否有收信人稱呼、所需產品及自我簡介做基本判斷。如果連基本項目都沒有，只表示對你公司有興趣者，必定如亂槍打鳥般發信，可不予理會。如果一開始就要樣品及報價者，則心態可議。倘若寄來的是其他投資合作的邀請訊息，極可能是詐騙陷阱（scam），不必給自己找麻煩。

篩選後的客戶才是目標客戶，接下來是發出一封如上提供之樣本反詢問函，要稱呼對方姓名，拉近距離，並製造多一點機會與客戶互動；在對方回覆而且充分確定更多可靠資訊及產品款式、材質、數量等各項交易條件後，才可以報價。

Note

Unit 2 Preparation for International Trade Fairs

國際參展準備

國外參展可主動拓展商機，而參展方式則直接影響效果：1. 參加展覽團雖方便，但廠商若未獲恰當攤位，則效果打折。2. 請國外代理參展，雖可省去開銷，但難盡如人意。3. 自行參展，可保有更多自主權，但展前數月就須開始籌備，從上網下載國外展場之申請表（application form）、報名（register）及閱讀「參展者指南」（exhibitor guide）及規章（份量不少，有疑問要儘早詢問），到安排展覽產品、寄送到國外展場倉庫、倉庫到會場、選攤、擺攤、公司及產品簡介、參展人員的國外機票飯店、服裝、禮節等，皆須適時預備及確認。商展本為營利單位，凡事都要收費。如能向國外當地客戶調來產品參展，互利互惠，準備就可簡單些。另外，若主辦單位出版買主名錄（buyers/importers directory），別忘了索取或購買。如要運回參展產品，須提前規劃交付貨物代理或當地代理辦理，撤場時間才來得及。

2.1 查看平面圖及選攤
Checking the Floor Plan and Choosing a Booth

Dialog 1 對話1

A: 嗨，我是泰瑞莎陳，我需要跟人談即將來臨貿易展的攤位。

A: Hi. I'm Teresa Chen. I need to talk to someone about booth space at the upcoming trade fair.

B: 哈囉，我是傑瑞泰勒。我可以幫你，你預訂了攤位嗎？

B: Hello. I'm Jerry Taylor. I can help you. Have you reserved a space yet?

A: 還沒，我需要搞清楚我們需要多少空間，空位在哪裡，以及價錢。

A: Not yet. I need to figure out how much room we need, the location of available spaces, and the price, too.

B: 好，跟我來。我會給你看一張電腦的平面圖。

B: OK. Come with me. I'll show you a map of the floor plan on the computer.

A: 好。

A: Good.

upcoming ['ʌp,kʌmɪŋ] adj. 即將來臨的
trade fair 貿易展
floor plan 平面圖

1. 我需要跟人談攤位。

   I need to talk to someone about booth space.

2. 你預訂了攤位嗎？

   Have you reserved a space yet?

3. 我需要搞清楚我們需要多少空間。

   I need to figure out how much room we need.

4. 我要知道空位在哪裡。

   I want to know the location of available spaces.

5. 聽起來我們需要兩個攤位。

   It sounds like we may need two spaces.

6. 我會給你看一張電腦的平面圖。

   I'll show you a map of the floor plan on the computer.

A: 我對平面圖有點困惑。可以請你解釋嗎？

A: The floor plan is a little confusing to me. Can you explain it please?

B: 好，我很樂意。這些線條表示你可以租賃的小區面積，標示較大的區塊不能變小。

B: Sure, I'll be happy to. These lines show the smallest area size you can rent. The larger areas shown can't be made smaller.

A: 那這些顏色呢？

A: What about these colors?

B: 相同產品會在同一區，所以它們代表不同廳及不同區有不同的產品。

B: The same products will be in the same section, so the colors represent different halls and different sections for different products.

A: 輪胎的區塊在哪裡？那個區塊每個攤位有多大？

A: Where is the tire section? How big is each booth in that section?

B: 在南區下層，攤位是 10 呎長 10 呎寬，也就是 100 平方呎的面積。

B: It's in the south hall lower level. The booth is 10 by 10 (feet). That is 100 square feet.

A: 我知道了。我可以租超過一個攤位嗎？

A: I see. Can I rent more than one booth?

B: 是的，你最多可以租不超過 5 個連續的攤位。

B: Yes. You can rent up to five consecutive spaces.

A: 平面圖內不同的區塊有任何價差嗎？

A: Is there any pricing difference between the different sections of the floor plan?

B: 靠近入口與飲食區價錢比較高。

B: The areas near the entrance doors and eating areas are priced higher.

A: 我明白了。

A: I see.

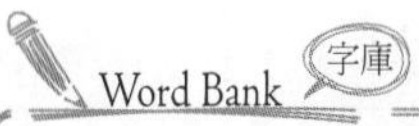

section ['sɛkʃən] n. 區塊
booth [buθ] n. 攤位
consecutive [kən'sɛkjətɪv] adj. 連續的
eating area 飲食區
price [praɪs] v. 定價

1. 那個區塊每個攤位有多大？
   How big is each booth in that section?
2. 我可以租超過一個攤位嗎？
   Can I rent more than one space?
3. 你最多可以租不超過 5 個連續的攤位。
   You can rent up to five consecutive spaces.
4. 有任何價差嗎？
   Is there any pricing difference?
5. 靠近入口的區域定價比較高。
   The areas near the doors are priced higher.

大型的展覽可能包含數十個展覽館，上千家廠商，以產業上下游或相關性分區，從零組件到成品甚至雜貨等分成不同展館，務必確認申請的攤位在適當的區域，不然損失就大了。價格決定攤位位置（site）的好壞，相同價格時有時還須抽籤（draw）。如果可以的話，選擇人潮進來或面對走道的地方。如在日本或英國等靠左行進的國家參展，務必確認展區進出的方向，並記得不要選擇有柱子或面對牆壁的地方。

另外，住宿遠近對於參展便利必然有所影響，挑選旅館的位置最好盡量靠近會場，雖然價格較高，但萬一碰到罷工（歐洲屢見不鮮），接駁車（shuttle bus）不開的話，可用步行方式順利到達會場，才不致大費周章消耗財力、人力到國外參展，卻完全無計可施。

2.2 租金與押金
The Rent and the Deposit

A: 租金包含什麼？

A: What is included in the rental cost?

B: 三天攤位的租金。

B: Three days of rent for your booth.

A: 有包含攤位其他的東西嗎？

A: Is there anything in the booth included?

B: 沒有，是空的，如果你需要裝潢布置，我們有簽約的團隊，其他的東西都可以用租的。

B: No, it is empty. If you need *décor*, we have contracted teams available. Everything else can be rented.

A: 你有服務的價目清單嗎？

A: Do you have a price list for the services?

B: 是的，在這裡，網站上也有。

B: Yes, we do. Here you are. It is also posted on the website.

A: 那讓我們的氣球升空呢？我們要多付費嗎？

A: What about flying our balloon? Do we need to pay extra?

B: 是的，你需要付氣球的天空租金。	**B:** Yes, you need to rent the sky for flying the balloon?
A: 那押金呢？	**A:** What about the deposit?
B: 大氣球押金要300元，但你需要買保險。	**B:** The big balloon takes a $300 deposit, but you need to buy the insurance.
A: 我可以用信用卡或公司支票支付嗎？	**A:** Can I pay by credit card or company checks?
B: 可以，我們收信用卡、轉帳以及某些支票。	**B:** Yes, we take credit cards, wire transfer, and certain checks.

décor ['dɛkɔr] 或 [de'kɔr] n. 裝潢布置（法文）
contract ['kɑntrækt] v. 簽約
available [ə'veləbl̩] adj. 可用的
balloon [bə'lun] n. 氣球
insurance [ɪn'ʃurəns] n. 保險
wire transfer 轉帳

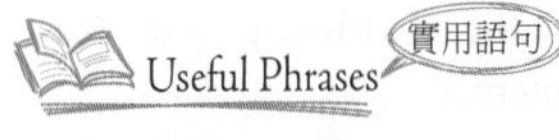

1. 租金包含什麼？
   What is included in the rental cost?
2. 有包含攤位其他的東西嗎？
   Is there anything in the booth included?

3. 你有服務的價目清單嗎？

Do you have a price list for the services?

4. 我要多付費嗎？

Do I need to pay extra?

5. 那押金呢？

What about the deposit?

6. 你需要買保險。

You need to buy the insurance.

7. 我可以用信用卡或公司支票支付嗎？

Can I pay by credit card or company checks?

有些展場要求現金交易或電匯轉帳，並非每個展場都願意收信用卡或支票。大型國際商展在展場前幾個月報名時就必須支付參展費用，繳費期限後才展開攤位分配或抽籤（draw）。爲求廣告效果，如果租用大型氣球或看板（signboard）、布條（banner）切記要買保險，氣球消氣後的重量或物品墜落皆足以傷人。

2.3 與參展大會接洽—確認水電、電話、網路 Contacting the Fair Agent - Confirming the Availability of the Utilities, Phone, and the Internet

A: 嗨，我需要跟你們確認水電、電話跟網路。

A: Hi, I need to confirm with you about the utilities, phone, and the Internet.

B: 你填申請單有填那些項目嗎？

B: Did you fill in those items in the application form?

A: 有。

A: Yes, we did.

B: 那應當在搭設的前一天就可以用了。

B: Then, they should be ready to use before the day of your set up.

A: 好，太好了！但是為了作展示，我需要確定在我攤位的某個位置有插座可以使用。

A: OK, that's great! But I need to make sure that an outlet will be available at a certain spot of my booth for the demo.

B: 你可以在搭設組幫你搭設時告訴他們。

B: You can talk to the set up team when they are setting up the booth for you.

A: 好，那網路呢？我需要無線網路密碼嗎？

A: Alright. What about the Internet? Do I need a password for the wifi?

B: 是的，你要給我看你的會展證件。

B: Yes, you do. But you need to show me your ID for the show.

A: 好的，在這裡。

A: OK, here you are.

B: 密碼是 semashow。

B: The password is semashow.

A: 多謝！

A: Thank you very much!

B: 當然，我很高興幫忙。	**B:** Sure, I'm glad to help.

utilities [ju'tɪlətɪ] n. 水電等公用設施
application [ˌæplə'keʃən] n. 申請
outlet ['aʊtˌlɛt] n. 插座

1. 我需要跟你們確認水電、電話跟網路。
   I need to confirm with you about the utilities, phone, and the Internet.
2. 我需要確定在我攤位的某個位置有插座可以使用。
   I need to make sure that an outlet will be available at a certain spot of my booth.

◎ 其他確認用語

1. 我要確認某事。
   I want to confirm something.
2. 請確認…。
   Please make sure that....
3. 我要確認…。
   I want to be certain that....
4. 我要確認…。
   I want to make sure that....

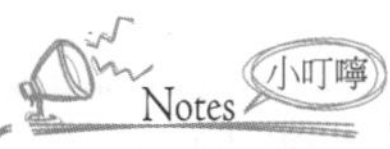

許多展覽的租金除了空間外，並不包含任何基本費用或配備。報名展場時就要填寫各項需要設備或備註，確認展場提供（或僅限使用展場提供）的設備收費多少，文件要攜帶備用，作爲已經申請的證明。

2.4 運輸（普通與特殊需求－車輛出入）Transportation (Regular and Special Needs, Vehicle Access - Entrance and Exit)

2.4a 詢問停車與入口 Asking about Parking and Entrance

A: 我會開車帶幾個客戶過來，最好在哪裡讓他們下車？	**A:** I will be bringing some clients here by car. Where is the best place to drop them off?
B: 四號入口最好，你可以直接開到門口，讓他們下車，直接進入室內。	**B:** Entrance 4 is best for that. There you may drive right up to the doors and let your clients get out of the car and go directly into the building.
A: 那裡有遮蔽嗎？	**A:** Is that area covered?
B: 有，他們（下車）不會受天氣影響。	**B:** Yes. They'll be protected from the weather.
A: 好，那停車呢？	**A:** Good. What about parking?

B: 因為你參展，可以免費停車，給停車服務員看你的通行證就可以了。

B: Because you are a participant in this show, you may park for free. Just show the parking attendant your pass.

A: 停車場在哪裡？

A: Where is the parking lot?

B: 在展區北側有一個八層樓的停車樓，南側有一個大停車場。

B: On the north side of the complex there is an eight level parking structure. On the south side there is a large parking lot.

A: 那無障礙入口呢？

A: What about handicap access?

B: 我們的停車場與入口都是無障礙的。

B: All of our parking facilities and entrances are handicap accessible.

A: 好，你幫了大忙。

A: OK. You have been a big help.

B: 沒問題，很高興為您服務。

B: No problem. Happy to be of service.

Word Bank 

participant [pɚˈtɪsəpənt, pɑr-] n. 參加者
attendant [əˈtɛndənt] n. 服務人員
pass [pæs] n. 通行證
complex [ˈkɑmplɛks] n. 展區，複合建築
handicap access 無障礙入口
accessible [ækˈsɛsəbl̩, ək-] adj. 可以獲得的

1. 最好在哪裡讓他們下車？
   Where is the best place to drop them off?
2. 停車場在哪裡？
   Where is the parking lot?
3. 那裡有遮蔽嗎？
   Is that area covered?
4. 他們（下車）不會受天氣影響。
   They'll be protected from the weather.
5. 那無障礙入口呢？
   What about handicap access?
6. 給停車員看你的通行證就可以。
   Just show the parking attendant your pass.
7. 讓他們下車。
   Drop them off.
8. 接他們上車。
   Pick them up.
9. 開到⋯。
   Drive up to....

2.4b 運輸（特殊需求）—卡車進入展場 Entering the Show Floor with a Truck

A: 早安，我們來搭設LH 集團的攤位，我們的卡車可以在哪裡進入會場？

A: Good morning. We are here to set up LH Group's booth. Where can we enter the show floor with our truck?

B: 你要從西側入口進入，那裡有大型車輛可以進入的大門。

B: You will have to go to the west side entrance. There is where the large doors are that large vehicles can come through.

A: 我知道了，我們到達的時候會有人在那裡嗎？

A: I see. Will somebody be there when we get there?

B: 我會打電話告訴他們你們到了。還有，你會看到入口左側門邊有一個電話箱。如果沒有人在那裡，就打電話，馬上有人會跟你對談。

B: I'll call and tell them you are coming. Also, you will see a call box on the left side of the entry door area. If no one is there, just pick up that phone. Someone will talk to you right away.

A: 聽起來很好，謝謝！

A: Sounds good. Thanks.

B: 不客氣。

B: Sure.

vehicle ['viɪkḷ] n. 車輛
call box 電話箱

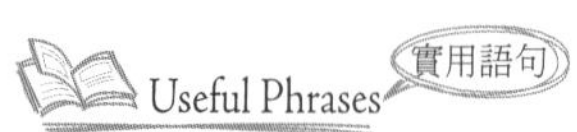

1. 我們的卡車可以在哪裡進入會場？

Where can we enter the show floor with our truck?

2. 我們到達的時候會有人在那裡嗎？

Will somebody be there when we get there?

3. 如果沒有人在那裡，就打電話。

If no one is there, just pick up that phone.

4. 拿起話筒。

Pick up the phone.

不要猶豫，只要提出來，展場應當都會協助載送產品或回應客戶的任何特殊需求，如果服務項目不包含在參展範圍，當然必須另外付費。展場幾乎都指定使用大會的機械器具（如舉升機），而不允許使用私人設備，一來展場有商業利益的因素，再者是安全的考量。

2.5 攤位設計、建造及裝潢
Booth Design, Construction, and Décor

A: 嗨，我們是參展的廠商，我們需要搭設攤位的人手。

A: Hi, we are participants in the show. We need people to set up our booth.

B: 好，我們有幾個簽訂合約的供應攤商可以滿足你們的需求。

B: OK. We have contracted with several supply vendors who can fill your needs.

A: 你可以告訴我們服務包含什麼嗎？

A: Can you tell us what kinds of services are included?

B: 好，我們提供你們服務，例如攤位設計、建造與搭設。

B: Sure. We have services available to you like booth design, construction, and set up.

A: 是的，那很好，很方便。那椅子呢？

A: Yes. That's great! It's very convenient. What about chairs?

B: 每個攤位包含四張椅子。

B: Four chairs are included with each rental space.

A: 可以有更多椅子嗎？

A: Are more chairs available?

B: 可以，如果你需要更多椅子可以用租的。

B: Yes. More chairs can be rented if you need them.

set up 搭設
contract ['kɑntrækt] v. 訂合約
supply vendor 供應攤商
fill [fɪl] v. 滿足
construction [kən'strʌkʃən] n. 建造

1. 供應攤商可以滿足你們的需求。
   Supply vendors can fill your needs.
2. 我們提供你們服務。
   We have services available to you.
3. 可以有更多椅子嗎？
   Are more chairs available?
4. （需要）更多椅子可以用租的。
   More chairs can be rented.

A: 嗨，我需要找人談貿易展攤位的裝潢。	**A:** Hi, I need to talk to someone about making *décor* for a booth at a trade show.
B: 好，請坐。	**B:** Certainly. Have a seat.
A: 謝謝。	**A:** Thank you.
B: 你可以敘述你要什麼嗎？	**B:** Can you describe what you want?
A: 我有些想法及幾個我畫好很簡單的圖給你看。	**A:** I have a few ideas and a couple of very simple drawings I can show you.
B: 好，我們看一下。	**B:** Good. Let's have a look.
A: 我們的攤位跟橫幅需要這些顏色。	**A:** We need these colors on the booth and banners.
B: 你知道你要什麼尺寸嗎？	**B:** Do you know what sizes you want?
A: 不太知道。	**A:** Not exactly.
B: 沒問題，我可以電腦模擬給你看這些看起來如何。	**B:** No problem. I can show you how these things might look by using a computer simulation.

A: 聽起來很有用。	**A:** Sounds very useful.

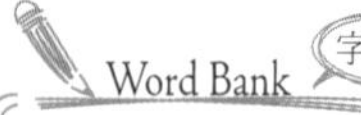

décor ['dɛkɔr] 或 [de'kɔr] n. 裝潢布置（法文）
banner ['bænɚ] n.橫幅，標語
simulation ['sɪmjə'leʃən] n. 模擬

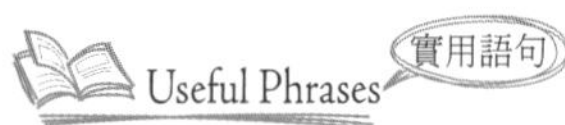

1. 我需要找人談裝潢。
   I need to talk to someone about making décor.
2. 我有畫簡單的圖。
   I have simple drawings.
3. 我們的攤位跟橫幅需要這些顏色。
   We need these colors on the booth and banners.
4. 我可以電腦模擬給你看。
   I can show you by using a computer simulation.
5. 聽起來很有用。
   Sounds very useful.

展場推薦介紹的裝潢商通常無法與你討論到細節裝潢，使用當地的裝潢公司，必須有良好溝通（可要求裝潢公司畫 3D 立體圖，可能須付費），才能得到想要的結果。通常標準裝潢是最常見的，如果到時自己動手改變裝潢的話，展場結束後要回復原狀。一般而言，展場的每樣事物都要費用，越方便的服務，費用就越高。

2.6 貿易展搭設資訊
Trade Show Set Up Information

A: 中心幾點開門？	**A:** What time does the center open?
B: 早上 8 點開。	**B:** It opens at 8 a.m..
A: 我們有多少時間搭設？	**A:** How much time do we have to set up?
B: 我們展場晚上 10 點關。這個展在開展前，你有 3 天可以搭設。	**B:** We close the show room at 10 p.m. For this show you have three days to set up before the event.
A: 我明白了，我需要現在開始。	**A:** I see. I need to get started now.
B: 讓我知道我們可以如何幫助你。	**B:** Let me know how we can assist you.
A: 好，我會打兩通電話再回來。	**A:** OK. I'll make a couple of phone calls and then be back.
B: 我們會在這裡。	**B:** We'll be here.

A: 好。

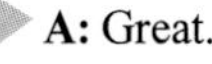

A: Great.

1. 我們有多少時間搭設？

   How much time do we have to set up?

2. 在開展前你有 3 天可以搭設。

   You have three days to set up before the event.

3. 我需要現在開始。

   I need to get started now.

4. 我會打兩通電話再回來。

   I'll make a couple of phone calls and then be back.

2.7 設攤 Setting Up a Booth

A: 這是我們的空間。

A: Here is our space.

B: 看來是個好位置。

B: Looks like a good location.

A: 對，我想是的，我們最好開始擺設。

A: Yes, I think so. We'd better get going on setting up.

B: 是，我們有好多事要做，但記得，還有兩個人會來幫忙。

B: Yeah. We have a lot to do, but remember. Two more people are coming to help.

A: 是，但他們明天才會來。

A: Yes, but they won't be here until tomorrow.

B: 對。

B: Right.

A: 希望今天好好展開頭緒。

A: I'm hoping to get a big head start on this today.

B: 好，什麼最先開始？

B: OK. What's first?

A: 我想我們先從該吊掛的開始做起，再往下。

A: I say we work on what has to be hung up first. Then, work down.

B: 聽起來很聰明。

B: Sounds smart.

A: 讓我們先掛好橫幅，再做別的。

A: Let's work on getting our banners hung up. Then, we can move on to other things.

B: 我們沒有步梯。

B: We don't have a step ladder.

A: 在卡車裡有一個，我們所需要的東西都在卡車裡。

A: There is one in the truck. Everything we need is in the truck.

B: 卡車來了！

B: Here it comes!

A: 時機正好，開始工作吧。

A: Good timing. Let's get to work.

head start 展開頭緒
banner ['bænɚ] n. 橫幅，標語
step ladder 步梯

1. 我們最好開始吧。
   We'd better get going.
2. 時機正好！
   Good timing!
3. 展開頭緒。
   Get a head start.
4. 聽起來很聰明。
   Sounds smart.

招牌看板（signboard）、海報（poster）等布置需與展場搭配得宜，及早開始擺設，才能爲可能遇到的問題預留處理的時間。

2.8 與客戶接洽準備參加國外展覽
Contacting the Local Client for Preparing an International Exhibition

A: LH集團，我可以幫你嗎？

A: LH Group. May I help you?

B: 嗨，我是山姆哈特，紐約的經銷商，回電給泰瑞莎陳女士談談即將來到的紐約市展覽。

B: Hi. My name is Sam Hult, the distributor in New York. I'm returning a call from Ms. Teresa Chen about the upcoming show in New York City.

A: 我為你轉接，請稍候。

A: I'll connect you. Please wait.

B: 謝謝。

B: Thank you.

A: 我是泰瑞莎陳。

A: This is Teresa Chen speaking.

B: 哈囉，我是在紐約的山姆哈特。

B: Hello. This is Sam Hult in New York.

A: 嗨，山姆，很高興聽到你的消息。

A: Hi, Sam. Good to hear from you.

B: 我也是，你那裡如何？

B: Same here. How are things in there?

A: 很好，你那裡呢？

A: Well enough. And there?

B: 一直都很忙，我打來是因為即將到來的展覽中心秀，這次公司要做什麼？

B: Busy as usual. I'm calling because of this convention center show that's coming up. What does the company want to do this time?

A: 我跟行銷部人員談了，他們說我們應該做跟去年差不多的展覽。

A: I talked to the marketing people about it. They said we should do about the same as last year.

B: 好，你有寄東西到這裡的辦公室了嗎？

B: OK. Have you sent anything to the office here yet?

A: 有，我們上週五寄了新的書面資料。

A: Yes. We sent new written materials last Friday.

B: 好，應該還沒到，但我會確認。

B: OK. I don't think they have arrived yet, but I'll check and make sure.

A: 如果還沒收到，告訴我。	**A:** Let me know if they didn't.
B: 我們展覽那裡還需要什麼？	**B:** What else do we want there?
A: 我們可以用去年的影片解釋我們的公司。	**A:** We can use last year's videos explaining our company.
B: 好，我會準備一些放映設備跟螢幕。	**B:** Sure. I'll arrange for a couple of video players and screens.
A: 我今天會電郵給你其他的東西，現在我得快點去開會了。	**A:** I'll email you about other things today. I have to rush off to a meeting right now.
B: 好，沒問題，讓我儘快知道，好嗎？	**B:** Sure. No problem. Let me know ASAP, OK?
A: 好，別擔心。	**A:** I will. Don't worry.
B: 好，泰瑞莎，晚點談。	**B:** OK, Teresa. Talk to you later.
A: 好，再見。	**A:** Soon. Bye.
B: 再見。	**B:** Bye.

Word Bank 字庫

exhibition [ˌɛksəˈbɪʃən] n. 展覽
distributor [dɪˈstrɪbjətɚ] n. 經銷商
upcoming [ˈʌpˌkʌmɪŋ] adj. 即將到來的
convention center 展覽中心
written materials 書面資料
rush off 趕忙
ASAP (as soon as possible) 儘快

Useful Phrases 實用語句

1. 很高興聽到你的消息。
   Good to hear from you.
2. 你那裡一切好嗎？
   How are things in there?
3. 我打來是因為即將到來的展覽中心秀。
   I'm calling because of this convention center show.
4. 你有寄東西到這裡的辦公室了嗎？
   Have you sent anything to the office here yet?
5. 我們展覽那裡還需要什麼？
   What else do we want there?
6. 我們可以用去年的影片解釋我們的公司。
   We can use last year's videos explaining our company.
7. 我會準備一些放映設備跟螢幕。
   I'll arrange for a couple of video players and screens.

2.9 與國外經銷商接洽共同設立攤位
Contacting the Local Distributor to Set Up the Booth Together

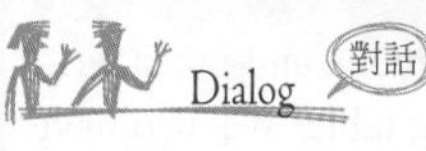

（電話鈴聲 Ring）

A: JC 公司，我是山姆哈特，如何為您效勞呢？

A: JC Company, Sam Hult speaking. How may I help you?

B: 嗨，我是泰瑞莎陳，我昨晚飛來紐約了，現在要開始搭設攤位，我打電話來問你們要帶什麼來。

B: Hi, Sam, this is Teresa Chen. I've flown in New York last night and will start to set up a booth right now. I'm calling to ask about what you want to bring out here.

A: 你來了！歡迎來到紐約！我在等你電話，你現在在哪裡？

A: Here you are! Welcome to New York! I was expecting your call. Where are you now?

B: 我在會議中心。

B: I'm at the convention center.

A: 好，我們會帶來足夠的小冊子與其他書面資料放在一個 8 英呎長的桌子上。我們也有兩個平面螢幕可以一直播放，你要求的產品也會帶過來，我也準備了橫幅標誌跟旗幟。

A: OK. We will be bringing enough brochures and other written material to cover an eight feet long table. We also have two flat screen monitors that will be playing all the time. The products that you asked about will be there, too. I've also prepared some banners and flags.

B: 好！我們帶了一些新模型跟廣告，並且待會按照我們的規劃開始擺設，你會何時過來？

B: Great! I have brought in some new models and ads. I'll start setting up later according to our plan. When will you be coming?

A: 我需要準備好東西然後載過去，需要一下子。

A: I'll need to get things ready and drive up. It will take a short while.

B: 好的，慢慢來，你記得我們攤位的位置嗎？

B: OK, take your time. Do you remember the location of our booth?

A: 是的，在南廳，B 區，第 1 層，105 號攤位。

A: Yes, I do. It is in the south hall, section B, level 1, booth 105.

B: 對，我應該兩小時後打電話給你嗎？

B: That's right. Should I call you after two hours?

A: 好，我可能到了。

A: OK. I'll probably be there.

B: 好，晚點聊。

B: Good. Talk to you later.

A: 好，再見。

A: OK, bye.

convention center 會議中心
brochure [broˈʃur] n. 小冊子
flat screen monitor 平面螢幕
banner [ˈbænɚ] n. 橫幅，標語
flag [flæg] n. 旗幟
ad (advertisement) [æd] n. 廣告

1. 我在等你電話。
   I was expecting your call.
2. 我們有兩個平面螢幕可以一直播放。
   We have two flat screen monitors that will be playing all the time.
3. 我準備了橫幅標誌跟旗幟。
   I've prepared some banners and flags.
4. 我待會按照我們的規劃開始擺設。
   I'll start setting up later according to our plan.
5. 你會何時過來？
   When will you be coming?
6. 需要一下子。
   It will take a short while.

7. 慢慢來。

Take your time.

8. 你記得我們攤位的位置嗎？

Do you remember the location of our booth?

國外參展可以選擇參加貿協或其他臺灣代理的國外展覽團（對區域、價錢等因素加以比較），或是自行報名國外展覽前往參展。如果當地有客戶或經銷商，可以向他們商借產品展覽，並且代訂飯店，我方給予當地附近的客戶名單做爲回饋，如此雙贏的作法可以省去許多麻煩（如不需要自己去運送產品、找翻譯等）。但重點是要能掌握彼此的合作，不要自己付錢辦展覽卻淪爲替國外客戶或經銷商免費打廣告，反客爲主，得不償失。

2.10 與國外展場接洽 Contacting the Exhibition Center Abroad

（電話中 on the phone）

A: 哈囉，科隆展覽中心資訊櫃臺，我可以如何幫你？

A: Hello, Cologne Exhibition Center information desk. How may I help you?

B: 嗨，我從臺灣打來問五月份的五金展，這是我第一次到德國參加的產品展，我有些疑問。

B: Hi, I'm calling from Taiwan to ask about the hardware exhibition in May. It will be my first time to be in Germany for a product exhibition. I have some questions.

A: 你有先上我們的網站下載「參展者指南」嗎？	**A:** Have you logged onto our website and downloaded *The Exhibitor Guide*?
B: 有，但是很難去搞懂超過 200 頁裡的資料。	**B:** Yes, I have, but it's hard to figure out everything in more than 200 pages.
A: 好，是什麼問題呢？	**A:** OK, what are the questions?
B: 你們有提供從倉庫把我的產品載到展場的服務嗎？	**B:** Do you have services provided to take my products from storage to the venue?
A: 有，你可以上網預訂服務或到現場訂都可以。	**A:** Yes, we do. You can book the service online in advance or at the venue.
B: 好，費用有包含在會展租金內嗎？	**B:** Good. Is the service included in the rent?
A: 沒有，你必須另外付，我們這裡有訂約的運輸商可以幫你。	**A:** No, you need to pay extra. We have contracted haulers here to help you.
B: 我明白了，我沒讀到這資訊，你可以為我指出在指南的哪裡嗎？	**B:** I see. I didn't read about the information. Can you point out to me where it is in the guide?
A: 運輸服務與如何收費列在「當地服務」的目錄內。	**A:** The hauling service and how it is charged are listed under the "local services" category.

B: 還有，展場有翻譯可以僱用嗎？	**B:** Also, are there translators to hire at the venue?
A: 有的，但你最好也先在網路上訂，在相同目錄內。	**A:** Yes, there are, and it's better for you to book first online, too. It's in the same category.
B: 我知道了，我一定是漏看那部分了！	**B:** I see. I must have overlooked that part!
A: 沒問題，我很高興幫得上忙。	**A:** No problem, I'm glad I could help.
B: 真感謝你，再見。	**B:** Thank you very much! Goodbye.
A: 再見。	**A:** Bye.

Word Bank 字庫

Exhibitor Guide 參展者指南
venue ['vɛnju] n. 展場，會場
hauler ['hɔlɚ] n. 運輸商
translator [træns'letɚ, trænz-] n. 翻譯
overlook [ˌovɚ'luk] v. 漏看

1. 你們有提供從倉庫把我的產品載到展場的服務嗎？
   Do you have services provided to take my products from storage to the venue?
2. 費用有包含在租金內嗎？
   Is the service included in the rent?
3. 你必須另外付。
   You need to pay extra.
4. 我們這裡有訂約的運輸商可以幫你。
   We have contracted haulers here to help you.
5. 你可以為我指出在指南的哪裡嗎？
   Can you point out to me where it is in the guide?
6. 展場有翻譯可以僱用嗎？
   Are there translators to hire at the venue?

知名的展覽很容易在貿協及工會網站查到時間表及主辦單位（organizer），但要注意有些寄生或地攤型的商展故意山寨知名展覽名稱，並開出較低參展價，大費周章到國外參展的結果當然是賠了夫人又折兵。因此，參展前務必對於該展覽歷年參展廠商、人數、或臺灣前去參加廠商及同業評價等加以了解，確認找對展覽及主辦單位，慎防展覽詐騙。國外展場指南說明通常又多又長，下載後要花時間看過，不了解的可以寫信或打電話去問，展場會有預訂機票、飯店、倉儲、運輸、翻譯、接駁車等各類服務，可在網路報名的時候就進行勾選。

Note

Unit 3 Participating In International Fairs

參加國際商展

商展目的爲開拓商機，是與潛在買主直接接觸及爲將來訂單成交鋪路的絕佳機會，其面對面的臨場感與專人介紹產品、示範、操作、即時問答、服務等特性，爲網路行銷難以取代。參加者需要計畫及多做準備，才能減少突發狀況。對於要展示的產品、操作及服務要瞭如指掌，不僅要能回答問題，並且要預測問題，甚至防止可能發生的問題。展示區配置及後勤在搭設時就要考慮完備，並且要確認產品展示時一切運作流暢。

3.1 展場顧客接待
Receiving Customers at the Trade Show

A: 嗨，歡迎來到 LH 的攤位，我是泰瑞莎陳，請來看看我們的產品陳列，如果有疑問，可以問我或我的同事。

A: Hi. Welcome to the LH booth. My name is Teresa Chen. Have a look at our product displays, and please ask me or one of my associates if you have any questions.

B: 謝謝，你有技術資訊我可以看嗎？

B: Thanks. Do you have any technical information available that I can look at?

A: 是的，我有。在這裡，坐一下讀這個，我也可以回答你有的任何疑問。

A: Yes, I do. Here you are. Have a seat and read this. I can answer any questions you have, too.

B: 好，我先花幾分鐘讀這個。

B: Good. I'll take a few minutes to read this.

A: 好，沒問題。

A: Sure, no problem.

Word Bank 字庫

display [dɪ'sple] n. 陳列
associate [ə'soʃɪ,et] n. 同事

1. 看一下我們的產品陳列。

   Have a look at our product displays.

2. 坐一下讀這個。

   Have a seat and read this.

3. 如果有疑問可以問我。

   Please ask me if you have any questions.

4. 我可以回答你有的任何疑問。

   I can answer any questions you have.

5. 你也可以問我同事。

   You can ask my associates, too.

參觀的買主多半是初次見面並且來去匆匆，在短時間內要讓雙方互相了解必須要靠充分的準備與體貼的臨場反應，同時要記錄及留下客戶資料或名片，爲進一步接洽鋪路。如果客戶留下手寫的聯絡資料，要即刻辨識與對方確認無誤。

3.2 即時介紹產品 Introducing Products Promptly

A: 嗨，你今天好嗎？	**A:** Hi. How are you today?
B: 好。你可以告訴我你的產品嗎？	**B:** Just fine. Can you tell me about your products?

A: 我很樂意，請到這邊來。

A: I'd be happy to. Step over here please.

B: 謝謝。

B: Thanks.

A: 我們的公司專門做家用工具超過 20 年了，我們在中國與臺灣都有工廠，這本目錄裡顯示我們全面的生產線。

A: Our company has specialized in home tools for more than twenty years. We have factories both in China and Taiwan. This is a catalog showing all of our production line.

B: 你這裡有工作樣品嗎？

B: Do you have working samples here?

A: 喔，是的，當然。我可以讓你檢查跟試用你有興趣的任何產品。

A: Oh, yes, of course. I can let you examine and try out any of them you are interested in.

B: 太好了。

B: Perfect.

A: 讓我替你解釋基本資訊。然後你可以問我任何型號，或者你可以試些樣品看看。

A: Let me explain the basic information to you. Then, you can ask about any model, or you can try some out.

B: 聽起來很好。

B: Sounds great.

catalog ['kætəlɔg] n. 目錄
working sample 工作樣品
model ['mɑdḷ] n. 型號，模型

1. 你可以告訴我你的產品嗎？
   Can you tell me about your products?
2. 我們的公司專門做家用工具超過 20 年了。
   Our company has specialized in home tools for more than twenty years.
3. 我們在中國與臺灣都有工廠。
   We have factories both in China and Taiwan.
4. 這本目錄裡顯示我們全面的生產線。
   This is a catalog showing all of our production line.
5. 你這裡有工作樣品嗎？
   Do you have working samples here?
6. 我可以讓你檢查跟試用任何產品。
   I can let you examine and try out any products.
7. 讓我替你解釋基本資訊。
   Let me explain the basic information to you.
8. 你可以問我任何型號。
   You can ask about any model.

參展無非要爭取各種機會向顧客展示產品，主動以兩三句簡短介紹公司後，讓他們仔細問你問題、試用、查看簡介、目錄及樣品。話說「嫌貨才是買貨人」，無論何種產品，顧客總是會找弱點來詢問比較。唯有適時的解說，誠懇的態度及服務，才能在競爭激烈的展場於顧客心中占有一席之地。

3.3 邀請與回答提問—關於服務
Inviting and Answering Questions - about Service

A: 如何？我可以回答你問題嗎？

A: How is it going? Can I answer anything for you?

B: 我有兩個問題。

B: I do have a couple of questions.

A: 好，是什麼？

A: Good. What are they?

B: 你的冊子說你公司現在有每天 24 小時每週 7 天為基礎的服務團隊。國際上真是如此或只有在美國是真的？

B: Your brochure says that your company currently has service teams available on a 24/7 basis. Is that true internationally or just in the U.S.?

A: 哪個國家的服務你想了解？

A: Which country are you wondering about service for?

B: 玻利維亞。

B: Bolivia.

A: 那個區塊我們有一個地區總部在巴西，可以很快支援你。

A: For that region of the world, we have a regional headquarter in Brazil that can reach you quickly.

B: 我了解了。

B: I see.

brochure [bro'ʃur] n. 冊子
24/7 每天 24 小時每週 7 天
Bolivia [bə'lɪvɪə] n. 玻利維亞
headquarter ['hɛd,kwɔrtɚ] n. 總部
Brazil [brə'zɪl] n. 巴西

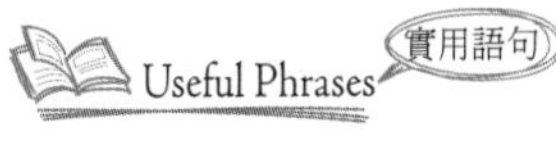

1. 我可以回答你問題嗎？
   Can I answer anything for you?
2. 你公司現在有永不打烊的服務團隊嗎？
   Does your company have service teams available on a 24/7 basis?
3. 國際上真是如此嗎？
   Is that true internationally?

4. 哪個國家的服務你想了解？

Which country are you wondering about service for?

5. 你們在加州有沒有代理商？

Do you have a distributor in California?

Tips 小祕訣

顧客關心的問題是最重要的問題，參展人員必然知道多數問題的答案，對於沒有太多把握或敏感的問題，可以反問客人希望的答案是什麼以探詢客人意向，關於敏感問題應該給予比較保險的答案來保留將來商議的空間。不知道的少數問題，不要亂回答，儘快確認後再回覆。

3.4 關於數量與運送 About Quantity and Delivery

Dialog 1 對話1

A: 我對你的產品有需求，但是我擔心運送時間。	**A:** I have a need for your product, but I am worried about delivery time.
B: 你需要多快呢？	**B:** How soon do you need it?
A: 兩個月內。	**A:** Within two months.
B: 你需要的數量是多少？	**B:** What quantity do you want?
A: 我們需要2,000單位。	**A:** We'll need 2,000 units.

B: 讓我打電話給總公司了解一下我們現在有多少存貨。

B: Let me call our headquarter and find out how many we have in stock right now.

A: 好。

A: OK.

B: 請坐這裡，我幾分鐘後回你。

B: Please sit here. I'll be back with you in a few minutes.

A: 謝謝。

A: Thank you.

A: 我剛才跟工廠的人談過，他們說三個星期內可以做好你的訂單。

A: I just talked to the guys at the factory. They say they can fill your order within three weeks.

B: 那樣很好，那是表示運送也會在三週內？

B: That's good. Does that mean delivery will be within three weeks too?

A: 我也問了他們關於運送的事，他們說在那之前可以運送給你。

A: I asked them about delivery too. They said they would have them delivered to you by that time.

B: 這樣聽來我們可以談訂單的細節了。

B: It sounds like we can talk about details of the order.

A: 好，我們開始吧！你要來杯咖啡嗎？

A: Great. Let's do it. Would you like a cup of coffee?

B: 好。

B: Yes, I would.

A: 我來給我們弄一些咖啡，請在這裡等一下。

A: I'll get us some. Just wait here.

B: 好。

B: Will do.

stock [stɑk] n. 庫存
fill [fɪl] v. 填滿，滿足
delivery [dɪ'lɪvərɪ] n. 運送

Useful Phrases 實用語句

1. 我擔心運送時間。
   I am worried about delivery time.
2. 你需要多快呢？
   How soon do you need it?
3. 你需要的數量是多少？
   What quantity do you want?
4. 讓我了解一下我們現在有多少存貨。
   Let me find out how many we have in stock right now.
5. 我幾分鐘後回你。
   I'll be back with you in a few minutes.
6. 他們三個星期內可以做好你的訂單。
   They can fill your order within three weeks.
7. 他們在那之前可以運送給你。
   They would have them delivered to you by that time.

8. 我們可以談訂單的細節了。
   We can talk about details of the order.
9. 好。
   Will do.

完成訂單及運送產品的時間兩者一定要釐清，交付出貨日、預計運送天數等也要一一確認，才不會出現溝通落差而影響交易。不確定的事不要亂回答，為了避免一時之快禍從口出，或是需要多一點考慮保留底線（bottom line）的時候，最好的辦法就是確定答案後再聯絡客戶。

3.5 介紹工廠與買主會面
Introducing the Supplier to a Buyer

A: 我們在這裡參展，我要介紹你與主要的供應商會面。	**A:** I'd like you to meet one of our main suppliers while we are here at this show.
B: 好。	**B:** OK.
A: 羅伯特西姆斯，這是保羅張，他是我們亞洲供應商之一。	**A:** Robert Sims, this is Paul Chang. He is one of our Asian suppliers.
B: 很高興認識你，張先生。（握手）	**B:** Nice to meet you, Mr. Chang. (Shaking hands)

C: 你好！	C: Ni hao!

Dialog 2 對話2

（介紹後 after the introduction）

A: 我們可以供應你需要的任何產品。	A: We can supply you with any of the products you want.
B: 你多快可以運送？	B: How fast can you ship?
B :你是說你多大的訂單？	A: How large of an order do you mean?
B: 3-4 萬單位。	B: 30 to 40 thousand units.
A: 我可以在兩個月內出那個數量的貨以及運送到你的地址。	A: We can have an order that size filled and delivered to your address within two months.
B: 那很快，你確定嗎？	B: That's pretty fast. Are you sure?
A: 我們保證。	A: We guarantee it.

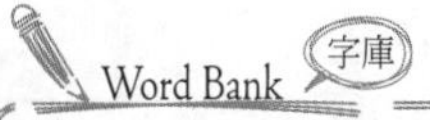

supplier [sə'plaɪɚ] n. 供應商，工廠

ship [ʃɪp] v. 運送，裝船

deliver [dɪ'lɪvɚ] v. 運送

guarantee [ˌgærən'ti] v. 保證

1. 我們可以供應你需要的任何產品。

   We can supply you with any of the products you want.

2. 你多快可以運送？

   How fast can you ship?

3. 你是說你多大的訂單？

   How large of an order do you mean?

4. 我可以在兩個月內出那個數量的貨以及運送到你的地址。

   We can have an order that size filled and delivered to your address within two months.

在網路發達、資訊透明的時代，貿易商的角色就是提供工廠與買主間的充分溝通服務。

3.6 顧客在展場議價下訂 Buyer Talking Price for an Order at the Trade Show

A: 我的公司要協商訂單的價格，我們覺得數量大到可以有一個售價的折扣。

A: My company wants to negotiate on the price of this order. We feel it is large enough to allow us a price reduction.

B: 當然我們可以談這個訂單的價格。你們希望多少折扣？

B: Of course we can talk price on this order. How much of a discount are you looking for?

A: 我公司相信這筆訂單的 85 折價格是合理的。

A: My company believes a discount of 15% is fair on this order.

B: 我知道了，我必須跟我的主管們討論。

B: I see. I'll have to discuss this with my superiors.

A: 好，我預計何時可以從你那聽到關於這件事的消息？

A: Of course. When can I expect to hear from you about this?

B: 我可以現在打電話討論，給我 10 分鐘。

B: I'll call them now and discuss it. Give me ten minutes.

A: 好。

A: Sure.

Word Bank 字庫

negotiate [nɪ'goʃɪ,et] v. 協商
reduction [rɪ'dʌkʃən] n. 降低
discount ['dɪskaunt]或[dɪs'kaunt] n. 折扣
fair [fɛr] adj. 合理的
superior [sə'pɪrɪɚ, su-] n. 主管，高層

Useful Phrases 實用語句

1. 我們可以談這個訂單的價格。
   We can talk price on this order.
2. 你們希望多少折扣？
   How much of a discount are you looking for?
3. 這訂單的 85 折價格是合理的。
   A discount of 15% is fair on this order.
4. 我必須跟我的主管們討論。
   I'll have to discuss this with my superiors.
5. 我預計何時可以聽到你的消息？
   When can I expect to hear from you?

Dialog 2 對話2

A: 我跟總公司談了，他們提供88折，但是也保證3週運送期。

A: I spoke to the head office. They are offering a 12% discount, but also guarantee a three week delivery date.

B: 我想我的部門主管應該會同意，但是如果運送期遲到一天，他會要求 15 %折扣。

B: I think my department head will accept this, but if the delivery is even one day late, he'll expect the 15% reduction.

A: 我會傳達你的還價給我老闆。

A: I'll pass your counter offer on to my boss.

B: 我會等回覆，我現在很餓了，我們晚點再談。

B: I'll wait for the reply. I'm pretty hungry now. Let's talk about this later.

A: 請讓我請你吃晚餐。

A: Please, let me buy you dinner.

B: 喔，不需要那樣的。

B: Oh, there is no need for that.

A: 拜託，我堅持。我知道這裡有一個好餐廳。

A: Please. I insist. I know of a very good restaurant near here.

B: 呃，好，有何不可？我們可以談更多關於這個交易的事。

B: Well. OK. Why not? We can talk some more about this deal.

A: 好，走吧。

A: Great. Let's go.

counter offer n. 還價
insist [ɪn'sɪst] v. 堅持

1. 我會等回覆。
I'll wait for the reply.
2. 我會傳達你的還價給我老闆。
I'll pass your counter offer on to my boss.
3. 請讓我請你吃晚餐。
Please, let me buy you dinner.
4. 喔，不需要那樣的。
Oh, there is no need for that.
5. 拜託，我堅持。
Please. I insist.

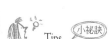

Tips 小祕訣

展場有些顧客會要求現場報價，但商場如戰場，爲免顧客只是來打探行情，對於詢問報價的回答最好是「看數量」或給一個參考價（rough price），所報參考價的高低可以根據顧客在意的是價錢還是品質來判斷（如產品依照數量或品質等級，大約落在幾元之間），報價預留吸引顧客的空間。另一個方式是給一個目前的參考價，表明將來下訂的話必須依照情勢調整訂價。如果顧客可以馬上下單的話，那麼數量跟價錢就可以馬上談。顧客多半會嫌價錢太高，如果不走削價競爭的路，就要站在對方立場想，說服買主接受你的產品，並強調他將能因選擇購買你的產品而獲得因此帶來的好處。（報價議價請見第七章）

3.7 展場議價條件—接受
Talking Price at the Trade Show - Terms of an Offer Accepted

（隔天電話 the next day on the phone）

A: 嗨，泰瑞莎，這是羅伯特。	**A:** Hi, Teresa. This is Robert.
B: 我從高層得到回覆了。	**B:** I got a reply from the higher-ups.
A: 他們說什麼？	**A:** What did they say?
B: 他們同意你的條件。	**B:** They agreed to your terms.
A: 真的？很好！	**A:** Really? Great!
B: 是，我也這麼想。我們何時可以一起看這筆交易的細節？	**B:** Yes. I think so, too. When can we get together and work out the details of the deal?
A: 今天下午 3 點好嗎？	**A:** How about this afternoon at 3:00?
B: 可以，我會準備一份合約給你審視。	**B:** Sounds fine. I'll have a contract ready for you to review.

A: 好，到時見。	**A:** Perfect. See you then.
B: 好，再見。	**B:** OK. Bye.
A: 再見。	**A:** Bye.

the higher-ups 高層，主管
term [tɝm] n. 條件
detail ['ditel, dɪ'tel] n. 細節
contract ['kɑntrækt] n.合約
review [rɪ'vju] v.審視，檢閱

1. 他們同意你的條件。
   They agreed to your terms.
2. 我們何時可以看這筆交易的細節？
   When can we work out the details of the deal?
3. 我會準備一份合約給你審視。
   I'll have a contract ready for you to review.

3.8 展場議價條件—需要再協商 Talking Price at the Trade Show - Further Negotiation Required

A: 嗨，泰瑞莎，我是羅伯特。	**A:** Hi, Teresa. This is Robert.
B: 嗨，羅伯特。我得到高層的回應了，他們拒絕你的條件。	**B:** Hi, Robert. I got a response from the higher ups. They rejected your terms.
A: 我知道了，他們有解釋為什麼嗎？	**A:** I see. Did they explain why?
B: 他們覺得你要求的時程要生產及運送太困難了，不可能做到。	**B:** They feel it will be too difficult to produce the product and deliver it within the timeline you requested.
A: 我會打電話給我的主管們報告，看看他們是否同意延後運送日期。	**A:** I'll call my superiors and report this. I'll see if they are willing to back-up the delivery date.
B: 我的主管說如果你們願意接受晚一個月的話就可以。	**B:** Mine said if you could accept delivery one month later, it could be done.
A: 好，我會跟他們說。	**A:** OK. I'll tell them that.

B: 我何時會知道你的回音？	**B:** When will I hear from you again?
A: 我會明天中午前打電話給你。	**A:** I'll call you before noon tomorrow.
B: 好，我們到時再談。	**B:** Alright. We'll talk then.
A: 再見，泰瑞莎。	**A:** Bye, Teresa.
B: 再見，羅伯特。	**B:** Bye, Robert.

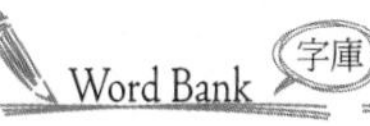

response [rɪ'spɑns] n. 回應
reject [rɪ'dʒɛkt] v. 拒絕
timeline ['taɪm,laɪn] n. 時程
superior [sə'pɪrɪɚ, su-] n. 主管
back-up ['bæk,ʌp] 或 [,bæk'ʌp] v. 後退，支持

1. 看看他們是否同意晚點的運送日期。
   I'll see if they are willing to back-up the delivery date.
2. 如果你們願意接受晚一個月的話就可以。
   If you could accept delivery one month later, it could be done.

3. 我何時會知道你的回音？

When will I hear from you again?

協商對買賣雙方而言都是測試底線，無論買賣是否做得成，都是在累積經驗。如果客人開出離譜的條件，每個案例背後都有許多可能原因，很難論斷。唯有誠意溝通努力爭取，如果客戶不接受你開出的最底限價格，那就只好保持聯絡，留待下回，並著手進行下個客戶可能的交易。買賣不成仁義在，客戶還是需要定期保持問候，提供市場資訊，將來還是有進行交易的機會。

3.9 關於品質控管—認證
About Quality Control - Certificates

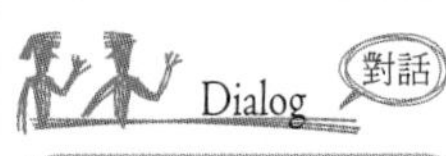

A: 你們有認證嗎？	**A:** Do you have any certifications?
B: 我們有好幾種，看你需要什麼？	**B:** We have several kinds. It depends on what you need.
A: 我們需要 CE 跟 ANSI。	**A:** We need CE and ANSI.
B: 讓我看看，我們有CE，但是沒有ANSI。	**B:** Let me check. We have CE, but no ANSI.
A: 好，你可以給我看 CE 的認證嗎？	**A:** OK. Can you show me your CE certification?

B: 好，我這裡正好有影本。	**B:** Sure, I have the photocopy right here.
A: 很好！	**A:** Great!

certification [ˌsɚˈtɪfəkɪtˈkeʃən] n. 認證
photocopy [ˈfotəˌkɑpɪ] n. 影本

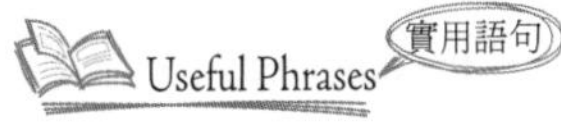

1. 你們有認證嗎？
   Do you have any certifications?
2. 看你需要什麼？
   It depends on what you need.
3. 我們需要 CE 跟 ANSI。
   We need CE and ANSI.
4. 我這裡正好有影本。
   I have the photocopy right here.

CE 歐盟認證 Conformité Européenne (French)，等於英文 European Conformity 意即符合歐盟的一致標準。

ANSI (American National Standards Institute) 即美國標準協會之認證。

3.10 關於品質控管—裝船前測試步驟 About Quality Control - Testing Procedures Before Shipment

A: 你們的測試步驟是什麼？

A: What is your testing procedure?

B: 我們在裝船前有三個按照 CE 規定的測試。

B: We have three tests following CE regulations before shipment.

A: 是哪三個？

A: What are the three tests?

B: 我們有硬度、密度及溫度測試。我們從 20 項產品裡隨機抽取 5 個樣本測試。如果有任何一個測試沒通過，更多的樣本就會被測試，所有的測試數據由品管員以書面報告記錄。

B: We have a hardness test, a density test, and a temperature test. We randomly choose 5 samples out of 20 to perform the tests on. If they fail any of the tests, more samples will be tested. All the test data is recorded in written reports by the inspectors.

A: 好，之後會做什麼？

A: OK. What will be done then?

B: 檢驗部門將通知生產部門提出解決辦法。

B: The inspection department will notify the production department about solutions.

A: 好，聽起來你們已經建立了品質控制的流程。

A: Alright. It sounds that you have established a quality control procedure.

B: 確實如此，經由這些測試及我們的先進研發，我們的品質居於業界的領導角色。

B: Indeed. Through these tests and our R&D advancement, our quality is in the leading role of the industry.

hardness ['hɑrdnɪs] n. 硬度
density ['dɛnsətɪ] n. 密度
randomly ['rændəmlɪ] adv. 隨機地
inspector [ɪn'spɛktɚ] n. 品管員
notify ['notə'faɪ] v. 通知
solution [sə'luʃən] n. 解決辦法

1. 你們的測試步驟是什麼？
   What is your testing procedure?
2. 我們在裝船前有三個按照 CE 規定的測試。
   We have three tests following CE regulations before shipment.
3. 我們從 20 項產品裡隨機抽取 5 個樣本測試。
   We randomly choose 5 samples out of 20 to perform the tests on.
4. 如果有任何一個測試沒通過，更多的樣本就會被測試。
   If any of the tests fail, more samples will be tested.
5. 所有的測試數據由品管員以書面報告記錄。
   All the test data is recorded in written reports by the inspectors.

6. 檢驗部門將通知生產部門提出解決辦法。
   The inspection department will notify the production department about solutions.

雙方品質條件的約定可依實物（standard object）、品牌（brand）、規格（specification）、樣品標準（sample standard）、說明書或使用手冊（guide or manual）等訂定，雙方約定並包含品質之確定、檢驗與寬容範圍（tolerance）。（有關產品品質對話，請另見5.10 及 8.1）

3.11 保證金退還 Returning the Deposit

A: 你要如何退回押金？	**A:** How would you like your deposit returned?
B: 我們要請你們入到公司銀行帳戶。	**B:** We would like you to credit our company bank account.
A: 好，那很容易，我們只需要銀行名稱及帳號。	**A:** OK. That will be easy. We just need to have the bank name and the account number.
B: 好，我會寫下來給你，多久可以辦好？	**B:** Alright, I'll write that information down for you. How long will it take to get it done?
A: 我們在 5-7 個工作日後會入帳。	**A:** We will credit that account in 5 to 7 business days.

B: 謝謝。	**B:** Thank you.
A: 不客氣。	**A:** You're welcome.

deposit **[dɪ'pɑzɪt]** n. 保證金，押金
credit **['krɛdɪt]** v. 入帳
business days 工作日

1. 你要如何退回押金？
   How would you like your deposit returned?
2. 我們要請你們入到公司銀行帳戶。
   We would like you to credit our company bank account.
3. 多久可以辦好？
   How long will it take to get it done?
4. 我們在 5-7 個工作日後會入帳。
   We will credit that account in 5 to 7 business days.

你可以以其他方式返還押金（例如，寄支票到你公司），但是銀行直接入帳可說是最安全又簡單的退還押金辦法。

3.12 商展後追蹤
Follow Ups after the Fair

（電話中 on the phone）

A: 哈囉，克拉克先生，我是 LH 集團的泰瑞莎陳，我們在貿易展見過面，您對我們的產品有興趣，我們想要跟您確認 150 及 155 號商品是您需要的。

A: Hello, Mr. Clark. This is Teresa Chen of LH Group. We met at the trade show and you were interested in our products. We'd like to confirm that two of the items, No. 150 and No. 155, were the items you needed.

B: 對，請寄給我報價。

B: Yes, just send me your quote.

A: 好，克拉克先生，我會立刻寄電子郵件報價。

A: Sure, Mr. Clark. I'll email a price quote right away.

A: 哈囉，克拉克先生，我是 LH 集團的泰瑞莎陳，我們在貿易展見過面，您對我們的產品有興趣，我們想要跟您確認 150 及 155 號商品是您需要的。

A: Hello, Mr. Clark. This is Teresa Chen of LH Group. We met at the trade show and you were interested in our products. We'd like to confirm that two of the items, No. 150 and 155, were the items you needed.

B: 嗯，不，是 150 及 152 號。

B: Um, no, they were No. 150 and 152.

A: 好，克拉克先生，我會立刻寄報價給您。

A: OK. Mr. Clark, I'll send you price quotes right away.

A: 哈囉，克拉克先生，我是 LH 集團的泰瑞莎陳，我們在貿易展見過面，您對我們的產品有興趣，我們想要跟您確認 150 及 155 號商品是您需要的。

A: Hello, Mr. Clark. This is Teresa Chen of LH Group. We met at the trade show and you were interested in our products. We'd like to confirm that two of the items, No. 150 and 155, were the items you needed.

B: 是的，泰瑞莎，但是今年我們不考慮賣這些產品。

B: Yes, Teresa, but we are not considering selling the products this year.

A: 克拉克先生，您有其他的計畫嗎？

A: Do you have other plans, Mr. Clark?

B: 是的，我們會專注在家用工具。

B: That's right. We will focus on home tools instead.

A: 那我寄給您家用工具的目錄，我們有超過 500 個項目可以選擇，您也可以上我們的網站找家用工具。

A: Let me send you our catalog of home tools. We have more than 500 items you can choose from. You can also visit our website for home tools.

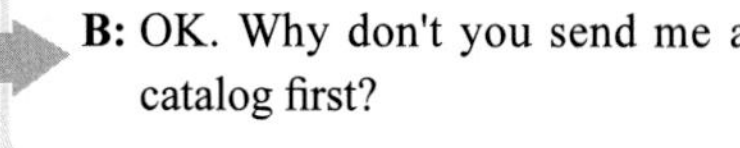

B: 好，你先寄給我目錄吧。	**B:** OK. Why don't you send me a catalog first?
A: 好的，克拉克先生，我會馬上去做。	**A:** Sure, Mr. Clark. I'll do it right away.

Word Bank 字庫

quote **[kwot]** n. 報價，報價單
catalog **['kætəlɔg]** n. 目錄

Useful Phrases 實用語句

1. 我們想要跟您確認兩個項目的商品是您需要的。
   We'd like to confirm that two of the items were the items you needed.
2. 請寄給我報價。
   Just send me your price quote.
3. 今年我們不考慮賣這些產品。
   We are not considering selling the products this year.
4. 您有其他的計畫嗎？
   Do you have other plans?
5. 我們有超過 500 個項目可以選擇。
   We have more than 500 items you can choose from.
6. 您也可以上我們的網站找家用工具。
   You can also visit our website for home tools.
7. 感謝您的資訊。
   Thank you for the information.

在展場收到的名片的當時，就記錄下客戶買賣哪方面產品的資料以利展後追蹤，並可試探性的挑選報價商品，依客戶的反應決定後續商機（如以上對話）。如果碰到客戶暫無買賣的興趣，掛電話前還是要向對方感謝他所提供的資訊，隔一陣子再試試看。

Why don't you send me a catalog first?

catalog

Sure,Mr. Clark. I'll do it right away.

Note

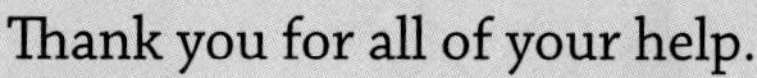

Unit 4 Receiving Clients

接待客戶

接待客戶是最直接的接觸，遠道而來又有決定權的客戶可能是公司的財神爺，除了解客戶本身的背景（與其切身的國際議題）、對產品的需求與過去接洽的重點外，尚須了解產業動態（industry trends）及預測客戶可能的提問，逐一記錄作好功課及推演，並準備資料圖表照片等以備不時之需。此外，事先與主管討論此次任務的授權及必須達成的目標或期望都是接待的前置作業。除了在商言商之外，業務人員應當能夠體貼遠行客戶的需求，確認他們對於下榻的旅館不會感到不舒服或免於爲了交通或通訊感到挫折，了解客戶是否有就近觀光（sightseeing）或購物的需求，做好適當的安排。你不必爲顧客買單，但任何可以增進商機穩固貿易夥伴情誼的可能性都該考慮。

4.1 到機場接客戶—自我介紹與寒暄 Picking Up a Client at the Airport - Self-Introduction and Small Talk

（在機場 at the airport）

A: 尼爾森先生？你是約翰尼爾森？	**A:** Mr. Nelson? Are you John Nelson?
B: 是的，我是。	**B:** Yes, I am.
A: 我是泰瑞莎陳，我為 LH 集團工作，我來這裡帶你到城裡的飯店。	**A:** I'm Teresa Chen. I work for LH Group. I'm here to escort you to your hotel in the city.
B: 我知道了，很高興與你會面，泰瑞莎。	**B:** I see. Nice to meet you, Teresa.
A: 我也很高興與你會面，我來幫你弄行李。	**A:** Nice to meet you, too. Let me help you with your luggage.
B: 好，謝謝。	**B:** Oh, thanks.
A: 我們有車子在外面等你，請跟我來。	**A:** We have a car waiting for you outside. Please follow me.
B: 好。	**B:** Certainly.

A: 你的飛行順利嗎？	**A:** Was your flight good?
B: 很好，我已經飛這麼多次了，現在感覺起來都一樣。	**B:** Good enough. I've flown so many times. It always seems the same now.
A: 我知道，我想就沒什麼驚喜吧。	**A:** I understand. I take it there were no surprises.
B: 也不盡然，每件事都很順利。	**B:** Not really. Everything went well.
A: 很好，我很開心聽到這樣。	**A:** Great. I'm glad to hear that.

client ['klaɪənt] n. 顧客
escort ['ɛskɔrt] v. 陪伴
luggage ['lʌgɪdʒ] n. 行李

1. 很高興與你會面。
   Nice to meet you.
2. 我為 LH 集團工作。
   I work for LH Group.
3. 我來這裡帶你到城裡的飯店。
   I'm here to escort you to your hotel in the city.

4. 你的飛行順利嗎？

Was your flight good?

5. 我很開心聽到這樣。

I'm glad to hear that.

接機前與客戶互留手機號碼，並且約定雙方在哪裡會面（例如：四號會面點meeting point 4 或詢問臺information center）萬一班機延誤或手機通訊有問題時，雙方才知道到何處等候。接到客戶時先聊聊輕鬆的話題，讓彼此拉近距離，並熟悉客戶的口音。

4.2 給予客戶行程表 Giving the Client a Schedule

A: 我們會先帶你到飯店，你可以在那裡休息，我也有個行程表給你，在這裡。

A: We will take you to your hotel first. You can rest there. I have a schedule for you, too. Here it is.

B: 謝謝，我需要這個，我知道我們下午 3 點有個會議，但我幾乎不知道其他的事。

B: Thanks. I need this. I know we have a meeting at 3:00 this afternoon, but I know little else.

A: 事實上會議被延後了半小時。	**A:** Actually that meeting has been moved back a half hour.
B: 真的，還好你告訴我。	**B:** Really? Good thing you told me.
A: 我無論如何必須告訴你，在去飯店路上我會讓你知道今天的行程。	**A:** I would have to anyway. On the way to the hotel I'll fill you in on what today's schedule is.
A: 聽起來很好。	**A:** Sounds good.
B: 車來了，我們可以放你所有的行李在後車廂。	**B:** Here's the car. We can put all of your luggage in the trunk.
A: 好，我只需要帶著公事包。	**A:** Fine. I just need my briefcase with me.
B: 當然，沒問題。	**B:** Of course. No problem.

fill ... in 告知（某人）
trunk [trʌŋk] n. 後車廂
briefcase ['brif,kes] n. 公事包

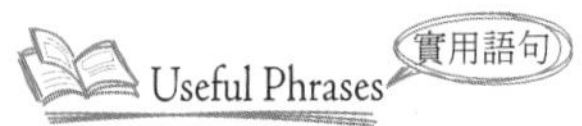

1. 你可以在那裡休息。

   You can rest there.

2. 我會讓你知道今天的行程。

   I'll fill you in on what today's schedule is.

3. 我有個行程表給你。

   I have a schedule for you.

4. 會議被延後了半小時。

   The meeting has been moved back a half hour.

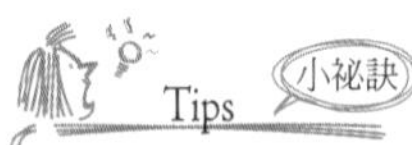

簡單口述行程，讓客人知道大概就好。注意行程若給得越細，讓客人知道越多公司或供應商的細節，對本身反而越不利。

4.3 前往飯店途中：確認行程
On the Way to the Hotel - Checking the Agenda

A: 交通很順暢。

A: The traffic is light.

B: 是的，我們會暢快無阻到達飯店。

B: Yes. We'll make good time to the hotel.

A: 很好，我想登記住宿並且看些文件。

A: Great. I want to get checked in and go over some papers.

B: 每樣東西都會為你準備好。	**B:** Everything will be ready for you.
A: 我可以有一份郵報嗎？	**A:** Will I be able to get a copy of *The Post*?
B: 沒問題，我會確定馬上會有一份送到你房間來。	**B:** No problem. I'll make sure one is delivered to your room immediately.
A: 謝謝，你知道王先生是否有空？我需要在今晚的活動之前跟他談話。	**A:** Thank you. Do you know if Mr. Wong will be available? I need to speak to him before tonight's event.
B: 我現在打電話去了解。	**B:** I'll call now and find out.
A: 謝謝。	**A:** Thank you.

Word Bank 字庫

make good time 以暢快速度通行
deliver [dɪ'lɪvɚ] v. 遞送
available [ə'veləbḷ] adj. 有空的
event [ɪ'vɛnt] n. 活動

Useful Phrases 實用語句

1. 交通很順暢。
The traffic is light.

2. 我們會暢快無阻到達飯店。

We'll make good time to the hotel.

3. 每樣東西都會為你準備好。

Everything will be ready for you.

4.4 車內聊天 Chatting

A: 你在 LH 集團服務多久了？	**A:** How long have you worked for LH Group?
B: 三年了。	**B:** Three years.
A: 你喜歡公司嗎？	**A:** Do you like the company?
B: 是的，很喜歡，那是個工作的好地方，我在那裡學到很多。	**B:** Yes, very much. It's a good place to work. I've learned much there.
A: 你打算待多久？	**A:** How long do you plan to stay?
B: 很難說，我不確定，到目前為止我沒有要離開的打算。	**B:** It's hard to say. I'm not sure. So far I have no plans to leave.
A: 這樣很好，要找到一個喜歡的工作環境很難。	**A:** That's good. It's not easy to find a place that you like to work at.

B: 我知道，我很幸運，我曾在許多不好的公司工作過，他們管理不佳，通常那就是問題。

B: I know. I'm very fortunate. I have worked for some pretty bad companies. They were poorly managed. That was usually the problem.

A: 我知道那情況，我也有過那種處境。

A: I know the situation. I've been in that spot, too.

spot [spɑt] n. 處境，困境

1. 你喜歡公司嗎？
   Do you like the company?
2. 你打算待多久？
   How long do you plan to stay?
3. 我在那裡學到很多。
   I've learned much there.
4. 到目前為止我沒有要離開的打算。
   So far I have no plans to leave.
5. 我知道那情況。
   I know the situation.
6. 我也有過那種處境。
   I've been in that spot, too.

如果客戶說話速度很快或是口音較難懂，抓重點或關鍵字（key words），聽不懂的地方可以適時請他重述，不必不好意思，讓客戶調整恰當的溝通方式對彼此都有幫助。業務方面的談話，如果不懂不要裝懂，裝懂可能會誤事，甚至導致彼此的損失，可以用自己得到的理解重述給客戶聽，確認你正確地了解他的意思。因爲雙方的專業用語未必相同，確認或澄清彼此的意思才能確保溝通及認知無礙。

商場如戰場，買賣雙方都想知己知彼，客戶可能向你打探，公司成立多久（答案不要與老闆不一致），你來公司多久，公司多少人，營業額多少等，碰到敏感問題，回答要很小心。回答「不知道」是不行的，有時你必須微笑著說「不便透露」（Sorry. I'm not supposed to answer this question.）。行車時間較長的時候，與客戶聊天經常會談到彼此國家的狀況，如正行進中之交通、建築物、庶民生活、薪資物價、經濟情勢等各種話題，另一個聊天的時候是用餐時間，兩者都是考驗及增廣自己知識見聞的機會。

4.5 到達飯店及入住登記 Arriving and Checking Into the Hotel

4.5a 爲房客登記入住 Checking Into the Hotel for a Client

A: 我們到了。	**A:** Here we are.
B: 很好。	**B:** Great.
A: 我們可以停在這裡及卸下東西。	**A:** We can park here and unload the car.

B: 好。（門房服務員走過來）啊！門房服務員來幫忙了。	**B:** OK. (the bellhop approaches) Ah! The bellhop is coming out to help.
A: 我來登記入住。	**A:** I'll go check in.
B: 讓我一起來，會快一點。門房會處理行李，我會告訴他放哪裡。	**B:** Let me go with you. It will be quicker. The bellhop will handle the bags. I'll tell him where to take them.
A: 好。	**A:** Fine.
B: 進去吧。	**B:** Let's go in.

（飯店櫃臺 front desk at the hotel）

A: 尼爾森先生要登記入住，他是 LH 集團的客戶。	**A:** Mr. Nelson is checking in. He's a guest of LH Group.
B: 很好，我看到他這裡的訂房，所有東西都好了。	**B:** Very well. I see his reservation here. Everything is ready.
A: 好，我們有點趕。	**A:** Good. We are in a bit of a hurry.

B: 沒問題，鑰匙在這裡，我們已經有所有資料了，請直走，電梯在那邊。	**B:** Certainly. Here is the key. We have all the details already. Please go up. The elevators are over there.
A: 謝謝。	**A:** Thank you.

4.5b 房客登記入住 Client Checking Into the Hotel

Dialog 對話

A: 哈囉，我可以幫你嗎？	**A:** Hello. May I help you?
B: 是的，我是約翰尼爾森，LH 集團有為我預訂了房間。	**B:** Yes. I'm John Nelson. I have a reservation made by LH Group.
A: 是的，尼爾森先生，歡迎。	**A:** Yes, Mr. Nelson. Welcome.
B: 謝謝。	**B:** Thank you.
A: 請在這裡簽名，我們已經有其他的必要資料。	**A:** Just sign here. We have all the other necessary information already.
B: 很好。	**B:** Great.

A: 這裡是你的鑰匙卡，歡迎入住。

A: Here is your key card. Enjoy your stay.

B: 謝謝。

B: Thank you.

unload [ʌn'lod] v. 卸下
bellhop ['bɛlˌhɑp] n. 門房服務員
reservation [ˌrɛzɚ'veʃən] n. 預訂
elevator ['ɛləˌvetɚ] n. 電梯
key card 鑰匙（感應）卡

1. 我來登記入住。
   I'll go check in.
2. 他是 LH 集團的客戶。
   He's a guest of LH Group.
3. 我們有點趕。
   We are in a bit of a hurry.
4. LH 集團有為我預訂了房間。
   I have a reservation made by LH Group.
5. 我們資料都有了。
   We have all the details already.
6. 歡迎入住。
   Enjoy your stay.

許多國家的飯店是無菸房，但目前中國仍分吸菸房及無菸房，不抽菸的人若被分配到吸菸房又無房間可換是很可怕的經驗。正因客戶住宿是否舒適直接影響其睡眠、體力與心情，在代訂飯店的時候須先確定飯店入住房間的房型、設備及客戶需求。

商務飯店通常有行李員服務行李，不需要搶著幫忙。如果沒看到行李員，可以讓客戶看著行李，自己去找人幫忙。如果要自己動手的話，應該先問該幫忙拿哪一件，手提行李雖然較輕，較適合女性幫忙提，但通常手提行李即是隨身重要物品，不適合別人代拿，除非你的客戶希望你這麼做。

4.6 客戶拜訪公司 Client Visiting the Company

（在公司 at the company）

A: 哈囉，葉女士，我是約翰尼爾森。	**A:** Hello, Ms. Yeh. I'm John Nelson.
B: 我很高興與你會面，請坐下。	**B:** I'm very pleased to meet you. Please sit down.
A: 謝謝，我只是想在今天會議之前順道過來介紹自己。	**A:** Thank you. I just wanted to stop by and introduce myself before tonight's meeting.
B: 我很高興你這麼做，我一直很期待與你會面，這裡每個人都是。	**B:** I'm glad you did. I've been looking forward to meeting with you. Everyone here has.

A: 我受寵若驚，也很期待見到及跟大家聊聊。

A: I'm flattered. I'm looking forward to seeing and speaking with everyone, too.

B: 呃，我們了解你有興趣成立密西根州的銷售團隊，所以大家想聽你有什麼看法。你要喝點什麼嗎？

B: Well, we've learned that you are interested in building a sales team in Michigan, so everyone wants to hear what you have to say. Would you like something to drink?

A: 不，沒關係。我真的不該久待，我要在會議之前多些準備。

A: No, that's OK. I really shouldn't stay long. I need to prepare more before the meeting.

B: 我了解，你需要什麼嗎？

B: I understand. Do you need anything?

A: 不，我很好，你已經提供我很大的空間來準備。

A: No, I'm fine. You've provided me with a great space to prepare.

B: 那很好，如果你需要任何東西，你知道要找誰了，對吧？

B: Good then. If you do need anything, you know who to ask, right?

A: 是的，沒問題，今晚見。

A: Yes. No problem. See you tonight.

B: 好。

B: Right.

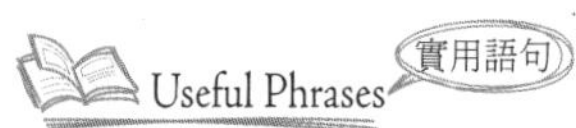

1. 我一直很期待與你會面。

   I've been looking forward to meeting with you.

2. 我受寵若驚。

   I'm flattered.

3. 大家想聽你有什麼看法。

   Everyone wants to hear what you have to say.

4. 我很期待見到大家跟每個人聊聊。

   I'm looking forward to seeing and speaking with everyone.

5. 你要喝點什麼嗎？

   Would you like something to drink?

6. 沒關係。

   That's OK.

7. 我真的不該久待。

   I really shouldn't stay long.

客戶來訪前把空間整理妥當，將設備及所需物品（冷氣、電腦、樣品、文件等）都準備好，務必給予客戶尊重及體貼的感受。I've been looking forward to meeting with you 與 meeting you 同樣是會面，但前者為正式及商業說法，隱含會面之餘，彼此可進一步合作之意。

4.7 為客戶介紹公司業務好手
Introducing a Top Sales Rep to the Client

A: 約翰，這是麗莎吳，她是我們的銷售員之一。

A: John, I'd like you to meet Lisa Wu. She is one of our sales people.

B: 很高興認識你，麗莎。

B: Nice to meet you, Lisa.

C: 我也很高興認識你，我們都很期待見到你及了解你對我們產品的想法。

C: Nice to meet you too. We've all been looking forward to seeing you and learning your ideas about our products.

B: 喔，我樂意與大家交換意見，謝謝你們招待我。

B: Oh, I'd love to exchange ideas with you all. Thank you for having me.

C: 歡迎至極，請享受你的來訪時間，並且隨時讓我們知道我們哪裡可以為你做得更好。

C: You're most welcome. Please enjoy your time here and let us know any time what we can do better for you.

A: 我要先帶約翰參觀，麗莎，我們晚點見。

A: I'll be showing John around first, Lisa. We'll see you later.

B: 好。

B: All right.

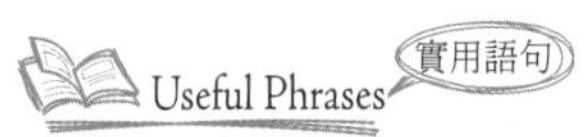

1. 我們都很期待見到你及了解你對我們產品的想法。

   We've all been looking forward to seeing you and learning your ideas about our products.

2. 歡迎至極。

   You're most welcome.

3. 請享受你的來訪時間。

   Please enjoy your time here.

4. 隨時讓我們知道我們哪裡可以為你做得更好。

   Let us know any time what we can do better for you.

5. 我要先帶約翰參觀。

   I'll be showing John around first.

4.8 銷售策略交流 Exchanging Marketing Strategies

A: 王先生，我知道你在 LH 集團這裡建立銷售團隊好幾年了。	**A:** Mr. Wong, I understand you've been developing the sales team here at LH Group for several years.
B: 呃，反正三年了，不是真的很久。	**B:** Well, three years anyway. Not very long really.
A: 但那大約是足以把事情帶到一個方向的時間。	**A:** Still, that's been long enough to head things in a certain direction.

B: 是，我想我有一些影響，我們的部門做得好，但最重要的是銷售的產品有競爭力。

B: True. I feel I've had an impact. Our department is doing well, and most importantly, the products are competitive.

A: 今年你們的目標是什麼？

A: What's your goal for this year?

B: 我們希望可以增加6%。

B: We hope to increase sales by six percent.

A: 那在今日不太容易，你打算如何辦到？

A: That's tough these days. How do you plan to do it?

B: 我們產品有一個新的廣告活動，並且我們希望從中獲得靈感，更了解國外的市場想要的是什麼。

B: We have a new ad campaign for our products, and we hope to gain insight to better understand what the foreign markets want exactly.

A :好點子，那是為何我在這裡的原因，不是嗎？

A : Good point. That is why I'm here, isn't it?

B: 是的，的確是。

B: Yes, indeed.

Word Bank 字庫

impact ['ɪmpækt] n. 影響
competitive [kəm'pɛtətɪv] adj. 有競爭力的
tough [tʌf] adj. 困難的
ad campaign 廣告活動
insight ['ɪn'saɪt] n. 靈感

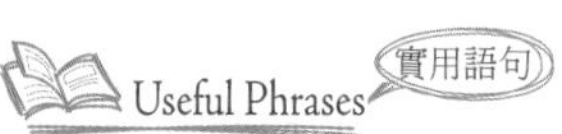

Useful Phrases 實用語句

1. 今年你們的目標是什麼？
   What's your goal for this year?
2. 我們希望可以增加 6%。
   We hope to increase sales by six percent.
3. 你打算如何辦到？
   How do you plan to do it?
4. 我們產品有一個新的廣告活動。
   We have a new ad campaign for our products.
5. 我們希望從像你一樣的客戶身上獲得靈感。
   We hope to gain insight from clients like you.
6. 我們希望更了解國外的市場想要的是什麼。
   We hope to better understand what the foreign markets want exactly.
7. 好點子（好理由）。
   Good point.

Tips 小祕訣

邊談邊做記錄，迅速寫下談話內容，事後再整理。要成爲好的觀察及學習者要把握機會，一邊記錄的是客戶直接表達的資訊、用語，另一方面也要觀察及學習客戶非文字（如舉止、儀態、應對、情緒）所透露的訊息。

4.9 帶領（另一客戶）參觀公司
Touring the Company (for Another Client)

Dialog

A: 讓我帶你看看我們的辦公室，卡爾登先生。	**A:** Let me show you around our company, Mr. Carlton.
B: 好，謝謝。	**B:** Sure. Thanks.
A: 跟我來，這邊是到主要的實驗室，我晚點會帶你看看全部。	**A:** Come with me. This way leads to the main lab. I'll show all of that later.
B: 好。	**B:** OK.
A: 現在我要帶你看主要的辦公大樓。	**A:** Right now I'll just show you around our main office building.
B: 聽來很好。	**B:** Sounds good.
A: 這裡是會議室。	**A:** Here is the conference room.
B: 很好。	**B:** It's quite nice.

A: 是的，我們喜歡它，它有開會或做報告的所有必要設備。	**A:** Yes. We like it. It has all the necessary equipment for having a meeting or giving a presentation.
B: 看起來很好，設計得也很好。	**B:** It looks very good. Well designed, too.
A: 謝謝，請到這邊。	**A:** Thanks. Come this way.
B: 好。	**B:** All right.
A: 這裡是我們較小的會議室之一，請看裡面。	**A:** Down here is one of the smaller meeting rooms. — Look inside.
B: 很好！	**B:** It's great!
A: 你今天會有機會用到它，王先生會在這裡跟你會面。	**A:** You'll get a chance to use it today. Mr. Wong will be meeting you here.
B: 好極了。	**B:** Wonderful.

Word Bank

lab (laboratory) [læb] n. 實驗室
conference room/meeting room 會議室

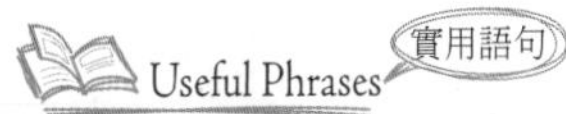

1. 我要帶你看主要的辦公大樓。

   I'll just show you around our main office building.

2. 這邊到主要的實驗室。

   This way leads to the main laboratory.

3. 王先生會在這裡跟你會面。

   Mr. Wong will be meeting you here.

4. 請到這邊。

   Come this way.

● （簡報——公司介紹請見 5.6）

4.10 帶領參觀產品展示間 Touring the Show Room

A: 你可以給我一個公司的目錄嗎？我想要在展示間這裡查詢項目。

A: Can you give me a company catalog? I'd like to check the items here in the show room.

B: 目錄在這裡，卡爾登先生。

B: Here you are, Mr. Carlton.

A: 這品項是什麼材質做的？

A: What is the material used to make this item?

B: 是鋼。	**B:** It is steel.
A: 表面處理是什麼？是漆或粉末噴塑？	**A:** What is the surface finish? Is it a paint or a powder coating?
B: 我查一下（幾秒鐘），是粉末噴塑。	**B:** Let me check. (a few seconds) It's a powder coating.
A: 這個項目的頁數是多少？	**A:** What is the page number of this item?
B: （翻頁）在這裡，你可以檢查一下規格確認。	**B:** (turning pages) Here you are. You can check the specs to be sure.

Word Bank 字庫

steel **[stil]** n. 鋼
surface finish 表面處理
powder coating 粉末噴塑
specs (specifications) **[spɛks]** n. 規格

Useful Phrases 實用語句

1. 這品項是什麼材質做的？
   What is the material used to make this item?
2. 表面處理是什麼？
   What is the surface finish?
3. 是漆或粉末噴塑？
   Is it a paint or a powder coating?

4. 這個項目的頁數是多少？

What is the page number of this item?

5. 你可以檢查一下規格確認。

You can check the specs to be sure.

事先從展示間裡整理好客戶需要的項目及準備好客戶所需的資料，雙方就可以直接展開交談，這也是客戶來訪前必須做好的功課之一。

4.11 帶領參觀內部餐廳 Touring the In-House Restaurants

A: 這是我們內部的餐廳之一。	**A:** This is one of our in-house restaurants.
B: 看起來很吸引人。	**B:** Looks inviting.
A: 是的，餐廳很舒適，而且食物很好又不貴。	**A:** Yes. It's comfortable and the food is very good and inexpensive.
B: 我會在你導覽後來試試看。	**B:** I'll try it out after your tour.
A: 我會給你一些餐券，這樣用餐就免費。	**A:** I'll give you some vouchers. That way it will be free.

B: 真謝謝你。

B: Thank you so much.

A: 當然要這樣。

A: We would not have it any other way.

B: 再次感謝。

B: Thanks again.

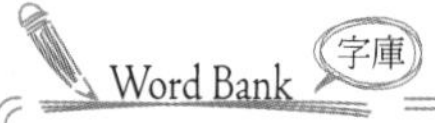

in-house ['ɪn,haʊs] adj. 內部的
inviting [ɪn'vaɪtɪŋ] adj. 吸引人的
voucher ['vaʊtʃɚ] n. 餐券

1. 這是我們內部的餐廳之一。

   This is one of our in-house restaurants.

2. 看起來很吸引人。

   Looks inviting.

3. 當然要這樣。

   We would not have it any other way.

4.12 關懷客戶住宿與需求
Checking a Client's Accommodations and Needs

A: 你的飲料來了。	**A:** Here is your drink.
B: 謝謝。	**B:** Thank you.
A: 你的住宿是否舒適呢？	**A:** Are your accommodations all right for you?
B: 是的，我對住宿很滿意，很方便。	**B:** Yes. I'm pleased with them. Very convenient.
A: 好，如果你需要任何東西讓我們知道。	**A:** Well, let us know if you need anything.
B: 謝謝，我想我在（飯店）那裡會沒問題。	**B:** Thank you. I think I'll be fine there.
A: 你已經有機會多了解一下我們的城市了嗎？	**A:** Have you had a chance to explore our city much yet?
B: 還沒，我已經走了一兩回，但還沒走遠些。	**B:** Not really. I've gone for a couple of walks, but I have not gone far.

A: 你真該看看大道區，很棒！	**A:** You really must see the Grand Avenue area. It's very nice!
B: 我需要買些東西，那裡有禮品店嗎？	**B:** I need to do some shopping. Are there any gift shops there?
A: 喔，是的，有一個很好的商店區及購物商場。	**A:** Oh, yes. It has a very good boutique area and a shopping mall as well.
B: 我得知它（大道區）有很好的公共藝術展示。	**B:** I've been told it has very good public art on display.
A: 是真的，有很多，而且是世界知名的藝術家所作。	**A:** Yes. It's true. There is a lot, all done by prominent artists from around the world.
B: 聽來很好。	**B:** Sounds good.

Word Bank 字庫

explore [ɪk'splor] v. 探索
gift shop 禮品店
boutique area 商店區
shopping mall 購物商場
public art 公共藝術
prominent ['prɑmənənt] adj. 知名的

1. 你的住宿是否舒適呢？

   Are your accommodations all right for you?

2. 如果你需要任何東西讓我們知道。

   Let us know if you need anything.

3. 你已經有機會多了解一下我們的城市了嗎？

   Have you had a chance to explore our city much yet?

4. 我對…很滿意。

   I'm pleased with ....

5. 我已經走了一兩回。

   I've gone for a couple of walks.

住宿 accommodations 爲複數概念。詢問客人住的是否舒適，給予關心，確定客人有你的電話號碼以備不時之需。

4.13 帶領參觀工廠 Touring the Manufacturing Plant

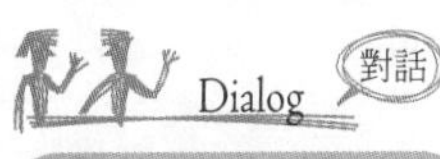

A: 嗨，泰瑞莎。	**A:** Hi, Teresa.
B: 哈囉，卡爾登先生。你準備好參觀工廠了嗎？	**B:** Hello, Mr. Carlton. Are you ready for a tour of the plant?
A: 是的。	**A:** Yes, I am.

B: 好，我們走吧。	**B:** Good. Let's go.
A: 請帶路。	**A:** Lead the way.
B: 在這裡你可以看到開始的過程。	**B:** Over here you can see where the process starts.
A: 這是新材料混合的地方嗎？	**A:** Is this where the new materials get mixed?
B: 是的，它們從那邊進來。	**B:** That's right. They come in from over there.
A: 你們每個月處理多少噸？	**A:** How many tons per month do you process?
B: 要看訂單多少，去年每個月我們處理大約 150 噸。	**B:** It depends on orders. Last year we took in an average of 150 tons per month.
A: 那樣很多。	**A:** That's a lot.
B: 是的，但是我們今年計畫增加產能，我們需要增產。	**B:** Yes, but we plan to boost capacity this year. We need to increase production.
A: 這樣很好。	**A:** That's good.

B: 是的。

B: Yes, it is.

Word Bank 字庫

order ['ɔrdɚ] n. 訂單
boost [bust] v. 增加，提高
capacity [kə'pæsətɪ] n. 能量，生產力

Useful Phrases 實用語句

1. 你準備好參觀工廠了嗎？

   Are you ready for a tour of the plant?

2. 請帶路。

   Lead the way.

3. 在這裡你可以看到開始的過程。

   Over here you can see where the process starts.

4. 你們每個月處理多少噸？

   How many tons per month do you process?

5. 我們今年計畫增加產能。

   We plan to boost capacity this year.

6. 我們需要增產。

   We need to increase production.

客人參觀前需先整理工廠，確認有條不紊的動線。熟悉各區域的設備及產品位置、操作、功能、特色等，並以英文演練介紹，這也是事前準備的一部分。（簡報——工廠介紹請見 5.8）

4.14 廠區及業務說明 Explaining a Section and Its Function

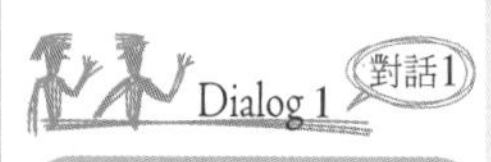

A: 現在我們在主包裝廠。

A: We're in the main packing plant now.

B: 這是你們多數產品輸出的地方？

B: Is this where most of your product gets shipped out?

A: 是的，這是所有產品準備好運出的地方。

A: Yes. This is where all the products are prepared for shipping.

B: 這個場所是否夠大可以處理工作？

B: Is this facility big enough to handle the job?

A: 現在可以，但是我們計畫下個月要開始擴展。

A: It is for now; however, we plan to expand it starting next month.

B: 那聽起來很好，這裡面似乎頗為擁擠。

B: That's good to hear. It seems pretty crowded in here.

A: 我們向來沒問題，但因為業務成長，業務部現在決定要在它變成問題之前擴展。

A: We've had no problems, but due to business growth, management has decided to expand now before it does become an issue.

B: 對。

B: Smart.

packing plant 包裝廠
shipping ['ʃɪpɪŋ] n. 裝運，運送
facility [fə'sɪlətɪ] n. 場所
expand [ɪk'spænd] v. 擴展
crowded ['kraudɪd] adj. 擁擠的
issue ['ɪʃu] n. 問題，爭議

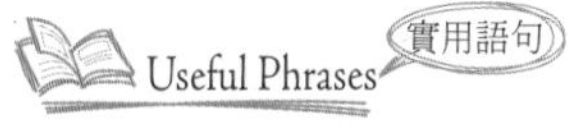

1. 現在我們在主包裝廠。
   We're in the main packing plant now.
2. 這個場所是否夠大可以處理工作？
   Is this facility big enough to handle the job?
3. 這是所有產品準備好運出的地方。
   This is where all the products are prepared for shipping.
4. 我們計畫下個月要開始擴展。
   We plan to expand it starting next month.

5. 這裡似乎頗為擁擠。

It seems pretty crowded in here.

Dialog 2 對話2

A: 就這樣了，你已經看了全部。

A: That's pretty much it. You've seen it all.

B: 很好，令我印象深刻。

B: Very good. I'm impressed.

A: 你有任何問題嗎？

A: Do you have any questions?

B: 或許晚些，我記了些筆記，我也會晚點在讀完筆記後問些事情。

B: Maybe later. I took some notes. I'll have some things to ask later after I read them over.

A: 沒問題，隨時歡迎。

A: No problem. Anytime.

B: 我現在確實有個問題。

B: I do have one question right now.

A: 是什麼？

A: What's that?

B: 我可以到哪裡弄點東西吃？

B: Where can I get something to eat?

A: 喔！跟我來，午餐正在等你，我們已經為你準備了一份午餐。

A: Oh! Come with me. Lunch is waiting for you. We already prepared a lunch for you.

B: 那是好消息，我餓慌了。

B: That's good news. I'm starving.

A: 跟我來。

A: Follow me.

impress [ɪm'prɛs] v. 印象
starve [starv] v. 挨餓

1. 令我印象深刻。
   I'm impressed.
2. 我記了些筆記。
   I took some notes.
3. 隨時歡迎（提問）。
   Anytime.
4. 我可以到哪裡弄點東西吃？
   Where can I get something to eat?
5. 我餓了。
   I'm starving.

6. 跟我來。

Follow me.

導覽工廠通常會從會議室開始，然後到不同的工作區，最後在展示間結束。工廠簡報是買主勘查工廠效率及種種條件是否值得合作的時候，同時也是供應商衡量買主是否識貨懂貨的時刻。彼此從規模、材料、機器等摸透看遍互相詰問，無非希望找到可靠買賣的對象，將本求利。

4.15 與客戶用餐 Having Dinner with a Client

Dialog 對話

A: 請坐下。	**A:** Please sit down.
B: 謝謝。	**B:** Thank you.
A: 我很高興你今晚能來。	**A:** I'm glad you could make it here tonight.
B: 我很高興來這裡。	**B:** I'm happy to be here.
A: 我可以給你弄點喝的嗎？	**A:** Can I get you something to drink?

B: 你有什麼？	**B:** What do you have?
A: 都有，你要雞尾酒嗎？	**A:** Everything. Would you like a cocktail?
B: 我不介意喝一杯，來杯伏特加可林如何？	**B:** I wouldn't mind a drink. How about a Vodka Collins?
A: 沒問題，我來準備。	**A:** No problem. I'll see to it.
B: 謝謝。	**B:** Thanks.

cocktail ['kak,tel] n. 雞尾酒

Vodka Collins 伏特加可林（含伏特加、甜橘酒、蘇打水之雞尾酒）

1. 我可以給你弄點喝的嗎？
   Can I get you something to drink?
2. 你要雞尾酒嗎？
   Would you like a cocktail?
3. 沒問題，我來準備。
   No problem. I'll see to it.

首先了解客人想要晚餐的種類？是否有飲食特殊需求？晚餐後是否想從事其他活動（關乎是否喝酒）或直接回飯店休息，無論活動安排爲何，務求賓主盡歡。輕鬆場合閒聊必然會談到產業或國際情勢，既是交換看法也是彼此詢問交手的時間，爲避免讓客戶感覺你在打聽他的業務機密，問題不宜單刀直入，而是轉個彎問大方向。也可從時事問起（如底特律破產、歐巴馬健保案對美國有什麼影響），從客戶閒聊的回答裡拉回你想從對方了解的問題。（見附錄——文化祕笈）

4.16 送機
Farewell

A: 我們到了，你的航空班機報到處在那邊。	**A:** Here we are. Your airline's flight check-in is over there.
B: 謝謝你所有的幫忙。	**B:** Thank you for all of your help.
A: 沒問題，我很樂意幫忙。	**A:** No problem. I'm happy to assist.
B: 我最好確認我的隨身行李沒有任何液體。	**B:** I'd better make sure I don't have any liquids in my carry-on.
A: 對，飛航安全現在很嚴格。	**A:** Right. Airline security is tight these days.

B: 呃，再次感謝你（握手），我真的很感激每件事。	**B:** Well, thanks again (shaking hands). I really appreciate everything.
A: 希望你在這裡過得愉快，並且覺得有收穫。	**A:** I hope you enjoyed your stay and found it productive.
B: 我有，保重。	**B:** I did. Take care.
A: 你也是，一路順風！	**A:** You, too. Have a good flight!

Word Bank 字庫

liquid ['lɪkwɪd] n. 液體
airline security 飛航安全
tight [taɪt] adj. 嚴格的
productive [prə'dʌktɪv] adj. 有生產力的，有收穫的

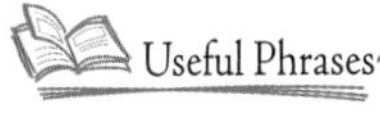

Useful Phrases 實用語句

1. 謝謝你所有的幫忙。
   Thank you for all of your help.
2. 我真的很感激每件事。
   I really appreciate everything.
3. 我很樂意幫忙。
   I'm happy to assist.
4. 希望你在這裡過得愉快。
   I hope you enjoyed your stay.

5. 一路順風！

Have a good flight!

親自送機是最好的，如果班機太早，可以體貼為客人準備早餐或請飯店準備，陪客人到登機櫃臺，進入安檢區前陪他聊聊天，這些都是送機基本的舉止。客人回國後，當然要持續保持聯繫為將來做準備。

Your airline's flight check-in is over there.

check-in

Unit 5 Giving Business Presentations

作商業簡報

即使對以英語做爲母語的人士而言，作商業簡報也可能是件令人害怕的事，爲了不被任務打敗，必須爲自己做好基本準備。本章提供簡報規劃指南及基本準則、簡報公司及工廠樣本、簡報產品與示範說明，以及簡報完成後如何掌握客戶問答。

5.1簡報規劃指南
Guide to Designing a Presentation

1. **爲觀眾列出你想爲他們達成的 3-4 項目標：**
你可能認爲你知道你想要完成的事，但是如果你不能爲自己弄清楚重點，別人就不可能知道你要表達什麼。例如：如果你的任務是爲他人介紹公司的成就或讓他們了解如何使用你公司的服務，那簡報就必須針對你想達成的目標來設定。
2. **了解你的聽衆及他們來聽你簡報的原因：**
出席簡報的人會立刻想知道他們是否會浪費時間聽簡報，你必須馬上爲他們搞清楚這點，如此有助於自己的思路清晰，並爲他們打造適合的內容。
3. **做一個清單，列出你要與聽衆溝通的重點：**
完成後，問自己——「如果聽衆明瞭了這些項目，我是否達到了目標？」
4. **搞清楚自己想在簡報裡創造的氣氛：**
例如：期望的、歡慶的、或激勵團隊精神的氣氛，如此將有助於與聽衆的情感連結。
5. **設計如何開場（占全部時間的 5-10%）：**
開場應包含:
(1)展現目標
(2)告知或爲聽衆釐清聆聽此簡報的好處
(3)解釋簡報的排序
6. **準備簡報的內容。**
7. **設計結語（占全部時間的 5-10%），總結重點。**
8. **預留時間給聽衆提問與意見交流。**

5.2 簡報資料準備指南 Guidelines for Preparing Presentation Materials

或許你會預先發給補充資料作為簡報參考（如報告或文章等），或是使用電腦簡報。

1. 如果使用電腦設備，要在聽衆入場前先確認相關設備、燈光按鈕、麥克風、音響、簡報筆等播放無誤。如果必須關掉燈光，須為自己準備小型照明。
2. 簡報畫面使用一致性的顏色或圖樣。
3. 投影片必須背景清晰，字體夠大（每張投影片最好不要超過 5 至 7 行，可設定順序一一出現），使聽衆閱讀時不會有困難。
4. 每張投影片使用 3 至 5 分鐘，不要更換得太快速或太頻繁，聽衆需要時間消化思考簡報的內容。
5. 如果簡報頁面插入按鈕連結網頁或影音，務必確認連結讀取有效迅速；為防止突發狀況，須有備檔，隨時待用。
6. 如果你在簡報中發給補充資料，聽衆可能會開始讀資料而不聽你簡報。為避免這種情形，可以在簡報結束後再發給聽衆。
7. 確認所有資料無誤。

5.3 簡報口說基本準則 Basic Guidelines about Your Delivery

1. 如果是對小衆（例如：4-15 人）簡報，要試著與每個人的眼光有幾秒鐘的接觸。
2. 不要一直看稿，多數時間應該看著聽衆。
3. 用略為大聲及比平常慢一點的速度說話。
4. 依照簡報內容調整音量、速度與語調，使聽衆凝聚注意力，並且不會感到乏味。

5.4 討論簡報目標 Talking about the Goals of the Presentation

A: 嗨，大衛，我需要跟你談一下關於週一的簡報。	A: Hi, David. I need to talk to you about next Monday's presentation.
B: 好，什麼時候？	B: Sure. When?
A: 今天比較好。	A: Preferably today.
B: 好，我下午有空。	B: OK. I'm free this afternoon.
A: 好，2 點你可以嗎？	A: Good. Is 2:00 good for you?
B: 好，你可以在我辦公室這裡碰面嗎？	B: Yes, sure. Do you want to meet here in my office?
A: 可以。	A: That would be fine.
B: 我們主要要討論什麼？	B: What will we be discussing mostly?

A: 我需要跟你一起決定我們這次簡報的主要目標是什麼。

A: I need to work with you on determining our main goals for this presentation.

B: 了解，2 點見。

B: Got it. See you at 2:00.

A: 好。

A: Great.

preferably ['prɛfərəblɪ] adj. 偏好地
determine [dɪ'tɝmɪn] v. 決定
goal [gol] n. 目標

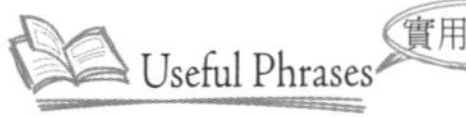

1. 我們將討論什麼？

   What will we be discussing?

2. 會面是關於什麼？

   What's the meeting about?

3. 我會買午餐給你。

   I'll buy you lunch.

A: 我們這次簡報想達成什麼？

A: What is it we want to accomplish with this presentation?

B: 我想我們需要為聽衆展現我們公司的背景與成就紀錄來為他們提供服務。

B: I believe we need to show the audience that our company has the background and success record to serve their needs.

A: 對，但我們也需要仔細說明我們在做什麼。

A: True, but we also need to show them specifically what we do.

B: 我不認為是這樣，這次簡報不需要。

B: I don't think so. Not in this presentation.

A: 真的嗎？為什麼？

A: Really? Why not?

B: 因為我們需要專注給他們刺激，並且先建立起他們的信心。

B: Because we need to concentrate on exciting them and building confidence with them first.

A: 他們會不想知道更多關於我們如何工作嗎？

A: Won't they want to know more about how we do things?

B: 是，但是首先我們需要讓他們相信我們可以做事。

B: Yes, but first we need to get them to believe we can do things.

A: 很有趣，我懂你的意思了。

A: Interesting. I see your point.

Word Bank 字庫

accomplish [ə'kɑmplɪʃ] v. 完成
audience ['ɔdɪəns] n. 聽衆
background [bæk,graund] n. 背景
success record 成就紀錄
specifically [spɪ'sɪfɪkəlɪ] adv. 細節地
confidence ['kɑnfədəns] n. 信心

Useful Phrases 實用語句

1. 我懂你的意思了。
   I see your point
2. 我不這麼認為。
   I don’t think so.
3. 我同意。
   I agree.
4. 我會讓你知道。
   I’ll let you know.
5. 我會再跟你談那件事。
   I’ll get back to you on that.
6. 我們需要專注給他們刺激，並先建立起他們的信心。
   We need to concentrate on exciting them and building confidence with them first.
7. 我們需要讓他們相信我們可以做事。
   We need to get them to believe we can do things.

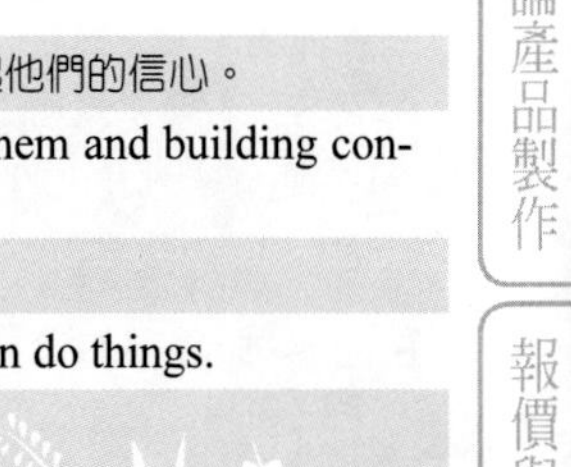

5.5 討論及確認簡報所有必要事項
Preparing and Confirming All Necessities for the Presentation

A: 看一下我準備的簡報資料。	**A:** Look at this PowerPoint material I've prepared.
B: 好。	**B:** OK.
A: 我昨天弄了整天。	**A:** I spent all day on this yesterday.
B: 我知道你很努力在做這個。	**B:** I know you've been working hard on this.
A: 好了，看吧！	**A:** Here we go. Look!
B: 那樣看來很好。	**B:** That looks nice.
A: 謝謝，你想字體夠大嗎？	**A:** Thanks. Do you think the words are big enough?
B: 對後排的人或許不夠。	**B:** Maybe not for the people in the back row.

A: 我稍後會改，你認為圖片夠清楚嗎？	**A:** I'll change it later. Do you think the picture is clear enough?
B: 是的，但我想那個圖表不好讀。	**B:** Yes, but I think that chart is hard to read.
A: 我了解你的意思，這些數字不容易讀得清楚。	**A:** I see what you mean. The numbers are not clear enough to read easily.
B: 對。	**B:** Right.

Word Bank 字庫

row [ro] n. 排
chart [tʃɑrt] n. 圖表

Useful Phrases 實用語句

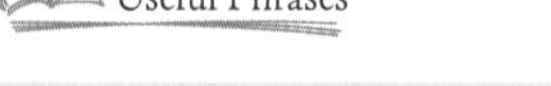

1. 我知道你很努力在做這個。
   I know you have been working hard on this.
2. 那個圖表不好讀。
   That chart is hard to read.
3. 這些數字不容易讀得清楚。
   The numbers are not clear enough to read easily.

Dialog 2 對話2

A: 這是我們簡報將使用的場地。	**A:** This is the room we will use for the presentation.

B: 不錯，有很多空間。	**B:** It's not bad. There's plenty of room.
A: 是，我們可以有幾張桌子給我們的銷售人員使用。	**A:** Yes. We'll be able to have several tables for our sales people to use.
B: 也有文件與點心桌。	**B:** Literature and refreshment tables, too.
A: 對，這裡很好。	**A:** Right. It's very good here.
B: 你認為照明系統恰當嗎？	**B:** Do you think the lighting system is adequate?
A: 還沒人有機會檢查那個跟音響系統。	**A:** No one's had a chance to check that or the sound system.
B: 那要何時（確認）？	**B:** When will that happen?
A: 設備組人員會在今天下午來這裡，一些技術人員也會來。	**A:** The set up crew will be here this afternoon. Some tech people are coming, too.
B: 好，聽起來很好。	**B:** All right. Sounds good.

Word Bank 字庫

literature ['lɪtərətʃɚs] n. 文獻（information handouts資料講義/pamphlets小冊子）
refreshments [rɪ'frɛʃmənt] n. pl. 點心（複數）
lighting system 照明系統
adequate ['ædəkwɪt] adj. 適當的
sound system 音響系統
crew [kru] n. 一組人員
tech people 技術人員

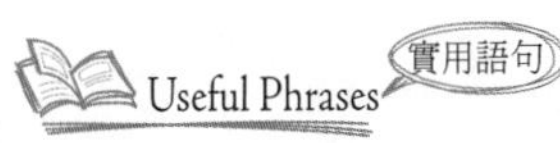

Useful Phrases 實用語句

1. 有很多空間。
   There's plenty of room.
2. 我們需要文件與點心桌。
   We need literature and refreshment tables.
3. 你認為照明系統恰當嗎？
   Do you think the lighting system is adequate?
4. 我們要檢查音響系統。
   We need to check the sound system.

5.6 簡報─公司介紹
The Presentation - Introducing the Company

5.6a 第一部分 Part 1

大家好，我是傑生林，謝謝你們今天來。

Hi, everyone. I'm Jason Lin. Thank you for coming today.

我知道今天你們寧可做別的事，但是我保證我要說的話對你們是有用的。讓我從介紹我服務的公司開始——LH 集團。我們精於讓各個部門藉由發展更多人性設計而更具有效率及生產力。我們擁有超過 20 多國的合約，並且現在在美國拓展我們的營運。

I know you'd rather be doing something else today, but I promise what I have to say will be useful to you. Let me start by introducing the company I work for—LH Group. We specialize in making departments more efficient and productive by developing more human compatible design into them. We have contracts in over twenty countries and are currently expanding our operations in the U.S..

我們到底做什麼呢？ 你可能會有此疑問，那是個很棒的問題，我即將開始解答。

What is it we do exactly? You are probably asking that question. It's a great question, and now I'm going to start answering it.

specialize ['spɛʃə,laɪz] v. 專精
efficient [ə'fɪʃənt, ɪ-] adj. 有效率的
productive [prə'dʌktɪv] adj. 有生產力的
compatible [kəm'pætəbḷ] adj. 相容的
expand [ɪk'spænd] v. 擴展
operation [,ɑpə'reʃən] n. 營運

5.6b 第二部分 Part 2

首先，請把 LH 集團想成一個製造商，在我們的案子裡，我們製造成功，我們藉由規劃與執行為個別公司、不同部門的設計來增加工作表現。我們派出一組專家、顧問、技師及其他人員的團隊來探究、觀察、評量及整編為了設計出使工作場所表現更好之所需資料。我們可以說是在打造一種客製化的方案，以適合特定的目標、區域、產品或服務及人員。如此我們可以做出你們公司所需，為你們公司創造有力的團隊，使你們在市場上更為成功。

To start with, think of LH Group as a manufacturer. In our case we manufacture success. We do that by designing and implementing the designs made for individual companies to enhance their performance, department by department. We send in a team of experts, advisors, technicians and others, to study, observe, evaluate, and compile the necessary data needed for designing a better performing workplace. We manufacture, so to speak, a custom made program that fits specific goals, regions, products or services, and people. In this way we can make what your company needs to further succeed in your market. We make powerful teams for your company.

Word Bank 字庫

manufacture [ˌmænjəˈfæktʃɚ] v. 製造
expert [ˈɛkspɝt] n. 專家
advisor [ədˈvaɪzərɪ] n. 顧問
evaluate [ɪˈvæljuˌet] v. 評量
compile [kəmˈpaɪl] v. 整編
custom made program 客製方案

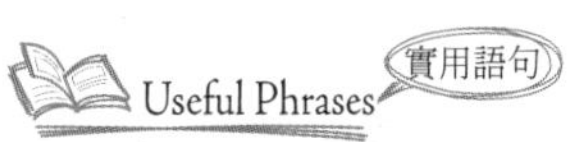

1. 我保證我要說的話對你們是有用的。

   I promise what I have to say will be useful to you.

2. 讓我從介紹我服務的公司開始。

   Let me start by introducing the company I work for.

5.7 客戶提問─設計方案 Q/A - Designing a Program

Dialog 對話

A: 好，現在誰有問題？	**A:** OK. Now, who has a question?
B: 我。	**B:** I do.
A: 好，什麼問題？	**A:** Great. What is it?
B: 你公司設計一個方案為時多久？	**B:** How long does it take your company to design a program?

A: 依照情況之複雜性而定，我們曾經最快兩個月，其他的我們需要一年。

A: It depends on the complexity of the situation. We have done it in as fast as two months, for other projects we needed a year.

B: 你可以猜想替設計工作制服的十人小組（做一個方案）要多久嗎？

B: Could you guess what it would be for a ten member team that designs work uniforms?

A: 這我真的很難說，我必須先跟你多談談，牽扯到太多因素，無法用猜的。

A: It's really hard for me to say. I'd have to talk to you more about it. There are too many factors involved to make a guess.

B: 好，我了解，謝謝。

B: OK, I see. Thanks.

尋找客戶
國際參展準備
參加國際商展
接待客戶
作商業簡報
討論產品製作
報價與議價

A: 好的，各位請記住，如我所提過的，在你們身後的桌子有聯絡資訊，你也可以在簡報後留下來跟我談一談。

A: Sure. And everyone remember, of course as I've mentioned, there is contact information on the tables behind you, and you can stay and talk to me after the presentation, too.

complexity [kəm'plɛksətɪ] n. 複雜
uniform ['junəˌfɔrm] n. 制服
factor ['fæktɚ] n. 因素
contact information 聯絡資訊

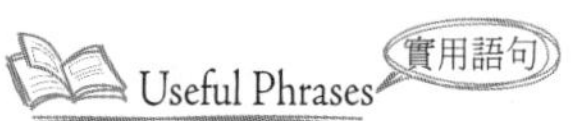

1. 我可以問一個問題嗎？
   May I ask a question?
2. 誰有問題？
   Who has a question?
3. 我有問題。
   I have a question.
4. 什麼問題？
   What is it?
5. 你想知道什麼？
   What would you like to know?

掌握及控制問答場面，採取聆聽及自然開放的態度及手勢（手臂不要抱在胸前或觸摸臉部及甩頭髮，手不要放在口袋或插腰，有瀏海者應將頭髮整理好），直視提問者，讓提問者問完後，可以停頓一兩秒再回答，讓人感覺你有經過思考。如果不等提問說完或一問完馬上丟出答案，可能會造成他人對你自以爲是的厭惡。如果提問的問題不清楚，以你的了解重述問題是否正確，回答宜簡明扼要，不要過度解釋，當然必須與確認客戶他是否了解你的答案，視情形補充說明。千萬別說「You are wrong!」激怒客戶。因爲你最了解產品也準備充分，你會知道多數的答案，對於少數不知道的答案，不要害怕回答「I don't know.」可以回問顧客他會怎麼做，聽聽對方的想法並留下聯繫方式，事後再回答。

5.8 簡報—介紹工廠
The Presentation - Introducing the Manufacturer

早安，大家好！ 讓我用幾分鐘時間介紹我們臺灣桃園的工廠。

Good morning, everyone! Let me take a few minutes to show you our factory in Tao Yuan, Taiwan.

我們的工廠在1985年設立後開始運作，幾度擴充規模後，目前廠區全部有70公畝，總共有10條生產線，每年生產100萬個產品。我們的產品賣到世界各地，主要是美國、歐洲及澳洲。我會展示每個區域給你們看不同的分工。在我介紹的時候，你們有任何疑問，請讓我知道。

Our factory started its operation in 1985. After several expansions, it is now 70 acres in total. There are 10 production lines, producing around 1,000,000 pieces of product each year. We sell our products worldwide, mainly in the US, Europe, and Australia. I'll show you each of the sections that perform different work processes. Please let me know any questions you have while I'm introducing them to you.

首先是備料區，我們有 85 公噸的備料可以應付買主的需求，並能穩定價格。去年因為低價，我們買進大量的鋼。當鋼的市場價格上漲，我們就可以持續供應具有價格競爭力的產品，而具有成本效率。

First of all, we are viewing the Material Section. We have 85 tons of material to meet our clients' demands and to stabilize our prices. Last year, we bought steel in bulk because of its low price. As the market price of steel goes up, we'll be able to continue providing competively priced products and be cost efficient.

（繼續介紹各區域 continuing each section）

裁切區：我們德國的雷射裁切機保證品質一致，不僅可以讓我們顧到細節，也可以加上更多控制點。

Cutting section: our German laser cutting machine guarantees consistent quality. Not only can we tend to detail, but we can also add more control points.

焊接區：我們使用機器人來澈底地焊接材質。

Welding section: we use robots to weld the material thourouly.

上漆區：自動粉末噴塑線路提供高品質的表面處理。

Painting section: automatic powder coating line provides a high quality surface finish.

組裝區：我們的新組裝線使我們可以達到一致性與高品質的組裝。

Assembly section: our new assembly line allows consistent, high quality assembly.

檢測區：在生產過程中，我們執行三回合的檢測。

Inspection and testing section: three inspection and testing rounds are performed during the production stage.

包裝區：我們的自動包裝線符合我們的高品質標準，有效率及堅固地包裝成品。

Packaging section: our auto packaging line meets all quality standards and packs the finished products efficiently and firmly.

裝運區：所有放置在這區塊的產品是準備好要輸出的。

Shipment section: all products located in this section are ready to go.

研發區：你可以看到我們的工程師正在鑽研開發最新產品，我們的研發部致力於為所有顧客達成最佳方案及永遠精進所有產品的最佳品質。

R&D section: you can see our engineers who are researching and developing the latest products. Our R&D strives for the best possible solutions for all customers and the advancement of the best quality ever for all products.

（即將結束導覽 Ending the tour）

最後，在我們的展示間裡，你可以看到最新的產品。我們目標在於發展及提供便利與高品質的產品供世人使用，我們很感激能與你們合作，將我們的產品進口到你們的市場。非常感謝！

Finally, you can see our latest products in our show room. It is our goal to develop and provide handy, quality products for people all over the world to use. We appreciate the opportunity to work with you to export our goods to your market. Thank you very much!

Word Bank 字庫

stabilize ['stebə,laɪz] v. 穩定
cost efficient 具成本效率的
consistent [kən'sɪstənt] adj. 一致的
welding [wɛld] n. 焊接
surface finish 表面處理
assembly [ə'sɛmblɪ] n. 裝配，組合
strive [straɪv] v. 致力

Useful Phrases 實用語句

1. 在我介紹的時候，你們有任何疑問，請讓我知道。
   Please let me know any questions you have while I'm introducing them to you.
2. 我們有 85 公噸的備料可以應付買主的需求。
   We have 85 tons of material to meet our clients' demands.
3. 我們德國的雷射裁切機保證品質一致。
   Our German laser cutting machine guarantees consistent quality.
4. 我們使用機器人來澈底地焊接材質。
   We use robots to weld the material thourougly.
5. 我們的研發部致力於為所有顧客達成最佳方案。
   Our R&D strives for the best possible solutions for all customers.

Tips 小祕訣

當客戶僅能從簡報簡介得知工廠資訊時，須確認工廠照片投影效果夠大夠清晰，簡報時的文字僅列簡單重要項目即可，使畫面清爽，讓顧客集中在重點上。如果在介紹前發給簡介，在介紹時可以導引顧客到該頁面，方便顧客提問及記筆記。

如果希望顧客專心聽取簡報，可以在簡報完畢後再給客戶書面簡介，無論做法爲何，在給予簡介的同時，務必請客戶惠賜名片。

5.9 產品介紹與示範 Introducing and Demonstrating Products

（後車廂腳踏車架 Trunk Bike Rack Installation）

嗨，大家早！你看到我手上拿的是我們的新腳踏車架，它是100%以再生塑膠做成，所以非常輕，中間手把是不鏽鋼做的，架子很輕，但很堅固。架子的塑膠手臂跟腳架是射出成型，是目前市場上最堅固的質材。整個架子重量為 1.5 公斤，也就是 3.3 磅，即使是女士們也可以不流一滴汗輕易地在車廂上安裝腳踏車架。

Hi, everyone. Good morning. Here you can see in my hand our new bike rack. It's made of 100% reclyclable plastic, so it's pretty light. The milldle bar is made of stainless steel. The rack is light, but very sturdy. The plastic arms and legs of the rack are injection-molded, using the strongest material on the market. The whole rack weighs only 1.5 kilograms or 3.3 pounds. Even ladies can easily install the bike rack onto the trunk of a car without a sweat.

它適合 90%市場上的車輛，並且因為是塑膠及不鏽鋼做的，完全不需要擔心生鏽的問題。如果你跟你的家人喜愛帶腳踏車到不同地方去騎，這腳踏車架一定可以贏得你的心。現在我開始展示給你看安裝有多簡單，只要幾個步驟。

It fits nearly 90% of the vehicles available on the market, and because it is made of plastic and stainless steel, there is absolutely no need to worry about rusting at all. If you and your family love to take your bikes to ride in different places, this is the one that is going to win your heart for sure. Now I'm going to show you how easy the installation is by simply following a few steps.

（站到車子後面 standing at the rear of a vehicle）

首先，握住腳踏車架，放到車廂上。將架子的橡膠腳直接放在保險桿上，橡膠腳會保護車漆。

First, hold the bike rack and put it on the rear of your car. Have the rubber feet of the rack directly put on the bumper. The rubber feet can protect the finish of your car.

再來，將上下側邊的帶子固定好，拉緊。

Next, attach the upper, lower, and side straps onto the trunk and tighten.

然後，調整手臂，確定角度略為水平。

Then, adjust the arms. Make sure they are somewhat horizontal.

現在你可以將腳踏車放到架子上，這個架子可以放兩臺腳踏車，你可以看到兩臺腳踏車的高度不同以確保它們在運送中最好的狀況，它們不會撞到彼此。

Now you can mount you bikes onto the rack. This rack can hold two bikes, and you can see the two bikes are on different levels to ensure their best condition during transport. They won't knock against each other.

最後，拉緊棘輪皮帶固定你的腳踏車使它們不會搖晃。

Finally, tighten the ratchet straps to secure your bikes to prevent them from swaying.

你剛剛看到你可以在一兩分鐘內快速完成安裝，這個理想的腳踏車架將帶給你戶外騎乘很多的樂趣，完全不用擔心會傷害你的車或你的腳踏車。

So you have just seen how quickly you can finish the installation in just one to two minutes. It is the ideal bike rack that is going to give you a lot of fun riding outdoors without worrying about damaging your car and your bike.

這個可以載兩臺腳踏車的架子是$59.99，載三臺腳踏車的也有，標價是$79.99。因為它很耐用跟完全不會生鏽，這是你唯一需要的，可以讓你到處騎車的腳踏車架。今天為了大家的方便，我們準備了車架規格的紙本介紹，我們的網站有車型適用表，謝謝大家的聆聽。現在如果你有任何問題或意見，請讓我知道，非常感謝！

This two bike rack is $59.99. The three bike rack is also available, priced $79.99. Because it's so durable and rust free, this is the only bike rack you will ever need for riding your bike anywhere you like. Today we have prepared paper copies of the specificaitons for your convenience. The fit chart is abailble on our website. Thank you for listening, everyone. Now if you have any questions or any comments, please let me know. Thank you very much!

Word Bank 字庫

recyclable plastic 再生塑膠
sturdy ['stɝdɪ] adj. 堅固的
injection-molded 射出成型
without a sweat 不流一滴汗
horizontal [ˌhɔrə'zɑntl̩] adj. 水平的
mount [maunt] v. 架置
ratchet strap 棘輪皮帶
secure [sɪ'kjur] v. 固定
sway [swe] v. 搖晃
durable ['djurəbl̩] adj. 耐用的

rust free 不會生鏽的
fit chart（車型）適用表

1. 架子很輕，但很堅固。

   The rack is light, but very sturdy.

2. 即使是女士們也可以不流一滴汗輕易地安裝腳踏車架。

   Even ladies can easily install the bike rack without a sweat.

3. 完全不需要擔心生鏽的問題。

   There is absolutely no need to worry about rusting at all.

4. 現在我開始展示給你看安裝有多簡單，只要幾個步驟。

   Now I'm going to show you how easy the installation is by simply following a few steps.

5. 今天為了大家的方便，我們準備了車架規格的紙本介紹。

   Today we have prepared paper copies of the specifications for your convenience.

6. 我們的網站有車型適用表。

   The fit chart is available on our website.

7. 現在如果你有任何問題或意見，請讓我知道。

   Now if you have any questions or any comments, please let me know.

5.10 客戶提問—生產、材料及品質控管問題
Q/A Time - Production, Material,and Quality Control

1. **問題**：鋼管是無縫鋼管嗎？

   回答：是的，這樣鋼管才能安全承受重量。

   Q: Is the steel tubing seamless?

   A: Yes, it is. So the steel tubing can withstand the weight very well.

2. **問題**：從收到訂單到交貨需要多久時間？

回答：大約 45-60 天，要看量跟出貨到哪裡。

Q: What's your lead time?

A: About 45 to 60 days, depending on the quantity and where the products are shipped.

3. **問題**：你們生產時的不良率多少？

回答：大約 3%。

Q: What is the production rejection rate?

A: About 3%.

4. **問題**：你們的消費者退回的不良率是多少？

回答：我們檢查三次以上才裝運，所以我們幾乎沒有銷售不良率。

Q: What is your consumer reject rate?

A: We have them inspected three times before shipment, so we have nearly 0% rejection rate.

5. **問題**：不良的原因是什麼？

回答：多數是包裝。

Q: What is the reason for rejection?

A: Mostly packaging.

6. **問題**：你有無法使用你們產品腳踏車架的車輛清單嗎？ 我們要怎樣才能確定你們的車架適合某一種車型？

回答：我們有清單，但可能無法完整，因為總是有新車上市。雖然我們可以包含將近 90%的車輛，我們仍然在為剩下的 10%建立清單。我們衷心希望研發部門努力開發，在不久的將來能開發出能百分之百容納所有車輛的理想車架。

Q: Do you have a list of vehicles that your product won't fit on? How can we make sure that your bike rack works for a particular model of car?

A: Yes, we do, but it may be impossible to have a complete list as there are always new vehicles coming out. While our racks fit nearly 90% of the cars, we are still building our database for the rest of the 10% that they won't fit. With high hopes our R&D Department strives to develop the ideal rack that fits all vehicles in the near future.

seamless ['simlɪs] adj. 無縫的
withstand [wɪθ'stænd, wɪð-] v. 承受
lead time 收到訂單到交貨（視交貨條件）所需時間
reject/rejection rate 不良率

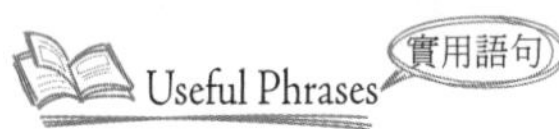

1. 從訂單到交貨期間需時多久？
   What's your lead time?
2. 你們生產時的不良率多少？
   What is the production rejection rate?
3. 你們的消費者退回的不良率是多少？
   What is your consumer reject rate?
4. 不良的原因是什麼？
   What is the reason for rejection?
5. 我們幾乎沒有銷售不良率。
   We have nearly 0% rejection rate.

客戶最關心的無非是成本、品質、交貨時間，對於這些問題及相關的細項及數字要詳加準備。如lead time爲備料、生產完畢到交貨的總和時間。注意，交貨時間視交貨條件而定，常見的條件爲船上交貨（FOB），含成本及運保費交貨（CIF），或是門對門交貨（door to door delivery），所需時間不一。

delivery date/day/time指的是出貨當天的日期/時間，加上transportation time是運輸時間長短（含船運及內陸），兩者爲出貨運輸重要資訊。關於lead time的時間條件均需與買方確認接受無誤。

另外要注意的是廠商在國外參展時（例如：美國），如果客戶指定 FOB 船上交貨（例如：舊金山）的話，等同臺灣廠商的CIF（含成本及運保費）或C&F（含成本及運費），意即報價須計算從臺灣到舊金山的運費負擔。如果搞錯了，勢必虧本。

Note

Unit 6 Discussing and Manufacturing Products

討論產品製作

對客戶有些基本了解（例如：是哪裡的客戶？公司性質？主要市場？買過什麼東西？是批發商還是零售商？經常購買的數量？），讓顧客明白你問這些問題才能推薦合適的產品。如因應客戶要求生產客製化產品（customized products），除技術考慮外、開模費、專利權、最低訂製額及安全性等其他相關成本亦須考慮在內。

6.1 客戶詢問—產品問題
Receiving Client's Inquiry - Questions about a Product

A: 哈囉，泰瑞莎陳女士在嗎？	**A:** Hello, is Ms. Teresa Chen there?
B: 請問您是哪一位？	**B:** May I ask who's calling?
A: 我是彼得紐頓從西雅圖打來，我們上星期在拉斯維加斯的貿易展會過面。	**A:** This is Peter Newton calling from Seattle. We met at the trade show in Las Vegas last week.
B: 好，紐頓先生，請等一下，我幫你接給她。	**B:** OK, Mr. Newton, one moment please. I'll get her for you.
A: 好。	**A:** Alright.

（電話轉接 call transferring）

A: 嗨，陳女士，我是彼得紐頓。	**A:** Hi, Ms. Chen. This is Peter Newton.

B: 是的，紐頓先生，我們確實在貿易展會過面，聽到你的消息真好。你好嗎？

B: Yes, Mr. Newton. We met at the trade show indeed. It's great to hear from you. How are you?

A: 我很好，請叫我彼得，你好嗎？

A: I'm fine. Just call me Peter. And how are you?

B: 我也很好，你可以叫我泰瑞莎，我今天可以幫你什麼嗎？

A: I'm fine, too. You can call me Teresa. What can I help you with today?

A: 我想問你地板腳踏車架，目錄裡 68 號。

A: I'd like to ask about the Floor Bike Stand, No. 68 in your catalog.

B: 好，請等一下，有什麼問題嗎？

B: Sure. Just a second. What is your question?

A: 是鋼製的嗎？

A: Is it made of steel?

B: 是的，沒錯，是粉末噴塑鋼管，你有確認規格嗎？

B: Yes, that's right. It is powder coated tubular steel. Have you checked the specs?

A: 有，20 × 18 × 30 吋及重 8.5 磅。

A: Yes, I have. It's 20x18x30 inches and weighs 8.5 pounds.

B: 對，它是我們銷售最好的產品之一，並且外銷到美國、歐洲、澳洲及其他市場。

B: That's right. It is one of our best selling products and is exported to America, Europe, Australia, and other markets.

powder coated 粉末噴塑的
tubular steel 鋼管
specs (specifications) 規格
export [ɪks'port, -'pɔrt] v. 外銷，出口

1. 我們確實在貿易展會過面。
   We met at the trade show indeed.
2. 聽到你的消息真好。
   It's great to hear from you.
3. 我今天可以幫你什麼嗎？
   What can I help you with today?
4. 是鋼製的嗎？
   Is it made of steel?
5. 它是粉末噴塑鋼管。
   It is powder coated tubular steel.
6. 你有確認規格嗎？
   Have you checked the specs?
7. 它是我們銷售最好的產品之一。
   It is one of our best selling products.

顧客詢問產品問題都是最基本的問題，包括材料、規格樣式、是否有現貨、價格、包裝、檢驗標準、下訂後多久可以交貨等等。

6.2 產品證明與專利 Product Certification and Patent

A: 你腳踏車架有產品認證嗎？	**A:** Do you have the product certification for the bike stand?
B: 有，你需要哪裡的認證？	**B:** Yes, we do. What kind of certification do you need?
A: 我需要歐盟的，你可以寄給我嗎？	**A:** I need CE. Can you send me the certification?
B: 當然了，我可以用電子郵件寄給你掃描檔，可以嗎？	**B:** Sure, I can send it by email with a scanned file. Is it OK?
A: 好，那行。	**A:** Yes, that's just fine.

對話2 Dialog 2

A: 你從哪裡得到想法？	**A:** Where did your idea come from?

B: 產品是我們的設計，我們有品質試驗，並且我們有它的專利。

B: The product is our own design. We have it tested for quality, and we have the patent.

A: 專利在哪個國家註冊？你可以給我專利號碼嗎？

A: In which country did you register the patent? Can you give me the patent number?

B: 我們在臺灣、中國、美國都有註冊，我們稍後可以給你每個國家的號碼。

B: We registered it in Taiwan, China, and the USA. We can give the number of each country to you later.

A: 很好。

A: Good.

product certification 產品認證
scan [skæn] v. 掃描
patent ['pætn̩t] n. 專利
register ['rɛdʒɪstɚ] v. 註冊

1. 你腳踏車架有產品認證嗎？
   Do you have the product certification for the bike stand?
2. 你需要哪裡的認證？
   What kind of certification do you need?
3. 你從哪裡得到想法？
   Where did your idea come from?
4. 專利在哪個國家註冊？
   In which country did you register the patent?
5. 你可以給我專利號碼嗎？
   Can you give me the patent number?
6. 產品是我們的設計。
   The product is our own design.
7. 我們有品質試驗。
   We have it tested for quality.
8. 我們有它的專利。
   We have the patent.
9. 我們在臺灣、中國、美國都有註冊。
   We registered it in Taiwan, China, and the USA.

申請專利或認證、公證（notarization）費用並不便宜，須衡量成本，如果是需額外付費的證書（certificate），費用須另計。千萬不要作假搞出黑心產品，後患無窮， 依照客人需求申請符合其市場或安全規格要求之認證才是正途。

6.3 介紹替代產品
Introducing a Product for Substitute

A: 我想問目錄裡 63 號女士皮包。

A: I'd like to ask about No. 63 lady's bag in your catalog.

B: 我們以前有賣，但現在不生產了。我們有出一批新設計的包款也許你會有興趣，你想要先收到更新過的目錄嗎？我待會兒也可以推薦一些皮包。

B: We used to sell it, but we no longer produce it any more. We have just come out with some newly designed bags that you would probably be interested in. Would you like to receive the updated catalog first? I can also recommend some bags later.

A: 好，我先看一下你的目錄。

A: Alright. I'll take a look at your catalog first.

B: 好，我先留你的聯絡資訊。

B: Sure, let me have your contact information.

A: 你可以告訴我 55 號女士皮包嗎？

A: Can you tell me about the catalog item No. 55 lady's bag?

B: 好，你有看過照片嗎？

B: Yes, have you seen the picture?

A: 有，但我需要確定材質、尺寸及放小東西像鑰匙、唇膏等的內部設計。

A: Yes, I have. But I need to make sure about the material, size, and the inner design that can hold small things like keys, lipsticks, etc.

B: 沒問題，袋子百分之百是棉做的，內袋是帆布，把手是聚氨酯（PU），30×36×30公分大，400 克重，又輕又流行的女士包，我們的最低訂貨量產量是 500 個。

B: No problem. The bag is made of 100% cotton. The inner side is canvas, and the handles are made of PU. It is 30x36x30cms, weighing about 0.4kg, a very light and fashionable lady's bag. Our minimum order quantity (MOQ) is 500 pieces.

A: 內袋呢？

A: What about the inner pockets?

B: 有四個內袋，這個包是女士們理想的大小，非常時髦又方便！

B: There are four of them. The bag is the ideal size for ladies. It's very chic and handy!

A: 哪裡做的？

A: Where is it made?

B: 中國。

B: China.

Word Bank 字庫

cotton ['kɑtn̩] n. 棉

canvas ['kænvəs] n. 帆布

PU(Polyurethane)[ˌpalɪ'jurəˌθen] n. 聚氨酯

ideal [aɪ'diəl] adj. 理想的

chic [ʃik, ʃɪk] adj. 時髦的

handy ['hændɪ] adj. 方便的

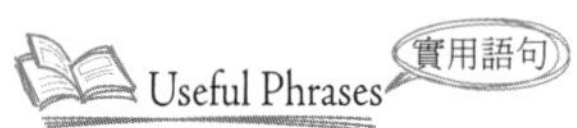

Useful Phrases 實用語句

1. 我們有出一批新設計的包款，也許你會有興趣。

   We have just come out with some newly designed bags that you would probably be interested in.

2. 你想要先收到更新過的目錄嗎？

   Would you like to receive the updated catalog first?

3. 我們的最低訂貨量產量是 500 個。

   Our minimum order quantity (MOQ) is 500 pieces.

4. 非常時髦又方便！

   It's very chic and handy!

6.4 客戶索取樣品—重要客戶 Client Requesting a Sample - Valued Customer

Dialog 對話

（電話中 on the phone）

A: 你可以寄給我減震腳踏車座墊樣品嗎？目錄的 58 號？

A: Can you send me a sample of your Cushioned Bicycle Seat, No.58 in your catalog?

B: 可以，因為你是我們的重要客戶，我們不會收樣品費。但是我們會需要你付海外郵資，你有 FedEx 或 UPS 的帳戶嗎？

B: Yes, and because you are a valued customer, we will not charge for the sample. However, we will need you to cover the overseas postage. Do you have a FedEx or UPS account?

A: 有，我可以給你我的 FedEx 帳戶來付郵資，我可以何時拿到樣品？

A: Yes, I do. I can give you my FedEx account to pay for it. When can I get the sample?

B: 我們今天稍後會電郵給你確定品項、照片及確實郵資後，兩天後空運。

B: We'll airmail it in two days after we confirm the item, the picture, and the exact postage with you later today by email.

A: 好，我晚點會收電子郵件。

A: OK. I'll check my email later.

Word Bank 字庫

cushioned ['kuʃənd] adj. 減震的
valued ['væljud] adj. 重要的，尊貴的
overseas postage 海外郵資

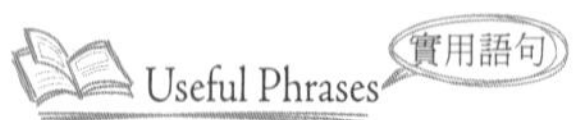

1. 我們會需要你付海外郵資。

   We will need you to cover the overseas postage.

2. 你有 FedEx 或 UPS 的帳戶嗎？

   Do you have a FedEx or UPS account?

3. 因為你是我們的重要客戶，我們不會收樣品費。

   Because you are a valued customer, we will not charge for the sample.

6.5 客戶索取樣品—新客戶 Client Requesting a Sample - New Customer

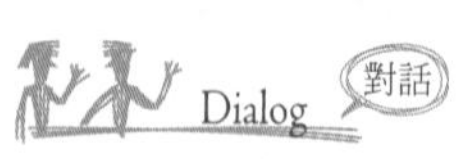

（電話中 on the phone）

A: 你可以先寄給我樣品嗎？

A: Can you send me a sample first?

B: 我們很樂意寄給我們的新客戶，但是為了要減輕我們的成本，我們的公司需要樣品費跟海外郵資。

B: We are happy to do that for our new customers, but in order to reduce our cost, our company requires a sample charge and overseas postage.

A: 總共多少錢？

A: How much is that altogether?

B: 樣品 20 元，郵資大約是 30 元，總共大約 50 元。

B: The sample is $20, and the postage is about $30. So it comes to $50 or so.

A: 好，我可以貨到付現嗎？

A: That's alright. Can I pay cash on delivery (COD)?

B: 沒有辦法，我們只有收事先電匯。

B: No, that's not possible. We only accept T/T advance.

A: 我可以何時拿到樣本？

A: When can I get the sample?

B: 我們收到金額兩天後會空運。

B: We'll airmail it in two days after we receive the amount.

A: 好，那樣聽起來可以。

A: OK. That sounds just fine.

B: 我們今天稍後會寄電子郵件跟你確認，還有樣品費會從將來的訂單金額扣掉。

B: We will confirm with you about details by email later today. By the way, the sample fee will be deducted from the amount of your order in the future.

A: 好，謝謝。那很合理。

A: Yes, thank you. That is reasonable.

B: 我們很樂意推薦好的產品給你。謝謝你，請你晚點確認郵件。

B: We are happy to recommend any good products to you. Thank you and please check your email later.

A: 我會的，再見。

A: I will. Goodbye.

B: 再見。

B: Goodbye.

Word Bank 字庫

overseas postage 海外郵資
cash on delivery (COD) 貨到付現
T/T (Telegraphic Transfer) advance 事先電匯

1. 為了要減輕我們的成本，我們的公司需要樣品費跟海外郵資。

   In order to reduce our cost, our company requires a sample charge and overseas postage.

2. 我可以貨到付現嗎？

   Can I pay cash on delivery (COD)?

3. 我們只有收事先電匯。

   We only accept T/T advance.

4. 我們會電郵給你確定項目後，兩天後空運。

   We'll airmail it in two days after we confirm the item.

5. 我們收到金額兩天後空運。

   We'll airmail it in two days after we receive the amount.

6. 樣品費會從將來的訂單金額扣掉。

   The sample fee will be deducted from the amount of your order in the future.

7. 那很合理。

   That is reasonable.

8. 我們很樂意推薦好的產品給你。

   We are happy to recommend any good products to you.

從客戶是否願意付樣品費及郵資，可以看出其是否有誠意，請客戶體諒你的成本問題。通常較大的公司或是較熟的客戶都有快遞帳號，可從帳號內直接扣除郵資。無快遞帳號者請對方先電匯樣品費及郵資再寄出樣品。

6.6 與客戶確認樣品—測試樣本
Checking the Sample with a Client - Having a Sample Tested

A: 嗨，泰瑞莎，我打來告訴你昨天樣品到了。	**A:** Hi, Teresa, I'm calling to tell you that the sample arrived yesterday.
B: 我們的產品很棒吧？！	**B:** Our product is great, isn't it?

A: 我們會先給工程部門測試。	**A:** We will have our engineering department test it first.
B: 好，我們期待不久聽到你的好消息。	**B:** Alright. We are expecting to hear good news from you shortly.
A: 要一些時間，但我們拭目以待。	**A:** It will take a short while, and we will see to it.
B: 你想多久會知道結果？	**B:** How long do you think you will get the result?
A: 大約一星期或更久一點。	**A:** Maybe a week or longer.
B: 到時我會聯絡你，如果你需要任何東西，讓我知道。	**B:** I'll contact you then, and if you need anything, just let me know.
A: 好，晚點聊，再見。	**A:** OK. Talk to you later. Goodbye.
B: 再見。	**B:** Bye.

A: 嗨，史丹，你知道測試結果了嗎？	**A:** Hi, Stan, have you learned about the result of the test?

B: 是，結果剛出來。	**B:** Yes, the result has just come back.
A: 很好，對嗎？	**A:** It is good, isn't it?
B: 呃，看起來可以。	**B:** Well, it looks fine.
A: 好，你需要多少量？	**A:** OK. What is the quantity you need?
B: 我會晚點回覆你。	**B:** I'll get back to you later.
A: 好，我會等你聯絡我。	**A:** Alright. I'll be waiting for your next contact .
B: 好，再見。	**B:** OK, goodbye.

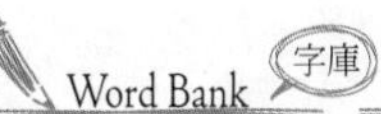

see to 照料，照顧

1. 我們會先給工程部門測試。

   We will have our engineering department test it first.

2. 我們期待不久聽到你的好消息。

We are expecting to hear good news from you shortly.

3. 要一些時間，但我們拭目以待。

It will take a short while, and we will see to it.

4. 你知道測試結果了嗎？

Have you learned about the result of the test?

5. 我們的產品很棒吧？！

Our product is great, isn't it?

6. 很好，對嗎？

It is good, isn't it?

7. 你需要多少量？

What is the quantity you need?

8. 我會晚點回覆你。

I'll get back to you later.

9. 我會等你聯絡我。

I'll be waiting for your next contact.

客戶測試樣品通常不一定會明說多久會知道結果。除非客戶對購買產品時間急迫，否則在測試時間上賣關子對他自己較爲有利。

6.7 討論客製品 Discussing Customized Goods

A: 哈囉，泰瑞莎，這裡是麥克大衛森。

A: Hello, Teresa, this is Michel Davidson.

B: 嗨，大衛森先生，你好嗎？聽到你的消息真好。

B: Hi, Mr. Davidson, how are you? It's great to hear from you.

A: 我很好，聽好，我對你寄給我的流行鎖頭照片感興趣。

A: I'm fine. Listen. I'm interested in the pictures you sent me about fashionable locks.

B: 是的，大衛森先生，它們是很棒的產品，對吧？！

B: Yes, Mr. Davidson, they are really good products, aren't they?

A: 對，但是我有些主意可以讓它們更受青睞。

A: They are, but I have some ideas that can make the locks even more popular to sell.

B: 真的？！ 你認為我可以怎樣幫你？

B: Really?! How do you think I can help you?

A: 我畫了一些特別訂製鎖的圖片，它們很漂亮，並且在所有節日場合都是很棒的禮物，我想我們可以一起把原型做好，然後量產。

A: I have drawn some pictures about specially designed locks. They are beautiful and could be great gifts for all occasions. I'm thinking we can work to get the prototypes done and put into production later.

B: 大衛森先生，這些鎖頭我聽起來很有趣，我們需要做多少原型？ 我們需要先行評估總成本。你的鎖頭材質及規格是什麼？

B: Mr. Davidson, these locks sound very interesting to me. How many prototypes do we need to make? We need to estimate the overall cost first. What are the materials and the specifications of your locks?

A: 呃，鎖頭是壓克力跟鋼做的，每個鎖頭表面有不同的雕刻。有四個圖樣：一個心型、一個太陽、一個月亮、一個星星，尺寸相似，大約 5×5×1 公分。

A: Well, the locks are made of acrylic crystal and steel. On the surface, each lock carries a different carving. There are four pictures: a heart, a sun, a moon, and a star, about similar sized within 5x5x1 centimeters.

B: 好，我明白了，大衛森先生，那就有四個原型。

B: OK, I see, Mr. Davidson, there are four prototypes then.

A: 對。

A: That's right.

B: 除了雕刻部分，我可以告訴你原型聽起來不會太難做。

B: Except for the carving part, I can tell you the prototypes do not sound too difficult to make.

A: 好，那是好消息，你要求的原型最低訂購量是多少？

A: OK, that is good news. What is the MOQ you request for making prototypes?

A: 每個原型的最低訂貨量是 2,000，但因有不同的雕刻，確實的最低訂貨量我必須晚點回覆你。

A: MOQ 2,000 for one prototype, but with different carvings, I'll have to get back to you later about the exact MOQ.

B: 你每個原型的成本是多少？

B: What is the cost of each prototype?

A: 我需要把你的圖樣給技術部門先看過，並且要他們對圖樣保密。	**A:** I'll have to have your pictures checked by the technical department first and also have them protect the pictures.
B: 好，我會電郵給你保密條款，讓你公司簽字後寄給你圖樣。	**B:** OK. I'll email you the confidential agreement for your company to sign and then send you the pictures.
A: 我了解，那我等你的電郵，再回覆後續。	**A:** I see. I'll be expecting your email then and get back to you with the follow ups later.
B: 好，泰瑞莎，再見。	**B:** Alright, Teresa. Goodbye.
A: 謝謝，大衛森先生，再見。	**A:** Thank you, Mr. Davidson. Goodbye.

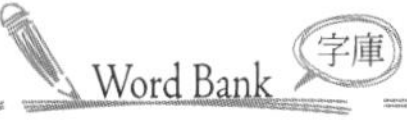

prototype ['protə,taɪp] n. 原型
acrylic [ə'krɪlɪk] adj. 壓克力的
carving ['kɑrvɪŋ] n. 雕刻
minimum order quantity (MOQ) 最低訂購量
confidential agreement 保密條款

1. 我們可以一起把原型做好，然後量產。

   We can work to get the prototypes done and put into production later.

2. 你的鎖頭材質及規格是什麼？

What are the materials and the specifications of your locks?

3. 你要求的原型最低訂購量是多少？

What is the MOQ you request for making prototypes?

4. 你每個原型的成本是多少？

What is the cost of each prototype?

5. 我需要把你的圖樣給技術部門先看過，並且要他們對圖樣保密。

I'll have to have your pictures checked by the technician department first and also have them protect the pictures.

6. 我會電郵給你保密條款，讓你公司簽字。

I'll email you the confidential agreement for your company to sign.

客戶要求小量生產之製模（molding）或模具（tooling）需由其支付費用，工廠須先收取訂金後，開製模具（mold）；大量生產的話，則由供應商支付開模費用（molding fee）或模具費用（tooling fee）。如果是個人創作或專利，當然需要相關人員簽訂保密條款（confidential/confidentiality agreement 或 non-disclosure agreement, NDA）。

6.8 製作原型及評估成本 Making the Prototypes and Estimating the Cost

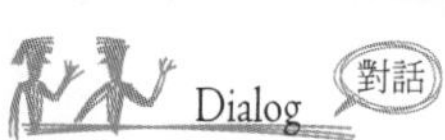

A: 大衛森先生，我技術部門有結果了。

A: Mr. Davidson, I have got the result from the tech department.

B: 是的，如何了？

B: Yes, how is it?

A: 好消息，我們可以在幾週內以合理價格製作原型。

A: Good news, we can have the prototypes made at a reasonable cost and within a few weeks.

B: 那很好，有包含雕刻嗎？

B: That's good. Does it include the carving?

A: 有，雕刻也評估進去了。

A: Yes, the carving work has been evaluated, too.

B: 每個原型多少錢？

B: How much does each prototype cost?

A: 是一個鎖頭有四種雕刻在上面。

A: It is actually one lock with four carvings on top.

B: 對。

B: That's right.

A: 鎖頭模具成本 500 元，每個雕刻模具 150 元，有四種模具，所以全部金額 1,100 元。

A: The lock mold costs $500, and each carving costs $150. There are four of them, so the total amount is $1,100.

B: 我明白了，你何時可以完成原型？

B: I see. When can you finish the prototypes?

A: 大概三週。

A: About three weeks.

evaluate [ɪ'væljʊ,et] v. 評估

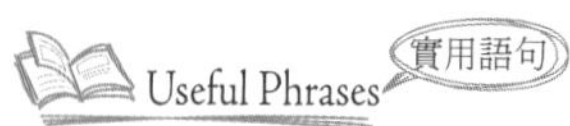

1. 我們可以在幾週內以合理價格製作原型。
   We can have the prototypes made at a reasonable cost and within a few weeks.
2. 每個原型多少錢？
   How much does each prototype cost?
3. 你何時可以完成原型？
   When can you finish the prototypes?

6.9 修改及確認原型 Altering and Confirming the Prototypes

A: 嗨，大衛森先生，原型已經完成了，並且我剛才用電子郵件寄照片給你讓你查看。

A: Hi, Mr. Davidson, the prototypes have been finished, and I've just emailed you the pictures for you to check over.

B: 好，泰瑞莎，我會查看，晚點再告訴你。

B: OK, Teresa. I'll look at them and talk to you later.

A: 好，大衛森先生，晚點聊。

A: Alright, Mr. Davidson. Talk to you later.

（稍後 later）

A: 泰瑞莎，我打電話來告訴你關於圖案的雕刻。

A: Teresa, I'm calling to tell you about the carving in the pictures.

B: 好，大衛森先生，有任何問題嗎？

B: OK, Mr. Davidson, are there any problems?

A: 雕刻需要再深 0.2 釐米，讓圖案看起來更生動。

A: The carving needs to go deeper about 0.2 millimeter to make them look more vivid.

B: 好，我會告訴技術部門看看他們可否這麼做。

B: Ok, I'll ask the technical department to see if they can do so.

A: 好，謝謝。

A: Alright. Thank you.

B: 沒問題，大衛森先生，晚點聊了。

B: Sure, Mr. Davidson. Talk to you later.

A: 大衛森先生，技術部門可以做調整，我會幾天後寄給你照片確認。

A: Mr. Davidson, the tech department can do the adjustment. I'll send you the pictures to confirm in a few days.

B: 好，謝謝，泰瑞莎。	**B:** OK, thank you. Teresa.
A: 沒問題。	**A:** No problem.

adjustment [ə'dʒʌstmənt] n. 調整

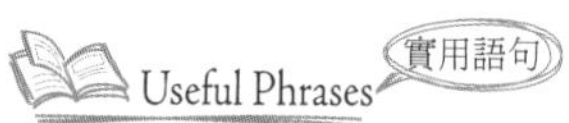

1. 我打電話來告訴你關於圖案的雕刻。
   I'm calling to tell you about the carving in the pictures.
2. 有任何問題嗎？
   Are there any problems?
3. 雕刻需要再深 0.2 釐米。
   The carving needs to go deeper about 0.2 millimeter.
4. 雕刻需要看起來更生動。
   The carving needs to look more vivid.

6.10 討論訂單—客製品 Discussing an Order - Customized Products

A: 嗨，泰瑞莎，我剛收到你的原型鎖頭。	**A:** Hi, Teresa, I've just received the prototyped locks.

B: 是的，大衛森先生，它們看起來很棒，不是嗎？

B: Yes, Mr. Davidson, they look wonderful, don't they?

A: 是的，我很興奮看到它們，你們何時可以量產？

A: Yes, they do. I'm excited to see them. When can you put them into production?

B: 我們確認數量之後，每個鎖頭我們的最低訂貨量是 2,000 個，你的訂單會在10,000 個或以上才能包含模具的成本。你要訂多少量？

B: After we check over our quantity. Our MOQ for each lock is 2,000. Your order will come to 10,000 or more in order to cover the cost of the tooling. What is the quantity you need?

A: 大概在10,000-20,000個鎖頭，要看我們同意的價錢。

A: Perhaps between 10,000 to 20,000 locks, depending on the price we agree on.

B: 是船上交貨或含成本運保費舊金山交貨？我明天會準備報價。

B: Is it FOB or CIF San Francisco? I'll prepare a quote tomorrow.

A: 含成本運保費舊金山交貨，我希望很快得到你的報價。

A: CIF San Francisco. I'll hope to get your quote soon.

B: 好，我會明天打電話給你報價。

B: OK, I'll call you tomorrow about the quote.

A: 謝謝你，泰瑞莎，再見。

A: Thank you, Teresa. Goodbye.

B: 再見，大衛森先生。	**B:** Goodbye. Mr. Davidson.

Word Bank 字庫

tooling ['tulɪŋ] n. 模具

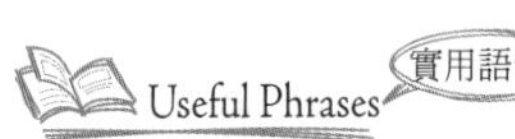

Useful Phrases 實用語句

1. 你們何時可以量產？
   When can you put them into production?
2. 你要訂多少量？
   What is the quantity you need?
3. 我明天會準備報價。
   I'll prepare a quote tomorrow.

Word Bank 字庫

國際買家千百款，無論如何，希望成交獲利的同時也必須有風險管理（risk management），賣方必須收取足夠的訂金獲得一些保障才不會掉入人心難測的交易陷阱（business trap）。

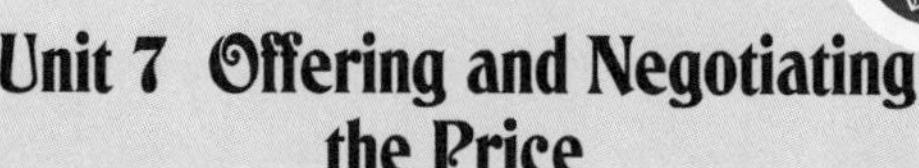

Unit 7 Offering and Negotiating the Price

報價與議價

在判斷詢價的人不是來打聽行情，而是確實有誠意進行交易後，才進入報價階段。報價重點是價格，但產品規格、品質、客戶交情、付款條件、佣金、成本及利潤等都是決定價格高低的因素。無論客戶是否只在乎價格，站在客戶立場爲其解釋下訂單給你的利基（niche），才能增加成交的機會。如果對方要找的是工廠，可以隨報價附上幾張工廠照片，並請對方瀏覽你的網站了解產品及規模。不管結果是否成交，請客人務必回覆讓你了解其決定及緣由，以做爲將來改善及因應之道。

7.1 處理客戶詢價
Handling Client's Inquiry

（電話鈴聲 Ring）

A: 哈囉，（我是）艾倫瓊斯。

A: Hello, Allan Jones.

B: 嗨，瓊斯先生，我是臺灣 LH 集團的泰瑞莎陳。

B: Hi. Mr. Jones, this is Teresa Chen calling from LH Group in Taiwan.

A: 嗨，陳女士，接到妳電話很好，你有我詢價的答案嗎？

A: Hi, Ms. Chen. It's good to get your call. Do you have answers for my inquiry?

B: 瓊斯先生，你可以叫我泰瑞莎，我們有很多種類的家用工具可以滿足你的需求， 並且我昨天已經傳送你詢價的規格及照片了。

B: Mr. Jones, you can call me Teresa. We have a variety of home tools that should be able to meet your needs, and I have already emailed the specifications and pictures for your inquiry yesterday.

A: 我知道了，請等一下，讓我確認有收到你的郵件。

A: I see. Just a second. Let me make sure I've got your mail.

B: 好，我要在線上等還是待會打來？

B: OK. Should I stay on line or call you later?

A: 你可以五分鐘後打來，我有幾個問題要問你。

A: You can call me after five minutes. I'll have a few questions to ask you.

B: 好，瓊斯先生，晚點談。

B: OK, Mr. Jones . Talk to you later.

A: 好，再見。

A: OK. Bye.

A: 我多久可以收到貨？

A: What is your lead time?

B: 我們的生產要 1 個月左右，運送要 30 天。通過海關要一週，所以收到貨要 70天左右。

B: Our production will take a month or so, and the shipment will take thirty days. Passing customs will take one week. So the lead time will be about seventy days.

A: 你產品有存貨嗎？如果沒有，你可以立即投入生產嗎？

A: Do you have the products in stock? If not, can you put them into production immediately?

B: 讓我看看，你可以等一下嗎？

B: Let me check first. Can you hold?

A: 好（一秒鐘）。

A: OK. (A second)

B: 我們存貨大概有700臺，你要多少量？

B: We have about 700 of this model in stock. What is the quantity you need?

A: 10,000臺，我需要8月15日前收到。

A: 10, 000 and I need the shipment by the 15th of August.

B: 好，我們收到你訂單確認後，可以在3-4星期完成生產。

B: OK. We can complete the production in about three to four weeks after we receive your order confirmation.

A: 你可以給我報最低，含成本及運保費在內，美國華盛頓州西雅圖交貨的價格嗎？

A: Can you quote me your lowest price, CIF Seattle, Washington, USA?

B: 可以，你會發現以我們的品質來說，我們的價格非常有競爭力。

B: Yes, you will find our price very competitive with our quality.

A: 希望是這樣。

A: I surely hope so.

B: 我明天再報給你，讓我複述你的詢價——10,000臺地板腳踏車架，含成本及運保費西雅圖交貨，8月15日前送到。

B: I'll get back to you tomorrow. Let me repeat your inquiry—10,000 Floor Bike Stands, CIF Seattle, delivered by Aug 15th.

A: 對。

A: That's right.

B: 好，我明天跟你談，再見。

B: OK. I'll talk to you tomorrow. Goodbye.

A: 再見。

A: Bye.

inquiry [ɪn'kwaɪrɪ, 'ɪnkwərɪ] n. 詢價
variety [və'raɪətɪ] n. 種類
in stock 存貨
CIF (cost, insurance, freight) 含成本保費運費在內的報價
competitive [kəm'pɛtətɪv] adj. 有競爭力的

1. 我多久可以收到貨？
   What is your lead time?
2. 你產品有存貨嗎？
   Do you have the products in stock?
3. 你可以立即投入生產嗎？
   Can you put them into production immediately?
4. 我們這個樣式大約有700個存貨。
   We have about 700 of this model in stock.
5. 你要多少量？
   What is the quantity you need?

6. 我們收到你訂單確認後，可以在 3-4 星期完成生產。

We can complete the production in about three to four weeks after we receive your order confirmation.

7. 你會發現以我們的品質來說，我們的價格非常有競爭力。

You will find our price very competitive with our quality.

8. 我需要 8 月 15 日前出貨。

I need the shipment by the 15th of August.

報價須有專業（了解產品製作、原料等各方面條件，告訴客戶你的報價是依據數量或原料、包裝等而定），預留適當利潤及協商空間，客戶還價時彼此才能繼續談下去，最後達成交易（專業報價甚至包含了解對手產品）。報價更要即時，客戶也許在等你答案才能給他的客戶報價，他要求越清楚的產品及條件要你報價，你就越可能有潛在成交的機會。所有時間及流程（下訂後生產、運輸、通關）的計算須與買方確認，以求彼此認知無誤。第一次報價到成功交易順利完成可說是未來是否能夠繼續交易的風向球，因此機會來了，要好好把握。

7.2 報價 Offering

A: 我需要知道你可以給我 250 個貨板什麼價錢。	A: I need to know what price you can give me on 250 pallets.
B: 每個 550 元。	B: $550.00 per pallet.

尋找客戶 國際參展準備 參加國際商展 接待客戶 作商業簡報 討論產品製作 報價與議價

A: 那樣對我們而言太貴了。	**A:** That's going to be too high for us.
B: 現在很難做，市場很不好。	**B:** The situation is difficult now. The market is not good.
A: 是的，我知道，但我們也受影響，我們沒法負擔。	**A:** Yes, I know, but we are suffering from it also. We can't go that high.
B: 我降到每個貨板 540 元，臺灣基隆港船上交貨，但那是最低了。	**B:** I'll drop it to $540.00 a pallet FOB Keelung, Taiwan, but that is as low as I can go.
A: 還是很貴。	**A:** That's still high.
B: 想想看我們跟別人比的產品品質。	**B:** Think about the quality of our product compared to others.
A: 好，我們訂每個貨板 540 元。	**A:** OK. We'll place the order at that $540.00 per pallet.
B: 謝謝，在投入生產前我要收到 30%的訂金。	**B:** Thank you. I'll need a 30% deposit of your order before we put it into production.
A: 沒問題。	**A:** No problem.

pallet ['pælɪt] n. 貨板
FOB (free on board) 船上交貨
deposit [dɪ'pɑzɪt] n. 訂金

1. 現在很難做，市場很不好。
   The situation is difficult now. The market is not good.
2. 我降到每個貨板 540 元，但那是最低了。
   I'll drop it to $540.00 a pallet, but that is as low as I can go.
3. 想想看我們跟別人比的產品品質。
   Think about the quality of our product compared to others.
4. 出貨前我要收到訂金。
   I'll need a deposit before we can ship.

Notes 小叮嚀

船上交貨的港口要在報價時就與買方說好，以免你要到基隆交貨，買主後來卻要你到高雄去併櫃。

7.3 客戶還價 Client Making a Counter-Offer

A: 你的價格 14.99 元太高了，其他的供應商報給我更低的價錢。

A: Your price $14.99 per unit is too high. Other suppliers are offering much lower prices.

B: 我恐怕那是不可能，你可以分辨我們的品質比其他的更好。

B: I'm afraid that's impossible. You can tell our quality is better than others.

A: 那是真的，但是以這麼高價我們無法拓展銷售。

A: That's true, but we cannot push the sales with such a high cost.

B: 各種增加的成本，報價已經到底了。但是如果你可以從 2,000 個增加到至少 5,000 個單位，我們可以降一點價。

B: With all kinds of increasing costs, the quoting price already hits the rock bottom. But if you can increase the quantity from 2,000 to at least 5,000 units, we can probably reduce the price a little.

A: 那你的價格呢？

A: What is your price then?

B: 我可以明天回你嗎？

B: Can I get back to you tomorrow?

（次日 The next day）

A: 嗨，早安，泰瑞莎，你好嗎？

A: Hi, Teresa, good morning, how's it going?

B: 我很好，謝謝，萊斯先生。我打來告訴你關於你的詢價。

B: I'm fine. Thank you, Mr. Rice. I'm calling to talk to you about your inquiry.

A: 是的，我期待聽到些好消息。

A: Yes, I'm expecting to hear some good news.

B: 呃，如果你採納我的提議的話，我就有好消息給你。如果你訂 2,000 組，價格為每組 14.99 元，但是如果你買 5,000 組，價格就降到每組 14.69 元。我們已經在賣成本價了，所以這是一個實盤，而且只有 3 天有效，也就是說，在這週結束之前。

B: Well, I do have good news for you if you take my proposal. If you order 2,000 kits, the price remains $14.99 per kit. But if you purchase 5,000 kits, the price goes down to $14.69 per kit. We are selling at our cost already. So this is a firm offer, and it is only good for three days; that is, by the end of this week.

A: 嗯，現在我必須想想。

A: Um, now I have to think.

B: 好，萊斯先生。我會馬上寄電子郵件給你報價的消息，並且會等你的決定。

B: OK. Mr. Rice, I'll email you with the price information in a minute and will be waiting for your decision.

A: 好，謝謝你，泰瑞莎。

A: Alright. Thank you, Teresa.

B: 不客氣，萊斯先生，再見。

B: No problem, Mr. Rice. Goodbye.

proposal [prə'pozl̩] n. 提議
firm offer 實盤

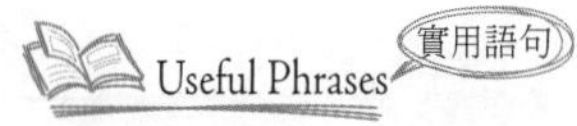

1. 如果你採納我的提議的話，我就有好消息給你。

   I do have good news for you if you take my proposal.

2. 你少來了，你在開玩笑。

   Come on. You're kidding me.

3. 我恐怕那是不可能的。

   I'm afraid that's impossible.

4. 我們的品質比對手的好。

   Our quality is better than our rivals.

5. 我們已經在賣成本價。

   We are selling at our cost already.

6. 以這麼高價我們無法拓展銷售。

   We cannot push the sales with such a high cost.

7. 報價已經到底了。

   The quoting price already hits the rock bottom.

8. 如果你買 5,000 組，價格就降到每組 14.69 元。

   If you purchase 5,000 kits, the price goes down to $14.69 per kit.

9. 這是一個實盤。

   This is a firm offer.

10. 只有 3 天有效。

    It is only good for three days.

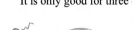

價格協商須制定有效期，但不要太急切催促，如果客戶在有效報價期將屆時尚未回覆，應給予友善提醒。

7.4 持續議價—給予新客戶折扣
Continuing Bargaining - Giving a Discount to a New Customer

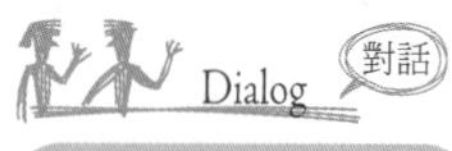

A: 嗨，泰瑞莎，早安，你好嗎？

A: Hi, Teresa, good morning! How are things?

B: 我很好，謝謝。紐頓先生，我打電話是要告訴你關於你的詢價。

B: I'm fine, Thank you. Mr. Newton, I'm calling to talk to you about your inquiry.

A: 是，我期待一些好消息，你開價太高了。

A: Yes, I'm expecting to hear some good news. The price you offered was too high.

B: 呃，你同意我們的品質比其他人好，我們的價格已經很合理，但如果你可以預先付款，我們可以給你 3% 的折扣。價格降到每單位 14.24 元，含成本及運保費，舊金山交貨。

B: Well, you agree that our quality is better than others. Our price is already very reasonable. But if you can pay the order in advance, we can give you 3% discount. The price comes down to $14.24 per unit, CIF San Francisco.

A: 我不認為那是可能的。

A: I don't think that's possible.

B: 或是如果你增加購買量到至少 1,000 個貨板，或是電匯預付貨款的一半，我們就給你 3% 的折扣。

B: Or if you increase the purchase to at least 1,000 pallets, and pay half of the amount by T/T advance, we'll give you 3% discount.

A: 嗯，現在我要想想。

A: Um, now I have to think.

B: 好，紐頓先生，慢慢來，我會為你準備電子郵件，備有這些選擇及付款條件。

B: Alright. Mr. Newton. Take your time. I'll prepare an email with the options and the payment terms for you.

A: 好，泰瑞莎。

A: OK, Teresa.

B: 請讓我知道你是否收到郵件及回覆給我關於你的決定。

B: Please let me know if you get the mail and get back to me about your decision.

A: 好，泰瑞莎，再見。

A: Alright, Teresa. Goodbye.

B: 再見，紐頓先生，祝你有美好的一天！

B: Goodbye, Mr. Newton. Have a nice day!

A: 你也是。	**A:** You, too.

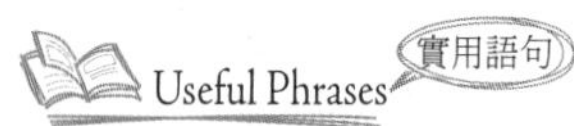

1. 你同意我們的品質比其他人好。
   You agree that our quality is better than others.
2. 我們的價格已經很合理。
   Our price is already very reasonable.
3. 如果你增加購買量到至少 1,000 個貨板，或是電匯預付貨款的一半，我們就給你 3%的折扣。
   If you increase the purchase to at least 1,000 pallets, and pay half of the amount by T/T advance, we'll give you 3% discount.
4. 慢慢來。
   Take your time.
5. 我會為你準備好電子郵件備有這些選擇及付款條件。
   I'll prepare an email with the options and the payment terms for you.
6. 請讓我知道你是否收到郵件及回覆給我關於你的決定。
   Please let me know if you get the mail and get back to me about your decision.
7. 請告訴我們你的意見或請你出價。
   Please let us know your comments or your price bid.

價格、品質、數量是相對的因素，也取決於買賣方市場、個別目標及自身條件（如追求利潤或是低價先打開市場，雙方資金成本等），能否成交也要看運氣或緣分。報價預留合理空間，讓客戶有議價的意願或請他出價，給客戶一些選擇配套或組合（以截長補短），或給予不同的付款條件，都是可行的辦法，但務必想好說詞來保護自己的底線（bottom line），如能成交，無論選項爲何公司都有訂單。若未能成交，也可從客戶回覆中了解原因，以利下一階段挑選其他合適產品之後的報價。

7.5 續訂折扣
A Repeat Order

A: 嗨，帕克先生，我為你的續訂打來。

A: Hi, Mr. Parker, I'm calling about your repeat order.

B: 是什麼呢？

B: Yes, what is it?

A: 我打電話來與你確認，因為你續訂，可以享受3%折扣。

A: I'm calling to confirm with you that you enjoy a 3% discount for this repeat order.

B: 那是好消息。

B: That's good news.

A: 是的，我們珍惜你的生意，並且希望與你在將來儘可能密切合作。

A: Yes, it is. We value your business and hope to cooperate with you as often as we can in the future.

B: 好，如果你繼續低價供應良好品質的產品，我們一定可以繼續保持好生意。

B: OK. If you continue to supply good quality products with a low price, we can surely continue doing good business.

repeat order 續訂
discount ['dɪskaunt] n. 折扣

1. 我為你與先前同樣的訂單打來。
   I'm calling about your repeat order.
2. 你因為重複同樣的訂單，可以享受 3%折扣。
   You enjoy a 3% discount because of this repeat order.
3. 我們珍惜你的生意，並且希望與你在將來儘可能密切合作。
   We value your business and hope to cooperate with you as often as we can in the future.

給予續訂客戶少許折扣優惠是常見的商業技巧（customer retention strategy），無非是抓住客戶的心理，進而培養固定訂購之顧客忠誠度（customer loyalty）。

7.6 報價含佣金
Offering with Commission Included

A: 哈特先生，早安，你詢問的女士皮包價格，我現在打來報價。

A: Mr. Hart, good morning. I'm calling you about the price for the lady's bag you asked about.

B: 好，多少錢？

B: OK. How much is it?

A: 你要求報價包含 3% 的佣金。

A: You requested the offer to include a 3% commission?

B: 對。

B: That's right.

A: 那是每個皮包 8.75 元，含成本運保費及 3% 佣金，舊金山交貨。

A: It is $8.75 per bag, CIF Commission 3% San Francisco.

B: 我明白了，你能降低到 8.50 元嗎？

B: I see. Can you go down to $8.50?

A: 最低訂貨量是不可能降價的，如果你訂 1,000 個皮包，我們或許可以降一點。

A: That is not possible with an order of minimum quantity. If you order 1,000 bags, we can probably go down a little.

B: 不，這事實上是試訂，我們要先看結果。

B: No, this is a trial order in fact. We have to see the outcome first.

A: 好，哈特先生，這報價有效日期 3 天，到 10 日為止，我們期待收到您的訂單。

A: OK. Mr. Hart, this offer is valid for three days, until the 10th. We look forward to receiving your order.

B: 謝謝你打來，我會考慮。

B: Thank you for calling. I'll think about it.

A: 我很高興幫忙，我今天晚點會電郵給你關於這筆報價。

A: Happy to help. I'll email you about the offer later today.

B: 好，謝謝，再見。

B: OK, thank you. Goodbye.

A: 我的榮幸，哈特先生，再見。

A: My pleasure, Mr. Hart. Goodbye.

request [rɪ'kwɛst] n. 要求
commission [kə'mɪʃən] n. 佣金
outcome ['aut͵kʌm] n. 結果
valid ['vælɪd] adj. 有效的

1. 最低訂貨量是不可能降價的。

   That is not possible with an order of minimum quantity.

2. 如果你訂 1,000 個皮包，我們或許可以降一點。

   If you order 1,000 bags, we can probably go down a little.

3. 這事實上是試訂，我們要先看結果。

   This is a trial order in fact. We have to see the outcome first.

4. 這報價有效日期 3 天。

   This offer is valid for three days.

5. 我們期待收到您的訂單。

   We look forward to receiving your order.

7.7 重新報價－調漲運費 Requoting an Offer - Adding Shipment Price Increase

A: 嗨，詹姆士，你的減震腳踏車座墊我們前天提供的報價要調整。	**A:** Hi, James, the price about the cushioned bike seat we offered the day before needs to be adjusted.
B: 為什麼？	**B:** Why?

A: 我們上星期沒有算到運費調漲，所以 5,000 個減震腳踏車坐墊報價，含成本運保費，西雅圖交貨，應該是每個 15.60 元，而不是 15.30 元。

A: We didn't add the shipment price increase last week. So the offered price should be 5,000 cushioned bike seats, $15.60 per unit CIF Seattle, instead of $15.30.

B: 那真是壞消息。

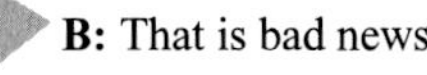

B: That is bad news.

A: 這對我們的成本也是壞消息，讓我們希望運費不會再上漲，報價只有 3 天有效， 到 18 日。

A: It is bad news for our cost, too. Let's just hope the shipment cost won't go up again. The price is valid for three days, until the 18th.

B: 好，我知道了，我會想想看。

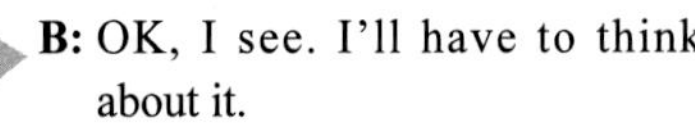

B: OK, I see. I'll have to think about it.

A: 好，關於報價調整今天我會電郵給你，並且在三天後聯絡你，希望聽到你的好消息。

A: Alright, I'll email you today about the adjustment and contact you in three days. Hope to hear good news from you.

B: 好，晚點談，再見。	**B:** OK. Talk later. Goodbye.
A: 再見。	**A:** Bye.

1. 我們沒有算到運費調漲。
   We didn't add the shipment price increase.
2. 我們沒弄對產品。
   We didn't figure the right product.
3. 我們沒有算對材積。
   We didn't calculate the volume correctly.
4. 我們沒有算到匯率升值。
   We didn't include the exchange rate appreciation.
5. 我們沒有加上正確包裝材料的成本。
   We didn't add the packing cost of the correct packing material.

報價時將預估的運費變動加上，或在訂單上加上備註變動可能，都有助於抵銷旺季交貨突然上升的運費漲幅。報錯價、看錯產品、錯估匯率、重量、材積等都有可能發生，除非有其他補救方式，馬上跟客戶坦承錯誤才是上策。

7.8 保留與催促下訂
Keeping an Offer Open and Pushing for an Order

A: 嗨，詹姆士，我打來問你關於減震腳踏車座墊的決定，報價到今天為止，是什麼原因讓你耽擱下訂？

A: Hi, James, I'm calling to ask about your decision on our offer for the cushioned bike seats. The offer expires today. What's holding up your ordering decision?

B: 是你的價錢，比其他人貴。	**B:** It's your price. It's higher than others.
A: 你可以接受的價錢是多少？	**A:** What is the price you can accept?
B: 你的價錢高出3%。	**B:** Your price is 3% higher.
A: 謝謝，我會問我的主管，然後在今天晚些用電郵回覆你。	**A:** Thank you. I'll ask my supervisor and get back to you later today by email.
B: 我還是需要時間做對的決定。	**B:** I still need time to make the right decision.
A: 好，我知道了，報價只到這週星期五，22日為止。	**A:** OK, I see. The offer will be open until the end of this week, Friday, the 22nd.

B: 呃，我會記得。

B: Well, I'll keep it in mind.

A: 我會電郵給你報價截止日期，並且希望聽到你的好消息。

A: I'll email you about the offer expiry date and hope to hear good news from you.

B: 好，謝謝，再見。

B: OK, thank you, and goodbye.

A: 再見。

A: Bye.

A: 嗨，費爾茲先生，我打電話來問你的決定如何，關於我們運動背袋的報價？有效期限到今天為止。

A: Hi, Mr. Fields, I'm calling to ask about your decision on our offer for the sports bags. The offer expires today.

B: 我還是需要時間做對的決定，事實上現在的價錢是太高了。如果你可以降低到 6.25 元，我可以馬上訂 700 個背袋。

B: I still need time to make the right decision. Actually the price is too high now. If you can lower the price to $6.25, I can place an order of 700 bags right away.

A: 嗯，以你的數量我不覺得有那可能，但我可以問我的主管後再回覆你。

A: Um, I don't think that's possible with your quantity, but I can ask my supervisor and get back to you later.

B: 好，謝謝你，再見。

B: OK. Thank you. Goodbye.

A: 再見。

A: Bye.

expire [ɪk'spaɪr] v. 到期
hold up 耽擱
expiry date 到期日

1. 報價有效期限到今天為止。
   The offer expires today.
2. 是什麼原因讓你耽擱下訂？
   What's holding up your ordering decision?
3. 你可以接受的價錢是多少？
   What is the price you can accept?
4. 以你的數量我不覺得有那可能。
   I don't think that's possible for your quantity.

5. 我可以問我的主管後再回覆你。

I can ask my supervisor and get back to you later.

7.9 接受報價/還價 Accepting an Offer / Counter-Offer

7.9a 接受報價 Accepting an Offer

A: 嗨，泰瑞莎，我們接受棒球球棒樣品的品質，並且同意接受你們的報價。

A: Hi, Teresa, we accept the sample quality of the baseball bats and agree to accept your offer.

B: 那是好消息——5,000 個棒球球棒，每支 3.50 元，船上交貨，洛杉磯，我會電郵你的訂單確認，接下來我們可以討論運送標誌及你的包裝需求。

B: That's good news—5,000 baseball bats, $3.50 per unit, FOB Los Angeles. I'll email your order for confirmation. And we can discuss the shipping mark and your packing requirements next.

A: 那聽起來很好，明天下午我會準備好後續。

A: That sounds good. I'll have the follow-ups ready tomorrow afternoon.

B: 好，我到時會聯絡你。

B: OK, I'll contact you then.

A: 好，再見。

A: OK. Goodbye.

B: 再見。

B: Bye.

7.9b 接受還價 Accepting a Counter Offer

Dialog 對話

A: 哈囉，費爾茲先生，早安。

A: Hello, Mr. Fields, good morning.

B: 嗨，泰瑞莎，你好嗎？

B: Hi, Teresa, how are you?

A: 我很好，謝謝。費爾茲先生，我打來告訴你我們接受你的還價，700 個運動背袋每個 6.25 元，船上交貨，澳洲雪梨。

A: I'm fine. Thank you. Mr. Fields, I'm calling to tell you that we accept your counter offer for the 700 sports bags at $6.25 per bag, FOB Sydney, Australia.

B: 好，那很好！

B: OK, that's good!

A: 我會電郵給你接受報價及跟你談後續事宜。

A: I'll email you the acceptance and talk to you about the follow-ups later.

B: 好，謝謝你打來。

B: OK, thank you for calling.

A: 不客氣，費爾茲先生，再見。

A: Sure, Mr. Fields. Goodbye.

B: 再見。

B: Bye.

shipping mark 運送標誌
packing requirements 包裝需求
follow-ups 後續事宜

1. 我們接受棒球球棒樣品的品質，並且同意接受你們的報價。

   We accept the sample quality of the baseball bats and agree to accept your offer.

2. 明天下午我會準備好後續。

   I'll have the follow-ups ready tomorrow afternoon.

7.10 客戶拒絕報價 Client Declining an Offer

A: 哈囉，彼得森先生，我打電話來問你我們的報價你決定如何？

A: Hello, Mr. Peterson, I'm calling to ask if you've made the decision about our offer.

B: 嗨，泰瑞莎，你的價錢太高了，我沒法接受。

B: Hi, Teresa, your offer is too high. I cannot accept it.

A: 彼得森先生，我們已經為你降價了，並且你已承認我們的好品質。

A: Mr. Peterson, we have already lowered the price for you, and you have already acknowledged our good quality.

B: 呃，看來我們沒法談成了。

B: Well, it looks like we cannot make the deal then.

A: 好，彼德森先生，謝謝你告訴我答案，我會報告給我的主管，並且希望很快聽到你的消息。同時，我會推薦其他你可能有興趣的產品。

A: OK, Mr. Peterson, thank you for telling me your answer. I'll report it to my supervisor and hope to hear from you soon. In the meantime, I'll recommend other products that you may be interested in.

B: 好，謝謝，泰瑞莎，再見。

B: Alright, thank you, Teresa. Goodbye.

A: 再見。

A: Goodbye.

lower ['loɚ] v. 降低
acknowlege [ək'nɑlɪdʒ] v. 承認

1. 我打電話來問你我們的報價你決定如何？
   I'm calling to ask if you've made the decision about our offer.
2. 我們已經為你降價了。
   We have already lowered the price for you.
3. 你已承認我們的好品質。
   You have already acknowledged our good quality.
4. 看來我們沒法談成了。
   It looks we cannot make the deal then.
5. 謝謝你告訴我答案。
   Thank you for telling me your answer.
6. 我會報告給我的主管，並且希望很快聽到你的消息。
   I'll report it to my supervisor and hope to hear from you soon.
7. 我會推薦我們其他你可能有興趣的產品。
   I'll recommend other products that you may be interested in.

7.11 供應商拒絕還價 Supplier Declining a Counter Offer

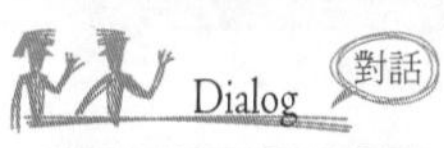

A: 哈囉，飛利浦先生，你好嗎？	**A:** Hello, Mr. Philips, how are you?
B: 我很好，謝謝你，你好嗎？	**B:** I'm fine. Thank you. How's it going?

A: 呃，飛利浦先生，我恐怕要告訴你我不能接受你要求的價格，這比我們的成本還低。

A: Well, Mr. Philips, I'm afraid to tell you that we cannot accept the price you requested. It is lower than our cost.

B: 好，泰瑞莎，那真是不妙，我們沒法談成了。

B: OK, Teresa. That's too bad. We cannot make the deal then.

A: 是的，飛利浦先生，謝謝你承認我們的品質，這次我們很遺憾。我會持續讓你知道我們可能會讓你感興趣的產品，我可以推薦幾個代替品。

A: Yes, Mr. Philips, thank you for acknowledging our quality, and we are sorry this time. I'll keep you posted about our goods that could be of interest to you. I can recommend a few substitutes.

B: 好，泰瑞莎，謝謝你。我不介意看看，如果它們值得考慮的話，就先寄給我照片吧。

B: OK, Teresa. Thank you. I don't mind having a look to see if they are worth considering. Just send me some pictures first.

A: 好，飛利浦先生，我下午會電郵它們給你，你還有需要什麼嗎？

A: Sure, Mr. Philips. I'll email you them this afternoon. Is there anything else you need?

B: 我想現在這樣夠了，謝謝你，再見。

B: I guess that's enough at this point. Thank you and goodbye.

A: 不客氣，再見。

A: Any time. Goodbye.

Word Bank 字庫

keep somebody posted 持續讓...知道

substitute ['sʌbstə,tjut] n. 代替品

Useful Phrases 實用語句

1. 我恐怕要告訴你我不能接受你要求的價格。

   I'm afraid to tell you that we cannot accept the price you requested.

2. 這比我們的成本還低。

   It is lower than our cost.

3. 那真是不妙，我們沒法談成了。

   That's too bad. We cannot make the deal then.

4. 謝謝你承認我們的品質，這次我們很遺憾。

   Thank you for acknowledging our quality and we are sorry this time.

5. 我會持續讓你知道我們可能會讓你感興趣的產品。

   I'll keep you posted about our goods that could be of interest to you.

6. 我可以推薦幾個代替品。

   I can recommend a few substitutes.

7. 如果它們值得考慮的話，我不介意看看。

   I don't mind having a look to see if they are worth considering.

眼見生意就要談成，但最後客戶沒有下訂可能有許多原因，可能他的訂單有狀況了，或是他只是在建立資料，亦或是他習慣信口開河。無論如何，未收到訂金或信用狀訂單之前什麼都可能發生，就當作累積經驗，爲將來作準備。

Your offer is too high. I cannot accept it.

We have already lowered the price for you.

Unit 8 Negotiation on Terms and Conditions of Transaction

協商交易條件

一樁交易要能夠完成，需經過價格、數量、品質、付款、品檢、專利、認證、包裝、運送、保險、保固等條件的溝通。客製化產品因受客戶委託訂製有其特殊性，開模費及技術、專利權等其他條件要考慮完整。本章包含這些交易條件協議的對話，逐項協商後列入合約，若不幸發生問題，才有處理依據。

8.1 品質條件—國際認證
Quality Terms - International Certification

A: 哈囉，紐頓先生，我是泰瑞莎。

A: Hello, Mr. Newton, this is Teresa.

B: 嗨，泰瑞莎，你好嗎？

B: Hi, Teresa, how are you?

A: 我很好，謝謝，你有收到我們腳踏車架的樣品嗎？

A: I'm fine. Thank you. Have you received our bike stand sample?

B: 有，樣品還可以，但是你可以再考慮價錢嗎？還有你有任何國際標準化組織或歐盟的認證，可以寄電子郵件給我嗎？

B: Yes. It was ok. But can you think about the price again? And do you have any ISO or CE certificates? Can you email them to me?

A: 好，我很快會準備給你。掃描檔可能很大，我應該寄到同樣的電郵帳號嗎？

A: OK, I'll prepare them shortly. The scanned files can be big. Should I send them to the same email account?

B: 是，同樣的帳號可以。

B: Yes, the same account is fine.

A: 嗨，瓊斯先生，你有收到我們的認證檔案嗎？那些是你需要的嗎？ 或者你需要其他的，請讓我知道。

A: Hi, Mr. Jones, have you received the certificate files? Were those what you need? Or if you need something else, please let me know.

B: 好，我收到了，但是我需要知道產品的細節。

B: Yes, I have gotten them, but I need to know the details about the products.

A: 你需要知道什麼細節？

A: What are the details you need to know?

B: 你的不良率是多少？

B: What is your reject rate?

A: 我們生產線的不良率低於1%。

A: Our reject rate on the production line is under 1%.

B: 那鋼管呢？你使用什麼鋼材？

B: What about the tubular steel? What kind of steel do you use?

A: 我們使用1045鋼材，噴末鋼管。

A: We use 1045 steel. Powder coated tubular steel.

B: 你的鋼材有認證嗎？

B: Do you have a certificate for the steel?

A: 我會準備一份副本給你，你還需要其他的嗎？

A: I'll prepare a copy for you. Is there anything else you need?

B: 現在不需要，我會再告訴你。

B: Not now, I'll let you know later.

A: 好。

A: OK.

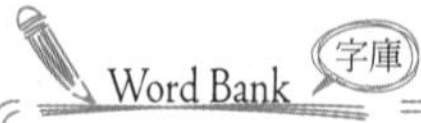

ISO (International Organization for Standardization) 國際標準化組織

CE certificate 歐盟認證

1. 你有收到我們腳踏車架的樣品嗎？

   Have you received our bike stand sample?

2. 你有任何國際標準化組織（ISO）或歐盟的認證嗎？

   Do you have any ISO or CE certificates?

3. 產品必須符合我們國家的檢驗標準。

   The products need to fit our national inspection standards.

4. 我需要知道產品的細節。

   I need to know details about the products.

5. 你的不良率是多少？

   What is your reject rate?

6. 你使用什麼鋼材？

What kind of steel do you use?

7. 你的鋼材有認證嗎？

Do you have a certificate for the steel?

8. 我們生產線的不良率低於1%。

Our reject rate on the production line is under 1%.

9. 我們使用 1045 鋼材。

We use 1045 steel.

8.2 依照客戶要求樣品投入生產 Putting Into Production According to a Client's Sample

A: 哈囉，泰瑞莎，你可以根據三天前我寄給你的樣品來生產嗎？

A: Hello, Teresa, can you produce my goods according to the sample I sent to you three days ago?

B: 可以，飛利浦先生，技術部門今天早上剛告訴我答案，但是我們需要確認樣品是否有專利問題。還有我們需要確認如果我們沒有得到訂單，你是否會支付初步樣品製作費？

B: Yes, we can. Mr. Philips. The tech department has just told me the answer this morning. However, we need to make sure if the sample has a patent issue and if you will pay for the primary sample making if we do not get your order.

A: 泰瑞莎，我有專利，並且有必要的話，我當然可以支付你們的初步樣品製作費。你可以在投入生產前寄給我你做的5個最初樣品嗎？

A: Teresa, I have the patent and I can of course pay for the sample making if I have to. Can you send me five primary samples first before we put into production?

B: 沒問題，飛利浦先生，我兩週內可以把它們寄給你。

B: No problem, Mr. Philips. We can send them to you in two weeks.

A: 嗯，好。

A: Um, that's fine.

B: 飛利浦先生，樣品準備好的時候，我會讓你知道。

B: Mr. Philips, I'll let you know when they are ready.

A: 好。

A: Good.

B: 我晚點會寄給你今天我們討論的細節給你確認。

B: I'll email you to confirm the details we discussed today.

A: 好，晚點談。

A: Alright. Talk to you later.

B: 好，再見。

B: OK. Bye.

（稍晚 later）

A: 哈囉，飛利浦先生，你認為我們的初步樣品如何？ 我們寄給你之前有做測試。

A: Hello, Mr. Philips, What do you think of our primary samples? We did testing before sending them to you.

B: 看起來可以，但我們還要把它們寄給我的三個經銷商測試性能。

B: They look ok, but we are also sending them to three of my distributors to test the performance.

A: 好，飛利浦先生，結果出爐的話讓我知道，你下訂之後我們會付測試的費用。

A: Alright, Mr. Philips. Let me know the result when the test results come out. We'll pay for the testing cost after getting your order.

B: 好的，謝謝。

B: OK. Thank you.

patent ['pætn̩t] n. 專利
issue ['ɪʃʊ] n. 議題
primary sample 初步樣品
distributor [dɪ'strɪbjətɚ] n. 經銷商
performance [pɚ'fɔrməns] n. 性能，表現

1. 我需要確認樣品是否有專利問題。
   We need to make sure if the sample has a patent issue.
2. 你認為我們的初步樣品如何？
   What do you think of our primary samples?
3. 我們要把它們寄給我的三個經銷商測試性能。
   We are sending them to three of my distributors to test the performance.
4. 你下訂之後我們會付測試的費用。
   We'll pay for the testing cost after getting your order.

產品規格標示公/英制（metric/English system）的換算（conversion）要清楚，賣方依照買方要求品質進行生產交貨，品質條件應明定政府或民間的權威檢驗機關（authoritative inspection organization）及寬容標準（standard tolerance）才能減少糾紛，因為買賣雙方立場對立，有時並非賣方交貨品質不佳，而是買家要求嚴苛造成的問題。

8.3 驗貨條件
Inspection Terms

A: 哈囉，飛利浦先生，我打來問最初樣品的 SGS 測試結果。	**A:** Hello, Mr. Philips, I'm calling to ask about the SGS testing result of the primary sample.
B: 泰瑞莎，你們通過了。我們可以開始生產了。	**B:** Teresa, you have passed. We can get the production started.
A: 是的，飛利浦先生，你的訂單會根據最初樣品投入生產。	**A:** Yes, Mr. Philips, your order will be put into production based on the primary sample.
B: 你們會如何做測試以保證品質？	**B:** How do you handle the inspection to guarantee the quality?
A: 我們的檢驗員會在每個生產日結束時隨機抽取10項來檢查以保證品質。	**A:** Our inspectors will randomly pick up ten items to check over at the end of each production day to ensure good quality.
B: 你們可以確認產品符合SGS標準及低於1%不良率嗎？	**B:** Can you assure your products meet SGS standards with a reject rate under 1%?
A: 是的，飛利浦先生，我們可以確定。	**A:** Yes, Mr. Philips, we can assure that.
B: 好。	**B:** Good.

A: 飛利浦先生，我會寄電郵給你確認今天我們討論的細節。

A: Mr. Philips, I'll email you to confirm the details we discussed today.

B: 出貨前，我要收到檢查報告。

B: Before shipment, I'd like to receive an inspection report.

A: 當然，飛利浦先生，沒問題。

A: Sure, Mr. Philips. That's no problem.

B: 好，謝謝你。

B: OK, thank you.

Word Bank 字庫

SGS (Société Générale de Surveillance) 總部位於瑞士日內瓦的檢驗認證機構

randomly ['rændəmlɪ] adv. 隨機地

assure [ə'ʃur] v. 確信，擔保

reject/rejection rate 不良率

1. 你會如何做測試以保證品質？

   How do you handle the inspection to guarantee the quality?

2. 我們的檢驗員會在每個生產日結束時隨機抽取10項來檢查以保證品質。

   Our inspectors will randomly pick up ten items to check over at the end of each production day to ensure good quality.

3. 你可以確認產品符合SGS標準及低於1%不良率嗎？
Can you assure your products meet SGS standards with a reject rate under 1%?

驗貨為確定品質之依據，有關何時、何地、由誰驗貨、驗貨次數等規定，須視訂單的交易條件（為出廠、裝運、抵岸、或門對門交貨）而訂。

8.4 數量條件—少於最低訂貨量
Quantity Terms - Lower than Minimum Order Quantity

A: 伍德先生，我們已經收到你的樣品，你的第一批貨數量多少？

A: Mr. Wood, we have received your sample. What is the quantity of your first order?

B: 我們每年可以賣出10,000個腳踏車架。

B: We can sell 10,000 bike stands each year.

A: 我們的產能當然可以達到你的需求，你的第一份訂單多少？

A: Our production capability can meet your demand for sure. What is your first order?

B: 呃，我們計畫買1,000個腳踏車架。

B: Well, we plan to have 1,000 bike stands.

A: 我們的最低訂貨量是2,000個。	**A:** Our MOQ is 2,000.
B: 你可以為我們將來的合作再想一下，為我們出1,000個嗎？	**B:** Can you think again for our cooperation in the future and make 1,000 for the first order?
A: 我要在會議裡提出你們的訂單加以討論。	**A:** I need to talk about it in the meeting to discuss your order.

production capability n. 產能

1. 你的第一批貨數量多少？
   What is the quantity of your first order?
2. 你要多少量？
   What is the quantity you need?
3. 我們的最低訂貨量是2,000個。
   Our MOQ is 2,000.
4. 你可以為我們將來的合作再想一下嗎？
   Can you think again for our cooperation in the future?
5. 我要在會議裡提出你們的訂單加以討論。
   I need to talk about it in the meeting to discuss your order.

賣方有生產數量須符合成本之考量，不妨在報價單上備註最低訂購數量或最低訂購金額（minimum purchase amount）。

8.5 原料成本與數量
Material Cost and Quantity

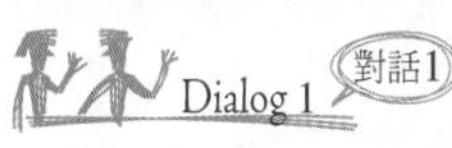

A: 飛利浦先生，我們已經考量你的要求，並且準備你一下單就開始生產你的貨。

A: Mr. Philips, we have gone through your requirements and are ready to put your goods into production as soon as you place your order.

B: 好，我需要10,000個產品。

B: Good. I'll need 10,000 units of the products.

A: 因為鋼價上漲很快，你有考慮要加量嗎？

A: Have you thought about raising the quantity because the steel price is going up rapidly?

B: 是啊，但我必須考慮我的存貨成本。

B: That's true, but I have to think about my inventory cost.

A: 飛利浦先生，如果你多訂5,000個，你的成本會下降。一到兩個月後買鋼材會又難又貴，我們下次可沒辦法依現在的價錢來生產你的貨。

A: Mr. Philips, if you order 5,000 units more. Your cost will go down. It will be hard and more expensive to get steel in a month or two. We won't be able to produce your goods at this price next time.

B: 我了解，我要考慮後再給你回覆。

B: I understand. I'll think about it and get you back later.

A: 好，飛利浦先生，晚點聊。

A: Alright. Mr. Philips. Talk to you later.

B: 謝謝，泰瑞莎，再見。

B: Thank you, Teresa. Goodbye.

A: 飛利浦先生，我們準備好要生產你的貨了，但是我們沒辦法生產20,000個給你。

A: Mr. Philips, we are ready to put your goods into production, but we wouldn't be able to produce 20, 000 units for you.

B: 為什麼？

B: Why?

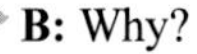

A: 鋼價上漲太劇烈了，我們的成本已經太高。	**A:** The steel price is going up so drastically. Our cost has gone too high.
B: 那你可以生產多少？	**B:** Then, how many can you make?
A: 10,000個。	**A:** 10, 000 units.
B: 那12,000個呢？	**B:** What about 12,000 units?
A: 我要先問，晚點才能答覆你。	**A:** I'll have to ask first and get back to you later.
B: 好，晚點聊，再見。	**B:** Alright. Talk to you later. Bye.

requirement [rɪ'kwaɪrmənt] n. 要求，需要
raise [rez] v. 增加，提高
inventory cost 存貨成本
drastic ['dræstɪk] adj. 劇烈

1. 我必須考慮我的存貨成本。

   I have to think about my inventory cost.

2. 我們下次可沒辦法依現在的價錢來生產你的貨。

We won't be able to produce your goods at this price next time.

3. 我們準備好要生產你的貨了。

We are ready to put your goods into production.

4. 鋼價上漲太劇烈了。

The steel price is going up so drastically.

5. 我們的成本已經太高。

Our cost has gone too high.

先行將成本可能上漲因素反映給客戶，讓雙方事先評估因應之道才能降低虧本的風險。

8.6 價格條件 Price Terms

A: 哈囉，瓊斯先生，我打來通知你我的主管同意降價，並且給你實盤價。

A: Hello, Mr. Jones, I'm calling to inform you that my supervisor has agreed to lower the price and give you a firm offer.

B: 好，你的最低單價是多少？

B: Ok. What's your lowest unit price?

A: 2,000 個運動袋，每個 4.50 元，含成本及運保費，雪梨交貨。	**A:** 2,000 sports bags, $4.50 per unit, CIF Sydney.
B: 我知道了。	**B:** I see.
A: 我們收到你訂單就可以馬上投入生產。	**A:** We can go into production right after we receive your order.
B: 好，我晚點聯絡你。	**B:** OK, I'll get back to you later.
A: 好，報價只有 3 天有效。我們會在收到訂單後，準備標籤等你認可。	**A:** Alright. The offer is open only for three days. We'll prepare the label print for your approval after receiving your order.
B: 好，晚點聯絡，再見。	**B:** OK. Talk to you later. Bye.

firm offer 實盤價
label print 標籤
approval [ə'pruvl̩] n. 認可

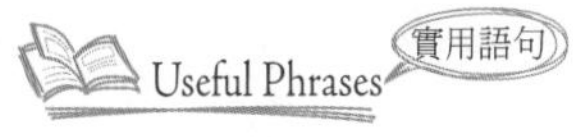

1. 我的主管同意降價，並且給你實盤價。
   My supervisor has agreed to lower the price and give you a firm offer.

2. 你的最低單價是多少？
What's your lowest unit price?
3. 我們收到你訂單就可以馬上投入生產。
We can go into production right after we receive your order.
4. 我們會在收到訂單後，準備標籤等你認可。
We'll prepare the label print for your approval after receiving your order.

報價單註明報價幣別及匯率基準，載明如果低於某匯率，報價須另議以規避匯兌風險。但能否在合約載明，仍由買賣方何者市場決定。

8.7 付款條件 Payment Terms

A: 我要跟你談付款條件。
A: I want to talk to you about payment terms.

B: 我們需要你在下訂單時支付 30%訂金，尾款於出貨前付清。
B: We request that you pay a 30% deposit wïthïn order, and the balance before shipment.

A: 我想是可以的，但我要跟我的主管確認。
A: I think that will be OK. I'll have to check with my director.

B: 好。
B: Very well.

Dialog 2 對話2

A: 你們接受何種方式付款？

A: What method of payment do you accept?

B: 我們接受銀行開出的現金支票或是轉帳。

B: We accept cashier's checks or wire transfers.

A: 我知道了，沒問題，我們兩個都做過。

A: I see. No problem. We have done both before.

B: 好，我會確認你有需要的全數名稱及帳號。

B: Good. I'll make sure you get all the names and account numbers necessary.

A: 謝謝。

A: Thank you.

Dialog 3 對話3

A: 我有何付款選擇？

A: What payment options do I have?

B: 我們每個月會寄給你有一個指定銀行帳號的帳單。

B: We'll send you a bill each month with a designated bank account number.

A: 日期呢？

A: What day?

B: 你會在每月 10 日前收到，每月 25 日到期。

B: You'll have it by the 10th of each month. The due date will be the 25th of each month.

A: 好，支票可以嗎？

A: OK. Is a check OK?

B: 保付支票可以，記住要允許交易時間。

B: Certified checks are fine. Remember to allow for transaction time.

A: 好，我會確認至少到期前 3 天就匯入。

A: Right. I'll make sure the remittance is in at least three days before the due date.

B: 好主意。

B: Good idea.

A: 如果我有其他付款條件或方式的問題，應該聯絡誰？

A: If I have any other questions about payment terms or methods, who should I contact?

B: 你可以隨時打電話給我。

B: You can call me anytime.

A: 謝謝。

A: Thanks.

request [rɪ'kwɛst] v. 要求
deposit within order 下訂單時付訂金
balance ['bæləns] n. 尾款
cashier's check (CC) 銀行開出的現金支票
wire transfer 轉帳
certified check (CC) 保付支票
remittance [rɪ'mɪtṇs] n. 匯款

1. 你們接受何種方式付款？

   What method of payment do you accept?

2. 我有何選擇？

   What are my options?

3. 我們需要你在下訂單時支付 30%訂金，尾款於出貨前付清。

   We request that you pay a 30% deposit within order, and the balance before shipment.

4. 我們接受銀行開出的現金支票或是轉帳。

   We accept cashier's checks or wire transfers.

5. 我要跟我的主管確認。

   I'll have to check with my director.

6. 我們會寄給你帳單。

   We'll send you a bill.

7. 記住要允許交易時間。

   Remember to allow for transaction time.

8. 我會確認匯入。

   I'll make sure the remittance is in.

9. 如果我有其他問題，應該聯絡誰？

   If I have other questions, who should I contact?

10. 隨時打來。

    Call anytime.

報價單註明付款方式，買方何時支付多少訂金，何時開信用狀等時間之詳載。即使做了客戶信用調查（client's credit check），也不表示貨款無虞。如果還沒收到訂金就投入生產，即可能掉入交易陷阱。無論訂金是否需要三催四請才下來，切記一定要等到訂金確定入帳後才可以投入生產。賣方可能面臨的不僅是未收到訂金就投入生產的風險太大，有些合約附註密密麻麻微小字體，甚至允許買方片面取消訂單完全不必負責（subject to cancellation without notice），因此務必確認訂單需經雙方同意才可撤銷。

8.8 包裝條件
Packaging and Packing Terms

A: 嗨，泰瑞莎，我們的裝運標記的主要標籤修改已經完成了。	**A:** Hi, Teresa, the revision of our main label for shipping marks is finished.
B: 好，瓊斯先生，我會查看新版本的郵件。	**B:** OK, Mr. Jones, I'll check my mail to see the new version.
A: 現在大一點了——3 吋寬 10 吋高，角落有 1 吋的三角形。	**A:** It is bigger now—3 inches wide and 10 inches high. The corners have a 1 inch triangle.
B: 好，你要印在什麼材質上？	**B:** OK. What kind of material do you want the label to be printed on?
A: 你可以印在既防油又讓標籤印得好的白色材質上嗎？	**A:** Can you find any oil resistant, white material that the label will print on well?
B: 我會問技術部門，晚點再回你。	**B:** I'll ask the tech department and get back to you later.

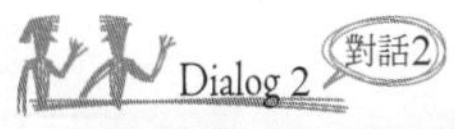

A: 瓊斯先生，你的標籤圖樣已經做成標籤膜了，現在準備讓你看是否核可。

A: Mr. Jones, your label artwork has been made into a label film. It's now ready for your approval.

B: 好，我會看。

B: OK, I'll have a look.

A: 我們也準備了你要求檢查的一個塑膠袋，包裝氣泡，及一個彩色的包裝盒。

A: We've also prepared a plastic bag, wrapping bubbles, and a colored packing box that you've requested to check over.

B: 先寄電郵照片給我，我會晚點檢查。

B: Just email the pictures to me first. I'll check them over later.

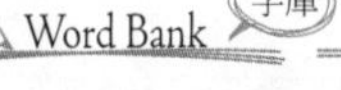

revision [rɪ'vɪʒən] n. 修改
label ['lebḷ] n. 標籤
shipping marks 裝運標記
oil resistant ['ɔɪl,rɪ'zɪstənt] adj. 防油的
film ['fɪlm] n. 膜
wrapping bubble 包裝氣泡
packing box 包裝盒

1. 你要印在什麼材質上？

   What kind of material do you want the label to be printed on?

2. 你的標籤圖樣已經做成標籤膜了。

   Your label artwork has been made into a label film.

3. 現在準備讓你看是否核可。

   It's now ready for your approval.

包裝方式關乎包裝成本，雙方當然必須協議。內包裝（packaging）用於保護貨物，外包裝（packing）用於辨別，以免在裝運時誤運或誤卸，審視標籤是否確實包含目的（卸貨）港（discharging port）、產地（country of origin）、編號（package number）、主標誌（main marks）、副標誌（counter marks 或 sub-marks）、側面標誌（side marks 標示重量、體積）及小心標誌（care marks）等訊息。

8.9 保險條件 Insurance Terms

A: 嗨，柯林斯先生，我們經常以含成本及運保費為報價基準，請告訴我們你的公司地址以便查看運費。

A: Hi, Mr. Collins, we usually quote on CIF basis. Please tell us your company address for freight checking.

B: 好，你晚點會收到我地址的郵件。

B: OK, you'll be receiving my mail later with the address.

A: 好，柯林斯先生。我們會以門對門配送，所以你不需擔心貨運。

A: OK, Mr. Collins, We'll do door to door delivery, so you won't need to worry about shipment.

B: 戰爭險有包含嗎？

B: Is war insurance included?

A: 有，而且保險包含送到你倉庫途中的任何海盜、天然災害及其他風險與延遲。

A: Yes, it is. Also, it includes insurance for sea pirates, natural disasters, and any other risks and delays on the way to your warehouse.

B: 好，那正是我需要的。

B: OK, that's what I need.

war insurance 戰爭險
sea pirate 海盜
natural disaster 天然災害
risk [rɪsk] n. 風險

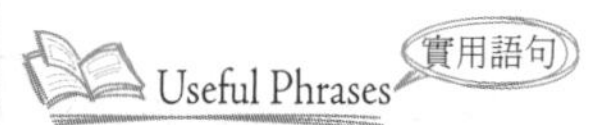

1. 我們會以門對門配送，所以你不需擔心貨運。

   We'll make door to door delivery, so you won't need to worry about shipment.

2. 戰爭險有包含嗎？

   Is war insurance included?

3. 保險也包含送到你倉庫途中的任何風險與延遲。

   It also includes insurance for any risks and delays on the way to your warehouse.

8.10 運送條件 Shipment Terms

A: 我需要跟你談運送條件。

A: I need to talk to you about your shipping terms.

B: 好，請坐。

B: Sure. Have a seat.

A: 謝謝。

A: Thanks.

B: 你需要知道什麼？

B: What would you like to know?

A: 我有什麼運送選擇？

A: What shipping choices do I have?

B: 那要看我們送貨到哪裡，我們可以報門對門，含成本及運保費，或船上交貨價。

B: It depends on what place we are shipping to. We can do door to door, CIF, or FOB.

A: 那如何影響價格？

A: How much does that affect the price?

B: 每個地方有所不同。

B: It varies from place to place.

A: 我知道了，我們要溝通不同交貨點的報價選項。

A: I see. We would have to communicate about pricing options connected to shipping differences.

B: 對，我會與你一起看每個方式的報價。

B: Right. We'll work with you on each.

door to door 門對門交貨
CIF(cost, insurance, and freight) 含成本及運保費
FOB(free on board) 船上交貨

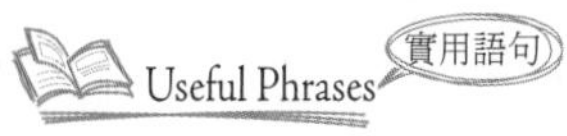

1. 我有什麼運送選擇？

What shipping choices do I have?

2. 那要看我們送貨到哪裡。

It depends on what place we are shipping to.

3. 每個地方有所不同。

It varies from place to place.

跟其他條件一樣，運送條件是可以溝通的，但是買賣雙方當然各有盤算，會考慮便利及成本等方式來選擇所需。如果交易條件含運送，報價註明另加運費旺季漲幅（freight surcharges），或將預計加價包含在內，才不會做賠本生意。

8.11 保固條件 Warrantee Terms

Dialog 1 對話1

A :早安，羅德。	A :Good morning, Rod.
B: 哈囉，泰瑞莎，你好嗎？	B: Hello, Teresa. How are you?
A: 還可以，謝謝。你呢？	A: Just fine, thanks. And you?
B: 我也好，請坐。	B: I’m OK. Please sit.
A: 謝謝你。	A: Thank you.

B: 你今天要跟我說什麼？

B: What do you want to talk to me about today?

A: 首先，保固條件。

A: First of all, warrantee terms.

B: 我明白了。呃，我們的標準保固是兩年零件與人工，但是在這個交易裡我們同意延長一年。

B: I see. Well, our standard warrantee is two years parts and labor. However, we agree to extend that by one year in the case of this deal.

A: 好，我確實在我們寫的合約裡看到那個（條件）。

A: OK, good. I did see that in the contract we wrote up.

B: 好，還有呢？

B: Fine. What else?

A: 我有另一個關於保固的問題。

A: I have another question about the warrantee.

B: 喔，好，是什麼？

B: Oh. Sure. What is it?

A: 保固是從我們訂購的設備到達開始，還是從設備裝好可以運作開始？

A: Does the warrantee begin when the equipment we ordered arrives, or does it start when the equipment has been installed and is operational?

B: 從裝好可以運作開始，我確定那點也有在合約裡。

B: Installed and operational. I'm sure that's in the contract as well.

warrantee [ˌwɔrən'ti] n. 保固
part [pɑrt] n. 零件
labor ['lebɚ] n. 人工
extend [ɪk'stɛnd] v. 延長
operational [ˌɑpə'reʃənl̩] adj. 運作

1. 你今天要跟我說什麼？
   What do you want to talk to me about today?
2. 我們的標準保固是兩年零件與人工。
   Our standard warrantee is two years parts and labor.
3. 在這個交易裡我們同意延長一年。
   We agree to extend that by one year in the case of this deal.
4. 保固是從設備到達開始嗎？
   Does the warrantee begin when the equipment arrives?

5. 還是從設備裝好可以運作開始？

Or does it start when the equipment has been installed and is operational?

保固書之保證含明示保證（express warrantee）及默示保證（implied warrantee）兩種，前者為保固書（或廣告）之明文記載，後者為隱含保證，即使未明文記載，但為社會所公認的保證。賣方可能在保固條件內註明免責條款（disclaimer of warranty），但須考量買方感受，除雙方所同意可排除條款外，賣方須負起保固時限內之瑕疵責任。

8.12 售後服務條件 After-Sales Service Terms

A: 我們關心的另一方面是瑕疵零件與組裝問題，我們可能無法馬上知道那一類的問題。

A: Another area of concern for us is defective parts and installation. We might not notice that type of problem right away.

B: 都包含在保固了，不用擔心。如果出現任何那些問題，我們會處理。

B: All covered by the warranty. No worries. If any problems like those come up, we'll take care of them.

A: 你的技師多快可以到達，如果需要修理的話？

A: How soon can your technicians arrive if repairs are needed?

B: 我們有合約經銷商負責保固內的所有維修。在接到通知後就會儘快安排維修時程，通常在 3-5 日以內可以完成，並且我們也保證所有服務 30 日內維修完畢。

B: We have a contracted distributor in charge of all the repairs. The schedule will be arranged as soon as the repair case comes in. Usually the repair can be done within three to five days, and we also back up all our services with a 30-day guarantee.

A: 過了保固期呢？

A: What about after the warranty period?

B: 經銷商也會修理，但是會收取零件費用與服務費。

B: The distributor offers the repair, too, but there will be a charge on the parts and the service.

after-sales service 售後服務
defective [dɪ'fɛktɪv] adj. 瑕疵的
contracted distributor 合約經銷商
in charge of 負責
back up 支持，後援
guaranty/guarantee ['gærəntɪ/ˌgærən'ti] n. 保證
charge [tʃɑrdʒ] n. 費用

1. 我們關心的另一方面是⋯。

   Another area of concern for us is ....

2. 我們可能無法馬上知道那一類的問題。

   We might not notice that type of problem right away.

3. 不用擔心。

   No worries.

4. 如果出現任何像那些的問題，我們會處理。

   If any problems like those come up, we'll take care of them.

5. 你的技師多快可以到達，如果需要修理的話？

   How soon can your technicians arrive if repairs are needed?

6. 我們有合約經銷商負責保固內的所有維修。

   We have a contracted distributor in charge of all the repairs.

7. 在接到通知後就會儘快安排維修時程。

   The schedule will be arranged as soon as the repair case comes in.

8. 通常在 3-5 日以內可以完成維修。

   Usually the repair can be done within three to five days.

9. 我們也保證所有服務 30 日內維修完畢。

   We also back up all our services with a 30-day guarantee.

10. 過了保固期呢？

    What about after the warranty period?

11. 會收取零件費用與服務費。

    There will be a charge on the parts and the service.

guaranty 為名詞也可拼成 guarantee，而guarantee 可當名詞與動詞。warranty 與 guaranty 都是「保證」的意思，如 The car is still under/out of warranty/guaranty. 這輛車還在/不在保固期限內。產品保固服務或保固書常用warranty（warranty card 保固卡, life-time warranty 終身保固），guarantee 尚有「承諾滿意」之意，多用在滿意保證（satisfaction guarantee）上，如 a money-back guarantee 退款保證。

8.13 退貨與退款條件
Terms for Returning Products and Refunds

A: 我需要問幾個退貨與退款的問題。

A: I need to ask a couple of questions about returning products and refunds.

B: 好，你想知道什麼？

B: Very well. What do you want to know?

A: 合約裡說如果我們雙方都覺得新設計的設備運作不夠好的話，可以退兩件設備。我的問題是我們要怎樣退以及要多久才能拿到貨款？

A: In the contract it states that we can return two of the pieces of equipment that are new designs if we both agree that they are not working well enough. My question is how do we return them and how long will we have to wait to get a refund?

B: 你的案子的話，我們會來取貨，並且是免費的，我們會在 3-5 天內收取。退款方面，我們要請你給我們 30 天。

B: In your case we will come and get them, and there will be no charge for doing so. And we would get them within three to five days. As for the refund, we ask that you allow us thirty days.

A: 我明白了，我會跟辦公室說。

A: I understand. I'll tell my office about this.

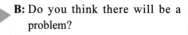

B: 你想會有問題嗎？	**B:** Do you think there will be a problem?
A: 我不知道，但是他們告訴我他們要知道那些問題的答案。	**A:** I don't know, but they told me they want to know the answers to those questions.
B: 我知道了。	**B:** I see.

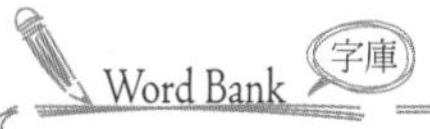

refund [rɪ'fʌnd] n. 退款
allow [ə'laʊ] v. 允許

1. 我需要問幾個退貨與退款的問題。
   I need to ask a couple of questions about returning products and refunds.
2. 我們要怎樣退以及要多久才能拿到貨款？
   How do we return them and how long will we have to wait to get a refund?
3. 這樣的服務免費。
   There will be no charge for doing so.
4. 我們會在 3-5 天內收取。
   We would get them within three to five days.
5. 我們要請你給我們 30 天。
   We ask that you allow us thirty days.
6. 你想會有問題嗎？
   Do you think there will be a problem?

保固條件是賣方給買方因為購買了你的產品而產生的承諾，除非買賣舊貨，賣方有責任供應買方無瑕疵產品，否則即為賣方違反承諾（breach of warranty）。因此，保固書等同賣方於保固期間內對買方在無瑕疵產品正常使用下所負擔之產品責任（product liability）。

8.14 不可抗力條件 Force Majeure ("Act of God")

A: 你如何保證我的產品安全無虞，並準時抵達？	**A:** How do you guarantee my products delivery safe and sound and on time?
B: 你的意思是？	**B:** What do you mean?
A: 不可抗力條件如颱風或意外都能輕易造成我公司的損失。	**A:** What about an act of God like typhoons or any accidents that can easily cause my company's loss?
B: 你有何建議？	**B:** What do you suggest?
A: （微笑）	**A:** (smile)
B: 你可以晚點告訴我們。	**B:** You can tell us later.

force majeure [ˌfɔrs mɑˈʒɚ](F.) 不可抗力（如天災、戰爭）
majeure（法文，即英文的 major）
safe and sound 安全無虞的

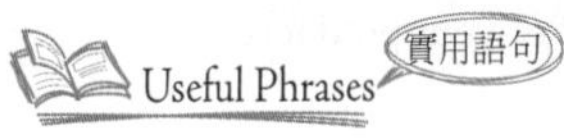

1. 你如何保證我的產品安全無虞，並準時抵達？
   How do you guarantee my products delivery safe and sound and on time?
2. 不可抗力條件如颱風或意外都能輕易造成我公司的損失。
   What about an act of God like typhoons or any accidents that can easily cause my company's loss?
3. 你的意思是？
   What do you mean?
4. 你有何建議？
   What do you suggest?

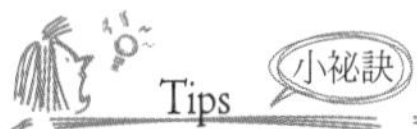

碰到商品行情正好的時候，進口商卻因不可抗力而無貨可賣，即使買足保險亦不足以賠償買方損失（例如：三百萬進口成本可賣九百萬，保險達到三百萬根本不足賠償進口商預計收益之白白損失）。買方希望賣方保多少險不會明講當然更不會直接建議，而是暗示賣方可做什麼，不懂潛規則（unspoken/unwritten rules）追問下文的話，即使條件全都談好，極有可能就是拿不到訂單。

8.15 著作權條件 Copy Right Terms

A: 你如何保證產品的著作權？

A: How do you guarantee the copy right of your products?

B: 我們的律師會確認，並且給你一份正式的著作權報告。

B: Our lawyer will check on that and give you a formal copy right report.

找律師出著作權保證書代價高，且必須自行支出，所以必須衡量成交是否值得。關於契約仲裁之訂定，除非是強勢賣方，否則幾乎由對方決定。

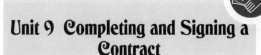

Unit 9 Completing and Signing a Contract

完成合約簽訂

用「魔鬼藏在細節裡」來說明合約細節的重要一點都不爲過。契約書簽訂應該包含各個銷售條件（產品數量、價格、付款條件、交貨日期、品質依據、品質檢驗、退貨處理、售後服務、糾紛仲裁等）。供應商與客戶有許多要達成共識及互相配合之處才能達成交易，爲免認知或解讀有誤，電話及郵件確認細節絕不可少。本章提供一些面對合約細節及簽訂合約時如何溝通的樣本。

9.1 檢查草約細節
Examining Details of a Contract Draft

（電話中 on the phone）

A: 哈囉，我是凱爾喬爾森。	**A:** Hello. This is Kyle Jolson.
B: 哈囉，我是從 LH 集團打來的泰瑞莎陳。	**B:** Hello. This is Teresa Chen calling from LH Group.
A: 哈囉，陳女士，你今天好嗎？	**A:** Hello, Ms. Chen. How are you today?
B: 好，謝謝你的問候。	**B:** Just fine. Thank you for asking.
A: 今天我可以幫你什麼忙呢？	**A:** What can I help you with today?
B: 接待員將我轉接給你，我想討論我們合約的條件。	**B:** Your receptionist transferred me to you. I want to discuss the terms of our contract.
A: 我知道了，讓我把它弄到螢幕上。	**A:** I see. Let me get it on my screen.
B: 好，我已經把它弄到我面前了。	**B:** OK. I have it here in front of me already.

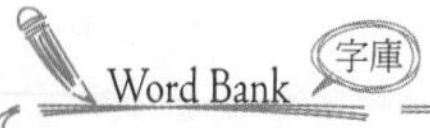

Word Bank 字庫

receptionist [rɪ'sɛpʃənɪst] n. 接待員，總機
transfer [træns'fɝ] v. 轉接

Useful Phrases 實用語句

1. 謝謝你的問候。

   Thank you for asking.

2. 今天我可以幫你什麼忙呢？

   What can I help you with today?

3. 我想討論我們合約的條件。

   I want to discuss the terms of our contract.

4. 讓我把它弄到螢幕上。

   Let me get it on my screen.

Dialog 2 對話2

A: 請看第 3 頁第 4 行。

A: Please look at Line 4 on Page 3.

B: 好，我看到了。

B: OK. I have it.

A: 這部分不正確，應該是「在碼頭運送與檢查結關」。

A: That part is incorrect. It should read, "on delivery and inspection clearance at dock."

B: 我會檢查這點。

B: I'll check on this point.

A: 好，另外一點，第 5 頁，第 22 行，「所有系統在裝置的第二期必須可以運作」。

A: Fine. On another point, on Page 5, Line 22, it says, "all systems must be operational by the second installment date."

B: 是，我看到了，那有問題嗎？

B: Yes, I see that. Is that a problem?

A: 我們先前已經同意在那之前的一星期，所有系統必須可以運作。

A: It was agreed that one week before that date, all systems would be operational.

B: 我了解，我也會檢查這點再回給你。

B: I understand. I'll look into this also and get back to you.

A: 謝謝，我何時可以得到你的回音？

A: Thanks. When will I hear back from you?

B: 我今天晚點會給你寄電子郵件。

B: I'll email you later today.

A: 好，謝謝。

A: OK. Thank you.

B: 沒問題。

B: No problem.

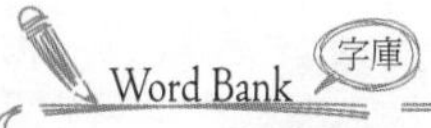

clearance ['klɪrəns] n.（船隻）結關
operational [ˌɑpə'reʃənl̩] adj. 運作的
installment [ɪn'stɔl mənt] n. 裝置
look into 檢查，深究

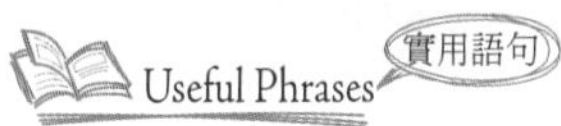

1. 這部分不正確。
   That part is incorrect.
2. （文字）應該是…。
   It should read.…
3. 我會檢查這點。
   I'll check on this point.
4. 那有問題嗎？
   Is that a problem?
5. 我們先前已同意…。
   It was agreed that.…
6. 我會檢查這點再回給你。
   I'll look into this and get back to you.
7. 我何時可以得到你的回音？
   When will I hear back from you?

以電話與不同國籍者進行交易因爲缺乏肢體訊號，表達要越清楚越好，所以將內容先寫下來並且確認重點，有組織及準備，需要的話應當先演練。事後以電子郵件作書面細節有其必要，一來可爲雙方確認，二來可作爲憑證。

9.2 協商未果—終止協商
Ending the Negotiation after Failure

（電話中 on the phone）

A: 這裡是泰瑞莎陳嗎？

A: Is this Teresa Chen?

B: 是的。

B: Yes, it is.

A: 我是吉姆桑德斯，你好嗎？

A: This is Jim Sanders. How are you this morning?

B: 很好，你呢？

B: Pretty good. How about you?

A: 喔，泰瑞莎，我很抱歉，但是我必須告訴你我們已經決定要結束協商。

A: OK. Teresa, I'm sorry, but I must tell you we have decided to end negotiations.

B: 我知道了，我很遺憾聽到這個。

B: I see. I'm sorry to hear this.

A: 是的，我知道你會感到遺憾，問題是價格，我的公司找到一個更好的交易。

A: Yes. I figured you would be. The problem is price. My company found a better deal.

B: 呃，我們試了，但我想我們無法達到你們的要求。	**B:** Well. We tried, but I guess we couldn't reach your requirements.
A: 對，或許將來我們能夠達成交易。	**A:** Right. Maybe in the future we'll be able to reach a deal.
B: 希望如此，跟你做生意很好。	**B:** I hope so. It's been nice doing business with you.
A: 我也覺得如此，你在我的聯絡名單裡。	**A:** I feel the same way. You are in my contact list.
B: 保持聯絡。	**B:** Stay in touch.
A: 當然了，我們再聊。	**A:** For sure. Talk to you later.
B: 再見。	**B:** Bye.

negotiation [nɪˌgoʃɪ'eʃən] n. 協商
deal [dil] n. 交易
contact list 聯絡名單
for sure 當然

1. 我必須告訴你我們已經決定要結束協商。

   I must tell you we have decided to end negotiations.

2. 問題是價格。

   The problem is price.

3. 我的公司找到一個更好的交易。

   My company found a better deal.

4. 我們試了。

   We tried.

5. 我猜我們無法達到你們的要求。

   I guess we couldn't reach your requirements.

6. 或許將來我們能夠達成交易。

   Maybe in the future we'll be able to reach a deal.

7. 跟你做生意很好。

   It's been nice doing business with you.

8. 你在我的聯絡名單裡。

   You are in my contact list.

交易要達成有許多因素，更需要機緣，交易雖未談成，彼此的情義還是在的。買方或許一時找得到倒店貨做低價買賣，但不一定找到好品質或長期穩定品質的供應商，保持良好關係，有利於將來客戶回頭，再度接洽進而達成交易。

9.3 交易談成—訂單準備
The Deal Is Done - An Order Will Be Ready

A: 好，所有的細節已取得一致意見了，我們可以準備訂單了。

A: OK. All the details have been agreed upon. We are set to prepare the order.

B: 好，我最關心的是出貨。

B: Good. I'm most concerned about delivery.

A: 我們會準時交貨，但是讓我強調一下你的信用狀必須最晚在出貨一個月前開出。

A: We'll get it delivered on time, but let me stress that your LC needs to be open no less than a month before the shipping date.

B: 沒問題，會的。

B: No problem. It will be open.

A: 很好。

A: Great.

B: 誰會做檢查？

B: Who will do the inspection?

A: 碼頭官員。

A: Port authority inspectors.

B: 我們也要所有的文件以雙語完成。	**B:** We'll also have to have all documents done in both languages.
A: 好。	**A:** Good.

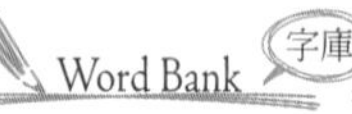

stress **[strɛs]** v. 強調
LC (letter of credit) 信用狀
port authority inspector 碼頭官員

1. 我們可以準備訂單了。
   We are set to prepare the order.
2. 我們會準時交貨。
   We'll get it delivered on time.
3. 誰會做檢查？
   Who will do the inspection?
4. 你的信用狀必須最晚在出貨一個月前開出。
   Your LC needs to be open no less than a month before the shipping date.

信用狀（LC）何時開出或何時收訂金，訂單確認後多久交貨，是否可分批出貨（運保費及報關等負擔將加倍）等同意條件皆須詳載。信用狀的每項內容必須確認及向開狀銀行查證，以免收到詐欺或不正確的信用狀，導致血本無歸。

9.4 交易條件轉成契約
Turning Trade Terms into a Contract

A: 哈囉，我要找傑克亞當斯。	**A:** Hello. I'm calling for Jack Adams.
B: 我是傑克。	**B:** This is Jack.
A: 嗨，傑克，我是LH 集團的泰瑞莎陳。	**A:** Hi, Jack. I'm Teresa Chen from LH Group.
B: 嗨，泰瑞莎，我可以為你做什麼？	**B:** Hi, Teresa, what can I do for you?

A: 我要你知道我們在依照我們所同意的交易條件打合約稿，應該下週會準備好給你看。

A: I just want to let you know that we are drawing up the contract based on the trade terms we have agreed upon, and it should be ready for you to look at next week.

B: 很好，準備好的時候讓我知道。	**B:** Great. Let me know when it's ready.
A: 會的，下週我會打電話給你。	**A:** Will do. I'll call you next week.

B: 好，那到時再跟你談了，再見。	**B:** Good. Talk to you then. Bye.
A: 再見。	**A:** Bye.

A: 嗨，傑克，我是泰瑞莎陳。	**A:** Hi, Jack. Teresa Chen here.
B: 嗨，泰瑞莎，情況如何？	**B:** Hi, Teresa. What's the situation?
A: 我們已經寄出給你了，用限時郵件。	**A:** We've mailed out the contract to you. We express mailed it.
B: 好，應該很快就到了。	**B:** Good. It should be here pretty soon.
A: 好，我們有一個追蹤號碼，我現在電郵給你。	**A:** Right. We have a tracking number. I'll email that to you now.
B: 好。	**B:** OK.
A: 讓我知道你是否有任何疑問。	**A:** Let me know if you have any questions.

B: 我會那樣做的，晚點聊。	**B:** I'll do that. Talk to you later.
A: 好，再見。	**A:** Right. Bye.

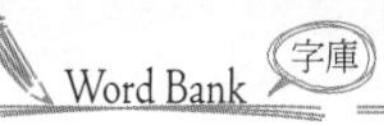

draw [drɔ] v. 打草稿
tracking number 追蹤號碼

1. 合約正在準備中。
The contract is being prepared.
2. 你想我何時會再聽到你們的消息？
When do you think I'll hear from you again?
3. 我們在依照我們所同意的交易條件打合約稿。
We are drawing up the contract based on the trade terms we have agreed upon.
4. 我們寄出限時郵件。
We express mailed it.
5. 我們有一個追蹤號碼。
We have a tracking number.
6. 一旦我們收到，我就會通知你。
I'll let you know once we get it.
7. （合約）寄到的時候，我們的法務部門會看。
We'll have our legal department look at it when it arrives.
8. 讓我知道你是否有任何疑問。
Let me know if you have any questions.

即使已有客戶徵信，也不表示沒有交易風險，如果收益成本划算，且當地治安無虞的話，安排簽約前先拜訪客戶將可降低風險。

9.5 合約錯誤更正
Correcting a Problem in the Contract

A: 哈囉，山姆，聽著。我們發現合約有個問題。	**A:** Hello, Sam. Listen. We found a problem in the contract.
B: 真的嗎？是什麼？	**B:** Really? What is it?
A: 第 4 頁的安裝日期有誤。	**A:** There is a mistake on Page four about the installation date.
B: 我這裡有一份合約，我看一下。	**B:** I have a copy of the contract here. Let me look at it.
A: 看第 4 頁。	**A:** Look on Page four.
B: 好，我看到今年 6 月20 日。	**B:** Alright—I see June 20 of this year.

A: 對，如果你看到我們的會議筆記，我相信你會看到我們同意的是 5 月 20 日。

A: Right. If you look back at the meeting notes I believe you'll see the agreement was for May 20.

B: 我要查一下，一個小時後跟你回覆。

B: I'll have to check. I'll get back to you in an hour.

A: 好。

A: Sounds good.

meeting notes 會議筆記

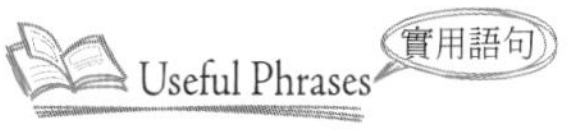

1. 我發現合約有個問題。

   We found a problem in the contract.

2. 第 4 頁的裝設日期有誤。

   There is a mistake on Page four about the installation date.

交易合約因爲多是買方所擬定（並經律師處理），對賣方較爲不利。如果財務許可，請商務律師爲合約把關是最妥當的。如果財力不允許的話，將合約充分閱讀後，不明白之處一定要問清楚。

9.6 回應合約更正
Calling Back on Contract Correction

A: 嗨，吉姆，我查了會議紀錄，發現有差異。	**A:** Hi, Jim. I've checked the meeting records and found the discrepancy.
B: 你打算怎麼做？	**B:** What are you going to do about it?
A: 我們儘快寄另一份合約給你，有你要的安裝日期。	**A:** We're rushing another contract to you with the date of installation you want.
B: 謝謝，何時會到呢？	**B:** Thank you. When will it be here?
A: 明天，我們馬上寄隔天送達。	**A:** Tomorrow. We'll send it overnight delivery right away.
B: 我知道了，很好。我們再次查看後會打電話給你。	**B:** I see. Good. I'll call you after we check it again.
A: 很好，我明天再跟你談。	**A:** Very well. I'll talk to you tomorrow.
B: 好，再見。	**B:** OK. Bye.

Dialog 2 對話2

A: 這是瑞歐工業的彼德華格納。

A: This is Peter Wagner from Red O Industries.

B: 嗨，彼得，我是泰瑞莎陳。

B: Hi, Peter. Teresa Chen here.

A: 哈囉，泰瑞莎，我只想讓你知道我們修改好合約，並且準備要寄給你。

A: Hello, Teresa. I just want to let you know we have revised the contract and are ready to have it sent over to you.

B: 好。

B: Good.

A: 明天會寄出去。

A: It will be delivered tomorrow.

B: 我會讓大家明天看一下。

B: I can have everybody look at it tomorrow.

A: 聽起來很好。

A: Sounds good.

B: 好，明天再聊。

B: OK. Talk to you later tomorrow.

A: 好，再見。

A: Right. Bye.

discrepancy [dɪ'skrɛpənsɪ] n. 差異
rush [rʌʃ] v. 趕緊
installation [ˌɪnstə'leʃən] v. 安裝
revise [rɪ'vaɪz] v. 修改

1. 我們會寄隔天送達。
   We'll send it overnight delivery.
2. 我們已修改好合約
   We have revised the contract.
3. 我會讓大家明天看一下。
   I can have everybody look at it tomorrow.

9.7 簽約
Signing a Contract

A: 我是彼德華格納。	**A:** This is Peter Wagner.
B: 嗨，彼得，我是泰瑞莎。	**B:** Hi, Peter. Teresa here.
A: 對，嗨，泰瑞莎，你好嗎？	**A:** Right. Hi, Teresa, how are you?

B: 很好，你有時間看過合約嗎？

B: Pretty good. Have you had time to look over the contract?

A: 是的，看過了，看起來可以。

A: Yes, we have. It looks fine.

B: 準備要簽約了嗎？

B: Are you ready to sign it?

A: 好。

A: Sure.

B: 很好。你要何時簽？

B: Great. When do you want to do it?

A: 明天下午，須到場的人會來這裡。

A: Tomorrow afternoon. Everyone needed will be here.

B: 好，幾點？

B: Alright. What time exactly?

A: 下午3點。

A: 3:00 pm.

B: 好，我們會到，期待明天見到你們。

B: Good. We'll be there. I look forward to seeing you all tomorrow.

A: 我也是，明天見。

A: Me, too. See you tomorrow.

Dialog 2 對話2

A: 嗨，泰瑞莎，請進來坐下。	**A:** Hi, Teresa. Come in. Please have a seat.
B: 謝謝，又看到你真好。	**B:** Thank you. Nice to see you again.
A: 我也很高興看到你。	**A:** Good to see you, too.
B: 我們準備好完成交易了。	**B:** We are ready to seal this deal.
A: 是的。	**A:** Yes, we are.
B: 好，我們來進行吧。	**B:** Great. Let's do it.
A: 好。	**A:** All right.
B: 這是合約，我們雙方公司的法務部都清楚了。	**B:** Here is the contract. Both your and my company's legal departments have cleared it.
A: 對，讓我們再一次確認合約條件。然後，就可以簽名了。	**A:** Right. Let's go over the terms one more time. Then, we can sign it.

B: 好。	**B:** OK.

seal **[sil]** v. 密封，蓋印
legal department 法務部

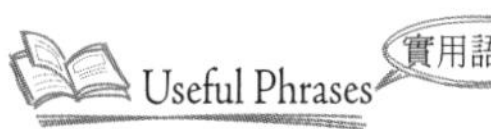

1. 你有時間看過合約嗎？
   Have you had time to look over the contract?
2. 準備要簽約了嗎？
   Are you ready to sign it?
3. 期待明天見到你們。
   I look forward to seeing you all tomorrow.
4. 我們準備好完成交易了。
   We are ready to seal this deal.
5. 我們雙方公司的法務部都清楚了。
   Both your and my company's legal departments have cleared it.
6. 我的公司同樣這麼告訴我。
   I've been told the same by my company.
7. 讓我們再一次確認合約條件。
   Let's go over the terms one more time.

英語合約條文密密麻麻又小又難懂，且買方多已請律師修改成對其有利之條件，供應商面對不利條件，只有搞清楚才能自保。

9.8 通知開始貨物生產
Informing the Starting Process of Making the Goods

A: 哈囉，休斯先生，我是 LH 集團的泰瑞莎陳。

A: Hello, Mr. Hughes. This is Teresa Chen of LH Group.

B: 嗨，泰瑞莎，你今天好嗎？

B: Hi, Teresa. How are you today?

A: 我很好，謝謝問候，我相信你也很好。

A: I'm good. Thanks for asking. I trust you are doing well, too.

B: 是的，謝謝，這通電話是為了什麼呢？

B: I am, thanks. What is this call about?

A: 我只想通知你我們今天開始生產你們公司下的訂單。

A: I just want to inform you that we started production today of the order your company placed.

B: 很棒！ 時間很剛好。

B: Wonderful! Right on time.

A: 是的，並且看起來我們可以早兩天完成生產流程。

A: Yes. And, it looks like we can finish the production run two days early.

B: 好消息，泰瑞莎。

B: Great news, Teresa.

A: 很高興告訴你，我會打電話來給進一步的資訊。

A: Glad to tell you. I'll call with further updates.

B: 請打來，謝謝你來電。

B: Please do. Thanks for calling.

A: 沒問題，晚點聊，再見。

A: No problem. Talk to you later. Bye.

B: 再見。

B: Good bye.

字庫

place [ples] v. 下（訂單）
production run 生產流程
update ['ʌpˌdet] n. 更新資訊

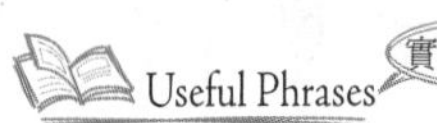

1. 這通電話是為了什麼呢？
   What is this call about?
2. 我只想通知你我們今天開始生產你們公司下的訂單。
   I just want to inform you that we started production today of the order your company placed.
3. 時間很剛好。
   Right on time.
4. 我們可以早兩天完成生產流程。
   We can finish the production run two days early.
5. 很高興告訴你。
   Glad to tell you.
6. 我會打電話來給進一步的資訊。
   I'll call with further updates.

Notes
小叮嚀

雖然合約已詳訂生產時程，但通知買方開始生產及後續消息使其放心是提供良好服務絕對必要的手續。

What is this call about？

I just want to inform you that we started production today of the order your company placed.

Unit 10 Handling Problems with Goods

處理產品問題

如何妥善處理問題是成功經營的重要關鍵，了解問題、解決問題、進一步避免問題的產生遠比追究誰造成的過失更有意義。買賣雙方因合約規範，在出現問題時，可使雙方有所依循。但產品有問題不免損害商譽，需極力挽救，以令人滿意的彌補措施挽回客戶的信心。拜網路之賜，許多過來人在網路貿易平臺或論壇裡分享各種經驗智慧（請見附錄），如果你提問，也可能得到有用的回應或建議做參考。相對地，網路資訊正確性及詐騙氾濫也必須時時留意。

10.1 客戶更改訂單 Client Changing Orders

10.1a 不增加成本 With No Cost Added

A: 嗨，我打來改我昨天發的訂單。

A: Hi. I'm calling to change an order I made yesterday.

B: 我明白了，您的大名是？

B: I see. What is your name?

A: 馬克瓊斯。

A: Mark Jones.

B: 謝謝，瓊斯先生。你有訂單號碼嗎？

B: Thank you, Mr. Jones. Do you have the order number?

A: 有，是 5T55995。

A: Yes. It is 5T55995.

B: 謝謝，我看到在這裡。是 200 個 S55s。

B: Thank you. I see it here. It's for two hundred S55s.

A: 對，我想把訂單從綠色改成藍色。

A: That's right. I'd like to change my order to blue ones instead of green.

B: 我知道了，沒問題，我現在馬上就改。

B: I see. No problem. I'll simply change your order right now.

A: 會添加任何一筆費用嗎？	**A:** Will there be any additional charge?
B: 不會，訂單價錢不會改變。	**B:** No. The price of your order will not change.
A: 好，謝謝。	**A:** Good. Thank you.
B: 沒問題。有其他問題嗎，瓊斯先生？	**B:** No problem. Will there be anything else, Mr. Jones?
A: 沒有，就這樣，謝謝。	**A:** No. That's it. Thanks.
B: 好，我幾分鐘後會寄給你電郵確認更改。	**B:** Alright. I'll email you to confirm the change in a few minutes.
A: 好，祝你有愉快一天！再見。	**A:** OK. Have a nice day! Good bye.
B: 你也是，再見。	**B:** You, too. Bye.

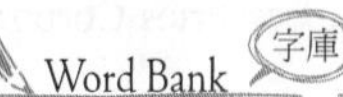

additional [ə'dɪʃənḷ] adj. 添加的
charge [tʃardʒ] n. 費用

1. 你有訂單號碼嗎？
   Do you have the order number?
2. 我想把訂單從綠色改成藍色。
   I'd like to change my order to blue ones instead of green.
3. 我現在馬上就改。
   I'll simply change your order right now.
4. 會添加任何一筆費用嗎？
   Will there be any additional charge?
5. 訂單價錢不會改變。
   The price of your order will not change.
6. 有其他問題嗎？
   Will there be anything else?

10.1b 增加一些成本 With Some Added Cost

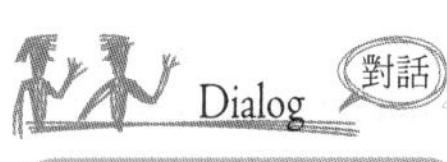

A: 哈囉，我打來改我們公司的訂單。	**A:** Hello. I'm calling to change an order our company made.
B: 請問大名是？	**B:** May I have your name please?
A: 好，我是約翰華勒斯，我代表哈奇飾品公司。	**A:** Yes. It's John Wallace. I represent Hatch Accessories Corporation.
B: 是的，華勒斯先生，你可以也告訴我訂單號碼嗎？	**B:** Yes, Mr. Wallace. Can you also tell me the order number?

A: 好，是 DSD55。	**A:** Yes. It's DSD55.
B: 謝謝，我這裡電腦上有了，你要更改什麼？	**B:** Thank you. I have it here on my screen. What is it you want to change?
A: 這些品項的柄要是黑的，而不是紅的。	**A:** The handles on those units need to be black instead of red.
B: 我們可以改，但會增加成本。	**B:** We can make that change, but it would add to the cost.
A: 為什麼？	**A:** Why?
B: 因為訂單已經在做了，我們要另外投入人工來改。	**B:** Because that order is already in production. We'd have to put additional labor into the changes.
A: 你可以給我另加的金額嗎？	**A:** Can you give me the amount extra it would cost?
B: 我要先聯絡生產線才知道答案，你要我回你電話嗎？	**B:** I'll have to contact production first to get that answer. Would you like me to call you back?
A: 是的。	**A:** Yes, please.
B: 沒問題。我會今天回你電話，大約一小時內。	**B:** No problem. I'll get back to you today, probably within an hour.

A: 很好，謝謝，再見。	**A:** Great. Thanks. Bye.
B: 再見。	**B:** Goodbye.

accessory [æk'sɛsərɪ, ək-] n. 飾品
handle ['hændḷ] n. 柄，握把
labor ['lebɚ] n. 人工

1. 你要更改什麼？
   What is it you want to change?
2. 這些品項的柄要是黑的，而不是紅的。
   The handles on those units need to be black instead of red.
3. 我們可以改，但會增加成本。
   We can make that change, but it would add to the cost.
4. 訂單已經在做了。
   That order is already in production.
5. 我們要另外投入人工來改。
   We'd have to put additional labor into the changes.
6. 你可以給我另加的金額嗎？
   Can you give me the amount extra it would cost?
7. 我要先聯絡生產線才知道答案。
   I'll have to contact production first to get that answer.

10.1c 太晚改訂單，無法更改 Changing an Order Too Late, Impossible

A: 嗨，我打來是關於一個我們下的訂單要更改。

A: Hi. I'm calling about an order we put in that needs to be changed.

B: 好，給我訂單號碼？

B: OK. Give me the order number.

A: GTY66.

A: GTY66.

B: 好，我這裡有，帕森氏公司，對嗎？

B: OK. I have it here. Parsons Company, right?

A: 對。

A: Right.

B: 要改什麼？

B: What is it you want to change?

A: 我們要改鋼管的長度。

A: We want changes to the length of the steel rod.

B: 我明白了，恐怕不可能，訂單早已投入生產了。

B: I see. I'm afraid that is not possible. The order is already too far into production.

A: 你確定嗎？

A: Are you sure?

B: 是，幾乎要完工了。	**B:** Yes. The whole order is almost complete.
A: 我知道了，我會跟上司們講這個情形，謝謝。	**A:** I see. I'll talk to my superiors about the situation. Thank you.
B: 沒問題，關於這點很抱歉。	**B:** You're welcome. Sorry about this.
A: 沒關係，晚點再說，再見。	**A:** It's OK. Talk to you later. Bye.
B: 再見。	**B:** Bye.

1. 我們要改鋼管的長度。

   We want changes to the length of the steel rod.

2. 恐怕不可能。

   I'm afraid that is not possible.

3. 訂單早已投入生產了。

   The order is already too far into production.

4. 幾乎要完工了。

   The whole order is almost complete.

訂單到生產前有一小段時間爲備料的緩衝期，爲避免客戶修改訂單導致問題，可約定買方在下訂幾日後，或一旦開始生產日期之後，即不可修改訂單的政策。

10.2 樣品損壞 Damaged Sample

A: 嗨，泰瑞莎，我們已經收到你的腳踏車架樣本。	**A:** Hi, Teresa, we have just received your bike stand sample.
B: 我們的產品很棒吧！？	**B:** Our product is great, isn't it?
A: 它底部損壞了。	**A:** It was damaged at the bottom.
B: 什麼意思？	**B:** What do you mean?
A: 底部凹進去了，因為凹進去，所以掉漆大約有一公分。	**A:** The stand was dented at the bottom, and the coating faded about 1 centimeter because of the dent.
B: 我很抱歉發生這樣的事，你可以電郵照片嗎？ 是包裝問題嗎？	**B:** I'm sorry for what happened. Can you email the picture? Is it a packing problem?
A: 或許包裝不能保護架子，或許運送員沒有好好運送。	**A:** Maybe the packing could not protect the stand, or perhaps the courier didn't take care during the delivery.
B: 你需要新的嗎？我會讓樣品準備好。	**B:** Do you want a new one? I'll have it prepared.

A: 好，但是這次你要付費。

A: OK, but you'll pay for it this time.

B: 當然，我會確認這次包裝妥當。

B: Sure, I'll make sure it is well packed this time.

dent [dɛnt] v. 凹
coating ['kotɪŋ] n. 塗層
fade [fed] v. 掉漆，褪色
centimeter ['sɛntəˌmitɚ] n. 公分
courier ['kurɪɚ] n. 運送員

1. 我們的產品很棒吧！？
   Our product is great, isn't it?
2. 它底部損壞了。
   It was damaged at the bottom.
3. 是包裝問題嗎？
   Is it a packing problem?
4. 我會確認這次包裝妥當。
   I'll make sure it is well packed this time.

客戶親自打電話來表示事態嚴重，一定要好好處理。除了道歉，馬上彌補過失外，了解爲何損壞的原因後要向客戶解釋，並防止出現同樣錯誤，接下來務必提供令人滿意的服務挽回客戶信心。

10.3 客戶拒絕收貨 Client Rejecting Reception of Goods

A: 哈囉，史丹，我是泰瑞莎陳。	**A:** Hello. Stan, Teresa Chen speaking.
B: 嗨，泰瑞莎，我必須要跟你說我們不收已經過季遲到的訂單。	**B:** Hi, Teresa. I have to tell you about a late order we cannot accept.
A: 怎麼了？有問題嗎？	**A:** What happened? What's the problem?
B: 運送太慢了，那是為了耶誕節購物季而下的訂單，但卻過了耶誕才到。	**B:** The delivery came too late. It was for the Christmas shopping season, but it was delivered after Christmas.
A: 我明白了，我會跟上司確認，並且看下一步怎麼做。	**A:** I see. I'll check with my supervisor and see what to do next.
B: 好，何時可以聽到你的消息？	**B:** OK. When will I hear from you?
A: 我會在半小時內回電。	**A:** I'll call back within thirty minutes.
B: 好，我會等。	**B:** Great. I'll be waiting.

A: 好。

A: Alright.

Dialog 2 對話2

（半小時後 thirty minutes later）

A: 嗨，史丹，我是泰瑞莎。

A: Hi, Stan, Teresa here.

B: 哈囉，是什麼情況？

B: Hello. What is the situation?

A: 你跟我這邊沒有問題，船運公司沒有照我們的合約履行。我們要跟他們處理這個問題。

A: There is no issue between your company and mine. The shipping company did not fulfill the agreement we had with them. We'll have to deal with them about this problem.

B: 那對我們是好消息，但我們要怎樣退回訂單？

B: That's good news for us, but how should we return the order?

A: 我們要安排取貨，我明天會打電話給你談細節。

A: I'm going to arrange for pickup. I'll call you back tomorrow with details.

B: 好，我明天很多時間會外出，但是我外出時會看電子郵件，你可以留言。

B: OK. I'll be out a lot tomorrow, but I check my email while out, and you can leave a message.

A: 好，沒問題。我有你的聯絡資料。

A: Sure, no problem. I have your contact info. already.

B: 好，再聊。

B: Good. Talk to you later.

A: 聽起來很好，再見。

A: Sounds good. Bye.

B: 再見。

B: Bye.

late order 過季遲到的訂單
issue ['ɪʃʊ] n. 問題，爭議
fulfill [fʊl'fɪl] v. 履行，實現

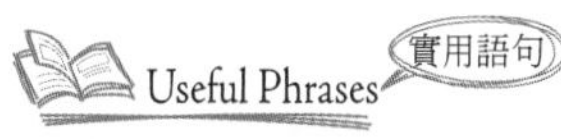

1. 是什麼情況？

   What is the situation?

2. 你跟我這邊沒有問題。

   There is no issue between your company and mine.

3. 船運公司沒有照我們的合約履行。

   The shipping company did not fulfill the agreement we had with them.

4. 我們要跟他們處理這個問題。

   We'll have to deal with them about this problem.

5. 我們要怎樣退回訂單？

How should we return the order?

6. 我們要安排取貨。

I'm going to arrange for pickup.

如果你被客戶咆哮，保持冷靜，並且繼續儘可能地幫忙。在困難的情況下更要保持專業態度，不要因爲挫折或生氣而失去控制。此時最重要的是如何留住客人信心，如果你不能滿足你的客戶，請客戶進一步與主管尋求解決之道。反之，如果你的供應商無法給你所需之幫忙或滿足你的期待，就要進一步找對方的主管。

10.4 貨物遲到與賠償 Late Delivery and Compensation

A: 我們沒收到訂單51326F的貨物。	**A:** We have not received order 51326F.
B: 我看一下紀錄（一秒）。我們的紀錄顯示三週前出貨。	**B:** Let me check our records. (One second.) Our records show it was shipped three weeks ago.
A: 沒送到。	**A:** It never got here.
B: 好，我會查這事及今天回電給你。	**B:** All right. I'll check on this and call you back today.

A: 謝謝你！

A: Thank you.

B: 好，沒問題。

B: Sure. No trouble at all.

A: 我要跟你談運送的事，貨物遲到了。

A: I want to talk to you about the delivery. It was late.

B: 真的？遲到多久？

B: Really? How late?

A: 10 天。

A: Ten days.

B: 我知道了，很糟。

B: I see. Very bad.

A: 我想你知道我們合約裡有補償條款。

A: I'm sure you know we have a compensation clause in our agreement.

B: 是的，我知道。我有看過協議。

B: Yes, I do. I've looked at the agreement.

A: 延誤已造成 10% 的總價損失，我們會在付款時扣除金額。

A: The delay has cost 10% of the total price. We will deduct the amount from our payment.

B: 好。

B: Alright.

compensation clause 補償條款
deduct [dɪ'dʌkt] v. 扣除

1. 我們的紀錄顯示三週前出貨。
   Our records show it was shipped three weeks ago.
2. 我會查這事及今天回電給你。
   I'll check on this and call you back today.
3. 我們合約裡有補償條款。
   We have a compensation clause in our agreement.
4. 延誤已造成 10%的總價損失。
   The delay has cost 10% of the total price.
5. 我們會在付款時扣除金額。
   We will deduct the amount from our payment.
6. 我們週末已經以符合標準的品質完成你的訂單。
   We have completed your order over the weekend with meeting quality standards.
7. 為了儘早送達，我們會用 UPS 寄出產品，由我們付費。
   To ensure the goods earliest arrival, we will ship them by UPS at our own cost.
8. 希望我們的安排能彌補你的損失。
   We hope our arrangement will make up for your loss.
9. 請接受我們最誠懇的道歉。
   Please accept our most sincere apology.
10. 我們會避免相同問題再發生。
   We will avoid this mistake from happening again.

11. 我們當然會盡全力符合你的需求。

We will surely do our utmost to meet your request.

12. 如果你有任何意見或疑慮，請告訴我們。

Keep us informed if you have any comments or concerns.

Tips

整批貨物運送的預計日期較易掌握，但載運散貨或拆貨運送時較可能發生預料之外的遲送。即使訂有賠償條款，仍導致商譽損失及客戶因延誤商機而造成的銷售收益損失，解決之道無他，惟誠意與將心比心。

10.5 貨物遺失 Lost Goods

Dialog 1

A: 我打來問一批遺失的貨物。	**A:** I'm calling about a lost shipment.
B: 你有運送號碼嗎？	**B:** Do you have the shipping number?
A: 有，是HJK73265。	**A:** Yes. It is HJK73265.
B: 我們的紀錄顯示上個月 15 日出貨。	**B:** Our records show it was shipped on the fifth of last month.
A: 我們是被告知這樣，但貨從沒到達。	**A:** We were informed of that, but it never arrived.

B: 好，我會調查這件事及一個小時內回電。

B: OK. I'll investigate this and call you back in an hour.

A: 謝謝你。

A: Thank you.

B: 沒問題。

B: No problem.

（稍後 later）

A: 我們打給運送人想找到這批貨，很不幸地，貨物遺失了，我們現在什麼也沒法做，只能等保險公司調查。

A: We have called the shipper to find out about the shipment. Unfortunately, the shipment is lost. There is nothing we can do now but to wait for the insurance company to investigate.

B: （嘆氣）好。

B: (Sigh) OK.

investigate [ɪn'vɛstə,get] v. 調查

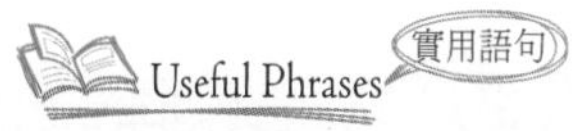

1. 你有運送號碼嗎？

   Do you have the shipping number?

2. 我們的紀錄顯示上個月 15 日出貨。

   Our records show it was shipped on the fifth of last month.

3. 我會調查這件事及一個小時內回電。

   I'll investigate this and call you back in an hour.

4. 我們現在什麼也沒法做，只能等保險公司調查。

   There is nothing we can do now but to wait for the insurance company to investigate.

現今貨物多已使用定位追蹤（GPS tracking），防止失蹤（missing）、失竊（theft），輸入提單或貨櫃號碼即可追蹤貨況，貨物損失率大為降低。

10.6 零件不全 Missing Parts

A: 貨送來了，但是六個螺栓不見了。

A: The shipment has arrived, but six bolts are missing.

B: 我跟包裝部門確認再回覆你。

B: Let me check with the packaging department and get back to you.

（稍後 later）

B: 格蘭特先生，我們會馬上寄六個螺栓給你，你應該三天以內可以收到。

B: Mr. Grant, we will deliver the six bolts to you right away. You should be receiving them in three days.

A: 好。

A: OK.

bolt [bolt] n. 閂，螺栓
packaging department 包裝部門

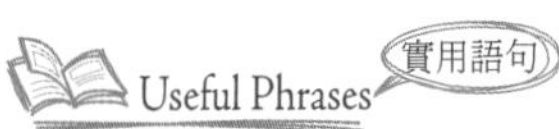

1. 我跟包裝部門確認再回覆你。
   Let me check with the packaging department and get back to you.
2. 我們會馬上寄六個螺栓給你。
   We will deliver the six bolts to you right away.
3. 你應該三天以內可以收到。
   You should be receiving them in three days.

10.7 檢驗貨物瑕疵與處理後續
Inspecting Defectives and Handling the Aftermath

A :嗨，艾琳。	A :Hi, Irene.
B :哈囉，史丹，你好嗎？	B :Hello, Stan. How are you?
A: 好，你呢？	A: Good. And you?
B: 很好，我看你這裡有一些瑕疵品。	B: Pretty good. I see you have the defective products here.
A: 是的，我們看看，好嗎？	A: Yes, we do. Let's have a look, OK?
B: 好，我們需要檢查它們。	B: Sure. We need to inspect them.
A: 你會注意這一個有個裂縫，還有這些遺失了一些螺栓。	A: You'll notice there is a crack on this one, and these are missing some bolts.
B: 我知道了，呃，遺失零件的產品可以在這裡補上。	B: I see. Well, the ones with missing parts can be fixed here.

A: 其他的呢？	**A:** What about the others?
B: 那些（有裂縫的）當然要換成新的。	**B:** Of course those will be replaced with new ones.
A: 我很高興聽到這樣，我也要問運送。	**A:** I'm glad to hear that. I want to ask about shipping, too.
B: 我們會付運費，很明顯的這是我們的錯。	**B:** We'll pay for it. Obviously this is our fault.
A: 我會把你的說明通知總辦公室，他們在擔心誰付運費。	**A:** I'll let my main office know what you've said. They were worried about who'd pay for shipping.
B: 別擔心，我們會付。	**B:** Don't worry. We'll cover it.
A: 謝謝。	**A:** Thanks.

Word Bank 

inspect **[ɪn'spɛkt]** v. 檢查
defective **[dɪ'fɛktɪv]** adj. 瑕疵的
crack **[kræk]** n. 裂縫
bolt **[bolt]** n. 螺栓
replace **[rɪ'ples]** v. 更換

1. 這些是有瑕疵的。

   These are defective.

2. 這一個有個裂縫。

   There is a crack on this one.

3. 這些遺失了一些螺栓。

   These are missing some bolts.

4. 遺失零件的產品可以在這裡補上。

   The ones with missing parts can be fixed here.

5. 那些當然要換成新的。

   Of course those will be replaced with new ones.

6. 我們會付款。

   We'll cover it.

7. 我們珍惜你的惠顧。

   We value your business.

10.8 客戶自行修理及要求償付費用 Client Handling Repairs and Requesting Reimbursement

A: 我們訂的貨有瑕疵品。	A: Our order has some defective goods.
B: 我們很抱歉造成你的不便，你可以清楚地描述是什麼問題嗎？	B: We are sorry for the inconvenience. Can you describe clearly what the problem is?
A: 無法恰當關閉。	A: They won't turn off properly.

B: 我明白了，你可以提供照片跟產品序號嗎？

B: I see. Can you provide photos and the products serial number?

A: 好。請等一下，序號是12523638。照片我等一下就可以傳電子郵件給你。

A: OK. Just a moment. The serial number is 12523638. I can email you the photos in a few minutes.

B: 你要我們如何幫你處理這些瑕疵品？

B: How can we help you with the defectives?

A: 我不知道是否只有這個產品損壞。

A: We don't know if these ones are the only defective ones.

B: 你可以明天早上告訴我有幾個損壞嗎？

B: Can you tell me how many are damaged tomorrow morning?

A: 好。

A: OK.

（第二天 the next day）

A: 我們初略統計了，目前大約有 26 個壞掉，我們的技術人員正在討論是否可以自行修理，如果可以弄到新開關的話。

A: We have quickly checked over them and found 26 defective ones at this point. Our technicians are discussing whether we can repair them if we can get the new switches.

B: 我知道了，你們可以幫我們在當地經銷商取得新開關嗎？還是要我們空運到你倉庫呢？數量要多少？

B: I see. Can you get the new switches from the local distributor ? Or do you want us to airmail them to your warehouse? And how many do you need?

A: 我們技術人員認為我們更換沒問題，我們需要 30 組的開關零件，請寄過來。我們會向你們公司收取修理費，一臺機器大約 230 元美金，乘以 26 臺。

A: Our technicians think we can fix the problem, and we need 30 sets of the switches. Please mail them to us. There will be a charge for our repair service to your company. Each unit $230. Times 26.

B: 好的，請於下次付款時扣除金額。我們明天就寄出 30 組開關零件。我們認為你們公司的技術維修能力是沒問題的，若有裝配順序的問題，我們會請技師拍一段影片放到 You Tube 供你們參考。

B: OK. Please deduct the amount from the next payment. We will mail 30 sets of the switches tomorrow. We think your company should have no trouble fixing the units. If the order of installation is a problem, we will have a video made by our technician and put it on You Tube for your reference.

A: 好。

A: Good.

reimbursement [ˌriɪm'bɝsmənt] n. 歸還費用
defective [dɪ'fɛktɪv] adj. 瑕疵的，n. 瑕疵品
serial number 產品序號
switch [swɪtʃ] n. 開關
deduct [dɪ'dʌkt] v. 扣除

1. 你可以清楚地描述是什麼問題嗎？
   Can you describe clearly what the problem is?
2. 你可以提供照片跟產品序號嗎？
   Can you provide photos and the products serial number?
3. 你要我們如何幫你處理這些瑕疵品？
   How can we help you with the defective ones?
4. 你們可以幫我們在當地經銷商取得新開關嗎？
   Can you get the new switches from the local distributor ?
5. 你要我們空運到你倉庫嗎？
   Do you want us to airmail them to your warehouse?
6. 我們會向你們公司收取修理費。
   There will be a charge for our repair service to your company.
7. 請於下次付款時扣除金額。
   Please deduct the amount from the next payment.
8. 我們會請技師拍一段影片放到 You Tube 供你們參考。
   We will have a video made by our technician and put it on You Tube for your reference.

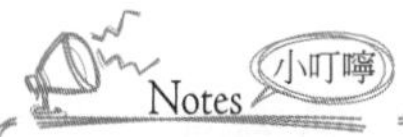

因爲國際貿易的退換貨有許多作業程序，最重要的是商譽（reputation）問題，生產時的品質把關才是避免麻煩的最要件。雙方處理時會按照合約條件做爲依據，因此有詳盡的條款雙方才知道該怎麼處理。如果客戶可以自行解決問題，供應商理當樂意協助，並從下次交易扣款，在認定瑕疵部分要能退讓一步，並進行品質改善，才能在客戶自行解決問題後，還願意與你再做生意。

10.9 客戶要求技術支援 Client Requesting Technical Support

10.9a 技術團隊 Tech Team

A: 哈囉，我是泰瑞莎陳。你是克特哈博嗎？

A: Hello. This is Teresa Chen. Is this Kurt Harper?

B: 是的，哈囉，泰瑞莎，你今天好嗎？

B: Yes, it is. Hello, Teresa. How are you today?

A: 好，克特，你呢？

A: Good. Kurt, and you?

B: 好，謝謝你上星期二給我們回覆，我們感謝你的迅速服務。

B: Just fine. Thanks for getting back to us last Tuesday. We appreciate the prompt service.

A: 沒問題，我的榮幸。

A: No problem. My pleasure.

B: 我有個問題要跟你談。

B: I have a problem I need to talk to you about.

A: 我明白了，是什麼？

A: I see. What is it?

B: 我們得知在安裝之後我們沒有操作設備的專門技術，我們需要談談從你們那裡弄來一組技術團隊來做額外訓練。

B: It's been realized that we do not have the technical expertise to operate the equipment after installation. We need to talk about getting a tech team from you for additional training.

A: 我想那可以辦得到，但是會增加成本。

A: I'm sure that can be done, but it will add cost.

B: 是，那個我也需要跟你談。

B: Yes. That I also need to talk to you about.

prompt [prɑmpt] adj. 迅速的
expertise [ˌɛkspɚ'tiz] n. 專門技術或知識
additional [ə'dɪʃənl̩] adj. 額外的

1. 我們感謝你的迅速服務。

   We appreciate the prompt service.

2. 我們需要你們的一組技術團隊來做額外訓練。

   We need to get a tech team from you for additional training.

3. 我想那可以辦得到。

   I'm sure that can be done.

4. 那會增加成本。

   It will add cost.

10.9b 討論可行性與成本 Discussing Execution and Cost

A: 你認為你們需要技術小組多久？	**A:** How long do you think you will need a tech team for?
B: 最好是一個月。	**B:** Ideally a month.
A: 你想你們會需要多少人？	**A:** How many people do you think you'll need?
B: 我們認為要 6 個人。	**B:** We think six.
A: 我要估計一下這個成本。	**A:** I'll have to estimate costs for this.

B: 我們心裡有一個估價。	**B:** We have a price in mind.
A: 真的？你可以告訴我是多少？	**A:** Really? Can you tell me what it is?
B: 是的，我被授權這麼做，是75,000元。	**B:** Yes. I'm authorized to do so. It's $75,000.
A: 好，這讓我可以做點事，今天我可以晚點給你回覆。	**A:** Good. This gives me something to work with. I'll get back to you later today.
B: 好，晚點談。	**B:** Great. Talk to you later.
A: 好，再見。	**A:** Right. Bye.

ideally [aɪ'diəlɪ] adv. 最好地，理想地
estimate ['ɛstəˌmet] v. 估計

1. 你們需要技術小組多久？
   How long will you need a tech team for?
2. 我要估計一下這個成本。
   I'll have to estimate costs for this.

3. 我們心裡有一個估價。

We have a price in mind.

4. 我被授權這麼做。

I'm authorized to do so.

5. 這可以讓我做點事。

This gives me something to work with.

為了生存，現在的公司必須提供好的產品與迅速的服務，買方有可能無法預知是否有操作設備的專門技術，因此賣方提供技術團隊來做額外訓練，也可能是買方期待的，賣方必須有此認知，並將成本問題列入考慮。

10.10 確認退款 Verifying a Refund

A: 嗨，泰瑞莎，我是TYN公司的約翰懷特，你今天好嗎？	**A:** Hi, Teresa, this is John White from TYN Company. How are you today?
B: 還可以，今天能幫你做什麼？	**B:** Just fine, John. What can I do for you today?
A: 我是為了一筆預計你們公司的退款打來的。	**A:** I'm calling about a refund that we are expecting from your company.
B: 我明白了，我幫你轉給會計部，他們會幫你。	**B:** I see. I'll transfer you to accounting. They'll be able to help you with this.

A: 好，謝謝。

A: OK. Thanks.

B: 沒問題。

B: No problem.

（轉接電話 Transferring call）

A: 哈囉，懷特先生，這裡是莎拉張，我被告知你打來是為了一筆預計的退款。

A: Hello, Mr. White. This is Sara Chang speaking. I've been told you are calling about a refund you are expecting.

B: 是的，是為了訂單 827G。

B: That's correct. For order number 827G.

A: 好，我們的紀錄顯示這筆退款今天早上已從我們的銀行轉到你公司帳戶。

A: All right. Our records show that the refund was transferred through our bank to your company's account this morning.

B: 我明白了，我猜是還沒入帳紀錄。我會打電話給我們的銀行確認。

B: I see. It has not been recorded yet I guess. I'll call our bank and confirm this.

A: 好主意，如果有任何問題，直接打電話給我，我分機是 235，我的名字是莎拉張。

A: Good idea. If there is any problem, call me directly. My extension is 235. Again, my name is Sara Chang.

B: 謝謝你，莎拉。我會確認，再次謝謝你，再見。

B: Thank you, Sara. I'll check it out. Thanks again. Bye.

A: 樂意服務，再見。

A: My pleasure. Bye for now.

refund ['rɪfʌnd] n. 退款
transfer [træns'fɝ] v. 轉帳，轉接
extension [ɪk'stɛnʃən] n. 分機

1. 我是為了一筆預計你們公司的退款打來的。
   I'm calling about a refund that we are expecting from your company.
2. 今天早上退款已從我們的銀行轉到你公司帳戶。
   The refund was transferred through our bank to your company's account this morning.
3. 我猜是還沒有入帳紀錄。
   It has not been recorded yet I guess.
4. 樂意服務。
   My pleasure.

Notes
小叮嚀

做好紀錄歸檔說來簡單，但失誤混淆卻經常發生，忙碌時單據遺失，送錯貨物，各種料想不到的延誤、閃失或物料人力技術等計算錯誤，不勝枚舉。將最基本的紀錄做好是預防措施的第一步。

I'm calling about a refund that we are expecting from your company.

Accounting

I See. I'll transfer you to accounting. They'll be able to help you with this.

Unit 11 Handling Crises

危機處理

企業經營將本求利風險無所不在，公司要能自保必須進行風險管理（risk management），使公司在可行範圍內迴避風險，預防風險或轉移風險才可能遠離風險。相對地，企業對於發生機率小，損失程度低的風險，可能選擇承擔。最怕的是因僥倖失算而被迫承受無法負擔的風險。採取法律行動追討欠款可說是公司經營最怕碰到的麻煩事，一開始就避免被欠款可說是公司追求利潤及永續經營的重要原則。

11.1欠缺人工
Lack of Labor

A: 嗨，萊瑞，我打來是因為你們的訂單，我們碰到生產問題。	**A:** Hi, Larry. I'm calling about a production problem we are having with your order.
B: 是什麼問題？	**B:** What's the problem?
A: 我們沒有足夠人工來準時完成工作，我們需要另外三星期。	**A:** We don't have enough workers to get the job done on time. We'll need an additional three weeks.
B: 真的，那對我們是個問題。我們很快就需要產品。	**B:** Really? That's a problem for us. We need the products soon.
A: 我們現在可以運出已完成的產品，並且會付額外的運費。	**A:** We can ship what we have finished now, and we'll pay for any additional shipping costs.
B: 我跟經理談話後，今天再打電話給你。	**B:** I'll talk to my manager and get back to you today.
A: 好，我會等你電話。	**A:** All right. I'll wait for your call.
B: 好，再見。	**B:** OK. Bye.

A: 再見。	**A:** Goodbye.

1. 我打來是因為你們的訂單，我們碰到生產問題。
   I'm calling about a production problem we are having with your order.
2. 我們沒有足夠人工來準時完成工作。
   We don't have enough workers to get the job done on time.
3. 我們需要另外三星期。
   We'll need an additional three weeks.
4. 我們現在可以運出已完成的產品，並且會付額外的運費。
   We can ship what we have finished now, and we'll pay for any additional shipping costs.

問題無法解決，必須報告客戶。分批交貨的結果多出的運保費、通關費等成本不僅足以造成血本無歸，連帶影響商譽造成客戶流失，必須謹慎以對。

11.2 罷工 On Strike

A: 哈囉，史丹，這是LH 集團的泰瑞莎陳。	**A:** Hello, Stan. This is Teresa Chen of LH Group.
B: 嗨，泰瑞莎，我今天可以為你做什麼？	**B:** Hi, Teresa. What can I do for you?

A: 我恐怕有壞消息。我們的工人出外去罷工了。	A: I'm afraid I have some bad news. Our workers have gone out on strike.
B: 我明白了，這真糟糕，你所有的生產設施都受影響嗎？	B: I see. That is bad. Are all of your production facilities affected?
A: 是的，我們不知道會持續多久。	A: Yes. We don't know how long this will go on.
B: 好，我會聯絡我主要的辦公室，告訴他們現況。	B: OK. I'll contact my main office and tell them what's going on.
A: 好。	A: Right.
B: 我們必須要談一談這個訂單的合約。	B: We'll have to have a conversation about the contract for this order.
A: 好，我了解。	A: Yes. I understand.
B: 我很快會打給你。	B: I'll call you back soon.
A: 好，晚點聊。	A: Right. Talk later.
B: 好，再見。	B: OK. Bye.

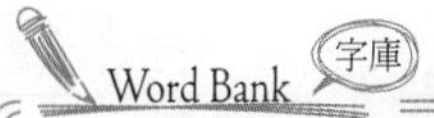

strike [straɪk] n. 罷工
facilities [fə'sɪlətɪz] n. 設施（複數）
affect [ə'fɛkt] v. 影響

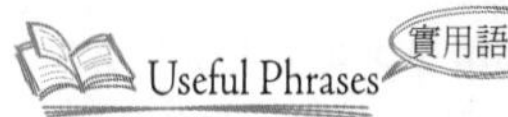

1. 我們的工人出外去罷工了。

   Our workers have gone out on strike.

2. 你所有的生產設施都受影響嗎？

   Are all of your production facilities affected?

3. 我們不知道會持續多久。

   We don't know how long this will go on.

4. 我們必須要談一談這個訂單的合約。

   We'll have to have a conversation about the contract agreements for this order.

發生緊急情況時，應該誠實告訴客人以免延誤他的生意，並先找出合約或購貨發票（purchase invoice, PI）條文關於延遲出貨的賠償。因爲缺工缺料的情況難以預期，如需分批出貨，勢必產生運費相關損失。若能尋求買方同意延期交貨，務必守信，保持商譽。

11.3 成本急升
Cost Soaring

（電話中 on the phone）

A: 哈囉，伍德先生，我打來通知你我們的生產停滯了。

A: Hello, Mr. Wood, I'm calling to inform that our production is running into a stall.

B: 怎麼了，泰瑞莎？

B: What happened, Teresa?

A: 我幾個月前跟你提過關於鐵價上漲。

A: I've mentioned to you a few months ago about the soaring iron price.

B: 對。

B: Yes.

A: 價格已經多出過去三個月的 50%，我們的生產也已經被鐵料短缺影響。我們已經完成你訂單的 1/3，如果你同意支付影響你訂單的昂貴鐵料成本，我們就可以儘快再投入生產。

A: The price has gone up 50% in the past three months. Our production has been affected because of the iron shortage, too. We have finished about 1/3 of your order, and we can go back into production again as soon as you agree to cover the expensive iron price affecting the cost of your order.

B: 那真是壞消息，但我們已經簽了合約。

B: That's really bad news, but we have signed our contract.

A: 伍德先生，合約也說如果材料上漲等於或超過 25%的話，買方負責支付多餘的成本，我們確定你注意到最近鐵價的飛漲。

A: Mr. Wood, it is also stated in the contract that it is the buyer's responsibility to cover the additional cost when the material price goes up equal or over 25%. We are sure you noticed the soaring price of iron recently.

B: 嗯。

B: Um.

A: 我們為了買昂貴的鐵料製作你的產品已經慘賠。沒有你平分成本，我們無法完成你的訂單。

A: We are actually losing our shirt for buying expensive iron to make your products. Without your fair share of the cost, we cannot finish your order.

B: 你在開玩笑？ 我確定你可以處理情況。

B: Are you joking? I'm sure you can handle the situation.

A: 不，我們是認真的，伍德先生。如果你提供鐵料所需的成本，我們可以解決問題，鐵料一進來就馬上再開始生產。

A: No, we are serious, Mr. Wood. We'll solve the problem if you provide the money to cover the cost of the iron. We can restart the production as soon as it comes in.

B: 嗯，我明白你的意思，成本飛漲我很難賣產品！

B: Um, I got your point now. It will be hard for me to sell the products because of the increasing cost!

A: 伍德先生，你寧可取消交易嗎？

A: Mr. Wood, would you rather call the deal off?

B: 我需要想出我現在真正面對的問題是什麼，你要我分攤多少成本？

B: I need to figure out what problem exactly I'm facing. How much do you want me to share the cost?

A: 25%，如果我們在 3 天內購買的話，但是鐵料運送加上完成生產會多出一個月。

A: 25% , if we buy iron in three days. But getting the iron delivered and finishing the production will probably take one more month.

B: 所以增加成本還會拖延出貨？我不認為可以接受！

B: So increasing cost plus delayed shipment? I don't think it is acceptable!

A: 好，伍德先生，如果你分擔 20%多出的成本，並且接受多 30 天再出貨，我們可以完成。如果不行，我們必須取消交易，將來有機會再與你合作。

A: OK, Mr. Wood. If you share 20% of the additional cost and accept additional 30 days before shipment, we will make it. If not, we will have to call it off and look for the next opportunity to work with you.

B: 那變動後到底成本跟出貨日期為何？

B: So what exactly would be the cost and the shipment date after the change?

A: 單價會從2.00元變成2.40元，出貨日期會從6月15日變成7月15日。

A: The unit price will go from $2.00 to $2.40, the shipment date from June 15 to July 15.

B: 我知道了，我要想一想再回覆你。

B: I got it. I'll have to think and get back to you later.

A: 好，謝謝你的體諒，我們晚點再談。再見。

A: OK. Thanks for your understanding. We'll talk later. Bye.

stall [stɔl] n. 停滯
losing one's shirt 慘賠
fair share 平分
call off 取消
acceptable [ək'sɛptəbḷ, æk-] adj. 可接受的

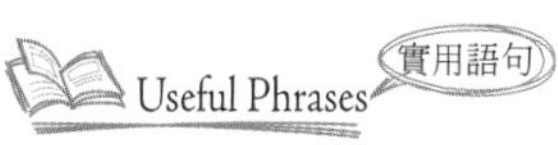

1. 我打來通知你我們的生產停滯了。
   I'm calling to inform that our production is running into a stall.
2. 價格已經多出過去三個月的 50%。
   The price has gone up 50% in the past three months.
3. 我們的生產已被鐵料短缺影響。
   Our production has been affected because of the iron shortage.
4. 如果材料上漲等於或超過 25%的話，買方負責支付多餘的成本。
   It is the buyer's responsibility to cover the additional cost when the material price goes up equal or over 25% .

5. 沒有你平分成本，我們無法完成你的訂單。

Without your fair share of the cost, we cannot finish your order.

6. 你寧可取消交易嗎？

Would you rather call the deal off?

7. 如果不行，我們必須取消交易。

If not, we will have to call it off.

如果合約載明成本上升的處理，就能保障自己。但是否能在合約載明，仍關乎買賣爲何方市場。

11.4 匯率劇烈變化 Exchange Rate Dramatic Change

A: 瓊斯先生，我是 LH 集團的泰瑞莎，我打來跟你討論我們對於劇烈匯率變化的分擔。

A: Mr. Jones. This is Teresa of LH Group. I'm calling to discuss our sharing on the drastic exchange rate.

B: 為什麼？

B: Why?

A: 我們契約上同意如果匯率波動劇烈的話要分擔成本，我相信你注意到最近新臺幣的升值。

A: We have agreed contractually to share the cost if exchange rates change drastically. I'm sure you have noticed the recent appreciation of the NT.

B: 嗯，我查看看。

B: Um, let me check.

A: 第二頁，第 3 條說當美金 1 元價值少於 30 元新臺幣時，買方會支付一半的損失。

A: On Page 2, Clause No. 3 says when 1 US dollar is worth less than 30 NT. The buyer will cover half of the loss.

B: 那你要我怎麼做？

B: So what do you want me to do?

A: 我們的交易是 240,000 元。今天美元兌新臺幣是 1:29，這交易使我們短收 24 萬臺幣，以今天匯率換算為 8275.86 元，你分攤一半我們的損失，也就是 4137.93 元。

A: Our deal is $240, 000. The US/NT exchange rate today is 1:29. We are paid $240,000 NT short from this deal. That is $8275.86 by today's rate. You share half of our lost. That is $4137.93.

B: 我明白了。	**B:** I see.
A: 我們明天會電郵給你正確的明細讓你確認。	**A:** We will email the correct statement to you tomorrow for your confirmation.
B: 好。	**B:** OK.

exchange rate 匯率
contractually [kən'træktʃuəlɪ] adv. 於契約上
drastically ['dræstɪkəlɪ] adv. 劇烈地
appreciation [əˌpriʃɪ'eʃən] n. 升值
clause [klɔz] n. 條款
statement ['stetmənt] n. 明細

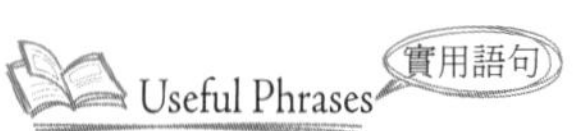

1. 我們契約上同意如果匯率波動劇烈的話要分擔成本。

   We have agreed contractually to share the cost of the exchange rate if it changes drastically.

2. 我相信你注意到最近新臺幣的升值。

   I'm sure you have noticed the recent appreciation of the NT.

3. 這交易使我們短收 24 萬臺幣。

   We are paid $240,000 NT short from this deal.

匯率影響進貨成本及競爭力，如能於合約載明匯率及震盪達 __%由雙方分擔，至少能將此風險減半。（例如：本報價以 1 美元兌換 30 元新臺幣為基準。如果匯率變動等於或超過 __%，我們保留匯率相關價格調漲的權利。The quotation is based on $1: NT30 exchange rate. We reserve the right to pass on exchange-rate related price increases should the exchange rate fluctuation equal or exceed __%.）

11.5 客戶要求整批退貨—安全問題 Client Asking for Returning the Order - Safety Issue

A: 哈囉，這裡是崔佛斯邦納，我要跟泰瑞莎說話。

A: Hello, This is Travis Burner. I'd like to speak to Teresa Chen, please.

B: 我就是。哈囉，邦納先生，你收到貨了嗎？

B: This is she. Hello, Mr. Burner. Have your received the shipment?

A: 嗨，泰瑞莎，我們上週收到腳踏車架了，並且檢查了 20 件產品。因為有問題，我們沒有辦法接受這批貨。

A: Hi, Teresa, we have received the bike stands shipment last week and have checked over 20 pieces. We cannot accept the shipment because there are problems.

B: 有何問題？

B: What problems?

A: 包裝不夠堅實，所以產品損壞了。還有噴漆刮到了，焊接不到位，組裝有安全疑慮。我們無法賣出產品，因為本季無產品可賣，我們將要蒙受巨大銷售損失。

A: The packing box is not strong, so the products are damaged. Also, the paint is scratched. The welding is improper, and the assembly has a safety concern. We cannot sell the products. We are going to lose a lot of sales because we have no products to sell in this season.

B: 你可以寄給我檢查影帶、照片及檢查報告嗎？ 我們看看接下來怎麼辦。

B: Can you send me an inspection video, photos, and the inspection report? Let's see what we can do next.

Dialog 2 對話2

A: 我們收到錄影了，我們可以寄零件讓你修理嗎？

A: We have received the video. Can we send some spare parts for you to fix the products?

B: 不，你瘋了嗎？這產品有安全問題可是會讓我坐牢的！

B: No, have you lost your mind? The products will put me into jail because of the safety problem!

A: 邦納先生，你公司希望我們如何處理這個問題讓彼此損失最少？

A: Mr. Burner, how would you like us to handle this problem and let us reduce the loss to the minimum?

B: 我們決定要退回這四個櫃子的貨，你們要儘快重新生產這四個櫃子，並且空運其中一個櫃子給我們檢查，然後鋪貨上市。

B: We have decided to return the four containers of goods, and you should reproduce them and airmail one of the containers first for us to inspect, then put on the market.

A: 可以給我一天的時間，我要先在公司開會提出你的案子，隔天回報給你。

A: Please allow one day for me to report your case in our company meeting first. I will get back to you the day after.

B: 好。

B: OK.

scratched [ˌskrætʃt] adj. 刮傷的
welding [wɛldɪŋ] n. 焊接
improper [ɪm'prɑpɚ] adj. 不適當的
assembly [ə'sɛmblɪ] n. 組裝
concern [kən'sɝn] n. 疑慮
inspection report 檢查報告
container [kən'tenɚ] n. 貨櫃

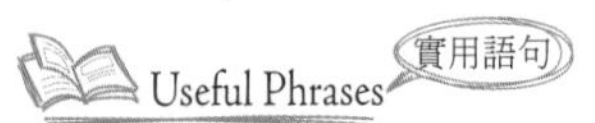

1. 噴漆刮到了。

   The paint is scratched.

2. 焊接不到位。

   The welding is improper.

3. 組裝有安全疑慮。

   The assembly has a safety concern.

4. 我們將要蒙受巨大銷售損失。

   We are going to lose a lot of sales.

5. 我們本季無產品可賣。

   We have no products to sell in this season.

6. 我們可以寄零件讓你修理嗎？

   Can we send some spare parts for you to fix the products?

7. 你公司希望我們如何處理這個問題讓彼此損失最少？

   How would you like us to handle this problem to reduce the loss to the minimum?

8. 我要先在公司開會時提出你的案子。

   I need to report your case in our company meeting first.

退貨牽扯到龐大的金錢、運費與時間成本，小規模的供應商甚至沒有能力解決，所以後續處理非同小可。

11.6 危機處理─搶修問題產品 Handling Crisis - Instant Repair for Problems

A: 嗨，這裡是客服中心，我可以幫你嗎？	A: Hi. This is customer service. May I help you?

B: 是的，我們向你們買了產品，並且產品有些問題。

B: Yes. We purchased products from you, and they have some problems.

A: 產品何時送到的？

A: When did you take delivery?

B: 三個月前。

B: Three months ago.

A: 我們的產品都有保固。

A: Our products are all covered by warranty.

B: 是，我知道，但是我們需要技術服務人員幫我們。

B: Yes, I know, but we'll need technical service people to help us.

A: 現在情形如何？

A: What is the situation right now?

B: 我們的生產進度現在已經被延誤了。

B: Our production schedule is being affected right now.

A: 你可以給我訂單號碼嗎？

A: Can you give me the order number?

B: 可以，合約號碼是S-09013583。

B: Yes. It's contract number S-09013583.

A: 好，我查看我們的紀錄。你可以在線上等嗎？

A: OK. Let me check our records. Can you hold?

B: 可以。 → **B:** Yes, I can.

A: 謝謝。 → **A:** Thank you.

Dialog 2 對話2

（等待中 waiting on line）

A: 哈囉，你還在線上嗎？

A: Hello. Are you still there?

B: 是的。

B: Yes, I am.

A: 很好，我這裡有紀錄，並且我要請你跟我們的工程組人員談話。

A: Great. I have the records here, and I'm going to have you talk to someone on our engineering team.

B: 很好，謝謝。

B: Fine, thank you.

A: 我現在為你轉接。

A: I'm transferring you now.

B: 謝謝。

B: Thank you.

（轉接電話 Transferring call）

（與工程部門對話 Talking to the Engineering Department）

A: 哈囉，這裡是工程部的珍妮唐。	**A:** Hello. This is Jenny Tang from Engineering.
B: 我是艾文莫菲。	**B:** I'm Evan Murphy.
A: 嗨，莫菲先生，我被告知你的公司最近向我們買的設備有一些問題。	**A:** Hi, Mr. Murphy. I've been told your company is having some problems with equipment you bought from us recently.
A: 是的，沒錯。	**A:** Yes, that's right.
B: 你可以告訴我你們現在有哪種問題？	**B:** Can you tell me what kind of problem you are having?
A: 是，我們買的設備，由你們公司裝設，無法與我們的生產線同步。	**A:** Yes. The equipment that we bought, and had your company install, is not operating in sync with our production line.
B: 我知道了，我們需要馬上派人去。	**B:** I see. We'll need to send somebody there immediately.
A: 是的，那正是我們需要的。	**A:** Yes. That is what we need.

B: 我會問你一些細節後，立刻安排派去兩位技術工程師。

B: I'll get a few more details from you, and I'll arrange to have a couple of tech engineers sent there right away.

A: 好。

A: That sounds good.

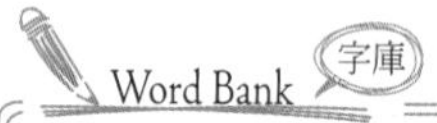

warranty **['wɔrəntɪ]** n. 保固
affect **[ə'fɛkt]** v. 影響
sync(synchronization)**['sɪŋk]** n. 同步

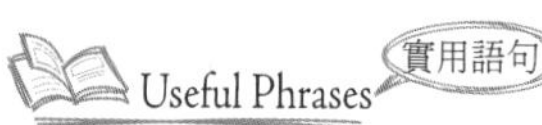

1. 我們向你們買了產品，並且產品有些問題。
   We purchased products from you, and they have some problems.
2. 產品何時送到的？
   When did you take delivery?
3. 我們的產品都有保固。
   Our products are all covered by warranty.
4. 現在情形如何？
   What is the situation right now?
5. 我們的生產進度現在已經被延誤了。
   Our production schedule is being affected right now.
6. 你可以給我訂單號碼嗎？
   Can you give me the order number?
7. 你可以在線上等嗎？
   Can you hold?
8. 你可以告訴我你們現在有哪種問題？
   Can you tell me what kind of problem you are having?

9. 設備無法與我們的生產線同步。

The equipment is not operating in sync with our production line.

10. 我會立刻派工程師過去。

I'll have engineers sent there right away.

11. 那正是我們需要的。

That is what we need.

基於業務需求，需要錄音的話，務必事先取得對方同意。例如：

我可以將有關於我們的談話錄音紀錄嗎？

A: May I record this conversation for purposes pertaining to our records?

好，可以。/我必須先問我的主管。

B: Yes, that's alright./I would have to ask my supervisor first.

無論如何，談話後發一封郵件確認內容，做爲雙方紀錄絕對有必要。

11.7 危機處理—工廠倒閉 Handling Crisis - Manufacturer Gone Bankrupt

A: 傑瑞，我剛才發現 GDQ 公司破產了。	**A:** Jerry, I just found out that GDQ Corporation went bankrupt.
B: 什麼？！真的嗎？	**B:** What?! Really?

A: 對，他們也向我們下了大訂單。

A: Yes. They put a big order in with us, too.

B: 那個訂單他們有付我們錢了嗎？

B: Have they paid us anything for that order?

A: 是的，付了 15%。

A: Yes. 15% down.

B: 我會打給約翰告訴他。

B: I'll call John and tell him.

A: 好，讓我知道接下來該怎麼辦。

A: OK. Let me know what to do next.

B: 我會的。

B: I will.

Dialog 2 對話2

A: 嗨，約翰，你找到什麼嗎？

A: Hi, John. What did you find out?

B: GDQ 沒有人接電話。關於這個（倒閉）問題，我已經打給我們的法務部了。

B: Nobody is answering the phone at GDQ. I've contacted our legal department about this problem.

A: 他們怎麼說？	**A:** What did they say?
B: 我們要等他們找到些東西再說。	**B:** We'll have to wait until they find something out.
A: 好。	**A:** OK.

bankrupt ['bæŋkrʌpt] adj. 破產的
legal department 法務部

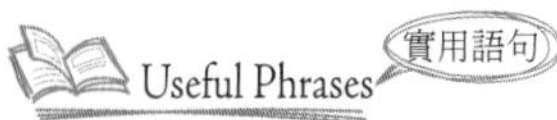

1. 他們也向我們下了大訂單。
   They put a big order in with us, too.
2. 他們那個訂單付錢了嗎？
   Have they paid anything for that order?
3. 付了 15%。
   Pay 15% down.
4. 關於這個問題，我已經打給我們的法務部了。
   I've contacted our legal department about this problem.
5. 我們要等他們找到些東西再說。
   We'll have to wait until they find something out.
6. 讓我知道接下來該怎麼辦。
   Let me know what to do next.

公司一旦破產，幾乎聯絡也很困難，事先的法律準備在這時就變得很重要，準備完善才能幫助回覆或賠償遭受的損失。

11.8 危機處理—分擔損失及處理客戶要求大筆理賠 Handling Crisis - Sharing Costs and Handling a Large Claim by a Client

A: 灰石工程，我可以幫你嗎？	**A:** Greystone Engineering. May I help you?
B: 我需要立刻跟人談一個很大的問題。	**B:** I need to speak to someone immediately about a major problem.
A: 是哪方面的問題？	**A:** What type of problem is it?
B: 我們向你們公司購買的新的安裝設備不能用。	**B:** Newly installed equipment we bought from your company is not working.
A: 我了解了，我幫你接到工程部門。	**A:** I see. Let me connect you with engineering.
B: 謝謝。	**B:** Thank you.

（一週後 a week later）

A: 嗨，馬特，請坐下。

A: Hi, Matt. Please sit down.

B: 多謝。

B: Thanks.

A: 我們查了這個事件全部的成本跟損失數字，我們承認你們的公司損失是因為我們錯誤的安裝所造成。

A: We've looked over the total cost and loss figures from this incident. We acknowledge that your company lost money due to the problems caused by our faulty equipment installation.

B: 好。

B: OK.

A: 我們當然會付修理費，但我們必須就銷售損失賠償繼續溝通。

A: We'll pay for all the repairs of course, but we will have to continue negotiations about lost sales compensation.

B: 我明白了，我們有一個銷售收益損失的成本估算，在這邊。

A: I see. We have a cost estimate on lost sales revenue. Here it is.

A: 好，我會拿給我的主管們看看他們怎麼說，然後打電話給你。

A: OK. I'll take it to my higher ups and see what they say. Then, I'll call you.

B: 好，大概需要多久時間？	**B:** All right, but how long will that take?
A: 你應該明天會接到我消息。	**A:** You should hear from me tomorrow.
B: 聽起來很好，我現在要去別的會議了。	**B:** Sounds good. I've got to go to another meeting now.
A: 好，我帶你出去。	**A:** Right. Let me show you out.
B: 謝謝。	**B:** Thanks.

Word Bank 字庫

acknowledge [ək'nɑlɪdʒ] v. 承認
lost sales compensation 銷售損失賠償
cost estimate 成本估算
lost sales revenue 銷售收益損失

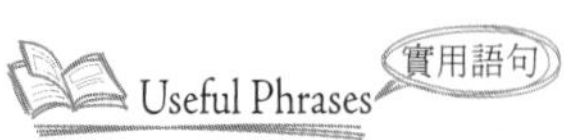

1. 我們當然會付修理費。

   We'll pay for all the repairs of course.

2. 我們必須就損失銷售賠償繼續溝通。

   We will have to continue negotiations about lost sales compensation.

3. 我們有一個銷售損失的成本估算。

We have a cost estimate on lost sales revenue.

11.9 催帳—接受延遲付款條件 Pressing for Late Payments - Accepting Terms for Overdue Payments

11.9a 催帳 Pressing for Late Payments

（電話中 on the Phone）

A: 哈囉，妥盼公司，我如何幫你？

A: Hello. Tollpan Company. How may I help you?

B: 哈囉，我是鮑伯陳，我替 LH 集團打來，我需要跟你們財務部的人說話。

B: Hello. I'm Bob Chen. I'm calling for LH Group. I need to talk to someone in your Finance Department.

A: 我為你轉接。

A: I'll connect you.

B: 謝謝。

B: Thank you.

（電話中 on the phone）

A: 哈囉，我是珍哈特曼。

A: Hello. I'm Jane Hartman.

B: 嗨，珍，我是鮑伯陳，替 LH 集團打電話來。我想要跟你談付款過期的事。

B: Hi, Jane. I'm Bob Chen calling for LH Group. I want to talk to you about late payments.

A: 是，我了解。我知道我們付你們公司的款項延遲了。

A: Yes, I understand. I'm aware that we are behind on payments to your company.

B: 我要跟你們談一個新的付款時程。

B: I'd like to talk to you about a new payment schedule.

A: 好，我可以談。

A: OK. I can do that.

B: 好，或許你可以提供一些你公司財務狀況的消息。

B: Good. Perhaps you can give some information about your company's financial situation.

A: 是，呃，我們承受（經濟）衰退嚴重打擊，但我們已經在逐漸地復甦中。

A: Yes. Well, we have been hit by the recession pretty hard, but we have been recovering slowly.

B: 聽起來很好，你認為你可以開始繼續付給我們款項嗎？	**B:** That's good to hear. Do you think you can start making payments to us again?
A: 是，但是我想跟你談最近半年減少我們每月必須支付的金額。	**A:** Yes, but, I'd like to talk to you about reducing the amount we must pay every month for the next half a year.
B: 好，我們可以談。	**B:** Sure. I can talk to you about that.

finance department 財務部門
recession [rɪ'sɛʃən] n. 衰退
recover [rɪ'kʌvɚ] v. 復甦

1. 我替 LH 集團打來。
   I'm calling for LH Group.
2. 我需要跟你們財務部的人說話。
   I need to talk to someone in your Finance Department.
3. 我想要跟你談逾期付款的事。
   I want to talk to you about late payments.
4. 我們需儘快收款。
   We need payment soon.
5. 我要跟你們談一個新的付款時程。
   I'd like to talk to you about a new payment schedule.
6. 我們承受經濟衰退嚴重打擊。
   We have been hit by the recession pretty hard.

7. 我們已經在逐漸地復甦中。

   We have been recovering slowly.

8. 你可以再度開始付款給我們嗎？

   Can you start making payments to us again?

9. 我想跟你談減少支付的金額。

   I'd like to talk to you about reducing the amount.

11.9b 取得共識 Reaching an Agreement

A: 看來我們取得共識。	**A:** It sounds like we have an agreement.
B: 是的。	**B:** Yes, we do.
A: 我們的公司未來六個月內的每月付款將比原本款項少繳35%。	**A:** Our company will make monthly payments that are 35% less than originally agreed for the next six months.
B: 是，沒錯，之後你會開始付最初同意之原本金額。	**B:** Yes, that is right. After that, you will start paying the original amount agreed upon at the start.
A: 同意，我們雙方的法務部會看過這個新協議，如果沒有問題就簽名。	**A:** Agreed. Our legal departments will both go over this new agreement, and if there are no problems, it will be signed.
B: 我想那需要一個禮拜。	**B:** I think all that will take one week.

A: 聽起來很合理。	**A:** That sounds reasonable to me.
B: 不久我就會打電話給你，確認進展良好。	**B:** I'll call you again soon to make sure everything is moving ahead well.
A: 好，謝謝。	**A:** Great. Thanks.
B: 好，再見。	**B:** OK. Bye.

monthly payment 月付款

1. 我們取得共識。
   We have an agreement.
2. 我們月付款少繳 35%。
   We will make monthly payments that are 35% less.
3. 之後你會開始付原本的金額。
   After that, you will start paying the original amount.
4. 聽起來很合理。
   That sounds reasonable to me.

一旦過了付款期，賣方初期催帳給買方時間通融時，請買方開出賣方「無過失證明」（no fault certification），若買方遲未付款，賣方則開出買方「欠款通知書」（notification of overdue accounts）。有了這兩個有效法律文件，即可展開私下（請收帳公司）或依法律途徑追討欠款。

11.10 催帳—催討嚴重過期債務 Pressing for Late Payments - Pressing for Seriously Overdue Payments

（電話中 on the phone）

A: BK 企業，我是艾琳，我如何幫你？	**A:** BK Enterprises. My name is Irene. How may I help you?
B: 我想跟財務長談話。	**B:** I'd like to talk to the chief financial officer (CFO).
A: 我要說誰打來呢？	**A:** Who should I say is calling?
B: LH 集團的鮑伯陳。	**B:** Bob Chen of LH Group.
A: 謝謝。我為你轉接，請等一下。	**A:** Thank you. I'll transfer you. Please hold.

B: 謝謝。

B: Thank you.

A: 哈囉，這是山姆湯普生。

A: Hello. This is Sam Thompson.

B: 嗨，山姆，我是鮑伯陳，你已經收到我昨天的催款電郵了吧？

B: Hi, Sam. I'm Bob Chen. Have you received my email about your overdue payment yesterday?

A: 有。

A: Yes, I have.

B: 我要跟你談這件事。

B: I need to talk about it with you.

A: 我了解。

A: I see.

B: 合約規定出貨後 90 天你就該付款，現在已經過了 30 天。我們已經等你付款等了一個月。

B: Your payment was due 90 days after shipment according to our contract. It's 30 days overdue now. We've been waiting for your payment for one month already.

A: 我了解，我知道有問題。

A: I understand. I know there is a problem.

B: 我們寄給你存證信函後，你也同意付款，但你還是沒付。我們不要再度協商支付款項，只要你們現在就付款。

B: After we sent you a legal attest letter, you agreed to pay, but you still have not made any payment. We don't want to renegotiate your payments. We just want you to make payment now.

A: 我們需要更多時間。

A: We need more time.

B: 請聽好，如果我們沒有在下週末前收到你們的款項，我們將立刻提出法律行動。

B: Listen. If we do not receive your payment by the end of next week, we'll take legal action immediately.

A: 我了解。

A: I understand.

B: 我們期待在這最後一通電話後，收到你的付款，再見。

B: We expect to receive your payment after this final call. Goodbye.

chief financial officer (CFO) 財務長
legal attest letter 存證信函
renegotiate [ˌrɪnɪ'goʃɪˌet] v. 再度協商
legal action 法律行動

1. 請等一下。

   Please hold.

2. 我們不要再度協商支付款項。

   We don't want to renegotiate your payments.

3. 我們只要你們馬上付款。

   We just want you to make your payment now.

4. 我們期待在這最後一通電話後，收到你的付款。

   We expect to receive your payment after this final call.

5. 如果我們沒有在下週末前收到你們的款項，我們馬上提出法律行動。

   If we do not receive your payment by the end of next week, we'll take legal action immediately.

雙方僅憑合約，在賣方出貨一定期限後（如 30/60/90 天後），買方才付款的賒帳交易（open account, O/A），因無信用狀或銀行制約，賣方必須承受財務壓力及可能血本無歸的風險。欠款時間越久對賣方越不利，萬一被倒帳，跨海官司勞民傷財，無須贅述。更令人無奈的是不能自認倒楣而不提出告訴，因爲壞消息傳得特別快，姑息養奸只會讓其他經銷商或客戶有樣學樣，危及自己與同業。

買方在合約規定期限未付款，賣方於欠款通融期間要儘快拿到買方開出的「無過失證明」證明賣出的產品無瑕疵，之後即寄出買方「欠款通知書」，於初期（約 2-3 週）追討無效後，儘快寄出存證信函（1 週內），一旦過了最後期限，所委託之收帳公司（debt collection agency）或法律追討行動隨即展開。因此，企業將本求利之前必須先求自保，惟有一開始就做好風險管理不被欠款，才能免於被倒帳的結果。

Note

Unit 12 Business Letters

商業書信

無論買賣雙方使用英語的程度為何，商業口語表達無論是面對面或在電話上都要以簡潔清楚為目的。書信則扮演彌補口語溝通的功能，商業經營諸多事項，舉凡確認、補充、更改、修正等等細節皆須有憑有據，面對面或電話上談好的條件後，需以郵件雙方確認無誤作為紀錄。如果有錯誤、道歉、賠償等棘手問題的處理，即使處理程序相同，但好的書信會考慮客戶讀信的感受，讓人感受誠意消彌怒氣，進而保住客戶。不幸碰到客戶拖欠賴帳甚至必須採取法律行動等措施，當然也必須有完備書面依據才有可能進行。本章提供以上所列情境之商業書信樣本。

12.1 書信格式與關鍵 Letter Formats and Keys

形式及目的

商業書信為機構公司行號間或公司與客戶間的書信往來，因此較為正式，但其正式程度要看彼此間的關係而定。正式的商業書信多見於法律方面信件，如合約或備忘錄，須以郵遞寄送（postal mail）。以溝通訊息為主的書信現今多採方便快速，但形式上較不正式之電子郵件（email）。

如果書信的目的是道歉或邀請，紙本（選擇優良質材）及郵遞信函讓人感受正式及真誠，電郵方式雖及時便利但較不正式及欠缺真誠溫情。寄信者需考慮何者為重加以選擇。如果形式較時間重要，使用郵遞信件；如果時間較形式重要，則用電子郵件。但無論寄送形式或溝通目的為何，商業書信的語言都必須客觀（objective）。

書寫祕笈

1. 時間就是金錢，商業人士多快速閱讀信件，因此應當為收件人寫上信件主旨（畫底線），以幫助收信人馬上了解信件重點。然而，如果是法律行動信件，你要當事人仔細讀，則另當別論。
2. 一封信只說明一件事，除非特殊情形，長度以一頁為原則。按照書信對象及目的決定書寫語氣，過猶不及顯得太生疏或太不誠懇都不恰當。（如果寫的是開發信，那麼書信就是你給人的第一印象。請見 1.7 銷售信，1.8 網路平臺回覆。）
3. 以收信人感受為出發點寫信，而不是以自己角度出發，收信人才可能被你打動。
4. 好的書信多用肯定句，少用否定句。

   例如：If you don't reply by May 10, there won't be any arrangements.「如果你不在 5 月 10 日前回覆，將不會有任何安排。」

   改成 Please call us by May 10 to make proper arrangements.「請在 5 月 10 日前打電話給我們以作恰當安排。」同樣的事情，收信

人讀起來的感覺完全不同。

5. 多用主動，讓人覺得彼此在對話，感覺直接而誠實，少用被動，似在閃躲引人猜測。以下主被動例子很經典，時常被引用：

   Any inconvenience caused is deeply regretted. 因為使用被動，不知道是「誰」在「遺憾」（非道歉）。

   改成 We apologize for any inconvenience. 直接了當說出 we「我們」apologize「道歉」，做錯了事造成別人的困擾，至少明白道歉誠意十足，不拐彎抹角。

6. 如果是催討欠款的信，一定要為受信人解決問題，提出對受信人可行的方案，才可能達到預期的效果。

7. 好的商業書信內容一定要符合公認的「商業書信 6C 原則」（the 6 Cs of Business Writing）：

   (1)簡潔（conciseness）
   (2)明瞭（clarity）
   (3)完整（completeness）
   (4)正確（correctness）
   (5)具體（concreteness）
   (6)婉轉有禮（consideration/courtesy）

   如果能夠加上能鼓舞他人（cheerfulness）及展現機構品牌（個人）個性（character）的話，實屬難得。

正因商業書信被期待具備這些原則，所以要注重形式、文法、標點、開頭、結尾。寫完後務必校正無誤，確定是否合格（顯現專業）才能寄出。

12.2 郵遞信函 Postal Mail

郵遞信函

1-10 為必要項目，未編號者為附帶項目：

1. 信頭（letter head）

2. 日期（date）
   檔案編號 Ref. No.（reference number）
3. 收件人地址（inside address）
   特定對象關注（Attention）：對象，人名

4. 稱呼語（salutation）

5. 主旨（letter subject）

6. 內文（body）

7. 結尾詞（closing/complementary close）

8. 簽名（signature）
9. 姓名（printed name）
10. 職稱（title）
   （使用有信頭之信紙，不必再寫公司名稱 Company name）
   打字員名字縮寫（typist initials）
   附件 Enc.（enclosure）：附件名稱。
   副本 cc（carbon copy）：副本收件人姓名。
   後註 P.S.（postscript）

說明

❶ 必要項目

1. 信頭為印好之公司名稱、品牌標章、創立年份、聯絡資訊等。

2. 日期：正式信函，月份不要簡寫。可使用美式順序（月日年），如 August 15, 2013 或英式順序（日月年），日期慣用序數，如 15th August, 2013 注意年份前使用逗點。不要用數字 05082013 表示，日期容易混淆。

3. 收件人（姓名及職稱）地址：信內地址為歸檔用，有加上姓名職稱的話，地址位於其後。

4. 稱呼語：正式稱呼抬頭加姓名，如 Dear Mr. Jack Adams, Dear Ms. Helen Sallace, 使用 Ms.稱呼女士（不指涉其婚姻狀況），名字後使用逗點或分號皆可。未知確切姓名者，特定人可使用 Dear Sir or Madam, Dear Manager, 一群人可使用 Dear Sirs, Dear Ladies, Dear Gentlemen,（字首需大寫，Gentlemen 必用複數）。不正式稱呼，直接使用名字，如 Dear Jack, Dear Tina, 或 Hi, David, 稱呼語的名字務必檢查拼字無誤。

5. 主旨：畫底線使收信人馬上了解信件重點。

6. 內文：現今潮流使用版面向左對齊（fully blocked layout）而不內縮段頭，使用 Times New Roman（較傳統及正式）或 Arial 及 12 號字體，單行間距（除非信很短），段與段間空一行方便閱讀。每段落只有一個中心思想，控制句子及段落長度，段落不要太長，並且不要連續以單行作為一段。每段落長度有變化。為求簡潔明確，句子也不要太長，句子長度須有變化。正式書信不要使用縮寫（如 we'll 應寫成 we will）。

7. 結尾詞：如 Sincerely, Truly, Very truly, Sincerely yours, Yours sincerely, Warm regards, Best regards, Best wishes, 結尾使用逗點 ","。

8. 簽名（signature）：正式簽名字跡須具備姓及名，而非只有名字。

9. 姓名（printed name）

10. 職稱（title）

➔ ❷ 附帶項目

- 信件使用檔案編號 Ref. No.（reference number），置於日期下方。
- 希望特定對象關注 att./attn.（attention），置於信內地址下方。

- 打字員名字縮寫（typist initials），置於發信人姓名職稱機構下方。也可使用 ABC/xyz 方式表示（左方 ABC 為發信人名字縮寫，右方 xyz 為打字員名字縮寫）。
- 附件 Enc.（enclosure）：附件名稱。
- 副本 cc（carbon copy）：副本收件人姓名。
- 後註 P.S.（postscript），書信以一信一事原則，最好避免使用後註。

信件極短時應酌於調整位置，以求版面美觀。

信　封

寄信人姓名 Sender's Name
公司行號 Company Name
門牌號碼，街名 Street No., Name
城市，郵遞區號 City, Zip Code
國家 Country

（附件註明 Attachment）
郵寄等級 Class of Mail
（信件類別 Classification）

收信人姓名 Receiver's Name
門牌號碼，街名 Street No., Name
城市，郵遞區號 City, Zip Code
國家 Country

說明：

1. 信封：使用公司行號已印製地址及商標之信封。
2. 郵寄等級：如航空 airmail、限時 prompt delivery、掛號 registered、印刷品 printed matter。

其他：

附件註明：如照片 photos、色版 color swatch、目錄 catalog、發票 invoice 等。

信件類別：如商業文件 commercial papers、機密文件 confidential papers、贈送本 complimentary copy。

傳　真

網路發達後，傳真需求大減，如需使用，可製作傳真首頁（Fax Cover Sheet），使收發件資訊、日期及檔案編號一目了然，再將首頁及信件內容傳真。

FAX COVER SHEET（傳真首頁）

Company Name（公司名稱）

Contact Information（聯絡資訊）

（電話、傳真號碼、地址、電郵、網址等）

To（收件人）＿＿＿＿＿＿ Fax（傳真號碼）＿＿＿＿＿＿

cc（副本收件人）＿＿＿＿＿＿ Regarding（主旨）＿＿＿＿＿＿

Date（日期）＿＿＿＿＿＿ Ref. no.（檔案編號）＿＿＿＿＿＿

From（傳送人）＿＿＿＿＿＿ Fax（傳真號碼）＿＿＿＿＿＿

Phone（電話）＿＿＿＿＿＿ Email（電郵）＿＿＿＿＿＿

No. of pages(including this page) 頁數（含本頁）＿＿＿＿＿＿

□Urgent 急件　□Please reply 請回覆　□Please comment 請評註

□For review 請檢閱　□For your record 請留記錄

Notes 備註：

12.3 電子郵件
Email

項目：

收件者地址（destination email）
副本 cc（carbon copy）
主旨（subject）
[附件 Enc.（enclosure）
稱呼語（salutation/greeting）
內文（body of message）

結尾詞（complementary close/closing）

姓名（printed name）
職稱（title）
公司/機構名稱（company/institution name）

[後註 P.S.（postscript）]

說明

1. 電子郵件項目內容與信件相似，但日期及地址為電腦設定，無須再註明。中括弧為非必要項目。
2. 注意他人隱私權及網路禮節（netiquette）。
3. 檔案編號可置於主旨欄內，便於歸檔。
4. 電子郵件同樣適用 6C 原則，但較紙本書信更求簡潔與口語化。
5. 不要隨意使用表情符號，與商業氛圍格格不入。
6. 寫給較熟悉對象的郵件結尾詞可用 Best regards, Warm regards, All the best, Best,等。
7. 電子郵件雖較不正式，但除非與對方已熟悉，否則仍須使用全名及職稱。

12.4 要求包裝材料
Requesting Packing Material

12.4a 買方寄來電郵 Email from the Buyer

註：郵件日期及雙方郵件帳號為電腦設定在此略去。

Subject: packing material—Styrofoam
主旨：包裝材料—保麗龍

Dear Jason,
親愛的傑生：

I want to let you know that the products must be packed in Styrofoam. It's important that the edges of the products are protected during shipping.
我要通知你產品要用保麗龍包裝，在運送過程中產品邊緣受保護很重要。

This is why we must insist on Styrofoam packing material.
這是我們為何堅持保麗龍包裝材料的原因。

Thank you.
謝謝。

Mark Stein
IJG Technologies
馬克史坦
IJG 科技

12.4b 供應商回覆郵件 Reply from the Supplier

Re: packing material—Styrofoam
回覆主旨：包裝材料—保麗龍

Dear Mr. Stein,
親愛的史坦先生：

I want to confirm that I received your email stating that the shipment must be packed in Styrofoam. I have informed the shipping department of your request. I will double check to make sure they meet your request.
我確認收到你電子郵件說明運送要以保麗龍包裝，我已經通知運送部門你的需求，我會再度確認他們符合你的要求。

Sincerely,
誠摯地，

Jason Lin
Sales Executive
LH Group
傑生林
銷售執行
LH 集團

Word Bank

Styrofoam ['staɪrə,fom] n. 保麗龍
insist [ɪn'sɪst] v. 堅持

1. 我已經通知運送部門你的需求。
   I have informed the shipping department of your request.
2. 我會再度確認他們符合你的要求。
   I will double check to make sure they meet your request.

12.5 產品顏色與數量 Product Colors and Quantities

12.5a 買方寄來電郵 Email from the Buyer

Subject: colors and quantities (order No. 122RT)
主旨：顏色與數量（訂單號碼 122RT）

Dear Teresa,
親愛的泰瑞莎：

Please note that one third of the order, number 122RT, must be gray, another third grass green, and the other third steel blue.
請注意編號 122R 的訂單，1/3 必須是灰色的，另外 1/3 草綠色，其他 1/3 鋼青色。

Best regards,
誠摯祝福，

Charlene Kirk
Collins Inc.
霞琳寇克
柯林斯企業

12.5b 供應商回覆郵件 Reply from the Supplier

Re: colors and quantities (order No. 122RT)
回覆主旨：顏色與數量（訂單號碼 122RT）

Dear Ms. Kirk,
親愛的寇克女士：

On order number 122RT the colors in the amounts you asked for(one third of the order in gray, another third grass green, and the other third steel blue)will be followed.
訂單編號 122RT 的顏色，依照你要求的數量（1/3 灰色，另外 1/3 草綠色，其他 1/3 鋼青色）進行。

The order will start production on Thursday of this week.
訂單將於本週四開始生產。

Sincerely,
誠摯地，

Teresa Chen
LH Group
泰瑞莎陳
LH 集團

1. 顏色與數量將依照你的指示進行。
   The colors in the amounts you asked for will be followed.
2. 訂單將於本週四開始生產。
   The order will start production on Thursday of this week.

雙方寫信時重述其被告知訊息很重要，對方才能確認其理解無誤，接下來再告知對方下一步的處理。

12.6 訂單細節確認 Confirming Details of an Order

12.6a 賣方發出電郵 Email from the Supplier

Subject: confirming details of an order
主旨：確認訂單商議的細節

Dear James,
親愛的詹姆士：

I want to confirm the details of our negotiations.
我要跟你確認商議的細節。

Order amount	2,500 units	訂單數量：2,500 單位
Order price	$28,500.00	訂單價格：28,500.00 元
Maintenance contract	$4,000.00 per year	維護合約：每年 4,000.00元
Delivery date	Sep. 15, 2013	運送日期：2013年9月15日
Delivery agreement	CIF San Francisco	運送條件：含成本及運保費，舊金山

Please acknowledge.
請確認。

Sincerely,
誠摯地，

Teresa Chen
LH Group
泰瑞莎陳
LH 集團

12.6b 買方回覆 Reply from the Buyer

Re: confirming details of an order 回覆主旨： 確認訂單商議的細節
Greetings Teresa. 泰瑞莎你好！ The details of our agreement you emailed are correct. I have checked over everything and found everything to be in order. We look forward to doing more business with you in the future. 你電郵過來我們合約的細節是正確的，我已經確認每件事無誤，我期待將來與你做更多的生意。 Best regards, 誠摯祝福， James Arnold 詹姆士阿諾

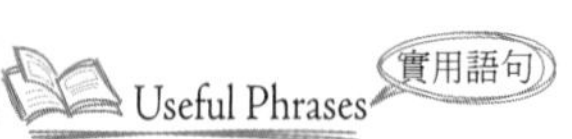

1. 請確認。

   Please acknowledge.

2. 我要跟你確認溝通的細節。

   I want to confirm the details of our negotiations.

3. 我已經確認每件事無誤。

   I've checked over everything and found everything to be in order.

Greetings David.（較 Dear David 不正式，可用在較熟的人）。

12.7 運送日期確認 Confirming Shipment Date

12.7a 買方寄來電郵 Email from the Buyer

Subject: confirming shipment date (order 878WS)
主旨：確認運送日期（order 878WS）

Dear Jason,
親愛的傑生：

Our records show that you will ship order 878WS on Aug. 7 of this year. Please confirm. You can email me at tswei@junline.com.
我們資料顯示你會在今年 8 月 7 日運送我們的訂單 878WS，請確認。你可以電郵到 tswei@junline.com。

Thank you.
謝謝。

Tom Miller
湯姆米勒

12.7b 供應商回覆 Reply from the Supplier

Re: confirming shipment date (order 878WS)
回覆主旨：確認運送日期（order 878WS）

Dear Mr. Miller,
親愛的米勒先生：

The production of your order 878WS has been finished last week. It will be ready to undergo shipping as soon as the packing is completed. We assure you that the order's shipment date Aug. 7 will be followed.
你的訂單 878WS 上週已經完成生產，包裝一完成就可以運送。請您放心，訂單會遵照出貨日期 8 月 7 日。

Sincerely,
誠摯地，

Jason Lin
傑生林

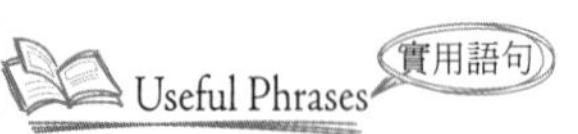

1. 我期待將來與你做更多的生意。
   We look forward to doing business with you.
2. 包裝一完成就可以運送。
   It will be ready to undergo shipping as soon as the packing is completed.
3. 請您放心，訂單會遵照出貨日期 8 月 7 日。
   We assure you that the order's shipment date Aug. 7 will be followed.

12.8 接受合作提議
Acceptance of Proposal

Subject: accepting proposal
主旨：接受提議
Attachment: agreement
附件：合約

Dear Sirs,
親愛的客戶：

Your counter proposal to the project we have been developing with you has been reviewed, and we find it acceptable in its entirety.
我們向你們提出的計畫，經過你們的還價與本公司之審視後，認為可以完全接受。

The agreement is attached in this mail for your reference. The paper agreement that requires your signature for completion will be air-mailed this afternoon.
我們在此郵件附上合約供您參考，紙本合約在今日下午會被寄出，需要您的簽名合約才能完成。

We are excitedly looking forward to this project and are pleased about having the opportunity to work with you.
我們很興奮地期待這份計畫，並且很高興有機會與你們合作。

Sincerely,
誠摯地，

Teresa Chen
LH Group
泰瑞莎陳
LH 集團

entirety [ɪn'taɪrtɪ] n. 全部

1. 你們的計畫經過審視後，我們認為可以完全接受。
   Your project has been reviewed, and we find it acceptable in its entirety.
2. 我們很興奮地期待這份計畫。
   We are excitedly looking forward to this project.
3. 我們很高興有機會與你們合作。
   We are pleased about having the opportunity to work with you.

12.9 停止協商 Stopping Negotiation

12.9a 客戶寄來電郵 Email from the Client

Subject: stopping negotiation
主旨：停止協商

Hi, Teresa,
嗨，泰瑞莎：

Sorry we couldn't reach an agreement this time. I expect that we will be doing business with each other in the future, however. I've got your contact information and will be in touch with you in the future when we need your product types.
很抱歉我們這次無法達成交易，但我期待我們將來會與彼此做生意。我有你的聯絡資料，並且在將來需要你的產品樣式時會與你保持聯繫。

Thank you.
謝謝。

Jim Sanders
吉姆桑德斯

12.9b 供應商回覆 Reply from the Supplier

Re: stopping negotiation
回覆主旨：停止協商

Dear Mr. Sanders,
親愛的桑德斯先生：

We are sorry to learn that we cannot reach an agreement on price this time. As you have already approved our product quality, we are sure that you understand the cost of producing quality goods. However, it is still possible for us to introduce other substitutes of your interest that will fit your market. If you are still looking for similar products, we can send you information right away.
我們很遺憾地獲悉這次我們無法在價格上達成協議，但您已經認可我們的產品品質，我們確信您了解製造好品質產品的固定成本。雖然如此，我們仍有可能為您介紹您感興趣並符合您市場的替代品，如果您仍在找類似產品，我們馬上可以寄給您資訊。

Please let us know about any questions you have any time. We will also keep you posted about our product information and market updates.
請隨時讓我們知道您有任何疑問，有關於我們產品的消息及市場資訊的更新，我們也會與您保持聯繫。

Sincerely yours,
誠摯地，

Teresa Chen
LH Group
泰瑞莎陳
LH 集團

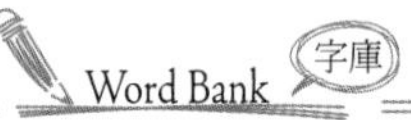

approve [ə'pruv] v. 認可，肯定
quality goods 優質產品
substitute ['sʌbstəˌtjut] n. 替代品

1. 我們確信您了解製造好品質產品的固定成本。
   We are sure that you understand the cost of producing quality goods.
2. 我們可以為您介紹您有興趣並符合您市場的替代品。
   It is possible for us to introduce other substitutes of your interest that will fit your market.
3. 如果您仍在找類似產品，我們馬上可以寄給您代替品的資訊。
   If you are still looking for similar products, we can send you information on some substitutes right away.
4. 我們也會與您保持產品消息的聯繫及市場資訊的更新。
   We will also keep you posted about our product information and market updates.

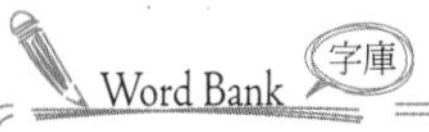

拒絕他人要爲對方找臺階下，想出配套方式使人比較容易接受。被拒絕是同樣道理，爲彼此找臺階下，並爲將來的可能性鋪路。

12.10 通知預計出貨及到達日期 Informing Estimated Shipment Departure and Arrival Dates

Subject: shipment notice
主旨：出貨通知
Attachment: photos of loading products onto vessel
附件：貨物裝船照片

Dear Mr. Wood,
親愛的伍德先生：

We are glad to inform you that your order No.13568 is on board. The estimated time of departure (ETD) is Jul. 2, 2013, estimated time of arrival (ETA) on Aug. 3, 2013 (32 days). The vessel is Everrich 3355. The forwarder is ABC. Their contact information in San Francisco is as follows.
我們很高興通知你，你的 13569 號訂單已經裝上船了，預計離港日是 2013 年 7 月 2 日，預計到達日是 2013 年 8 月 3 日（32 天）。船舶是永富 3355 號，承運公司是 ABC，以下是他們舊金山的聯絡資訊。

Everrich (San Francisco)：contact information
永富（舊金山）：聯絡資訊
ABC(San Francisco)：contact information, contact person
ABC（舊金山分公司）：聯絡資訊及聯絡人

Best wishes,
誠摯祝福，

Teresa Chen
LH Group
泰瑞莎陳
LH 集團

Word Bank

on board 裝上船
ETD (estimated time of departure) 預計離港日
ETA (estimated time of arrival) 預計到達日
vessel ['vɛsḷ] n. 船舶
forwarder ['fɔrwɚdɚ] n. 承運公司

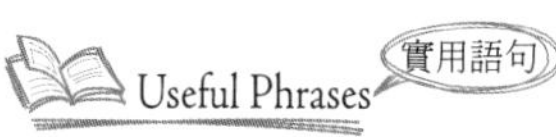

1. 我們很高興通知你，你的訂單已經裝上船了。
   We are glad to inform you that your order is on board.
2. 他們的聯絡資訊如下。
   Their contact information is as follows.

Tips

船務公司會通知買賣雙方船運日期，供應商再次通知買方提醒日期，並提供進出口地船務公司名字地址，給予良好的服務。

12.11 提貨文件寄出
Delivery Documents Air-Mailed

Subject: documents for picking up your order air-mailed today
主旨： 提貨文件今日寄出

Attachment: scanned invoice and packing list
附件：掃描之訂單發票、包裝單

Dear Jack,
親愛的傑克：

Please check our delivery documents for passing customs:
請確認我們的文件以利通關：

1. The forwarder will send you a telex release for your BL.
   船務公司會寄給你電放提單。
2. The invoice and the packing list have been scanned and attached in this mail for your reference. The original documents will be sent to you today by airmail. You should be receiving them within a week.
   發票跟包裝單已經掃描並且附加在郵件裡給你參考，原始文件今天會用空運寄給你，你應該在一週內會收到。

Best regards,
誠摯祝福，

Teresa Chen
LH Group
泰瑞莎陳
LH 集團

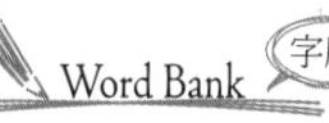

telex release n. 電放提單
BL (bill of lading) 提單
invoice ['ɪnvɔɪs] n. 發票
packing list n. 包裝單

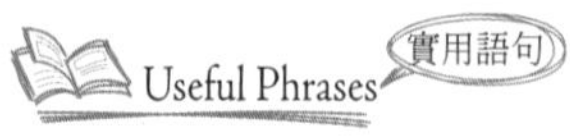

1. 請確認我們的文件以利通關。
   Please check our delivery documents for passing customs.
2. 船務公司會寄給你電放提單。
   The forwarder will send you a telex release for your BL.
3. 原始文件今天會用空運寄給你。
   The original documents will be sent to you today by airmail.

買方付款後，供應商發出電郵，通知買方收取所需文件（delivery documents）以便提貨清關，所需文件包含提單、發票、包裝單或是買方要求的其他文件如檢驗報告、大使館/領事簽證（consular visa）等。提貨文件應在貨物到達前適時寄出，一來客戶不會找不到或搞丟，二來貨物即可提領，無須支付倉儲費。

12.12 準備提貨通知 Notice - Ready for Lading

Subject: notice— ready for lading
主旨：通知一準備提貨

Dear Jack,
親愛的傑克：

Your order No. 33668 has arrived at San Francisco Port and is ready for you to pick up. Please contact the forwarder as soon as you can. The forwarders contact info. is as follows.
你的 33668 號訂單已經在舊金山港口等你提貨，請儘速聯絡船務代理。聯絡資料如下。

Forwarder Company Name 船務代理公司名稱
Contact person 聯絡人
Phone 電話
Address 地址

Sincerely,
誠摯地，

Teresa Chen
LH Group
泰瑞莎陳
LH 集團

12.13 客戶要求先不出貨 Client Requesting to Hold Shipment

12.13a 買方寄來郵件 Email from the Buyer

Subject: please hold the shipment until we get the license
主旨：請等我們執照下來再出貨

Dear Teresa,
親愛的泰瑞莎：

Please do not ship out the cargo until we get the import license. It should be done within two weeks. We will notify you as soon as it is ready. You must hold the shipment until we get the license.
請先別讓貨櫃放行，要等到我們進口執照下來，應該在兩週以內。執照下來我們會馬上通知你，你務必保留貨櫃直到我們拿到執照。

It is a serious matter. Please let me know if you have any questions.
這是很重要的事，請讓我知道你是否有疑問。

Thank you.
謝謝。

Paul Johnson
保羅強森

12.13b 供應商回覆郵件 Reply from the Supplier

Re: please hold the shipment until we get the license
回覆主旨： 請等我們執照下來再出貨

Dear Mr. Johnson,
親愛的強森先生：

Your request on holding up the shipment has been received. We understand it is a serious matter for you to get the license and hope you will get it as early as possible.
你提出先將貨品留住不放行的要求，我們已經收到了。我們了解拿到執照這件事對你很重要，並且希望你能儘快拿到。

We will continue waiting for your instructions.
我們會隨時等待你的指示。

Best regards,
誠摯祝福，

Teresa
泰瑞莎

import license 進口執照
notify ['notəˌfaɪ] v. 通知

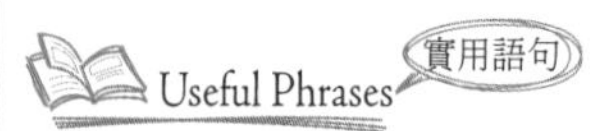

1. （執照）一下來，我們會馬上通知你。

   We will notify you as soon as it is ready.

2. 我們會隨時等待你的指示。

   We will continue waiting for your instruction .

12.14 出貨延誤 Shipment Delay

12.14a 買方寄來郵件 Email from the Buyer

Subject: wrong shipping date
主旨：錯誤出貨日

Dear Teresa Chen,
親愛的泰瑞莎陳，

It has been brought to my attention that the shipping date you stated in your last email is not the one we previously agreed to. Your email says that order 5667H will be shipped on May 22 of this year. Our previous agreed shipping date is May 12 of this year. We expect shipment on May 12.
我注意到你們上封電子郵件所說的出貨日期，並非我們先前同意的日期。你們的電子郵件說訂單 5667H 會在今年 5 月 22 日出貨，我們先前同意的出貨日期是今年 5 月 12 日，我們期待 5 月 12 日出貨。

Thank you.
謝謝。

John Parker
Grand Tech
約翰帕克
格蘭科技

12.14b 供應商回覆郵件 Reply from the Supplier

Re: wrong shipping date
回覆主旨：錯誤出貨日

Dear Mr. John Parker,
親愛的約翰帕克先生，

We have reviewed the agreement and must inform you that we cannot meet the May 12 shipping date. The production line division got the wrong date. Please accept our most sincere apology. We can have your shipment ready by May 17. Please inform me of what you think of this date.
我們審視了合約，並且必須通知您我們無法在 5 月 12 日出貨。生產線部門搞錯了日期，請接受我們最誠懇的道歉。我們可以在 5 月 17 日前準備好出貨，請告知你對此日期意下如何。

Sincerely,
誠摯地，

Teresa Chen
LH Group
泰瑞莎陳
LH 集團

12.15 出貨延誤賠償 Compensating the Shipment Delay

12.15a 買方寄來電子郵件（後續）Email from the Buyer (Cont.)

Re: wrong shipping date
回覆主旨：錯誤出貨日

Dear Teresa Chen,
親愛的泰瑞莎陳，

I am disappointed to hear about the late shipping date. Our company expects some financial compensation for this delay. Our contract was for May 12. We expect a reduced price on the product or some other form of acceptable compensation for this breach in the contract.
我很失望聽到遲到的出貨日期，我們公司期待得到這次拖延產生的財務賠償。我們的合約是 5 月 12 日，我們因為這樣違約應當得到減價，或是其他可以被接受的方式賠償。

Thank you.
謝謝。

John Parker
Grand Tech Auto
約翰帕克
格蘭科技汽車

12.15b 供應商回覆郵件（後續）Reply from the Supplier (Cont.)

Re: wrong shipping date
回覆主旨：錯誤出貨日

Dear Mr. John Parker,
親愛的約翰帕克先生，

After informing my supervisor of your position about the delayed shipping date, I have been authorized to offer your company an additional one-fifth more of the product you ordered at no additional cost to your company. Please let me know if this is acceptable as soon as possible.
在通知我的主管你被延宕的出貨日情況之後，我被授權免費額外提供你公司訂單的五分之一產品，請儘快讓我知道這樣是否可被接受。

Sincerely,
誠摯地，

Teresa Chen
LH Group
泰瑞莎陳
LH 集團

compensation [ˌkɑmpənˈseʃən] n. 賠償
breach [britʃ] n. 破壞，違反
authorize [ˈɔθəˌraɪz] v. 授權

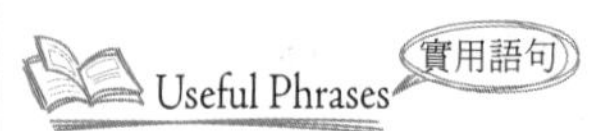

1. 我們公司期待得到這次拖延產生的財務賠償。

   Our company expects some financial compensation for this delay.

2. 我們應當得到減價，或是其他可以被接受的方式賠償。

   We expect a reduced price on the product or some other form of acceptable compensation.

3. 我被授權免費額外提供你公司訂單的五分之一產品。

   I have been authorized to offer your company an additional one-fifth more of the product you ordered at no additional cost to your company.

4. 請儘快讓我知道這樣是否可被接受。

   Please let me know if this is acceptable as soon as possible.

找出錯誤的原因，把事情交代清楚是基本要求，站在客戶的立場設想，他也必須對其客戶負責。訂單或合約裡幾乎都訂有延誤賠償罰則（例如：每遲到一天賠償貨款之某千分或百分比），因此要求延誤賠償是正常的，以眞誠及負責的態度才能再度贏得客戶的信任。

12.16 處理產品修理與更換 Handling Product Repairs and Replacements

供應商發出郵件 Email from the Supplier

Subject: technician coming to handle faulty units
主旨：技師將到達處理問題產品

Hi, Sid,
嗨，席德，

I want you to know that we got your email about the faulty units in order 7765R received on July 23. We will repair or replace those units depending on the results of our technician's inspection. Our technician will be there on Monday, July 30.
我要你知道我們收到你的郵件了，是關於你 7 月 23 日收到訂單 7765R 有問題產品。我們會根據技師檢驗結果來修理或更換那些產品，我們的技師會在7 月 30 日（週一）到達。

Please let me know that you received this email.
請讓我知道你收到這封郵件。

Regards,
誠摯祝福，

Jason Lin
LH Group
傑生林
LH 集團

12.17 帳戶錯誤 Accounting Error

供應商發出道歉信（郵政信函）Letter of Apology from the Supplier (by Postal Mail)

（簡化之故，以下信件章節之公司抬頭、收信人地址、日期略去）

Dear Sirs,
親愛的客戶，

Subject: accounting error reason
主旨：帳戶錯誤原因

This is an explanation for what went wrong in our accounting department. We hope that this letter will serve to resolve recent difficulties.
這是為何會計帳戶錯誤的解釋，我們希望這封信可以解決最近的困難。

We know that you can appreciate the fact that it has taken time to find exactly what was wrong. Please accept our apologies for the delay in responding.
我們知道你們可以體會要查出到底是什麼出差錯需要時間，請接受我們因延誤而回應的歉意。

Apparently, your payment was received on time, but it was credited to an account that has a similar name. Therefore, we started sending you our standard notices requesting payment. After posting the error, our accounting department failed to notify our credit department. That is why you continued to receive our correspondence demanding payment.
很明顯地，你的付款準時入帳，但是款項被歸入一個類似姓名的帳戶內。因此，我們才開始進入標準通知請求付款。在找出錯誤後，我們的會計部門沒有通知信用部門，那是你們持續收到要求付款信件的原因。

We know how exasperating this has been. We are deeply sorry about this problem. While there is a procedure within our firm to prevent this type of error, we are now reinforcing this procedure.
我們了解這個過程多麼令人不悅，我們為此問題深感抱歉，雖然在公司內部有一個步驟防止這類錯誤，我們現在正在加強這個程序。

You are a valued customer and have been for a long time. We appreciate you giving us the opportunity to serve you. You may rest assured that this problem will not happen again.
您一直是我們的貴賓，我們感謝您給我們機會服務，您可以放心這個問題永遠不會再發生。

Sincerely,
誠摯地，

Teresa Chen
LH Group
泰瑞莎陳
LH 集團

appreciate [ə'priʃɪ,et] v. 體會，感謝
correspondence [,kɔrə'spɑndəns] n. 信件
exasperating [ɪg'zæspə,retɪŋ] adj. 使人惱怒的
reinforce [,riɪn'fors] v. 加強
rest assured (be assured) 放心

1. 我們希望這封信可以解決最近的困難。

   We hope that this letter will serve to resolve recent difficulties.

2. 請接受我們因此延誤而回應的歉意。

   Please accept our apologies for the delay in responding.

3. 我們了解這個過程多麼令人不悅。

   We know how exasperating this has been.

4. 我們現在正在加強這個程序。

   We are now reinforcing this procedure.

5. 我們感謝您給我們機會服務。

   We appreciate you giving us the opportunity to serve you.

6. 您可以非常確定這個問題永遠不會再發生。

   You may rest assured that this problem will not happen again.

道歉信函內容必須保證錯誤不會再發生，並且應體貼當事人被錯誤導致的不悅心情，爲了顯示愼重及誠意，道歉函避免使用缺乏溫情的電子郵件，而應以正式信函（及優質紙材）印出，並以優先快捷方式郵寄。

12.18 逾期帳款
Account Overdue

供應商發出信函 Letter from the Supplier

Dear Sirs,
親愛的客戶，

We have written to you several times in the past month. We have requested an explanation on why you have failed to pay $50,000 on your account with us. It needs to be paid on.
我們已經在過去的一個月好幾次寫信給你，要求解釋為何你不付 50,000 元欠款給我們，款項必須馬上支付。

By ignoring our requests, you are damaging the credit history you had previously built with our company. In addition, you are incurring additional expense to yourself. I must mention our costs increase, too.
你輕忽我們的（支付）請求，正在損害你先前在我們公司建立起來的信用。另外，你在增加自己的成本，我必須向你聲明，你也在增加我們的成本。

We must hear from you within ten days. If we do not, we will have no other choice but to turn your account over to a collection company. We are sorry that we must take drastic action, but we see no other alternative. You can preserve your credit rating by remitting your check today for the amount stated above.
我們在十天以內必須收到你的回應，如果沒有，我們沒有其他選擇，只能將你的帳戶交給收帳公司，我們很遺憾必須採取激烈行動，但我們沒有其他選擇。你要保留你的信用評等就在今天匯款上述金額。

Thank You.
謝謝。

Bob Chen
Legal Department
LH Group
鮑伯陳
法務部
LH 集團

incur [ɪn'kɝ] v. 招致，惹起
collection company 收帳公司
take drastic action 採取激烈行動
alternative [ɔl'tɝnətɪv, æl-] n. 選項
preserve [prɪ'zɝv] v. 保留
credit rating 信用評等
remit [rɪ'mɪt] v. 匯款

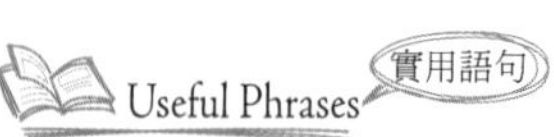

1. 我們已經要求解釋為何你不付款給我們。
   We have requested an explanation on why you have failed to pay us.
2. 我們沒有其他選擇，只能將你的帳戶交給收帳公司。
   We will have no other choice but to turn your account over to a collection company.
3. 我們很遺憾必須採取激烈行動，但我們沒有其他選擇。
   We are sorry that we must take drastic action, but we see no other alternative.
4. 你要保留你的信用評等就在今天匯款。
   You can preserve your credit rating by remitting your check today.

12.19 採取法律行動向客戶追討欠款
Taking Legal Actions for Collecting Payments

供應商發出信函 Letter from the Supplier

Dear Mr. Ron Baker,
親愛的朗貝克先生，

This letter is to inform you that we are starting legal procedures against DXD Corporation for past due payment of products delivered. We have contacted you on numerous occasions and have not reached any acceptable arrangement about past due accounts. We feel we have no other choice. You will be receiving legal documents pertaining to this matter soon.
這封信是通知你們，我們因為已送達貨品被欠款，現在正對 DXD 公司開始進行法律程序。我們已經在許多場合接洽你們，但從沒有獲得任何關於欠款可以令人接受的安排。我們覺得毫無選擇，你們很快就會收到關於此事的法律文件。

Yours Truly,
真誠地，

Bob Chen
Legal Department
LH Group
鮑伯陳
法務部
LH 集團

legal procedure 法律程序
numerous ['njuməros] adj. 許多的
pertain [pɚ'ten] v. 關於

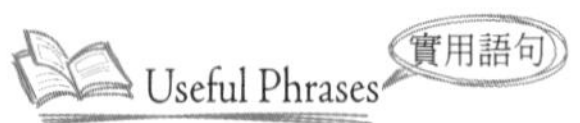

1. 我們現在正對 DXD 公司開始採取法律程序。
   We are starting legal procedures against DXD Corporation.
2. 我們已經在許多場合接洽你們，但從沒有獲得任何關於過期帳款可以令人接受的安排。
   We have contacted you on numerous occasions and have not reached any acceptable arrangement about past due accounts.
3. 我們覺得毫無選擇。
   We feel we have no other choice.
4. 你們很快就會收到關於此事的文件。
   You will be receiving documents pertaining to this matter soon.

12.20 新付款政策 New Payment Policy

供應商發出信函（郵政信函）Letter from the Supplier(Postal Mail)

Dear Sirs,
親愛的客戶，

Subject: New Payment Policy
主旨：新付款政策

In the past our policy was to supply our customers when their machines broke down. We have many customers now who are

paying late. We are forced to change company policy. Our new policy will go into effect on Jan. 1, 2014. It is as follows:
以前我們的政策是當顧客的機器故障時，我們提供（機器）給顧客。現今我們有許多顧客付款延遲，我們被迫改變公司政策。我們的新政策會在 2014 年 1月 1 日生效，政策如下：

If a customer is more than 20 days late in their monthly payment and the machine is not working, we will not supply. We will repair the machine, and the number of days in which the machine has not been in service will be credited to the customer's account. At the time of our service call, we will expect payment in full of any unpaid balance due. There will also be a surcharge on accounts falling more than 30 days behind.
如果顧客每月延遲付款超過 20 天，而他們機器故障了，我們將不會再提供（機器）給顧客。我們會修理機器，但需要幾天修理無法運作機器的費用會被計入顧客的帳戶中。當有服務需求時，我們預期收到全數未支付款項，並且對延遲超過 30 天的帳款加收費用。

We are sorry we must go to the above stated policy, but we are afraid that there is no alternative. Our company policy still is, and always will be, to provide the best service to our customers.
我們很遺憾必須做出上述政策，但我們恐怕沒有其他辦法。我們的公司政策仍是，也永遠是，提供給顧客最好的服務。

If there are any questions regarding our new policy, please call us.
如果有任何關於新政策的疑問，請來電。

Thank You.
謝謝。

Rick Wong Manager
LH Group
瑞克王經理
LH 集團

effect [ə'fɛkt, ɪ-] v. 生效

credit ['krɛdɪt] v. 計入帳戶

surcharge ['sɝ,tʃɑrdʒ] n. 額外費用

1. 當有服務需求時，我們預期收到全數未支付款項。

   At the time of our service call, we will expect payment in full of any unpaid balance due.

2. 我們的公司政策仍是，也永遠是，提供給顧客最好的服務。

   Our company policy still is, and always will be, to provide the best service to our customers.

3. 如果有任何關於新政策的疑問，請來電。

   If there are any questions regarding our new policy, please call us.

Appendices

附錄

1. 國際貿易進出口流程圖
2. 聯合國（電子化）貿易文件一覽表
3. 度量衡轉換表
4. 美國中央情報局「世界概況」（世界人口資料）
5. 各國肢體語言須知
6. 文化祕笈—帶客戶用餐須知
7. 文化祕笈—聚會派對禮節與文化了解
8. 外交部領事事務局全球資訊網（急難救助）
9. 臺灣經貿資訊站
10. 中國經貿資訊站

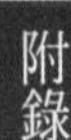

1. 國際貿易進出口流程圖
International Trade Transaction Flow Chart

http://content.edu.tw/vocation/business/ks_sm/111.htm（教育部數位教學資源）

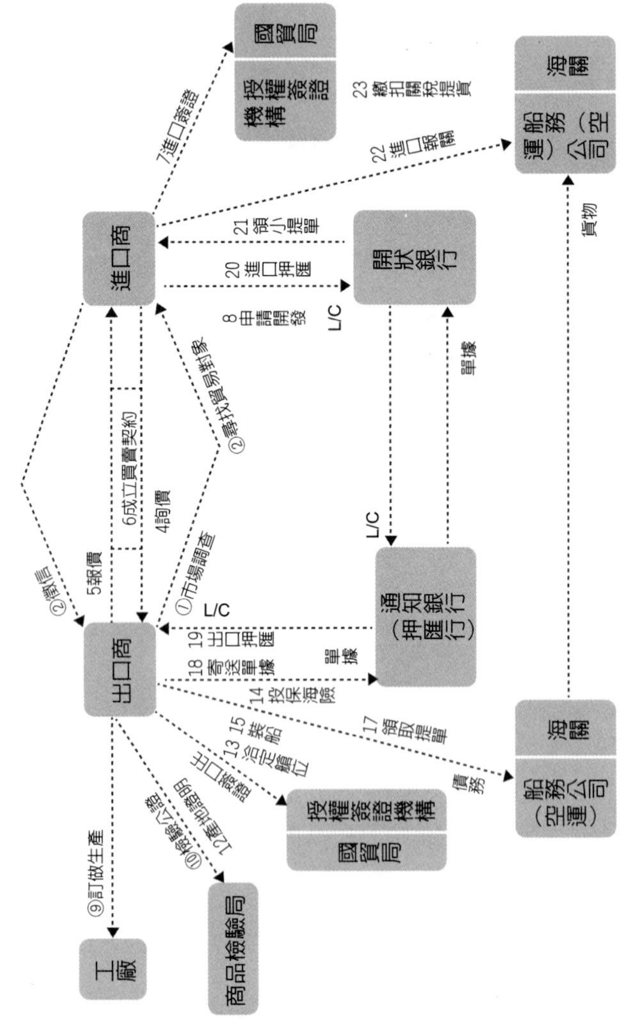

國貿局
授權簽證機構
海關
船務（空運）公司
7進口簽證
23 繳扣關稅提貨
22 進口報關
進口商
開狀銀行
21 領小提單
20 進口押匯
8 申請開發 L/C
貨物
單據
②尋找貿易對象
6成立買賣契約
4詢價
5報價
②徵信
①市場調查
L/C
通知（押匯行）銀行
出口商
19 出口押匯
18 寄送單據
單據
14 投保海險
17 領取提單
15 裝船
13 洽定艙位
出口簽證
12產地證明
⑩檢驗公證
⑨訂做生產
貨物
海關
船務公司（空運）
授權簽證機構
國貿局
工廠
商品檢驗局

2. 聯合國（電子化）貿易文件一覽表
The United Nations electronic Trade Documents (UNeDocs)

聯合國爲便捷國際貿易，依使用情形將貿易文件分爲以下九大類（資料來源－經濟部國貿局）：

1.生產（Production）

訂購單（Purchase order）
製造指示（Manufacturing instructions）
物料供應（Stores requisition）
商業發票資料單（Invoicing data sheet）
裝箱單（Packing list）

2.採購（Purchase）

詢價（Enquiry）
意願書（Letter of intent）
訂單（Order）
運送指示（Delivery instructions）
運送放行（Delivery release）

3.銷售（Sale）

報價（Offer/Quotation）
合約（Contract）
訂單確認（Acknowledgement of order）
發貨單（Performa invoice）
送貨通知（Dispatch order）
商業發票（Commercial invoice）

4.付款–銀行（Payment–Banking）

銀行匯款通知（Instructions for bank transfer）
收款單（Collection order）
付款單（Payment order）
押匯信用證申請（Documentary credit application）
押匯信用證（Documentary credit）

5.保險（Insurance）

保險證明（Insurance certificate）
保險單（Insurance policy）
保險用發票（Insurer's invoice）
承保單（Cover note）

6.仲介服務（Intermediary services）

運送指示（Forwarding instructions (FIATA-FFI)）
承攬業通知出口商（Freight Forwarder's advice to exporter）
承攬業收據證明（Forwarder's certificate of receip t(FIATA-FCR)）
港口收費相關文件（Port charges documents）
運送單（Delivery order）

7.運輸（Transport）

綜合運輸文件（Universal (multipurpose) transport document）
海運提單（Sea waybill）
提單（Bill of Lading）
訂單確認（Booking confirmation）
貨物到港通知（Arrival notice (goods)）

8.出口規定（Exit regulations）

輸出許可證申請（Export license application）
輸出許可（Export license）
貨物出口通關（Goods declaration for exportation）
貨物報關（Cargo declaration）
檢驗證明申請（Application for inspection certificate）

9.進口及過境規定（Entry and transit regulations）

輸入許可證申請（Import license, application）
輸入許可證（Import license）
外匯許可（Foreign exchange permit）
家用物品通關（Goods declaration for home use）
海關貨物即時放行（Customs immediate release declaration）

3. 度量衡轉換表 Measurement Conversion Charts

下載智慧型手機度量衡換算應用程式是另一便利

Length/Distance 長度/距離

1 centimeter (cm)公分	= 10 millimeters (mm)公釐/毫米
1 inch 英寸	= 2.54 centimeters (cm)公分
1 foot 英尺	= 0.3 meters (m)公里
1 foot 英尺	= 12 inches 英寸
1 yard 碼	= 3 feet 英尺
1 meter(m)公尺/米	= 100 centimeters (cm)公分
1 meter(m)公尺/米	= 3.28 feet 英寸
1 furlong 弗隆（1/8 英里）	= 660 feet 英尺
1 kilometer (km)公里	= 1000 meters (m)公里
1 kilometer (km)公里	= 0.62 miles 英里
1 mile 英里	= 5280 ft 英尺
1 mile 英里	= 1.61 kilometers (km)公里
1 nautical mile 海里	= 1.85 kilometers (km)公里

Area 面積

1 square foot 平方呎	= 144 square inches 平方吋
1 square foot 平方呎	= 929 square centimeters 平方米
1 square yard 平方碼	= 9 square feet 平方呎
1 square meter 平方米	= 10.7639104 square feet 平方呎
1 Ping 坪（日本、臺灣）	= 35.58 square feet 平方呎 3.3 square meters 平方米
1 acre 一英畝	= 43,560 square feet 平方呎
1 hectare 公頃	= 10,000 square meters 平方米
1 hectare 公頃	= 2.47 acres 英畝
1 square kilometer 平方公里	= 100 hectares 公頃
1 square mile 平方哩	= 2.59 square kilometers 平方公里
1 square mile 平方哩	= 640 acres 英畝

Weight 重量

1 milligram (mg)毫克	= 0.001 grams (g）公克
1 gram (g)公克	= 0.001 kilograms (kg)公斤
1 gram (g)公克	= 0.035 ounces
1 ounce 盎司	= 28.35 grams (g)公克
1 ounce 盎司	= 0.0625 pounds 磅
1 pound (lb)磅	= 16 ounces 盎司
1 pound (lb)磅	= 0.45 kilograms (kg)公斤
1 kilogram (kg)公斤	= 1000 grams 公克
1 kilogram (kg)公斤	= 35.27 ounces 盎司
1 kilogram (kg)公斤	= 2.2 pounds (lb)
1 short ton 美噸/短噸	= 2000 pounds 磅
1 long ton 英噸/長噸	= 2240 pounds 磅
1 metric ton 公噸	= 1000 kilograms (kg)公斤

Volume 容量

1 US fluid ounce 液盎司	≅ 29.57 milliliters (ml)公撮/毫升
1 US pint 品脫	= 0.473 liter 公升（473ml 毫升）
1 US quart 夸脫	= 2 US pints 品脫
1 liter 公升	= 1000 milliliters (ml)毫升
1 liter 公升	= 0.24 US gallon 美加侖
1 US gallon 美加侖	= 4 US quarts 夸脫
1 US gallon 美加侖	= 3.76 liters 公升

Temperature 溫度

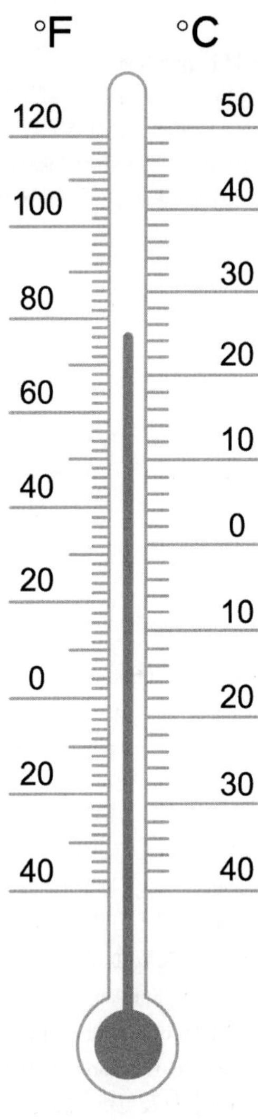

$$°C\,(\text{Celsius}) = (°F - 32) \times \frac{5}{9}$$

$$°F\,(\text{Fahrenheit}) = (\frac{9}{5}°C) + 32°$$

4. 美國中央情報局「世界概況」（世界人口資料）
CIA - The World Factbook (The World Population Data)

世界總人口 the World Population：

約 71 億 7 千萬（2014 年 7 月）前 10 大人口國：①中國 China 13.6 億，②印度 India 12.4 億，③美國 United States 3.2 億，④印尼 Indonesia 2.5 億，⑤巴西 Brazil 2.03 億，⑥巴基斯坦 Pakistan 1.96 億，⑦奈及利亞 Nigeria 1.8 億，⑧孟加拉 Bangladesh 1.7 億，⑨蘇俄 Russia 1.4 億，⑩日本 Japan 1.3 億。

世界人口宗教信仰（Religions）比例：

基督徒 Christians 33.39%
- 天主教徒 Roman Catholics 16.85%
- 新教徒 Protestants 6.15%
- 東正教徒 Orthodox 3.96%
- 英國國教徒 Anglicans 1.26%

回教徒 Muslims 22.74%
印度教徒 Hindus 13.8%
佛教徒 Buddhists 6.77%
錫克教徒 Sikhs 0.35%
猶太教徒 Jews 0.22%
大同教 Baha'is 0.11%
其他宗教 other religions 10.95%
無信仰者 non-religious 9.66%
無神論者 atheists 2.01%
(2014 年）

世界人口語言（Languages）比例：

中文 Mandarin Chinese 12.44%
西班牙語 Spanish 4.85%
英語 English 4.83%
阿拉伯語 Arabic 3.25%
（北）印度語 Hindi 2.68%
葡萄牙語 Portuguese 2.66%
孟加拉語 Bengali 2.62%
俄語 Russian 2.12%
日語 Japanese 1.8%,
標準德語 Standard German 1.33%
法語 French 1.25%
(2009 年）

註：1.將人口數乘上百分比可得人口數。例如：基督徒近 24 億人，回教徒約 16.3 億人，印度教近 10 億人，佛教徒約 4.85 億人。
2.語言為母語人口（Native Speaker）之比例。
3.CIA - The World Factbook，網址爲https://www.cia.gov/ibrary/publications/the-world-factbook/，由美國中情局（Central Intelligence Agency）發行及更新（2010 年起資料每週更新），可以 APP 下載，提供世界及 195 個國家與 72 個政治實體（共 267）之檔案查詢，包含簡介、地理、人口、政府、經濟等各方面之統計資料與排名。

5. 各國肢體語言須知

Body Language Speaks Louder than Words

從事國際商務的人士，除了主要溝通語言的需求外，應當學幾句當地語言，馬上拉近與客戶的距離。對於國際政經情勢及當地歷史文化宗教必須有所認識，不僅到國外出差能入境隨俗，接待遠行而來不同國籍的客戶，如有更多了解，才能在對的時間做對的事說對的話，避免踩到對方地雷或碰觸禁忌（taboos），能把商業服務做得更體貼，商機自然更為寬廣。另外絕不能忽略的是肢體語言，因為行為動作表達的意涵比語言更快更直接，必須非常注意不要給人錯誤的訊息。

美國是個大熔爐，在初見面介紹的場合，最常見的是握手禮，將右手空出準備握手。被介紹時不要害羞，眼神要直視對方（代表自信、誠實），並且主動伸手與對方握手（力道須展現熱誠，避免誇張或草率）。朋友間以握手、拍肩表示鼓勵或熱誠，彼此不會稱兄（姊）道弟（妹），除非雙方都是非裔，男士間不會勾肩搭背，女士間不會勾手表示熱絡，除非是同性戀人。美國人的身體距離（personal space）比我們寬得多，說話時不要靠得太近，保持一隻手臂的距離，以免對方有壓迫感而往後退。

除了握手禮之外，西方人表示關心與友好的禮節尚有擁抱禮、貼面禮與親吻禮，英國還有吻手禮。但在見面時是否適合要看人們的關係及場合而定，多數人不會在初次見面就與陌生人擁抱、貼面或親吻。擁抱禮可能出現在迎賓、祝賀、道謝、或道別的場合，平輩間的貼面禮與親吻禮是以貼面及親吻空氣（air kiss）表示友好。女士們與男女之間貼面與親吻次數各地不一，城鄉有別，男士間是否貼面與親吻也有文化之別。

某些文化如泰國（Thailand）、印度（India）、尼泊爾（Nepal）、柬埔寨（Cambodia）等，打招呼不用握手而是行雙手合十（wai）的合掌禮，從手放在胸前到眼前的程度表示尊敬的程度，慣於握手的人拜訪這些地區要入境隨俗。

許多亞洲與中東地區，對肢體碰觸相當保守，切記避免趨身向前與婦女握手，女士們可能感到受冒犯。回教文化中男女壁壘分明，異性之間即使是禮貌性的口頭稱讚（如未婚男士稱讚已婚女士表示有興趣了解對方）便可能惹惱對方配偶，與已婚女士照相更需取得對方先生同意。回教眞主阿拉並無形象，所以保守的回教徒不拍照。

衣著也是肢體語言的一部分，到回教世界衣著要保守，到極爲保守的回教國家（如伊朗）旅遊，女士在入境時就要包起頭巾至出境爲止，宗教警察一樣會糾察外國女子的衣著（不要露出頭髮、手臂、小腿或身體線條），男士衣著也要遮住手臂與小腿以贏得他人尊重。進入清眞寺或搭乘公共交通工具要跟同性別的人坐在同一邊，男女有別，左右不同，不可亂坐。中東地區人民較歐美國家對亞洲人熱情好客得多，許多古文明與民族風情更是截然不同，對國人可謂極具吸引力，另一方面，中東地區因爲反對以色列與美國的情節高漲，對於相關國際議題必須敏感小心。

此外，印度、尼泊爾、柬埔寨、阿拉伯地區或某些宗教（如回教）裡有禁用左手與他人互動的習俗，慣用左手的人一定要記住不用左手與來自這些文化的人握手、進食、付錢或傳遞物品。

某些文化肢體語言使用廣泛，美國人與義大利（Italy）南部人習慣說話時比手畫腳且表情豐富幫助語言傳達，中東男士間經常彼此碰觸，但英國人則少用肢體語言。國人經常使用的手勢在世界各地需要特別注意之處，列舉如下：

1. 豎起大拇指在許多地方是「棒極了」，但在澳洲、大部分中南美洲、及義大利南部等於是比中指的髒話。
2. 拇指豎起朝後方比的搭便車（hitchhiking）的手勢，在希臘(Greece）與土耳其（Turkey）幾乎等同中指髒話。
3. 我們常比的「OK」手勢，在許多地方意爲「沒問題」，在法國（France）代表「零」、「沒價值」，日本（Japan）代表「錢」或「零錢」（年輕人代表 OK），但在土耳其（Turkey）代表「同性戀」（homosexual），在德國某些地區與一些中南美洲國家如墨西哥（Mexico）、巴西（Brazil）、委內瑞拉（Venezuela）、巴拉圭(Paraguay）代表肛門，引申爲「混蛋」。
4. 勝利的 V 手勢手的背面要向著自己，如果在英國手背向著他人代表髒話，如果是在餐廳要點兩杯咖啡，比錯手勢，侍者不可能爲你服務。

5. 在希臘（Greece）向別人比出數字 5 的手勢是侮辱之意，爲歷史上侮辱戰敗敵人塗抹穢物的手勢，手掌朝對方臉越近，程度越嚴重。避免此手勢，要引起侍者注意、叫計程車或說再見，舉起手，手腕上下擺動。
6. 在馬來西亞（Malaysia）、印尼（Indonesia）、中東地區（the Middle East），以食指指他人是不禮貌的表現，要用拇指代替。
7. 在泰國及中東，腳部是一個人全身最低的地方，代表不乾淨，所以不要將腳底或鞋底示人，用腳推、指東西，是不禮貌的表現。
8. 泰國人認爲頭部最高也最神聖，所以不要摸任何人的頭部上方，當然包括小孩的頭。

商機稍縱即逝，肢體語言的重要性絕不亞於眞正的語言，用錯了肢體語言將造成誤會，用對了馬上拉近距離，彼此心神意會盡在不言中。使用適切的肢體語言不僅有助於溝通，並能超越國界及語言文化之藩籬。

6. 文化祕笈─帶客戶用餐須知
Cultural Tips—Treating Clients to Dinner

因爲華僑遍布海外，中國菜在世界各地可說是最物美價廉的異國餐廳，但國外客戶吃過的中國菜多爲酸甜口味，與臺灣、香港、中國等眞正道地的中國菜不同。客戶來到本地當然可以把握機會介紹本地美食，但任何人出差在外最不想要的事情就是身體不適，多數人的味蕾及腸胃還是受其文化及飲食習慣影響，所以除非客戶心胸開放特別希望嘗試新奇食物，作東請客還是以體貼客戶熟悉的飲食習慣才能賓主盡歡。客戶通常會請你做主，你可以請客戶做些選擇，一來可投其所好，二來你也做了美食外交，介紹了好吃的本地食物。

要注意的是如果帶國外客戶到中餐館用餐，告訴餐廳不要放味精(MSG)，許多老外對味精過敏（be allergic to MSG）。美國人不喜歡帶骨或刺的菜肴（除非是牛排或肋骨），多數人不能吃辣，且頂多只能接受一點點辣，設計菜單要盡量使賓客方便食用。可請中國菜館先上湯，雖然這是美國人的西餐順序。多數美國人能用筷子，但不要讓他們用餐時爲難或必須要動手吃，所以選擇雞胸肉會比選擇帶骨頭的翅膀或雞腿好。

如果要點魚或蝦，可以請餐廳去掉魚頭、蝦頭，魚蝦最好做成魚片、魚排或蝦鬆，沒有魚刺或蝦殼最受歡迎。如果沒有特別的原因，要避免請他們吃不敢吃的食物。美國人不希望看到或吃到生畜、家禽或海鮮的頭部、眼睛或其他如內臟（intestines, guts）、血（blood）、蹄(hooves)、腦（brains）等部分，以減少對食物的罪惡感（肝臟例外，如牛肝、鵝肝醬）。西方許多國家如希臘、德國、法國等食材或多或少都包含以上一些部分，並非完全排斥。主流的美國文化認爲除了衛生問題外，食用這些部位與人類獸性有關。附帶一提，除了西方國家外，東南亞（如泰國、越南、柬埔寨）及一些拉丁美洲（如墨西哥、巴西）、非洲（如辛巴威）國家有吃蟲的文化。

如果客戶是素食者（vegetarian），佛教徒（Buddhist），當然必須爲其準備素菜；如果賓客來自其他文化及宗教，例如：猶太教徒 Jews、回教徒 Muslims、印度教徒 Hindus，對於可食肉類種類、來源、宰殺方式、食用部位、飲食器具、食物及餐廳認證有特別規定。例如：回教有清眞/哈拉認證（halal），猶太教徒有猶太認證（kosher），印度教徒受其宗教與種姓制度（caste system）制約。此外，回教徒不可飲酒及吸菸，每日必須按時朝拜，並有齋戒月（Ramadan）白天禁食（fasting）等風俗，要當主人之前必須先做功課或詢問客人適合的食物，以避免觸犯禁忌造成尷尬。

7. 文化祕笈—聚會派對禮節與文化了解

Cultural Tips—Attending Parties Etiquette and Cultural Understanding

以下說明以美國爲主，其他地區爲輔。

紳士行為：

美國雖是平權社會，男士的紳士風度仍然存在，爲女士開門，爲最鄰近自己的女士拉椅子都是被期待的行爲。紳士行爲在世界各國同樣存在並且被期待（含各種場合），沒有紳士習慣的男士必須學習。

用餐時間：

美國人用餐時間與臺灣差不多，但不重視午餐也不午休，晚餐是一天中最豐盛的一餐。

許多歐洲、中東、拉丁美洲、東南亞國家晚 1-3 小時才用餐，有些國家重視午餐，用餐時間長得多（可能邊吃邊聊兩三個鐘頭及午休），晚餐則是 8-9 點以後才開始（夏季太陽晚下山），所以黃昏時會先吃點心。晚餐後如有派對可能在晚上 10 點後（甚至更晚）才開始。

用餐禮儀：

1. 有些人用餐前要先祈禱（say grace），別急著開動。
2. 如果是受邀到客戶家中，注意（女）主人是否開動了才開動，因爲（女）主人要花時間爲大家上菜，如果上菜時賓客已經都開動了，（女）主人準備許久要與大家共餐，（她）才開始用餐時，大家卻已經吃飽了，（女）主人在此時可能會感到很失落。
3. 餐巾打開表示用餐開始，中途離開餐巾放椅子上，用餐結束放桌上。
4. 用餐及喝湯時，身體不要向前傾，而是坐正將食物送入口中。
5. 體貼的將食物或餐盤傳給較遠的一方，或請對方傳過來，而不是伸長手去取食物。
6. 用餐時不要先聞食物，否則美國人會感到受冒犯。如果不確定使用哪個刀叉，看主人怎麼做。
7. 要有「公筷母匙」的概念：如果奶油是共用的，使用奶油刀將奶油放在自己的麵包盤上，再用晚餐刀在麵包上塗上奶油。直接將共用的奶油塗上你的麵包感覺不太衛生。麵包要先撕成小片再入口。

8. 不要滿口食物時說話，咀嚼時要閉口，也不要在他人正放入食物要咀嚼時問問題。要使用刀叉，不要用手拿起食物兜在刀叉上食用，湯匙是爲喝湯及甜品專用，食用主菜時不使用。
9. 美國人不喜歡帶骨或刺的菜肴（除非是牛排或肋骨），所以碰到骨頭與刺的機會不多，如果有的話，要用叉子接著放在自己的盤子邊（水果有子也一樣），不可直接吐在盤子上或放在桌上。
10. 刀叉擺放要注意，如將刀叉各擺在5及7點鐘位置，表示仍在進食。兩者擺在5點鐘位置爲用餐完畢，兩者都在7點鐘位置表示食物不合胃口或不好吃，可能會讓主人很難過。（在法國若將麵包沾醬料完全吃完，主人會很高興，但在埃及留一小口表示不貪心。）

坐姿：

坐直，勿彎腰駝背。坐下時就打開餐巾放在腿上。坐下時慣用右手的人要將左手放在腿上，而不是桌上，否則會被認爲是不體貼或是水準欠佳。（法國人則是雙手置於桌上。）

其他舉止：

分享的餐盤或蛋糕剩最後一口的話，應當徵詢旁人後再取用。擤鼻、剔牙、或女士補妝要到洗手間，萬一打噴嚏（sneeze）、打嗝（hiccup）、打哈欠（yawn）都要說抱歉（Excuse me），最好再加個解釋。他人道歉時可說沒關係（It's OK.），別人打噴嚏時，可以說「保佑你」（Bless you.）或「保重」（Take care.）。

吸菸/禁菸：

按國際潮流及健康概念當道，許多公共場所全面禁菸，私人聚會想抽菸要先問主人在屋外抽菸是否妥當，如果主人家沒有菸灰缸（ash tray），他們可能不希望你抽菸，或你必須在外面抽。但在吸菸人口多的國家，對於吸菸禁菸的空間規定執行並不嚴格。

合宜應對：

社交禮儀其實是實用又有趣的話題，眞正的社交禮儀在於如何適切應對，使自己舉止合宜，而不在於背誦社交規則。文化形成與先天氣候土地條件及後天政治歷史信仰等相關，抱持多少文化也有個人與時代的差異，因此不該懷有族群刻板印象（stereotype）。以上歐美適用的聚會派對禮節，其他文化未必適用，入境隨俗，尊重彼此的文化價值才是國際人士的行爲準則。

在文化迥異情況下，如果心裡忐忑該怎麼做才能不使自己困窘，不如坦承不了解當地社交禮儀（social etiquette），請教他人該如何表現才恰當，例如：沒吃過的食物，如何用手抓飯，或是哪種食物該用手吃（炸雞、蝦子、比薩…）？或許其他賓客也不知道該怎麼辦。利用機會提出這些問題（及文化風俗），可以讓大家自在地談論，有助於拉近距離。

時間觀與生活/工作觀：

除了用餐時間的不同，某些民族看待時間的觀念也不相同。對準時要求極高的北美北歐人士，時間爲絕對值，遲到沒有藉口。但在西班牙、南歐、拉美國家、泰國、菲律賓、馬來西亞、越南等國家，時間並非絕對，而是參考，是相對的概念，極有彈性。因此，「現在」不一定是現在，「5 分鐘」可能代表一個鐘頭，因其民族性是放輕鬆慢慢來，如果與這些國家的人訂定會面時間，務必與他們確認預計及實際的時間是幾點。請教這類文化差異問題會讓人覺得你在意他們的文化，並且樂意告訴你。

另外，出差除了時差之外，也要注意某些國家（如北美、歐洲、南美部分國家、紐、澳洲南部及非洲少數）因應季節（南北半球季節相反）在春分左右實施日光節約時間 DST(daylight saving time）將時間撥快一小時，秋分時再調慢一小時。因亞洲多數國家（除伊朗、敘、約、黎、以、土外）早已不實施，國人可能不會注意，但出差到上述地區，尤其搭乘飛機交通工具或有重要會議者不能不慎。

對時間的看法不同，加上國情與生活型態不同，即反映在工作態度、效率與公私生活的界線上。講求時間效率者一見面馬上談生意講重點，且上下班時間與公私界限分明；凡事慢慢來的生活型態，則人與人要先建立關係，再談生意。歐美國家下班後就是私人時間，亞洲人士則經常工作生活不分，下班時間繼續工作或爲了建立關係應酬。

隱私與面子：

與歐美人士閒聊受歡迎的話題（如興趣、休閒活動），避免問及他人隱私是妥當社交活動的不二法門，如果眞有必要知道某些私人訊息，透過轉個彎而非單刀直入的問法或先談論自己，對方或許就聊開。

遇到隨口就問隱私甚至馬上給你一番忠告的民族也不必意外，有些社會即使對沒有親屬關係的人，也以親屬稱謂及互動模式對待他人。隱私對他們有不同意義，也可說是人情味的一種展現。詢問隱私的原因很多：(1)某些社會階級貧富差異大，必須了解他人社會位階（social hierarchy）決定互動方式。(2)有些社會對階級高者必須使用敬語（honorific expressions），必須馬上了解對話者社會位階。(3)有些國家居住空間較擁擠，沒有隱私或個人空間。(4)某些社會集體意識（collectivism）大於個人意識（individualism）。(5)有些文化必須透過隱私交換才算朋友，問及他人隱私被視爲是關心或友善的表現。遇到直問隱私者，不需覺得被冒犯，而是應當合宜應對順其自然（go with the flow），回問「How about you?」，顯示你對他們同樣感興趣，他們會樂意回答。

國情不同也顯示在如何看待面子（face）問題及溝通時明示及暗示的差異上。沒有面子問題的社會多半直接了當，就事論事，接受拒絕或對錯是否等問題與面子是兩回事。相對地，有面子問題的社會，爲了和諧（harmony），有些人不會直接說「不」，而是要爲他人保留面子，這當然要靠你的敏感度（sensitivity）去體會。

結語：

除了在商言商的場合外，用餐聚會派對等社交活動是國際文化多樣性（cultural diversity）的展現與交流地。如果你的產品夠好，對產品市場也非常透徹，對客戶市場是否具備足夠的文化了解（cultural understanding），將是客戶在貨比三家後對你最後加分的決定關鍵。

8. 外交部領事事務局全球資訊網（急難救助）
Website of Bureau of Consular Affairs, Ministry of Foreign Affairs(Emergency Assistance)

旅外國人緊急服務專線+886-800-085-095。（諧音「您幫我您救我」，非緊急勿撥打，以免占線）

外交部緊急聯絡中心：「旅外國人急難救助全球免付費專線」電話+886-800-0885-0885，目前可適用歐、美、日、韓、澳洲等 22 個國家或地區。撥打方式如下：

專線電話

國家或地區	專線電話
日本	001-010-800-0885-0885 或 0033-010-800-0885-0885
澳洲	0011-800-0885-0885
以色列	014-800-0885-0885
美國、加拿大	011-800-0885-0885
南韓、香港、新加坡、泰國	001-800-0885-0885
英國、法國、德國、瑞士、義大利、比利時、荷蘭、瑞典、阿根廷、紐西蘭、馬來西亞、澳門、菲律賓	00-800-0885-0885

護照、簽證及文件證明等問題，請於上班時間撥打外交部領事事務局總機電話(02)2343-2888。

外交部一般業務查詢，請於上班時間撥打外交部總機電話(02)2348-2999。

註：外交部領事事務局自 101 年 2 月 29 日起提供「旅外救助指南（Travel Emergency Guidance）」智慧型手機應用程式（APP）免費下載，結合智慧型手機之適地性服務（Location-Based Service），可隨時隨地瀏覽前往國家之基本資料、旅遊警示、遺失護照處理程序、簽證以及我駐外館處緊急聯絡電話號碼等資訊。

9. 臺灣經貿資訊站 Business-Related Websites(Taiwan)

(1)中華民國對外貿易發展協會 Taiwan External Trade Development Council(TAITRA)—全球資訊網（Global Trade Source）

http://www.taitraesource.com /可查詢 168 國各國基本資料、主要產業狀況、市場投資環境、與我國經貿關係、當地商展活動等。

(2)臺灣經貿網（Taiwantrade）

http://www.taiwantrade.com.tw/CH/ch-index.html
提供焦點商情活動、商機撮合、全球採購網、發燒議題、網路安全詐騙實例、貿易百寶箱等資訊。

(3)中華民國經濟部國際貿易局經貿資訊網 Bureau of Foreign Trade

http://www.trade.gov.tw/ 經濟部國貿局負責掌理我國國際貿易政策之研擬、貿易推廣及進出口管理事項，提供會展資訊、線上申辦表格，查詢貿易法規或政策，並提供每日全球商情等訊息。

10. 中國經貿資訊站 Business-Related Websites (China)

(1)江蘇外貿論壇 http://bbs.jsiec.cn/

中國外貿人氣網站，提供交流互動討論與商務及其他外貿相關討論區，如外貿業務交流區、國外採購商資料區、外貿知識學習區、外貿生活感受區、產品推薦、展會訊息、貨運物流、涉外法律等。

(2)福步外貿論壇（FOB Business Forum）http://bbs.fobshanghai.com/

中國外貿人氣網站，提供外貿業務、外貿區域市場、外貿行業交流、電子商務、外貿經理人、外貿配套服務、外貿急診室等交流。

(3)跨國採購論壇（Global Importer）http://bbs.global importer.net

中國外貿人氣網站，提供綜合交流、外貿問答、外貿展會、外貿新聞、商務中心、外貿博客（部落格）等訊息。

(4)合眾外貿論壇 http://bbs.yicer.cn/

中國外貿人氣網站，提供進/出口論壇、外貿展會、電子商務、外貿防騙、世界各國習俗禮儀等討論區。

(5)阿里巴巴商人論壇（1688.com）http://club.1688.com/

中國外貿人氣網站，提供論壇、生意經、商友圈、博客（部落格）等資訊。

國家圖書館出版品預行編目資料

開口就會商貿英語/黃靜悅, Danny Otus Neal 著.
——初版. ——臺北市：五南, 2015.04
面； 公分

ISBN 978-957-11-8049-6（平裝附光碟片）

1. 商業英文 2. 會話

805.188 104002949

1AF4

開口就會商貿英語

作　　者　黃靜悅、Danny Otus Neal
發 行 人　楊榮川
總 編 輯　王翠華
企劃主編　鄧景元
責任編輯　吳雨潔
內頁插畫　吳佳臻
地圖繪製　吳佳臻
封面設計　吳佳臻

出 版 者　五南圖書出版股份有限公司
地　　址：台北市大安區 106 和平東路二段 339 號 4 樓
電　　話：(02)2705-5066　傳真：(02)2706-6100
網　　址：http://www.wunan.com.tw
電子郵件：wunan@wunan.com.tw
劃撥帳號：01068953
戶　　名：五南圖書出版股份有限公司

法律顧問　林勝安律師事務所　林勝安律師

出版日期　2015 年 4 月　初版一刷

定　　價　450 元整

WORLD MAP

NORTH
AMERICA
PACIFIC
OCEAN
CARIBBEAN
SEA
SOUTH
AMERICA
PACIFIC
OCEAN

ARCTIC OCEAN
EUROPE
ASIA
PACIFIC OCEAN
AFRICA
OCEANIA
INDIAN OCEAN
ANTARCTICA

開口就會系列

到美國long stay及遊留學的必備生活指南&實用會話工具書

開口就會社交英語 附贈MP3

+

開口就會美國校園英語 附贈MP3

+

開口就會旅遊英語 附贈MP3

+

開口就會美國長住用語 附贈MP3

生活資訊、語言學習、社交禮儀、疑難解決，全都帶著走

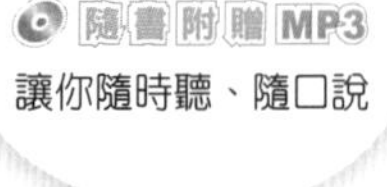

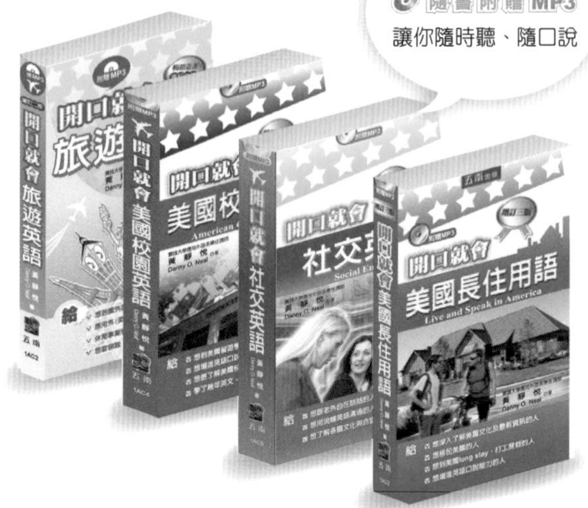